VAN ~ Y
~DE~

P9-DMD-193

DISCARDED

The Innocent Libertine

DISCARDED

HEIRS OF ACADIA

-TWO-

T. DAVIS BUNN
&
ISABELLA BUNN

The Innocent Libertine

BETHANYHOUSE

Minneapolis, Minnesota

Bun

The Innocent Libertine
Copyright © 2004
T. Davis Bunn and Isabella Bunn

Cover design by UDG Designworks, Inc.

Scripture quotations are from the King James Version of the Bible.

All rights reserved. No part of this publication may be reproduced, stored in a retrieval system, or transmitted in any form or by any means—electronic, mechanical, photocopying, recording, or otherwise—without the prior written permission of the publisher and copyright owners.

Published by Bethany House Publishers
11400 Hampshire Avenue South
Bloomington, Minnesota 55438
www.bethanyhouse.com

Bethany House Publishers is a Division of
Baker Book House Company, Grand Rapids, Michigan.

Printed in the United States of America

ISBN 0-7642-2858-7 (Trade Paper)
ISBN 0-7642-2929-X (Hardcover)
ISBN 0-7642-2930-3 (Large Print)
ISBN 0-7642-2931-1 (Audio)

Library of Congress Cataloging-in-Publication Data

Bunn, T. Davis, 1952-
    The innocent libertine / by T. Davis Bunn & Isabella Bunn.
      p. cm. —(Heirs of Acadia ; 2)
    ISBN 0–7642–2929–X (alk. paper) —ISBN 0–7642–2858–7 (pbk.) —ISBN 0–7642–2930–3 (large-print pbk.)
      1. Acadians—Fiction. 2. Scandals—Fiction. 3. Americans—England—Fiction. 4. London (England)—Fiction. I. Bunn, Isabella. II. Title II. Series: Bunn, T. Davis, 1952- . Heirs of Acadia ; 2.
    PS3552.U4718I56   2004
    813'.54—dc22   · 2004012185

9/04
BQT

This book is dedicated to
Susan & Ken Wales
Our gifted and exuberant friends

T. DAVIS BUNN is an award-winning author whose growing list of novels demonstrates the scope and diversity of his writing talent.

ISABELLA BUNN has been a vital part of his writing success; her research and attention to detail have left their imprint on nearly every story. Their life abroad has provided much inspiration and information for plots and settings. They live near Oxford, England.

By T. Davis Bunn

The Gift
The Messenger
The Music Box
One Shenandoah Winter
The Quilt
Tidings of Comfort & Joy

Another Homecoming*
Tomorrow's Dream*

The Dream Voyagers
Drummer in the Dark
The Great Divide
The Presence
Princess Bella and the Red Velvet Hat
Return to Harmony*
Riders of the Pale Horse
To the Ends of the Earth
Winner Take All

Song of Acadia*

The Meeting Place   *The Birthright*
The Sacred Shore   *The Distant Beacon*
The Beloved Land

Heirs of Acadia†

The Solitary Envoy
The Innocent Libertine

*with Janette Oke   †with Isabella Bunn

PART
ONE

Chapter 1

Abigail Aldridge tried to ignore the thrill she felt stepping off Shaftesbury Avenue and entering the forbidden world of Soho. Three paces were enough to cast her into another realm. The rutted cobblestones led her into a place deep in shadows and adventure. Here even the laughter was different.

Abigail stepped carefully over a water-filled trench, her skirts held in one hand. Thankfully the rain had finally ceased. But the sky overhead remained blanketed by clouds turned orange in London's evening lights. Though it was early July of 1824, they had scarcely known any summer at all. Abigail could see her breath as she walked. There were even reports of snow covering the Scottish dales. From the countryside came accounts of yet more ruined crops, the third such season in a row. The previous year the harvests had been particularly disastrous, bringing much of rural England to the brink of starvation.

A pair of fancy ladies approached with arms linked, dancing their way around a puddle. They giggled meaningfully and spoke a man's name with the derisive calm of women who knew things Abigail dared not even consider.

The two deserved the title of fancy, for they both wore dresses with far more frills than Abigail's. But their petticoats were bedraggled, and the silk trimmings were stained and frayed. Abigail had selected her plainest gown for this outing.

Her abundant red hair was primly tied back in a new ribbon, and her face and hands were scrubbed clean. Unlike the pair who now were directly in front of her.

They drew up sharp on catching sight of Abigail. One of them said, "Here now, what's this? Down for a bit of slumming, are we?"

The two could not have been older than Abigail's own eighteen years. Yet their eyes were as ancient and world-weary as the crumbling buildings to either side of where they stood.

"I–I'm here meeting a friend, actually," Abigail murmured.

"Oh, a friend, is it?" The one who spoke was the shorter of the pair, with pale locks spilling out from beneath a frowsy hat. "That what we're calling 'em these days, a friend?"

"Bet she don't have a clue how to keep her friend happy." The second woman smiled to reveal several missing teeth. "We could show you a thing or two, couldn't we, darlin'. Oh my, yes."

Abigail smelled the gin on their breaths as they giggled. Added to this was the odor emanating from their clothing—old perfume and smoke and something rank. "D-do either of you ladies know the saving grace of Jesus Christ?"

The two of them seemed to find that hilarious. The smaller woman took in the street with a grand sweep of her arm. "Don't recall seeing him 'round these parts before."

The other agreed. "If you've spied 'im in Soho, missy, best you believe 'e's got 'imself good and lost."

"But He is everywhere," Abigail declared earnestly, "and always."

"Abigail!" Another young woman ran breathlessly toward them. "I feared I had lost you entirely! Why did you not wait for me to arrive?"

The two ladies realized their game with Abigail was over. The smaller woman's face hardened. "Take your manners and your religious chatter and get back where you belong, missy. There's danger stalking these roads. Perils the likes of which you can't imagine."

The newcomer waited until the pair had departed to say, "I fear they are correct, Abigail. We do not belong here."

"If we do not try, how are they to hear the Word?" Abigail tugged her friend Nora's arm. "Remember, the harvest is great and the workers few."

"But—"

"Come!"

Abigail was well aware that Nora would have much preferred to remain safe in the West End. Nora had been Abigail's friend since their school days. A quiet girl by nature, she was a perfect daughter and the light of her mother's life. Nora was in love with a young man earning his charter in accountancy, and her face bloomed every time his name was mentioned. She loved him so much she almost wept with joy whenever she spoke of their coming wedding. Everyone said she would make a splendid wife and mother.

Abigail, however, had never loved any young man as Nora did this one. She could not imagine what it might be like. The only time she ever gave such feelings a second thought was when she listened to Nora prattle on. To give up her independence was unthinkable. She was not jealous of Nora. How could she be, when she had no interest in living a life tied to some man's interests and future? But Abigail prided herself on her honesty. Abigail was forced to admit that she was a bit jealous of this young man for stealing away her best friend.

"Do hurry on, Nora," she said as she moved forward.

"Oh, all right." Nora took hold of her skirt with one hand and the printed pamphlets with the other. "I suppose it would be too much to ask you to hold to the main roads for a change."

"You know where we're going. We've had this planned for days and days."

"*You've* had it planned."

Abigail did not respond because there was nothing to say. In the past, Nora had willingly gone along with all of Abigail's plans. That was how their relationship had always been. Abigail was the person with ideas, Nora with the steadfast support. Abigail was impetuous and eager and bursting with a great desire to improve her world. Nora was calm and unwavering in her friendship. Even Abigail's mother, who worried constantly about her willful daughter, always said that Nora would keep them out of harm's way.

Only now there was a change in the wind. Nora's husband-to-be, Tyler Brock, did not approve of Abigail Aldridge.

Abigail's father ran a trading concern that was a major client of Tyler's accountancy firm. Samuel Aldridge initially had been brought to England as deputy minister plenipotentiary for the United States. But when his stint with the government was concluded, Samuel had remained on to open a British arm of his family's highly successful trading empire. Since her arrival here as a young child, Abigail had traveled back to the United States only once, four summers past. England was where she had spent most of her life. If she stopped to think about it, Abigail Aldridge would have had difficulty determining which was more of a true homeland. Then again, Abigail rarely stopped and thought deeply on much of anything. Abigail was one for action and forward motion, with loyal Nora by her side.

Only Tyler was quietly intent upon changing all this.

Tyler was never direct in his criticisms. He was a cautious man with an accountant's way of examining things, picking them apart with delicate precision and wearing a body down with his unending questions. Abigail found Tyler to be a most trying sort of person. She tolerated him only because Nora was so deeply in love. At first she had expected this particular romance to follow the path laid down by all of Nora's earlier infatuations. First there was a great flame of dreaming and yearning and sighing and talking. Then came niggling doubts which mounted until the romance died. Poof. Like a candle snuffed. There one moment, mere smoke and forgotten brilliance the next. Only this particular romance had remained and even strengthened. Now Nora approached her long-sought goal of marriage and a family. With Tyler Brock, of all people.

Tyler had the irritating habit of asking Abigail questions she could not answer. For instance, were he here now, he would be inquiring in that mild voice of his about why she insisted upon walking down a dark street in the middle of London's dangerous Soho district. Was it truly because she wished to offer salvation to those shunned by society? Or was it perhaps something else entirely? Could she be after a glimpse of what was forbidden to her, except under this guise? Yes, most certainly, William Wilberforce urged them all to embrace those crushed by modern society. But were there not other ways she could serve, places where she might be included in an established group and thus kept safe? Why must she insist upon taking Nora down. . . . Oh, it really was entirely too much.

"Oh, I don't like the looks of this alley," Nora whispered. "Let's turn back, Abigail. Please."

Nora had recently begun expressing a mind of her own. Only they weren't her opinions, they were Tyler's. The accountant might as well have been there with them now, needling Abigail with his questions, driving his ink-stained wedge between her and her very best friend. "All right, Nora. Come along. There. We're back on the main road again. Do you feel better?"

"No, actually, I really would prefer it if we returned to—"

"Well, well, well. What have we here?"

Nora's face actually brightened at the voice, which was infuriating in itself. And the way she greeted him was far too much to bear. "Reverend Aimes! What a delightful surprise."

"I wish I could say the same."

Abigail refused to acknowledge the newcomer. "He's not a reverend yet, Nora. Don't provoke the man."

Derrick Aimes was a thickset man who affected a fighter's stance when irate. Such as now. "Did I not say that you lambs should never venture down here alone?"

Abigail had no choice but to greet him. "Forgive me, Mr.

Aimes. I was not aware you had been appointed the new sheriff of Soho."

Derrick, as usual, traveled with three of his mates. They all grinned at her response. She knew most by name. Derrick Aimes was well known by those close to William Wilberforce. Derrick and his band of Soho believers were perfect examples of how far Wilberforce's influence reached. Though a master politician and leader of the national opposition, Wilberforce had the uncanny ability to draw support from all levels of society. At Wilberforce's request, Derrick Aimes organized efforts among a number of London's wealthier churches to help the poor and the infirm. Abigail and her family attended one such church. Her parents, however, assumed Abigail's only connection to Derrick and his work was in the protected confines of their Audley Street church.

Derrick replied, "I have no need of earthly authority to protect innocent lambs such as yourselves."

"Have I not implored you never to call me that?"

"Lambs I said and lambs I meant. Why you insist upon venturing down these ways, tempting someone to wield the slaughtering knife, is beyond me."

"Don't talk like that; it frightens Nora," Abigail responded.

"As it's intended to." She saw his eyes widen as he realized where they had been standing. "Don't tell me you were headed down Blind Man's Alley."

Abigail was about to deny it when she spotted Nora's hand-wringing assent. "And if we were?"

"Did you not hear of the stabbing there just last week?"

"Forgive me, I really must go," Nora spoke, her voice unsteady, as she turned away.

"Nora, please."

"No, Abigail. The reverend is correct in what he says. We don't know what we're facing down here."

"This is no place for two young ladies such as yourselves, out wandering after dark and alone." Derrick Aimes snorted his derision. "I can scarcely believe your good families know what you're about."

Abigail drew her friend to one side. "You can't possibly intend to desert me, Nora," she whispered softly.

"No, Abigail. I want you to come with me."

"But we've only just arrived!"

"Abigail, you are my dearest friend. I want you to attend me at my wedding. Come away from here. Mr. Aimes is right. We don't belong."

The man called to them from farther down the lane, "Listen to your friend, Miss Aldridge. Go back to your world of thoroughfares and carriages and silk-lined drawing rooms."

"I was not addressing you, Mr. Aimes." She turned her back to him. "Nora, we've done this dozens of times before."

"And every time I've felt we were doing something wrong."

"Wrong to spread the Gospel in a world of darkness?"

"Wrong to do anything of which we fear to tell our parents."

Nora was leaving her, Abigail realized. There was nothing she could do to change her mind. No matter that her best friend had never stood up to her in such a fashion before. Abigail felt a painful wrenching inside. "Or at least so your Tyler says?"

"Tyler has every right to speak his mind, Abigail." Nora's voice was filled with hollow sadness. "Now come along."

"Oh, give me the pamphlets."

"Abigail, please, you can't possibly mean to stay here alone and—"

Abigail plucked the leaflets from her friend's hands. "I suppose you're going to report all this to Tyler and your parents."

"You know I won't. Why should I wish for you to be in more trouble than you already are?"

"But I'm not in any trouble, am I, Nora?"

"Let's hope and pray it remains so." Without another word, Nora turned and walked away. Back toward the well-lit West

End boulevards. Back to safety and the world they knew. Back to her Tyler Brock.

Derrick Aimes had moved back toward the two and now watched Abigail with open-mouthed astonishment. "You don't mean to tell me you're staying!"

"I most certainly am." If only she could make her eyes stop stinging so. "Now if you'll excuse me, I have these leaflets—"

"You're not going anywhere in Soho alone."

"Oh, and I suppose you intend to stop me?"

"I most certainly do." He blocked her path with his muscular presence. Derrick Aimes had been many things before seeing the light, as he put it. He had spent almost two years touring the countryside as a prizefighter known as the Soho Smasher, taking on all comers for the contents of a small leather purse. His legend still lived on within these noisome alleys and lanes, part of the lore that enveloped London's red-light district. Once he had gone nineteen rounds with Slammin' Jack Crouch, a boxer of infamous strength with fists like anvil hammers. But Derrick had left all that behind, and he presently was within a year of completing his ministerial studies. He worked and lived out of the church on Soho Square, and he had a way about him that made even the roughest highwayman sit and listen to the Gospel message. "You'd best be turning around and heading home, missy."

"And if I don't?"

"Then I'll be escorting you out to where it's safe again."

"Fine. Then I'll simply wait until you've passed and return to my duties."

"Duty, is it?" Derrick took another step closer. "Why ever do you insist upon coming down here? It can't be the Lord's calling."

Abigail decided she had heard enough. "Never you mind. It's not your approval that I'm after here tonight. It's being a light in the darkness."

To her surprise, Derrick's massive shoulders slumped in

defeat. "If I let you come with us, will you promise to stay close and not wander?"

Abigail wished she did not feel such relief at his reluctant invitation. But in truth the dark cobblestone lane with its rancid puddles and strange screeching laughter frightened her utterly. Nora was no longer there to support her. She had never felt quite so forlorn as now. Had Derrick and his merry band not been observing, she most certainly would have followed Nora back to home and safety. As it were, being allowed to accompany those whom she could trust meant a very great deal indeed. "Yes, all right. Agreed."

"Jack, stick close to the lady, will you?"

"A finer task I've never been offered." He was the oldest of the bunch and bore the seamy face of a very hard life. He respectfully doffed his tattered hat and gave an awkward bow. "At least not in the Lord's service."

"Hello, dear Jack." Abigail knew the man from earlier forays and liked him well enough. "Will you entertain me with stories of your ill-spent youth as we walk?"

"We're not here for idle chatter," Derrick admonished. "Or have you already forgotten your duty, as you call it?" Before Abigail could respond, he stomped away.

But once they were well underway and handing out Gospel leaflets to all who passed, Derrick sidled up alongside Abigail. "Straight up, now. Why is it that you venture down Soho way?"

She countered with a question of her own. "Does the Soho Square Church now claim all this territory as its own?"

"Of course not. Don't be silly."

"Are you so successful at turning the dark tide that you do not need help?"

"That's not what I'm about and well you know it." He gestured at her form. "Just look at you. Fancy silk dress, hair all nice as you please, smelling of some scent what cost more than any of these folks are like to see in a month of hard labor."

"The dress is linen and old," Abigail defended. "And the only thing I smell of is soap."

But Derrick was not to be put off so easily. "You're good at reaching out to folks, I'll give you that. But you don't belong in these parts. Don't look at me that way. You know it as well as I do." He tucked a folded page into the pocket of a passing gentleman, one doing his best to ignore them entirely. The man started to protest, then took one good look at Derrick's form and hurried away. Derrick went on, "All I'm asking is why you come at all."

"You sound as bad as Tyler Brock."

"Who?"

"Never mind."

"Is that a proper sort of answer to a proper sort of question?"

Abigail sighed. The truth was simple. Life at home bored her to distraction. She felt coddled and imprisoned. It mattered little that her cell was lined with striped wallpaper and that sunlight spilled over the high elms of Grosvenor Square. Nor that her parents loved her and wished for her the best that life could bring. They sought to protect her. She had heard that word so often she could scream. *Protect.* It sounded so nice in their mouths. They only wished to protect her from what she could not understand. How on earth was she to learn about life so long as she was trapped within these bonds of silk and velvet?

"Miss Abigail?"

Derrick said he wanted the truth. The truth was she yearned for adventure and she yearned to do good. To be a missionary in the darkest depths of Africa would satisfy both longings. She yearned to set out upon the high seas. She yearned, oh, how she yearned!

"Well, if that question is so difficult, answer me this. Why do you dress for these occasions as you would for the admiral's table?"

She was so caught up in her internal longings that she spoke without conscious thought. "It is the only way my parents would allow me to escape for an evening."

"And where do they think you are this night?"

"At a Drury Lane concert with Nora and her family."

Derrick flashed her a hard look but kept his tone level. "So you lie to your kith and kin and still claim to do the Lord's work?"

"I didn't lie. Well, not precisely. I . . . I allowed them to think thusly."

"A falsehood by any other name is still an abomination, lass." It was Derrick's turn to sigh. "What would happen if I went and addressed my concerns to your father directly?"

Abigail froze. "You wouldn't!"

Derrick scuffed the toe of his boot across the rough stones. "Perhaps I should. But it's not my nature to meddle in others' homes and affairs."

She felt weak with relief. Her father would be mortified. And her mother would be so disappointed. There would be further restrictions, holding her fast in their protective embrace until she utterly choked with despair. "Please don't," she said weakly.

"I should," Derrick repeated. "But I'll hold hard so long as you do one thing for me."

"Which is?"

"Never walk Soho's streets alone again. Always come first to the church. Always venture out with a group of us who've earned the hard knocks and know what's what."

"Very well."

"Just you wait, lass, I'm not done. You're claiming to want to help in the manner of Wilberforce's teachings. Well, then. I want you to become involved in a group we're setting up to minister to orphans. There's crowds of them roaming east of Oxford Street. We're looking for volunteers. Which you just did."

"Of course I'll help." A thought flashed so brilliantly it shone from her face. "But I'll need to change into a less formal gown at the church."

To her surprise, Derrick laughed aloud. "Are you that eager to leave behind what most of this lot would give their right arms to possess?"

"I am. So terribly much."

"Very well. But I'll be writing a letter to your father, all very formal, just letting him know where his daughter is occupied."

He won't like it, Abigail wanted to say. But she refrained. Because she could see Derrick was ready for argument, and she did not wish to quarrel. In truth, with Nora gone she needed new friends. She felt a stab of renewed sorrow over how her dearest ally had left her. "Thank you, Reverend Aimes."

He smiled at her. "Ah, lass. When you look at a man like that, you could melt stone."

"What—what do you mean?"

Without answering he turned to his grinning companions. "All right, brethren. It's back to the harvest we go."

Chapter 2

The dowager countess Lillian Houghton sat in the alcove serving as her dressing room and gave her face a critical examination. It never ceased to astonish her how all that she had endured remained hidden from view. At age thirty-three she was the mother of a fifteen-year-old boy, now happily settled in as a boarder at Eton. She was the widow of Grantlyn Houghton, fifth lord of Wantage and former equerry to His Royal Highness, now King George IV. She was heir not to the count's fortune, as most assumed, but rather to his enormous debts. Further, she was chased by the most dire scandal she could have imagined and was being blackmailed by a vile creature. She risked losing everything, including her reputation. She lived night and day with terrors so vast she could scarcely name them.

Yet even the most careful study of the face in the mirror revealed no hint of her woes. She remained untouched by time's hand or the ravages of ill fortune.

The upstairs maid knocked upon her open door. "Excuse me, mum, but you wanted to know the moment the gentleman arrived. I just spied his carriage pulling up in front."

"Thank you, Tilly. Please show him into the front parlor."

"Shall I be serving him anything? Tea, perhaps?"

"Most certainly not."

"Excuse me, mum, but what if he asks?"

"You will pretend to have heard nothing, you will take his coat, you will shut the door, and you will not reenter the room except upon my command. He is to receive nothing in this house, do you hear me? Nothing." Her tone said even more than her words. The maid curtsied and fled.

Lillian took a step back from the mirror and critically reviewed her entire form. She wore a dress of pale blue that perfectly matched her eyes. Some said her eyes were her finest feature, being large and round and clear as a young maiden's. They were framed by an unlined face, separated by a faultless nose, and bordered by a shining mass of dark curls. Her figure was as fine as her features, her hands as dainty as her feet, her lips a perfect cupid's bow. At her last visit to Court, one of the prince's consorts had bowed low over her hand and described her as the finest example of English beauty alive today.

She left the safety of her boudoir and descended the regal central staircase. Her London home was in one of the half-hidden cul-de-sacs off Pall Mall, as agreeable an address as any. Her husband's fortune had brought them many a fine bauble, until the appalling news had arrived that his investments in Portugal had been lost. All lost. Every penny he had and more. Considerably older than his young wife, Grantlyn's heart had not withstood the shock of learning that he was soon to be destitute. For Lillian, one sorrow had been followed by another. Then, just nine days earlier, had arrived the worst blow of all.

The banker now waiting for her in the front parlor was dressed in black. He always wore black save for some absurd trifle. Today his somber form descended to gray silk stockings and matching shoes buttoned up the side. They were polished to a mirror sheen, such that she could see herself approaching. "Good evening, Mr. Bartholomew. I trust you are well?"

"Seeing you again, my lady, would be sufficient to revive me from any ill health." He offered a modest bow. "And yourself?"

"Other than being plagued by matters which are not of my

own making, quite well, thank you." Pointedly she did not offer Simon Bartholomew a seat as she lowered herself into the chamber's most ornate armchair. She leaned back slightly, a lady of power settling into her throne. "You wished to speak with me about some matter?"

"Indeed so." He flipped back the tails of his coat and settled himself into the chair opposite. "I find myself in need of your assistance."

"Forgive me." She approved the frosty note in her voice. There was nothing to be gained by having this man know the fear he generated. In the sixteen years she had been wed to the count, she had learned many a lesson about letting others know their proper place. "I thought your occupation of my late husband's country estate was all the assistance I should ever be expected to offer."

"Were that only so, my lady." Simon Bartholomew was head of Bartholomew's Merchant Bank, which managed the finances of many at Court. At first glance, he did not cut an altogether repellent figure. Smallish in stature and narrow faced, his age was impossible to determine, for he looked both old and timeless. His fingers were long with oddly flattened cuticles. His nose ended in a rather blunt fashion, as though he had poked his attention in one too many hidden crevices and someone had cut off the tip. His dark hair was laced with silver, somewhat like that of a wild fox entering its winter's cave. His voice was mild like the breath of a killing freeze.

"I fear you have come for no good reason, sir. No matter—"

"Permit me to continue, my lady?"

She bridled at being interrupted. But she had little choice save to respond "Pray make it swift, then. I am due elsewhere within the hour."

"I am indeed grateful for the smallest portion of my lady's valuable time." He settled further into his seat. "As you are no doubt aware, relations between our king and his opposition in Parliament have reached a crisis point."

"I fear I have no interest in politics, sir."

"Were it only possible for me to share your distance, my lady. The opposition is led by one William Wilberforce—you have heard of him?"

"The name, perhaps. But I know him not."

"Be glad of that, my lady. A most contemptible gentleman. He leads the drive to abolish the slave trade."

Despite herself, Lillian found herself becoming fascinated. She had made it her business to learn as much as she could about this man who had become her greatest foe. Bartholomew's Merchant Bank was heavily invested in the slave trade. Although slavery had been banished from England itself for twenty years, British vessels still trafficked in human misery. Some of the empire's richest men, and the king's staunchest supporters, lived off of vast estates in the Caribbean colonies and South America. These men stood to lose massive fortunes if slavery was completely abolished. Bartholomew's could be wiped out entirely—not an unhappy circumstance since that would mean her own problems would evaporate.

But Lillian held to the languid tone of one who could scarcely be bothered to hear the man out. "How anyone could be so despicable as to profit from such a wretched commerce is utterly beyond me."

Simon Bartholomew flushed mightily as he sought to control his anger. "Those in power see things differently, my lady. And tonight it is their opinion which holds sway."

"I fail to see how this should interest me."

"Indulge me a moment longer. One of the opposition's allies and principal financiers is an American by the name of Samuel Aldridge. This is most certainly a name with which you are familiar."

"How would you be knowing this?"

"I have made it my business to know."

"And why, might I ask?" Lillian felt a growing sense of alarm that she took pains to conceal.

"For just such a moment as this." He leaned forward. "I

wish for you to use your connection with Lavinia Aldridge and her daughter—forgive me, I seem to have forgotten the daughter's name."

"Abigail," she said before she could stop herself.

"Thank you. Mother and daughter are bound to know what the former ambassador is about. And through him, we seek to know the schemings of William Wilberforce and his cadre of troublemakers."

"But why not focus your efforts directly at Wilberforce himself?"

"The Aldridge family and I share a bit of history. I seek to redress a past error, as it were."

Something in the banker's demeanor left Lillian shifting uncomfortably in her seat, as though a certain foulness had invaded her parlor. "Yet I still fail to understand precisely what it is you wish for me to find."

"A chink in the family's honor. A weakness through which I might insert the dagger of public disgrace." A fevered flame rose upon his features and just as swiftly vanished. He smiled at her. "There. You see how we have come to trust each other with our darkest secrets?"

She repressed a shudder. "And if I refuse?"

"Oh, Countess." The eyes gleamed dark as midwinter night. "I do so very much hope you would not entertain such perilous thoughts. Think of your son's good name."

Lillian resisted the urge to press at the spot in her chest where her heart seemed ready to burst from its confines. Fear filled her being, and she clasped trembling fingers together in her lap. "And if I do as you wish?"

"You would no doubt gain the undying gratitude of my humble self."

"I want more than that," she stated flatly. "I want you off my country estate and out of my life."

Eleven months earlier, Simon Bartholomew, a man she had only known superficially, had inserted himself into her life. While still in mourning over her husband's untimely passage, this despicable character, who formerly had done little more than shuffle letters of credit before her husband's pen, had announced himself in the boldest of manners. He had acquired a list of all her husband's outstanding debts. He had walked her through precisely what her husband owed. He had demanded that she lease to him her beloved country estate or the bank would foreclose.

Then, only nine days ago, Bartholomew disclosed that he had obtained knowledge of her deepest secret. A secret that, if revealed to the world, would destroy what remained of her cherished life.

"I want this matter buried and ended," Lillian repeated.

She might as well not have spoken. The banker rose to his rather short height. Yet from where she sat he loomed as huge and menacing as anything she could imagine. "Your assistance would be most certainly appreciated by all concerned. No, do not rise, my lady," he continued, though she had made no movement to do so. "I can see myself out."

Lillian sat in her lovely chamber for almost an hour after, staring at her hands and imagining them caught in chains fashioned by secrets and rumors and scandals yet unmasked. Every moment of this latest confrontation played out before her unseeing eyes. Simon Bartholomew had relished her anger. He had lashed her with his silken words, pleasuring in her helplessness. She was trapped, she was humiliated, she was left with no choice.

Oh, the shame of it all!

It was only after the third turning down another unmarked alley that Abigail realized Derrick Aimes had a specific goal in mind. The young minister had a fighter's bearing, with his great shoulders and a waist to nearly match her own. When he waved a pamphlet before someone's face, the person took it, no questions asked. His cry was loud enough to fill the street from one end to the other, lifting his call to Jesus above the hawkers and the singers and the good-time lads spilling boisterously from the taverns. Derrick led his well-intentioned little group with purpose.

Their course paralleled Shaftesbury Avenue, which formed the border between Soho and the more fashionable West End. Soho's streets were far from straight. Abigail was being led down lanes and alleys she had never seen before. Recent rains had left their glistening imprint upon the buildings and the cobblestones. Torches flickered at the entranceways to music halls and taverns. Along darker lanes the lanterns carried by two of their members offered their only light. She found this all an exciting glimpse into a very different world.

All manner of people filled the cramped ways. The so-called fancy ladies, with their garish outfits and brash voices, strolled with cutpurses and princes alike. Hawkers sold wares from shadowy booths, claiming they had perfumes from Paris and gold baubles from Constantinople. Pamphleteers and beggars vied for space on the street corners. The night was noisy, crowded, smelly—and thrilling. Every breath Abigail took smelled of untold adventure. Every sight revealed mysteries her mother tried so hard to keep from her.

They entered Cambridge Circus, a far smaller and more dreary affair than the better-known Piccadilly Circus further west. Two new theatres had recently opened. One sought to emulate the West End halls with their grand performances. The other, however, was something else entirely.

It was toward this second hall that Derrick now headed.

For the first time, Abigail hesitated. She had heard whispered tales of this place. Word of Cambridge Theatre's rank reputation reached even into the most respectable of drawing rooms. How could it not, when the king's own cronies consorted there? It was rumored the royal highness himself attended on occasion, masquerading as one of his own staff. The place held to a vile reputation. The term *music hall* was a mere guise for acts no decent person would ever care to witness.

Jack, her appointed escort, leaned down. "Leicester Square is but a stone's throw from here, Miss Aldridge."

Well did she know it. Abigail stared at the side street beckoning her back to the world she knew. She felt a tug of fear.

"None would think the worse of you for leaving us here, you know," he encouraged.

She glanced ahead. Derrick was already marching down the alley leading to the hall's side entrance. "N-no, I'll accompany you."

Jack started to say more, then subsided. "Stay close, then."

Chapter 3

As fate would have it, the first person Lillian saw at that evening's dinner party was none other than Lavinia Aldridge. They knew one another in the casual manner of ladies who occasionally attended the same events. The former U.S. deputy minister plenipotentiary's wife was slipping from her outer wrap, revealing a modest high-necked frock of taffeta and cream lace. Lillian was filled with a pressing desire to return home, bolt the doors, and wait for all the world to disappear. But her son's face swam there before her eyes, as did the promise she had made to her late husband on his deathbed to do her best by the boy. She had never truly loved Grantlyn, not in the manner described by all the novels she so enjoyed reading. There had never been any great sense of bonding with the man. Grantlyn had been more than twice her age and showed all the mottled signs of hard-lived years. But Grantlyn had been direct and honest with her, what they would term a thoroughly straight man. He had made Lillian an offer and stuck to his side of the bargain. And she would do the same by him, even though it turned out he had left her penniless and chained to the despicable Simon Bartholomew.

"Countess?" Lavinia Aldridge walked over and touched Lillian lightly upon the arm. "Are you quite all right? You look as though you've taken a chill."

The unexpected gift of sympathy was almost enough to

shatter her internal barriers. But Lillian must not speak of her secrets. For the sake of her son, she must not. "Life," she replied, hearing the hoarse tremble to her own voice, "is not what it should be, I fear."

Almost any other woman and certainly all the men would have taken this as their cue to recite all the wondrous advantages held by the lovely young dowager countess, even considering her widowed state. But Lavinia examined her with a face of deepest sympathy. "I am sure this must be a difficult time, just over a year since your late husband's demise. I do so hope you haven't received an additional shock."

"Of the worst possible sort."

"Would it do some good to talk it through?"

"Thank you, but none whatsoever."

"Then I will say no more about it, except for one question, which I fear will plague me all night unless I speak it aloud. Nothing has happened to your child?"

"No. Byron is safe at boarding school." She spotted a tall figure aimed like a dark-suited arrow her way. She turned her back to the room. "Oh my goodness, please spare me."

"I beg your pardon?"

"No, forgive me, I referred to the gentleman headed our way. Lord Avery will pester me all night, asking for my hand. I believe he feels he's being humorous, but I cannot abide his heavy-handedness this night."

"Then we must stop that before it has a chance to begin. Come." Lavinia took a firmer grip upon Lillian's arm. "Let us pay our formal respects to our host."

The approaching gentleman was what Lillian's late husband would have described a middling sort—middling nobility, middling wealth, middling honesty. His every phrase was accented by a slight sniff, as though he scorned even himself. "My dear Lady Houghton," he called as he rushed over, "had I but known you were attending, I would have spared no effort to ensure you were my partner for dinner. How thrilling it would be to escort—"

"Do please excuse us, sir," Lavinia said quickly, hurrying past him with the countess safely in hand. "We must pay our respects to the host without further delay."

"He will do everything in his power to have me seated beside him," Lillian whispered, resigned to a tedious and endless night.

"Then we must move swiftly." The women passed through the two side parlors with their roaring fires and milling guests. They entered the rear chamber, scarcely more than an alcove in size, but domed by a grand cupola and ringed by glass doors fronting an interior courtyard.

The marble fireplace was smaller, to fit the size of the room. Before it sat a very erect man, whose sharp features had scarcely been marred by his advancing years. "Mrs. Aldridge, what a delight it is to see you. Do come sit here beside me. And Countess Houghton, what an honor. Forgive me for not rising. Nathan, bring us another chair."

Lavinia Aldridge permitted the footman to hold her chair, then waited for Lillian to be seated alongside. "How are you, sir?"

"Oh, there are good days and bad, you know." The earl of Lansdowne kneaded the top of his cane, his attempt at hiding the palsy that shook his limbs. "Where is my good friend Samuel?"

"I fear my dear husband has been called to Brussels, sir. A crisis that could not wait. Our representative and partner has passed away quite suddenly."

"How tragic. Do please extend to him my deepest sympathy."

"Thank you, sir. He asked me to convey his sincere regrets. He was looking forward to another of your far-ranging discussions."

"Then we shall arrange for precisely that immediately upon his return. And in quieter surroundings than these."

Despite his age and infirmities, the earl of Lansdowne was an immensely popular figure in some circles. His father, the former earl, had been first minister to King George III, the present monarch's father. The former king's portrait hung over the mantel in this small parlor. It was in this very same room where the Declaration of Peace, ending the war between the former American colonies and the Crown, had been signed.

When Thomas Jefferson had arrived in London to seal the peace treaty, King George III had claimed that illness kept him from attending the negotiations. In truth, the king did have numerous bouts of ill health. But on this occasion, the monarch was livid over the loss of his American colonies and refused to accept the credentials of Thomas Jefferson, the American representative. It was this very same attitude which resulted in the War of 1812, which in turn had brought Lavinia and her husband, Samuel Aldridge, to England.

The old king was dead, the new king now four years upon the throne. And never had there been a more divisive rule. King George IV was known far and wide for his licentious behavior and the immorality of his court. Many of the former ruler's closest allies were openly critical of George IV and his cronies, the earl of Lansdowne among them. The present earl was a devout Anglican and he openly condemned the new rulers. As a result, he was attacked by those who sought favor with the Crown.

Some of the assaults he endured were scandalous. The Lansdowne estate formed one corner of Berkeley Square. It had been his beloved wife's cherished home, a place she had transformed into a haven of beauty and peace and good friends. But she was gone now. And with a sweep of his pen, the current first minister had decreed that Curzon Street, a fashionable road lined with clubs and shops frequented by the royal's new set, would extend into Berkeley Square. To do this, the first minister had chopped away one side and the entire front of the Lansdowne home. Gone were the pillars and entrance stairs. One wing had been partially gutted. No court would dare overturn an act that clearly held the king's own invisible seal.

Despite it all, the earl of Lansdowne maintained his criticisms of the regime and its loose morals. And he was admired far and wide for his courageous stand.

"My husband did so regret missing this opportunity to visit with you," Lavinia repeated.

"There will be other times, God willing." The earl turned to Lavinia's companion. "My dear Countess, I hope you will not consider it untoward of me to say how lovely you look tonight."

"Thank you, sir."

"Are you keeping well?"

Lavinia answered for her. "It is for this reason I am approaching you, sir. The Lady Houghton would prefer an evening away from, how shall I put this . . ."

"Gentlemen who might view her as a fox would a wandering chicken," the earl finished with a smile. "Were I but a few years younger myself, I fear I might be tempted to do the same."

"I was hoping you might allow us to be seated together," Lavinia finished, "so that we might continue our discussion and permit the lady a peaceful repast."

"Only if you agree to have me at your other side, Countess."

"I would be honored. Thank you."

"Splendid. I shall publicly apologize for the incorrect spacing of men and women at the table's head by saying the countess is standing in for my absent friend, Samuel Aldridge." The earl turned to his footman. "Nathan, see to the rearranging of the place cards, would you?"

"Of course, sir."

"Good man." His smiling gaze flickered back to the parlor's opposite corner. "And not a moment too soon. I spy a gentleman waiting for the chance to pounce."

"We are in your debt, sir."

"Nonsense. Whoever would consider it an imposition to be accompanied by two such lovely ladies?" He leaned heavily upon his cane and pushed himself to his feet. "Perhaps now would be as good a time as any to lead everyone to table."

Abigail and Jack hurried to catch up with the others further down the alley. She spied the young pastor having words with a woman, one scarcely more than a child yet bearing the world-weary gaze that seemed Soho's unique stamp. This one was different, however, for as they spoke together Abigail saw a light come into the young woman's eyes. One that shone even in this place.

The side alley led to a set of crumbling brick stairs, and they to a narrow door propped open. A pinch-faced lad lolled in the doorway. When the young woman tried to lead the group past, he drew himself erect and cried, "Here now, what's this? You know the rules good as me. No outsiders during the performance."

"Use your eyes," the lady snapped. "Don't you recognize this bloke?"

The boy squinted suspiciously. "No, I don't, and even if I did his name ain't down."

"Wouldn't do any good if it was, would it. Seeing as how you can't read a lick." She cocked her thumb at the squat pastor. "This here's Derrick Aimes, the Soho Smasher."

The lad's eyes widened. "Go on. He's not."

"He is, I tell you. Show him your fist, Derrick."

"I don't raise my fists unless I'm going to hit someone," Derrick replied, cool as the night.

The awestruck lad stepped aside. "I suppose it's all right, then."

"'Course it is." The young woman led them all inside, then heaved a great sigh. "There goes me job."

"You don't want to stay on here," Derrick reminded her. "You told me that yourself."

"Aye, but it's not just the job I'm leaving behind. It's the life."

"A tough but necessary step."

The girl studied his face, and she must have seen something there that gave her the strength to grin and ask, "Is it always so hard to leave the old ways behind?"

"Always," Derrick solemnly agreed.

"Right." The girl led them down the cramped hall. "This way."

Abigail followed the others through the chaotic dressing areas. She scarcely saw what she passed, both because she kept her eyes aimed downward and because of the exchange she had observed back at the side entrance. The truth was clear on that young woman's face. Derrick Aimes could reach these people. Abigail could not. The honest directness of Derrick's question stabbed at her anew. Why was she here? Was the Lord's work merely a convenient guise to venture out against her parents' wishes?

She realized the others had stopped. Abigail raised her eyes and gasped aloud.

They had arrived at the edge of the stage. From where she stood, Abigail could see both the audience and the performers. She was deeply shocked by both groups.

The stage held a five-piece string orchestra and a new type of spectacle that had gained great favor with the court. It was called a *tableau vivant* and was a scene as from a painting, yet formed by living people. The critics, and there were many, declared it was merely a means of keeping unemployed actresses' names in light. Abigail had seen one such display before, but nothing so dramatic as this. There must have been two dozen actresses and four or five actors filling the stage. They were set as gods and goddesses lolling about a disused temple. There was so much to look at Abigail's mind could not take it all in.

Then she gasped a second time. For she realized that the ladies were unclothed.

She swiveled away, her face aflame. Yet the hall was scarcely any safer a place to look. The chamber rose up in four tiers of gilt and red velvet. Tallow candles burned from any number of gilded chandeliers and sputtered upon the walls. Their black smoke competed for space in the crowded air with plumes rising from hundreds of clay pipes. The men were elegantly dressed, either in evening wear or officers' uniforms. They packed the hall with their noise and their laughter and their fancy ladies. There were many of them, all dressed in peacock finery and all bawdy in their manner. The longer Abigail looked, the more she saw, and the more she saw, the greater was her shame.

"Greetings in the name of the Most High God!"

This was no mere shout. This was a fighter's roar. Derrick's power was enough to silence the entire hall. A single violin scraped one last note. Someone coughed. A woman tittered nervously. Then a hush descended.

"The apostle Paul once stood before the pagan temple and proclaimed the God unknown!" Each word was a verbal fist of authority. He stood at the center of the stage, planted upon legs as strong as the hall's supporting pillars. "The people who heard Saint Paul that day were innocents, for they had never heard the Messiah's call. But you! You have been raised in a land that dares call itself Christian! Even so, you are gathered in a temple dedicated to your own sin."

One of the younger women at the closest border of the tableau vivant slipped out of the vines that offered her a semblance of modesty. She covered herself as best she could and came toward Abigail. She could see the woman was weeping. Abigail swept off her own coat and slipped it over the woman's bare shoulders. She whispered, "Would you care to pray with me?"

The woman hesitated a moment, long enough to cast Abigail a single tearful glance. Then she fled for the dressing rooms.

More women were moving from their positions and escaping in shame and tears. Most took aim for the exit opposite where Abigail and her fellows stood.

Derrick Aimes paid them no mind. He kept his back to the stage and gave the hall the full brunt of his righteous wrath. "Brothers and sisters, I stand before you this night to say that it is not too late! Jesus Christ has died so that we sinners might find a path to glory!"

A woman, somewhat older than most, spat on the floor by her feet and shrilled, "Ah, you Methodist! Why don't you go have yourself a bath!"

Derrick's authority was such that it halted the laughter before it managed to form. "Shame on you, I say, shame! You threaten to pull down not just your own houses, but the house of this great land!"

An officer in glittering uniform drawled, "Do find yourself another soapbox; that's a fine lad. I've paid good money for this table."

This time the laughter was louder. But Derrick was not cowed. "The Lord calls to each of us. Do not harden your hearts to His plea! All you need do is turn! Turn from your sinful ways, and embrace the Cross!"

The theatre manager appeared from the other side, flapping his arms in a futile attempt to both shoo Derrick from the stage and keep the ladies from departing. But the actresses and actors and now even the musicians were slipping away. The hall's mood suddenly changed, from irritation to genuine fury. Abigail could almost feel the abrupt shift.

The officer, flushed in anger by Derrick's roaring invective, plucked up a potato from the half-finished meal upon his table and flung it at the stage. A woman slipped off her shoe and tossed that as well. These were followed by a hail of vegetables and tankards of ale and gnawed bones and pipes. The theatre manager backed away from the sudden barrage, but Derrick merely stood with arms outstretched and called, "Repent, I say, repent!"

The angry officer turned and shouted to the back of the hall. "Sergeant!"

"Sir!"

"Round up your troops and arrest that man!"

From Abigail's left, Jack muttered, "That tears it proper."

"And while you're at it," the officer yelled, "round up his compatriots and arrest them as well!"

"Time to fly," Jack hissed.

"Straightaway to Newgate Prison with the lot!" The officer roared, his voice carrying above the fray. "Give them a taste of something they won't soon forget!"

Chapter 4

Once they were seated at the dining table, Lillian said, "You really are too kind to me."

"Nonsense," Lavinia Aldridge replied. "I am only doing what any person should, which is offer a friend a helping hand."

To many in London society, Lavinia Aldridge was a paradox. She now sat regal as a queen in her realm, though many thought she did not belong in such upper echelons. After all, her husband's former political power was gone. Now he was merely a merchant trader, and an American at that. They seldom invited anyone to their home on Grosvenor Square. They lived like social hermits. Yet here she sat, at the head of one of London's finest tables, certainly the nicest of those banished from the current royal court. And she was not merely calm and collected. She looked as if she *belonged*.

But the oddness only began there. Lavinia dressed in a style that was only a half shade removed from severe. There was no adornment to her dress. No plunging neckline, no silver buttons, no embroidered design. She did not even wear jewelry, save for a relatively modest wedding ring. Yet the ivory taffeta was of the finest quality, and Lavinia Aldridge held herself with regal bearing. She had the poise and assurance to defy current standards. Though Lillian was dressed in the height of fashion, and though she was considered a woman of startling beauty, somehow she was the one who felt tawdry seated beside this calm, strong lady.

And Lillian's current objective only made her feel the worse.

She looked at her bejeweled hands, the perfectly buffed nails reflecting light from the chandeliers and the table's candelabra. She scarcely whispered the word *friends*.

"Indeed so." Lavinia gave her the scarcest nudge. "Friend enough to warn you that eyes are upon you right the table round."

Lillian straightened in her chair. "I hadn't noticed."

"So I thought. Now smile and tell me about your boy."

Lillian felt herself relax. "Byron is a grand, healthy fifteen-year-old. Four years ago he was utterly miserable going off to boarding school. This year he could not depart for Eton soon enough. He is adorable and intelligent and proud to be so independent of his poor mama. I am the one who pines for him now."

Lavinia observed her with an odd smile. "Excuse me for saying. But I still have difficulty believing you are of an age to have a fifteen-year-old son. You scarcely look a day older than my own Abigail."

It was on Lillian's lips to speak the truth. She so yearned to confess all to this woman. How she was being blackmailed by a scoundrel who wished ill upon this fine woman and the Aldridge family. But if she did, her own existence would come crashing down around her. And even worse, her son's future would be destroyed.

Lillian dropped her eyes, the movement enough to dislodge one tear.

"Forgive me, my dear Countess. I had no idea what I was saying."

Even her title seemed a lie in this fine woman's mouth. "You must call me Lillian."

"I will, and gladly, but only if you call me Lavinia and will smile for me once more."

Lillian did so. "Perhaps I should not have come."

"Nonsense. What a lovely smile you have; you should reveal it more often. Now then. I do not recall learning your birth family's name."

"It is seldom mentioned." Lillian took the hardest breath of a very hard day and spoke a lie she hated before it was uttered. "I was born to clergy in the north of Lincolnshire."

Lavinia was genuinely delighted. "You are a believer, then."

She would taint this evening with no more falsehoods than absolutely required. "I-I fear not."

Lavinia's obvious disappointment disappeared behind her own bright smile. "There is always hope."

"Hope?" Their host leaned forward far enough to peer over and take in both ladies. "What hope is there in enduring this meal when my two beautiful guests insist upon keeping their heads together and excluding me from their conversation?"

Lillian turned all her charm upon the elderly gentleman. "Forgive me, sir, it was hardly intended—"

But Lillian was never granted an opportunity to complete her thought. For the ruckus rising from the front hall was such their host had no choice but to turn to the nearest footman and say, "Go see to that and report back, will you."

"Certainly, my lord."

Before he could depart, however, the majordomo came hurrying through the salon's main entrance and aimed straight for where the earl sat. The entire table pretended not to listen as he leaned forward and said, "I beg your pardon, my lord. But there appears to be a matter which can't wait."

"Speak up, will you, Nathan. You know how hard of hearing I've become."

The majordomo did no such thing. In fact, he seemed to be directing his low tone toward the two ladies seated on the earl's left. "There is a representative of the Aldridge household, with another gentleman. And they bring the most distressing report."

Lavinia was already on her feet. "Dear Father above, tell me my children are safe."

Lillian rose in the same instant. Nathan included her in the even more muted discussion. "I fear he has ill tidings with respect to your daughter, Mrs. Aldridge."

Lavinia's eyes were already searching the night beyond the elegant drawing room with its gleaming silverware and brilliant candlelight. "I must go to her."

"Of course you must." Lillian turned back to their host. "My lord, I beg you forgive us for—"

"Please, my dear lady. Say nothing more. You will accompany her?"

"Perhaps it would be best."

"Most definitely. Only promise to send me a note tomorrow and confirm that all is well in the Aldridge household." The earl raised his voice for the benefit of all the table. "Godspeed to you, my dear Mrs. Aldridge. And my very best regards to your husband. Now off with you both."

The only sound in the room was the rustling of their starched petticoats. They passed through the great double doors, descended the main staircase, and entered the front foyer. Lavinia reached for the uniformed gentleman waiting by the porter's stand, but did not quite touch him. "Tell me my Abigail is all right!"

The man, no doubt in his late fifties, had the seamed face of one who had lived through hard times. A former foot soldier, was Lillian's guess. But the other man who stood in the shadows by the front doorway was something else entirely. His own features were so scarred and battered he looked almost demented. His hair was long and so scraggly it looked greased by the rain which had again started to fall.

The man from the Aldridge household said, "This fellow appeared at the front gates nigh on an hour ago, ma'am. What he claims, well, I don't have any way of knowing—"

"It's true, your ladyship. Every word from my lips, as God is my witness."

Lavinia clearly suffered mightily from not knowing her daughter's fate. Still she managed to draw herself erect and address the stranger in a clear voice. "And you are?"

"The name is Jack, your ladyship. A scallywag and thief what deserves nothing better than the hangman's noose and the bottomless pit. But saved and sanctified by the grace of our Lord and Savior."

"You are a believer?"

"Aye, your ladyship. That I am. Thanks be to God."

Lillian decided it was time to move things onward, as clearly Lavinia was fearful to ask the necessary questions. "Tell us how you come to know the young Miss Aldridge."

"I've been lodge porter to the Soho Square Church for nigh on six years now, ma'am."

Lavinia protested, "B-but my Abigail has never set foot in Soho."

"Well, ma'am, that is, I . . ."

Lillian touched her new friend on the hand. Let me take care of this, the gesture said. "Never mind that now. The Soho Church, you say."

"We was out spreading the Word tonight." Nervously the man directed his explanation toward Lillian. "And we wound up in a spot of bother."

When the man hesitated, Lillian urged him with, "Bother, you say?"

"Aye, well, more than a spot." Jack wavered, then confessed, "They was all arrested, like."

Had Lillian not been there to hold her aloft, Lavinia would have gone down. She feebly protested, "B-but that's impossible. My Abigail, she wouldn't, she couldn't—"

Lillian squeezed the arm she held more tightly. She inquired, "How did you manage to evade capture?"

"I've been a night scavenger since I fled the borstal, ma'am. I know how to give the peelers the nick."

"You're certain they were arrested?"

"Saw them taken away, I did. The reverend and me best

mate and young Miss Aldridge."

"Did you hear where they were taken?"

"I heard the officer give the order," the man reluctantly replied.

Lillian dreaded the response, but she had to make certain. "Go on, man, out with it."

His eyes shone with a fearful light. "They was all taken to Newgate Prison."

"Then there's not a moment to lose." Lillian knew she had to take charge. Lavinia was not in any state to address these issues, particularly when time was of the essence. She addressed the man by the door, "You there. You're of the Aldridge household?"

"That I am, your ladyship."

"Your name and position?"

"Ben Talbot, your ladyship. Mr. Aldridge, he calls me the houseman, but I suppose you could say I'm general dogsbody. The Aldridges don't hold with a house full of servants—"

"You have a carriage outside?" she inserted quietly into the conversation.

"That I do, ma'am."

"Very well." She turned to Lavinia, whose face had gone ashen. "Listen to me, Lavinia. We don't have a moment to lose. Do you count a magistrate among your close friends?"

Lavinia shook her head dumbly. "Surely there has been a mistake," she finally forced out.

"For all our sakes, I hope so. But we must act upon what we know." She tightened her grip further and shook the woman gently. "You must help me here, Lavinia."

Her eyes unclouded. "Abigail!"

"Precisely." Lillian made certain the woman actually saw her. "You heard what the man just said. Your daughter is being held at Newgate."

Clearly these words had no meaning to Lavinia, but Lillian's tone was enough to bring the world into focus. "What do I do?"

"A magistrate. I know of one, but he and his family are on a tour of the Continent."

"Th-there is an elder in our church."

"He is a friend?"

"Yes. But must we speak of such a thing? That is, well . . ." Lavinia's breath came with as much difficulty as her words. "People will *know*."

"Listen to me, Lavinia. What people will or will not be saying tomorrow is the last of your worries just now."

"Her ladyship is right, Mrs. Aldridge," Ben Talbot chipped in. "A young lady such as Miss Abigail spending the night in Newgate Prison, it doesn't bear thinking about."

"Yes. Of course." Lavinia fastened a pleading gaze upon Lillian. "You know what must be done?"

"I do."

"Please help me."

"I will." She asked Mr. Talbot, "You are familiar with this magistrate?"

"Aye, ma'am. Know him well, I do."

"You will take us there." She ushered Lavinia toward where the earl's footman held their wraps. "We must make all possible haste."

Once in the carriage, however, Lillian had a sudden thought. She leaned out the window and spoke up to where Ben Talbot was urging the horses to greater speed. "I say, would it take us far out of our way to stop by the Aldridges?"

"The magistrate lives just the next park over, ma'am."

"Then stop by the Aldridge residence first, please." She pulled her head back inside and started to explain her intentions. But Lavinia's face bore the stricken expression of one already overburdened. She simply grasped the woman's hand in both of hers.

Lavinia asked weakly, "Can this be happening?"

"Let us see ourselves through this night, and then tomorrow we can ask all the questions we care to."

"Oh, that this would happen while my husband is out of the country!"

"Speaking of the gentleman, does Mr. Aldridge keep a sum of money on hand in the house?"

Once more there was the confused expression of a woman seeking to make sense of a foreign tongue. "I beg your pardon?"

"We need money, Lavinia. Gold coin would be best, but anything will do."

"My husband does much business from the office he keeps in our home. He keeps a strongbox."

"Do you have a key?"

The night's horror seemed to grow in Lavinia's features with each question. "Of course, but the magistrate will not seek recompense, particularly not this time of night."

Lillian decided there was nothing to be gained by explaining further. "I want you to fill a purse with gold coin." The carriage halted before a townhouse bordering Grosvenor Square. Lillian flung open the door. "Now hurry!"

The townhouse was one of a series, all of them stout Georgian brick in design, four sash windows wide, and bordered with square-cut granite block. A night watchman strolled the broad sidewalk and touched the rim of his hat with his stick. Tallow wicks burnished the night from within their well-cleaned lampposts. The trees of Grosvenor Square were tall and stately. Lights burned a warm welcome from many a window. Another carriage passed with the mellow sounds of horses' hooves and smooth-rolling wheels. The night air was scented with fires to ward off the damp, some of them burning fragrant cedar chips. The scene was one of calm and safety and wealth. But nothing could hold the danger at bay. Nor all the memories that pressed Lillian forward with such apprehension.

She helped Lavinia manage the front stairs. A maidservant opened the door. "Oh, Mrs. Aldridge, I'm so very—"

"Has there been any word from my daughter?"

"No, ma'am. Nothing at all from Miss Abigail."

Lillian stepped up close to remind the distraught mother, "Your husband's office, Lavinia. The strongbox. A purse. Quickly."

She let her go forward alone. Lillian turned to the maid-servant and said, "I am the Countess Houghton, a friend. Do you know what is amiss?"

"Yes, I'm afraid I do, my lady. I heard the man say Newgate Prison!" Her voice broke.

"I need two good stout robes. Black would do best. Something utterly without adornment."

"Mrs. Aldridge has just such a one. She keeps it for Sabbath occasions." The maid examined Lillian. "I suppose my own might fit your ladyship. But it's hardly suitable."

"That is not something which concerns us this night."

"No, of course not, my lady. I won't be a moment."

Lillian was helping Lavinia back into the coach when the maid hurried down the front stairs, her arms gripping a bundle black as the cloudy sky overhead. "Here you are, ma'am."

"Thank you." She lifted her voice. "The magistrate's!"

"Right you are, ma'am." Ben Talbot flicked his whip. "Hyah!"

Chapter 5

Edward Huffington resided in a townhouse of brick so dark it looked black in the flickering streetlights. Ben Talbot bounded down from the carriage's high seat and raced up the front steps. He hammered the big brass knocker and hallooed the house.

Light finally glimmered in the curved window over the door. Lavinia started to move as soon as the door cracked open. Lillian placed two fingers upon Lavinia's arm and said quietly, "Let your man handle this."

"But you said it was urgent!"

"Lavinia, I do not know you well enough to ask this, but ask I must. I want you to trust me utterly tonight."

Lillian was prepared for vehement protests. Instead the other woman examined her for a very long moment, then said quietly, "I have no idea what I would do were you not here beside me."

"I am quite certain you would have coped splendidly." Lavinia captured the hand upon her arm. "God's hand was upon our meeting tonight."

Had Lavinia slapped Lillian's face, the shock could not have been any harsher. "What are you saying?"

Ben Talbot's ruddy features appeared in the carriage door. "His honor ain't pleased about it, but he'll see you, ma'am."

Lillian forced her legs to carry herself up the front steps,

Lavinia at her side, and through the confined foyer. Then she turned back long enough to call out through the front door, "Jack—did you not say that was your name?"

"Indeed so, your ladyship." The man lifted a tattered hat.

"I think you had best join us."

The butler was minus his powdered wig, and his long coat was buttoned up incorrectly. He glared at the pair of ladies as he held the candle aloft. "The kitchen stove is cold, ma'am, and the cook is abed. I fear—"

"Never mind that, Harry," said a man behind the butler. "Mrs. Aldridge knows this household keeps to early hours." The heavyset Mr. Huffington's hair was mussed, his bulk fitted into an ancient housecoat. But his eyes were warm as he came forward with hand outstretched. "I am certain she would only be here with something urgent."

The kindness of Huffington's greeting was enough to dissolve Lavinia's fragile hold. She burst into tears and gripped the magistrate's hand with both of hers.

"My dear Mrs. Aldridge, what ever is the matter?"

"A-Abigail!"

"Your daughter? What's amiss with the lass?"

Lillian replied because Lavinia could not. "She has been arrested."

The magistrate stared open-mouthed at her. "When?"

"This very night. What is worse still, she has been taken to Newgate."

Huffington showed genuine shock. "Why is she not being held in the magistrate's cells at the Old Bailey?"

"I have no idea."

"Forgive me, you are?"

"Countess Lillian Houghton."

"Of course, forgive me, madam. It is the hour. You have been pointed out to me on several occasions." Nestling Lavinia's hand beneath his arm, he guided them into the parlor. "I would say it is an honor, ma'am, were it not for the circumstances."

Lillian motioned Jack to follow them. "Jack was apparently there when it happened."

"Mrs. Aldridge, perhaps Harry should light the stove—"

"Forgive me, sir. But we do not have the time."

"No. Of course not." He offered Lavinia his own handkerchief as he looked at the man hovering in the parlor's doorway. "Jack, did you say?"

"Aye, your worship, sir."

The magistrate might have been raised from his bed, but his mind obviously was still very sharp. "You've stood in chains before the bench a time or two, I warrant."

"That I have, your worship, sir. Too often to count, if truth be known. But all that's behind me now, thanks be to the good Lord Jesus and His saving grace."

"Ah, a believer. Excellent. Which church do you claim?"

"Soho Square, your worship, sir."

Lillian suggested, "You may address him as Mr. Huffington or Your Honor."

Huffington helped Lavinia settle into the sofa before saying, "All right, I'm listening."

"We was passing pamphlets out down Soho way, your wor . . . Mr. Huffington. Our reverend had a new convert working out of a theatre on Cambridge Circus."

"Who was your leader this night?"

"Derrick Aimes, Your Honor."

"The former boxer?"

"The very same." Jack was clearly proud of the recognition. "Reverend Aimes is as powerful a man with the Spirit as he was with his fists."

"And which theatre did you approach?"

Jack glanced at Lavinia, then reluctantly allowed, "Cambridge Theatre, Your Honor, sir."

Clearly the name meant nothing to Abigail's mother. The magistrate, however, looked appalled. "You dragged that innocent girl into the Cambridge? Why, it's hardly better than a bawdy house."

"Forgive me," Lavinia said, her voice a full octave lower than normal. "A what?"

Huffington quickly said, "It's a figure of speech, my dear woman." He frowned a warning at Jack. "Really, this is quite extraordinary."

"We didn't drag the lass nowhere, Your Honor. Matter of fact, I suggested she take herself off to Leicester Square. But she wasn't having none of it. And you know what Miss Abigail's like when she gets her dander up."

Lavinia leaned forward. "You know my daughter?"

Jack scuffed his boot across the floor.

"Speak up, man. Answer the lady."

"She's been with us a time or two," Jack grudgingly allowed.

Lavinia said shakily, "I–I don't understand. My daughter has entered Soho on more than one occasion?"

Huffington patted her hand. "We can worry about such things later, my dear Mrs. Aldridge. Right now we must concentrate upon freeing your daughter." He turned back to Jack. "Would you care to have a seat?"

"No thank you, Your Honor." Jack remained stationed by the doorway. "So we came into the theatre by the back entrance, and our guide led us up to the stage. I held back when I spied what was what, if you catch my meaning. So did the lass, Abigail. But Reverend Aimes, why, he marches straight out in front and gives them both barrels."

"I can well imagine," Huffington said. "I had the occasion to hear him speak a while back. The man was astonishing."

"Aye, that's our reverend in a nutshell. So off he goes, and they give it straight back at him, but the pastor, why, he just stands there and shows what it means to turn the other cheek, until . . ."

"Yes, go on, man."

"There was an officer in the crowd. He didn't take lightly to the reverend interrupting the night's entertainment, such as it was. He called back to his men in the upper tiers, and they came tromping down like the footsteps of doom itself."

"An officer. Did you notice which regiment?"

"Not me, Your Honor. Soon as I saw them soldiers, I was off like a shot. I tried to take the lass with me, and we got partway back to the exit. But then the soldiers came pushing into the backstage area and it was sixes and sevens, your honor. Sixes and sevens. All the ladies screaming and the soldiers shouting and grabbing hold of whoever they can get. But Abigail, she stands out, like. There's no question but what the little missus don't belong in that crowd. They latched on to her."

"And the reverend?"

"Aye, they got him as well. I hung back, found myself a mop and a bucket and stood holding it like it was the rope to heaven itself. The reverend called out for them to let the lass go, begged them. But the officer wasn't having none of it."

"You're certain of where they were taken? This is crucial, man. The officer ordered them straight to Newgate Prison?"

"Heard it with my own ears, I did. The officer, he writes out this paper for the sergeant to hand to the head peeler."

The magistrate stroked his beard. "He must be with the Royal Horse Guards. Someone with considerable clout. Which makes matters quite serious indeed."

Lavinia protested, "But surely my daughter has done nothing wrong!"

The magistrate did not bother to respond. Instead, something in Lillian's expression seemed to catch his eye. Huffington studied her so intently she was tempted to turn away. But she resisted the urge and met the penetrating gaze head on, not attempting to hide anything.

Huffington ventured, "You are familiar with Newgate?"

"By name and reputation. I have, however, visited other such places."

"You understand the situation?"

She nodded. "I do indeed."

"What?" Lavinia turned frantically from one to the other. "What is there to understand?"

Huffington's gaze did not waver. "I cannot be seen to appear in the night, a magistrate taking a personal interest in someone arrested by an officer of the royal household."

"Indeed not," Lillian agreed. "It would serve no purpose in regard to Miss Aldridge's freedom, and destroy your career in the process."

Huffington's lips tightened in a grim smile of approval. "I think perhaps Mrs. Aldridge is well served to have you at her side tonight, my lady."

"You will prepare the request?"

"Most certainly." Huffington rose and walked to his desk. He drew over a sheet of fresh parchment and dipped his quill into the polished inkwell. He said as he wrote, "Mrs. Aldridge, I would advise you to do whatever the countess suggests."

"Very well. But what is it you are not telling me?" Her frantic question fell into a long silence.

Huffington finished writing, inspected his work, then dusted the paper before replying. "All you should concern yourself with this night is your daughter's safe release. Are we clear on this matter?"

Lavinia's eyes tracked back and forth once more. Something in their set expressions caused her frame to shudder. "Of course I shall do as you advise."

"Excellent." He rose from his desk, walked over, and handed the paper to Lillian. "Do be so kind as to have your man report to me once this matter is resolved."

"It may be quite late, sir."

"No matter what the hour," Huffington replied. "I shall not sleep a wink until I hear from you." He steered Lavinia toward the door with a hand set gently upon her shoulder. "Until that time, I shall be praying as fervently as I know how."

Chapter 6

The carriage ride from the magistrate's home to Newgate Prison was a dark and endless trek. They left the fashionable districts behind with their bright streetlamps, carefully tended boulevards, fine townhouses, and broad sheltering trees. For Lillian, they ventured not just into the cramped and fetid lanes of London's impoverished East End. They also entered a realm that brought on a nightmare of memories.

Lavinia was too anxious to notice. "Abigail has always been an impulsive girl. Not bad natured, nor immoral in her intent. Never that. Which has made it so hard sometimes to discipline her. She is as strong a believer as ever I have met. But tied to this is a nature which—oh, it is so hard to explain."

Lillian fastened her attention upon the handkerchief Lavinia knotted and coiled with her fingers. But ignoring the scenes outside the carriage did not help. Everywhere she looked, she saw the same thing. "She attracts danger," Lillian finally said.

"No, not that exactly. But she does so enjoy questioning everything."

"She seeks out the wrong sort of folk to call friends," Lillian continued.

"H-how do you know Abigail so well?"

Lillian merely continued, "She launches herself into anything that might appear to offer what her staid life does not."

The carriage jounced them hard as it pulled to a halt, and

56

then Ben clambered down from up top. "Newgate Prison, ma'am!"

"I must go." Lillian moved for the door Ben held open.

"You must wait here."

"But shouldn't I—"

"Remember what I said, Lavinia." Lillian reached for the dark hooded garment resting on the opposite seat. "It is vital that you do as I say."

"Wait." Lavinia extended one hand. "Pray with me."

"I beg your pardon?"

"Oh, I know you do not share our faith. But if you are to act as my emissary in this matter, I must at least know you are shielded by prayer." She motioned Ben forward and then waited while he in turn brought the former thief into their circle. "Oh my dear Lord God," Lavinia began earnestly, "I have turned to thee on occasions beyond count. But never with a greater need than now. Guide the steps and actions and words of this dear woman, whom I am certain thou hast brought to us in this hour of direst need. Shield her from all who seek to do her harm. Open all locked doors, as thou hast done for other believers before us. Let her speak, and let them hear thy command. Set my daughter free."

"Amen," their carriage driver intoned, and Jack as well. "Yes, Lord, and amen."

"Give me the coin purse," Lillian said, her voice sounding distant to her own ears. She knotted the purse's leather strap around a button on her left cuff, then slipped it up her sleeve. Those accustomed to danger carried money in this manner. Normally a small knife with a razor's edge would be strapped alongside the purse, so a weapon might be drawn when supposedly reaching for money. She saw Jack's eyes widen at the practiced motions. Lillian did not care what Jack thought. She was so stunned by being prayed over that her mind could scarcely capture any thought at all.

Lillian drew the housemaid's cloak about her and fastened it at the collar and waist. She pulled the hood far over her face, careful to tuck in every strand of hair. "Jack, you will come with me."

"Aye, your ladyship."

"From this point on, you are to address me simply as 'mum.'" She looked back at Ben. "You will guard your lady."

"With my life, my lady—"

"And I shall pray for you as hard as I know how," Lavinia said, gripping Lillian's hand once more. "Thank you, sister. Thank you."

Save your words for when I return, Lillian wished to say. But she found herself unable to speak at all.

Lillian slipped her hand free and strode into the night.

Newgate Prison fronted the street with a façade as grim as a medieval fortress. The octagonal stone turrets were flat at the top, from which the peelers could stare down into the central press yard. This time of night, the main gates were shut. Even so, the stench hit Lillian long before she reached the keeper's lodge.

The head turnkey was always referred to as the keeper. This man was busy with his dinner when Lillian peered through the cracked window. The keeper was obviously accustomed to being disturbed by late-night visitors. He paid no attention to either the faces by his window or the loud knocking upon his door.

"I'll go in and suss out the man," Jack said.

"No, let him play his little game," Lillian responded, and waited.

Memories swirled about her like the tendrils of night mist. When she had been nine years old, her aunt had dressed Lillian in her darkest clothes. Together they had left the house an hour after her uncle had departed for some church meeting. Her aunt had spoken little—she had always been sparse with her speech. They had taken a transom to a portion of town the young Lillian had never seen before, a place of hovels and silence and gloom. They had halted before the porter's lodge of a prison very much like this one, though that distant night had been far colder. The air had tasted metallic, a dangerous flavor spiced by the same fetid smell that filled her nostrils now. That night, the keeper had not wanted to let them in either. But Lillian's aunt had insisted. The man had relented only when Lillian's aunt had slipped coins into his palm. Which was another astonishment. Her aunt had always been tight with her silver.

Lillian was brought rudely back to the present by a deep voice braying, "Well, what is it that can't wait for the proper hour?"

Lillian shuddered with the force it required to push the memories aside. "I come with an urgent request."

"Why should yours be any different?" The keeper laughed at his own joke. The room behind him was empty save for a battered pewter plate and mug, and a flickering tallow candle upon a rickety table. He wore unlaced boots and a stained leather apron over filthy trousers. His belly was enormous and shook as he laughed. He did not care that Lillian remained silent through his humor. He no doubt had grown used to laughing alone.

The keeper turned away long enough to drain his mug. "Aye, it's always the urgent ones what can't wait for morning." His eyes squinted in their attempt to pierce the shadows cast by Lillian's hood. Then he turned his attention to Jack. "Have I seen you round these parts before?"

Lillian halted Jack's response with an upraised hand. "I have a magistrate's order for you to discharge a prisoner brought here falsely."

"False arrest, is it?" The keeper was not impressed. "Walk these lanes, you'll find not a one of these vermin deserve to be here. They're all innocent. Every one."

"I am concerned with a young lady. Brought here earlier this very same evening."

"Ah." His eyes gleamed. "A proper looker, highborn and haughty. That the one?"

Lillian handed over the parchment. From the way the keeper frowned over the paper, it was evident the man could not read.

"Abigail Aldridge is the young woman's name," she said.

"That's as may be. But like I said, the prison's shut until—"

"I can pay."

The keeper examined the coarse dark robe covering Lillian's form. "Going against orders, that carries too dear a charge for the likes—"

Lillian slipped her fingers into the sleeve and drew out a single coin. "In gold."

The keeper licked his lips. "Let's be having it, then."

Lillian let the candlelight flicker over its gleaming surface. "Tell me the girl is all right."

"I let her stay in the association room, didn't I." He kept his eyes on the coin. "Didn't send her off to the cells, where anybody might trap her in the night."

"You thought there was a chance someone would come and offer good coin for such as her," Lillian interpreted. She pressed the coin into his hand. "Take me to her."

"A gold guinea won't take you far in these parts."

"Five more when we pass back through these gates."

"Aye, well . . ." He glared at Jack. "Your man stays back here. Can't be letting just anyone walk these halls."

Jack started to protest. Lillian cut him off. "Very well. Let us go."

The keeper hefted his lantern, grabbed the billy club from its place above the door, and set off across the press yard. He tapped the cobblestones as he walked, a hammering tone that marked his speech. Lillian knew the man was talking to her, but she could not make out the words. She pressed a handkerchief to her mouth to keep out the worst of the stench. If only she could hold off the memories as well.

They passed down a long stone hall lit only by the keeper's lantern. He used one of his jangling keys to open a stout oak door, which he slammed back on its hinges. "Here we are, then," he declared. "Right as rain, she is too. Get up there, lass. There's someone come to take you back to the land of the living." The keeper laughed anew at his own joke.

"Y-you're here for me?"

Lillian forced herself back to the present moment. A young woman was rising from her crouched position in the far corner, between the side wall and the unlit fireplace. But the shadows were so deep it was impossible to see more than a vague form. "Are you Abigail Aldridge?" she asked.

"Thank God," the young woman moaned as she rushed forward. "Thank the good Lord above."

In her haste to flee the chamber, Abigail struck the central table hard and almost went down. But she managed to stay aloft and rushed over. Her eyes apparently were adjusted to the gloom, and she came in close enough to peer under the hood. Her gaze widened in surprise. "Why, you are Coun—"

Lillian placed a hand upon the young woman's lips. "Your mother has sent me."

"Aye, it's a good thing the woman's come for you. There's every manner of disease and danger awaiting those who step on the wrong side of the law."

Abigail clenched Lillian fiercely as she cried, "I did nothing wrong!"

The keeper found that most humorous. "What did I tell you. There ain't a guilty one among 'em."

Quietly Lillian said, "Let us be rid of this place while we are able."

But Abigail held Lillian closer still. "What of my companions?"

Thankfully, the keeper spoke before Lillian could. "There ain't been nothing said of any others."

Lillian inspected the face before her. Flaming red hair

tumbled about features that remained strong and defiant, even when terrified. The eyes were impossibly clear, the expression alight with an innocence Lillian had never known. Certainly not by the time she had reached this woman's age.

Abigail protested, "I can't just leave them here to rot in this vile place!"

Lillian thought swiftly. This young woman was not going to come easily without her companions. There was nothing to be gained by arguing. She turned to the keeper. "Surely you noticed the other names written upon the magistrate's document."

The keeper gaped at her. "Other names?"

"The Reverend Derrick Aimes and his assistant, Peter Wise," Abigail offered quickly. "They did nothing wrong either."

"Of course not. Why should they be any different from all the others jailed here?" He kneaded the grip of his weapon. "You'll be paying for them as well?"

"I will."

He said nothing more. The keeper locked the door behind them, then left them standing in the press yard as he entered the north wing, where the men were kept. The wait was endless. The two women stood and clutched each other, surrounded by their own private worlds of fear and calamity.

Finally the keeper reappeared, leading two other figures. Lillian could not make out their faces in the misty gloom. But as soon as the keeper's lantern fastened upon the two women, one of those following the man cried out, "Abigail?"

"Pastor Derrick!"

"Praise be to God above!"

"Are you all right, Reverend?"

"Why should I not be, when our gracious Father has released us from our shackles and wrought another miracle?"

"One paid for by this woman's gold," the keeper said, his eyes fastened meaningfully upon Lillian.

She was already reaching for her purse. "Let us be free of this vile realm."

Chapter 7

Six days later, Abigail sat in the very same chair she had claimed as her own the first time she had come to this house. It had a high, curved back, a chair intended to nestle the occupant within its padded comfort. Abigail recalled that first visit to the Wilberforce manor very clearly. She had been nine years old. Her parents had been invited to come and have lunch with William Wilberforce in his home. During the carriage ride her mother had warned repeatedly not to speak out of turn or discuss matters which should be left until they were alone. She was to be a proper young lady, her mother had said, and for once Abigail had sincerely agreed, for she had seen how important this meeting was to both her parents.

They had decided to bring Abigail along that day, because William Wilberforce had been such a dear friend of Erica Langston. Erica and Abigail had grown extremely close during Erica's stay in England, despite an age difference of more than ten years. Erica had recently returned to her home in Washington, accompanied by her fiancé, Gareth Powers. Abigail had missed her terribly. Introducing Abigail to Erica's dear friend Mr. Wilberforce was her parents' way of trying to make her feel better. And it had. Oh, how much better she had felt after the visit. William Wilberforce had not been anything like Abigail had expected. She had imagined a great and powerful man after everything she had heard. Instead, the little man's eyes had fastened upon her with such gentle intelligence she had felt as though she had known him for years. He had spoken for a time with her parents, then selected the seat closest to Abigail. He had taken her hand in both of his, looked deep into her eyes, and said how he imagined she missed their mutual friend quite as much as he did.

The memory was enough to bring on new tears.

Fortunately, Abigail was the only person in the front parlor that day. Normally it bustled with visitors and guests and the quiet murmur of discreet conversations. Today, however, the drapes were partly drawn upon a rain-swept garden. The entire house seemed swathed in a muted light. Abigail forced herself to regain control and used her handkerchief to wipe her eyes. Occasionally people passed before the doors leading to the rear offices and the rest of the house. A few cast glances her way, swift looks that did not linger.

The previous few days had been the most wretched of Abigail's entire life. Her nights were riven by fearful dreams. Her days were filled with silent condemnation. When her mother had asked for details about her forays into Soho, Abigail had responded with the resignation of one who was beyond all desire to hide. Her mother had said very little more, not even asking how Abigail had come to lie to her parents. Which of course was precisely what Abigail had done. One falsehood piled upon another. The worst were the ones she had told herself. How she was doing this for a higher purpose. How she was behaving this way for God.

Her mother's silence was more profound than anything she could have said.

Everything else would wait until her father returned from Brussels. The thought of this had added a feverish edge to her nightmares and filled her every morning with dread.

Then the broadsheets with the awful headlines had appeared, and there was no way they could wait any longer for her father.

She knew why Wilberforce's household was avoiding her.

For two days now, the newspapers loyal to the Crown had spouted the most scurrilous lies. Articles claimed a leading Dissenter had been captured in a raid on a notorious bawdy theatre. "One Aldridge," the newspapers said. The articles made no mention that she had been the visitor. In fact, one implied that it had been her father who had actually been a member of the audience. They claimed this Aldridge had been captured in a general sweep, one carried out by the Crown at the public's demand for decency and reform. They suggested this Aldridge had actually been on the verge of entering the stage itself. A stage where most of the performers were without clothes.

Abigail buried her face in her hands. The shame was just too much to bear. Her father was due back in three days. She did not know which meeting she dreaded the most, that with her father or with Mr. Wilberforce.

Notice had come this morning, a written request from Wilberforce himself. When Abigail had read the note, she had resisted a sudden urge to break into hysterical laughter. No matter how awful the situation was, it insisted upon becoming worse still.

"Miss Aldridge? Mr. Wilberforce will see you now."

Abigail was once more filled with a desperate desire to flee the dark house and these hushed people. But where was she to go? She forced herself to rise and follow the young gentleman she scarcely saw. They entered the front hall and passed through the main gallery. She noticed people to either side, but no one spoke. People moved in funereal solemnity. And perhaps this was appropriate. She walked toward her own public humiliation.

The young gentleman opened one of the sliding doors leading to the formal library, the chamber Wilberforce used as his personal office. "Miss Aldridge, sir."

"Ah, Abigail. What a delight it is to see you again." The voice came from within a room darker than the rest of the house. "Forgive me for not rising. Do please come in. Will you take tea?"

"N-no thank you, sir."

"Thank you, Herbert. That will be all."

"Very good, sir."

When the door closed, the room's only light came from a tight slit in the window drapes. Abigail remained where she was, allowing her eyes to become adjusted.

"A wretched state of affairs, I do agree. Can you see where to put your feet? Perhaps I should have Herbert bring you a candle."

"No, sir. Thank you." She saw him now, a small figure reclining upon a daybed in the far corner. He wore his customary dark suit, but as she approached she saw his coat was being used as a pillow and his shoes were off. "Are you all right, sir?"

"I shall not begin this conversation with a lie. I am unwell. I have these dreadful attacks of pain in my forehead and temples, you see. They come without warning and wreak the most awful havoc upon my hours. Then they depart, and for a day I am weak as dishwater. After this it is as though the pain had never appeared."

"I am so very sorry, sir." Of course. She had heard her parents speak of the vengeance with which such attacks lay the ever-active Wilberforce low. They came, they left. There was nothing anyone could do but move softly and wait for the attack to cease. Sometimes they lasted for a few hours, other times for days. It was only as she started across the floor that she noticed the older woman in the far corner. She knitted with the calm certainty of one who had done this task for so long she scarcely needed her eyes at all. She glanced up and nodded at Abigail, then returned to her work. And said not a word.

"I am sorry for the dark," Wilberforce said. "It is the light, you see. I am so sensitive to the light during these weak times."

Weakness. Abigail bowed her head as she sat in a chair close to his. Her own weakness was there on glaring display. And now their enemies were using it to attack this good man.

"You are sad."

Her head was bowed, such that her tears fell upon the hands in her lap as she nodded.

"And I have so cherished your visits because of your joy. It hurts me to see you in such a state of sorrow."

This was just like the man, to be suffering himself and to have his life's work threatened by her own errors. And all he spoke of was her happiness. Her sorrow. Her tears fell faster still.

Wilberforce said nothing more until she managed to regain control. His voice held none of its normal strength and timbre when he said, "Life is so difficult at times, is it not? We feel so wronged. If only we could see and understand in advance just where we are headed, what lies in store. But do you know, the Scriptures say that all the Lord our God promises is to be a light unto our feet. One step at a time. Do you see? Perhaps it is not our charge to be looking further ahead than this one step, this one day."

"I am very, very sorry for all the trouble I have caused," Abigail whispered.

But Wilberforce did not seem to hear her. "Perhaps our task is to look upon this one day alone. Perhaps we must concentrate upon the one thing that is clearest in our mind and heart. This one duty. This one problem. And trust that our God can make sense of the grand scheme, the long road of days and tasks ahead."

"How can God make sense of all the woe and trouble I have brought?"

"Ah. Well. Were I to be a perfect man, with all the strength and wisdom in the world, perhaps I might be able to answer that for you. As it is, I fear I am just another humble servant. I am far too aware of my own failings to condemn you for being who you are."

"I am such a foolish child."

"Indeed, we all act foolishly from time to time." Wilberforce shifted slightly and pressed one hand to his left temple. "Would you be so kind as to pour me a glass of water?"

"Certainly." She then discovered it was necessary to help steady him so that he might straighten and drink.

"Thank you, dear child." His weary smile beckoned through the gloom. "I suppose I should stop thinking of you as such. For a child you are no longer."

"How can you say that, after all the damage I have caused?"

"Tell me," he said, again acting as though he had not heard her at all, "tell me who you are."

The strangeness of the question somehow drew her away from the dull pain in her heart. "Sir?"

"Oh, I know who you *were*. I know the child you are no longer. Tell me now, who are you becoming? Who is the woman, this Miss Abigail Aldridge?"

"I-I don't understand."

"I know, I know, it sounds like the vague ramblings of an ill old man. But indulge me, if you will. Were you able to speak of your heart's deepest longings, what would you say? Above all else, Miss Abigail Aldridge, what do you seek?"

The question took her breath away. Breath and tears both, and the pain besides. Which was so remarkable a sensation that it took a silent span of several minutes for Abigail to realize what she was feeling. It was forgiveness. Abigail found herself thinking of a word she had often heard in church but never understood until that very moment. The word was *shriven*. The burdens she had carried since that dreadful night were stripped away. The guilt and the pain and the sorrow were gone.

She looked at the man supine on the couch before her. He looked so frail, this gentleman. So very small for all the burdens he bore. His eyes were closed, and he seemed asleep. The only sound in the room was the soft click of the knitting needles. Abigail knew that Wilberforce was waiting. What an astonishing man he was.

Abigail took the first free breath she had drawn since all this had begun. What did she yearn for above all else?

She spoke a word she had scarcely admitted even to herself. She said, "Adventure."

Chapter 8

The sun was a brilliant gift the afternoon of the Aldridges' return to Wilberforce's home. It was five days since Abigail had visited, and the first since her dreadful night that it had not rained. There was an air of welcoming charm to the Wilberforce manor. The gardens were a shambles, as always. The weeds stood almost waist deep in places, and the trees were burdened with overripe fruit. The manor itself rambled in a rather haphazard manner. Everywhere Abigail looked she saw things in need of repair.

She sat in the carriage beside her mother with her father on the seat opposite. Her brother was playing at a friend's house. She took careful note of the outside surroundings because it kept her from staring at her father's stonelike expression.

Three other carriages waited in the forecourt as they pulled up and halted. Abigail waited while her father helped her mother down, then slipped out unaided. She moved around so she stood behind her parents. She kept her eyes upon the ground. It was safer thus. She followed them up the stairs and into the entrance hall. She recognized the young aide's voice, though she saw nothing more than his shoes and trouser legs as Herbert greeted them. She followed her parents into the front parlor and moved swiftly to the far corner. The padded high-backed chair embraced her in the same way it had when she was a child. The sunlight played over the carpet by her feet. She settled her hands into a tight ball in her lap and forced away the warm memories of another time. She would not cry.

Today was only the second time she had left her room since her father's return. He had spoken to her once since his arrival. It had been far from a pleasant conversation. He had stood over the chair where she had sat in their own front parlor. He had asked her questions, most of which she could not answer. How had she ever thought of doing such a thing? Was it true she had repeatedly lied to her parents? What had they done to deserve such treatment? Abigail had responded with little more than an apology, repeated over and over. Then as now, she had struggled hard and remained dry eyed. Why she felt it was so vital not to weep, she could not say.

The first time she had emerged from their home had been for church the previous day. The only time she had threatened to break down was when she had gazed into her young brother's eyes. Horace had been so hurt, so confused. She would never do anything to harm him, yet he now suffered through these tense hours because of her. She had turned away, unable to look at him. Church had been most dreadful. She had avoided the shocked and angry glares cast her way by seeing nothing more than the few steps ahead of her own feet. But she could feel their ire. Of course they were upset. The broadsheets loyal to the Crown were using her presence in the theatre to condemn them all. The king's allies within the press continued to lambaste the Dissenters for the actions they claimed she had done. The congregants at the chapel she had attended since childhood treated her as a stranger. As one who did not belong.

Now the parlor doors creaked open. The voice she had known since childhood exclaimed, "My dear Samuel, how good it is to see you again." And Wilberforce himself came into the room, obviously fully recovered from his recent bout of illness.

Abigail rose with the others but kept her face downcast.

She heard her father say, "I wish I could say I am glad to be home, William."

"Yes, yes, I do understand. Lavinia, my dear. How lovely to have you back in my home once more."

"How are you feeling, William? I understand you have been unwell."

"Indeed, yes, but it has passed, as it always does. So let us not dwell on it any longer." The diminutive figure moved over to where his bright eyes could peer up into Abigail's own. He patted her arm and said simply, "Hello, my dear."

She bit her lip and curtsied. His unspoken sympathy was a lance to her heart.

"Come, come, are we not friends? Let us relax and talk as such. Look, here is Cook with tea. And she has made her special shortbread. I find it quite the most delicious shortbread I have ever tasted. Lavinia, perhaps you will be so kind as to pour for us."

Abigail accepted her cup but did not taste it. She could not have swallowed just then. She could not capture all of what was being said. Mostly she heard the tones. William Wilberforce spoke in a warm and diplomatic manner. Her father responded with hard dignity. Her mother sounded resigned and sad.

Her father's words abruptly came into focus. "I am mightily surprised that you would ask such a question, William. How has she damaged me? What am I without my reputation, without my standing in the community?"

"Forgive me, old friend. But it seems from where I stand that the foment is being caused by His Majesty's minions and rumormongers, not your dear daughter."

"Only because she has supplied them with ammunition." Samuel Aldridge's words thudded like stones in the sunlit room. "They are attacking you and all our causes as well because of this. A fact certainly you are aware of."

Abigail's thoughts drifted away, carried by Wilberforce's soothing response. Her father's words had become a painful litany, one she heard even when he was not around. One she heard even in her dreams.

Then she realized William Wilberforce had spoken to her. She was so startled she looked up before she could catch herself. Her father sat across the room from her. They were as far apart as they had ever been in her entire life, it seemed. His gaze was dark and brooding, his brow so furrowed his eyes seemed to want to join together and bore straight through her. Her mother sat in a straight-backed settee and stared at nothing.

"Forgive me," Abigail said. She wanted to continue and say that she had not heard what had been spoken. But her throat clenched up tight.

"I was just telling your dear parents of the conversation we began the other day. And how I had been unable to continue because of my ailment. But how fascinating it was for me, my dear. And how illuminating." Wilberforce chatted on with the ease of one who noticed nothing whatsoever wrong with the day or the scene. "I was wondering if I might ask you to continue now."

She dropped her eyes and shook her head. Not that. Surely.

"Oh, do please. It is so vexing when my illnesses lay me low. I have thought of little else since our talk. I would so very much like to know how it would have continued had I been in better form."

The silence dominated for a long and heavy moment. Then her father said, "Do proceed, Abigail. Answer the gentleman."

"There, you see? Your parents are just as fascinated with what you have to say as I." If anything, Wilberforce sounded more cheerful than before. "Now then. Remind me what it was you said before I had to beg off and rest. I had asked you what it was you wanted most out of life. Not you, the child we all hold so dear. I referred to you as the adult you are becoming."

"I scarcely see how her actions grant her any such—" Her

father's voice sounded like the angry murmur of a brooding storm.

Abigail did not need to look up to realize Wilberforce must have halted her father's words. Her throat was so dry she could scarcely breathe, much less speak. Abigail took a sip of her tea. She tasted nothing.

She spoke the word to the cup resting once again in her lap. "Adventure."

"Adventure!" Wilberforce's repetition of her answer added the volume she could not provide. "Splendid!"

Lavinia asked, "How can you say that? What is splendid about any urge that causes her to disobey her parents?"

"My dear friend, you misunderstand me. I condone nothing. I seek merely to understand what is behind this behavior. Let me remind you, please. Your daughter is one of the finest people it has ever been my honor to know."

"Honor?" The rumbling thunder grew in force. "Honor?"

"Honor I said and honor I meant. Hear me out, I beg you both. Look beyond the moment's pain. We have sat together for these few minutes and already we have captured two essential elements. First, she is a child no longer. Perhaps, just perhaps, part of what we face here today has been caused by our desire to hold her within an impression that is no longer correct. So to understand what I face, because I do *not* know and do *not* understand, I have asked her. What does she want? Is this not a good manner of speech? Should we not seek understanding of such vital matters?"

This time, the silence was not so taxing. Abigail dared not raise her eyes. But she was listening now. Intently.

"My dear Abigail. Please tell me something. Do you believe in God? Do you accept Jesus Christ as your Lord and Savior?"

"With all my heart," she whispered.

"Do you feel that what you did, these forays into Soho and perhaps elsewhere, were done as a part of your Savior's calling?"

"I wanted to think that." The heat burned against her eyes once more. She blinked fiercely, willing it away. "But I was wrong to do so."

"So you justified actions you now acknowledge were wrong."

"Yes."

"And the justifications themselves you also accept as wrong."

"Yes. They were lies. The worst kind of lies."

"Why do you say that?"

She had to take another sip of tea to force air through the lump in her throat. "Because I was lying to myself, to my parents, and to my God. I lied to everyone I hold dear."

Her mother sobbed. The sound tore at her so, Abigail was forced to raise her eyes. Despite her own best efforts, she could not keep the heat from blurring her vision entirely. She spoke to vague forms she could not see. "I am so sorry, Papa. Mama. Please forgive me."

But her father's thunder had not diminished. "You have severely damaged—"

"Yes, yes, we are all aware of this," Wilberforce chided, surprising them all. "My dear Samuel, I shall speak to you as a friend. Which I hope and pray you shall remain for all our days here on this earth, and beyond. Samuel, you are too close to this matter to see the solution."

"I beg your pardon?" Louder still. "Solution, you say?"

"Just so. Samuel, everyone who knows you speaks of your abilities as a diplomat. And what is a diplomat's key role, I ask you? Why, it is to discover a solution to matters of conflict, is it not? Yet here in this critical juncture, where you address the needs of your own child, you—"

"You consider her lying to us and damaging our cause a need?"

"Has she not already apologized for this? I beg you, Samuel, consider what I am saying. Allow me to continue." Wilberforce permitted her father a moment further to object.

When Samuel remained silent, their host returned his attention to Abigail. "I am confused about one point, my dear."

Samuel Aldridge snorted his derision.

Wilberforce waited for silence to return without shifting his gaze. "Why have you not given yourself over to work with one of our numerous charities?"

"I have tried." Her voice did not seem to belong to her at all. It was scarcely above a whisper, the vague hush of a stranger. "But my parents . . ."

"Yes? Do please go on."

"My parents have restricted me at every turn." Her mother looked at her. "I'm sorry, Mama. But you know this is true. You allow me to venture forth only when I am so coddled and protected I have no chance of speaking to those in need. Or truly knowing them. Or doing anything of real value. I am held to teas and the chatter of well-intentioned ladies who do almost nothing for those in need. They only see the poor through the closed windows of their carriages. They pray for them in the safety of their parlors. They *do* nothing."

Her father demanded, "You think this excuses you for lying and slipping away and endangering yourself by consorting with riffraff in the worst regions of our city?"

Abigail dropped her gaze. "No, Father. Nothing excuses me. Nothing."

"Just so," Wilberforce exclaimed. "But we are now searching for the reasons, are we not? The condemnation has been set aside for a moment. So tell me, dear Abigail. What would you wish to do?"

"Go where I could be of genuine help. Act in ways that make a difference to this world. Help to further . . ." The voicing of her long-held dreams had caused her to look up once more. And that first glimpse of her father's face was enough to silence her utterly. There was no agreement there. No understanding. Nothing save disapproval.

Wilberforce sighed. "My dear, would you be so kind as to grant me a moment alone with your parents? Perhaps you might care to walk my garden paths, such as they are. For once in a very long while, the day is at least dry."

Abigail rose and crossed the room. At the doorway she turned back, her heart filled with a silent plea. Nothing hurt that day quite so severely as how neither of her parents would even meet her gaze.

Chapter 9

The banker paced up and down the parlor carpet in a rare rage. Had Lillian been in any other position than this, she might have even been a bit pleased to see him so furious.

"Eight days I have sent word requesting this meeting. Eight days!" Simon Bartholomew spun about to aim a finger at her. "And don't you attempt to tell me the messages weren't received. I sent them by my best man!"

"I shall tell you nothing at all so long as you remain in this state."

The finger leveled at her began to tremble. His fury was a molten force in his gaze. "Do not be so foolish as to think I am incapable of using the information at my disposal."

"I have every confidence you are as vile and despicable a creature as has ever walked the face of the earth," Lillian calmly assured him.

His face registered disbelief. "What did you say?"

"Stop being tiresome and sit down." She spoke as quietly as if she were discussing the weather with a neighbor. "I shall not speak with you further so long as you act like the spoiled child you no doubt were."

"How *dare* you speak to me in such a manner!"

"How else am I to speak with you? You storm into my house without a by-your-leave, you wear a trough in my best carpet, you rail at me over all sorts of nonsense. Precisely how would you prefer I address you?"

"As the man who holds your future, and that of your son, in his grasp!"

"Lower your voice," she said, speaking sharply for the first time. "Unless you wish to lose your presumed hold by proclaiming your abominable secrets to all the world."

He glanced at the closed door, then slitted his gaze and bore down on her. "I want—"

"Sit down, Mr. Bartholomew." She watched as reluctantly he lowered himself into a chair. "Now then. We are able to address one another as reasonable adults. Tell me what it is that you must have."

His voice held the barely controlled heat of a hissing kettle. "I want to know why I had to learn about the Aldridges' misery from the broadsheets!"

"None of the reports is accurate," Lillian replied.

But the banker was not finished. "Your task was to insert yourself into the affairs of this family and keep me abreast of anything that might be used as ammunition in my attack!"

"What ever have they done to you to deserve such harsh measures?"

"That is none of your concern!"

"Really, I must ask that you take a better hold upon your temper, sir." She picked up the little silver bell on the side table and rang it. When the maid appeared, Lillian said, "Our guest requires tea."

"Certainly, mum."

"I need no such thing."

"Nonsense. It will do you a world of good. Everyone knows there is nothing like good Ceylon tea for calming the nerves."

She did not care whether the banker had tea. She certainly had no intention of drinking a cup with him. But she needed a moment. She had to come to grips with what was happening.

It was the strangest sensation she had ever known, this calm in the face of such fury. And such peril.

For reasons she could not fathom, Lillian began recalling the evening with Lavinia. How despite the urgency and the worry, Lillian had found herself drawing away. She had felt split in two, one part riding in the carriage and the other deeply fearful of this man and the power he held over her.

The maid reentered with the tray. Without raising her eyes from her lap, Lillian said quietly, "Pour our guest a cup, if you please."

"Yes, mum."

Lillian wore a day dress of blue silk so reflective it looked almost silver in the sunlight. Her hands bore two rings, both gifts from her husband. One had a central ruby the size of a quail's egg. Around her neck were three long strands of over-sized pearls. She sat upon a gilded chair crafted in what was known as the Napoleonic style, backed in a tapestry cloth embroidered with the French fleur-de-lis. Her front parlor was not the largest nor the grandest of such London chambers, but it was a fine place indeed. She was in fact one of the most envied ladies in England—for her titles, for her beauty, for her supposed wealth.

During the previous week and a half, ever since that disas-trous night marking the last time the banker Bartholomew had entered this room, she had reflected upon what it should mean to lose everything. Her looks might as well be lost with her wealth and titles, for she most certainly would be unable to use her beauty to any great advantage. She might marry another older man, someone willing to take on a scandal-riven wife with a son. But it would not be a happy marriage, and the circumstances would be meager indeed. Even so, she did not wish to wed again. But she might be forced to in order not to starve.

And yet, despite all the fears that whispered through her dark hours, still there had been this remarkable calm.

Lillian realized the banker had spoken. "Forgive me, sir. I was lost in thought."

"So I see." Simon Bartholomew was as disconcerted as ever

she had seen. Clearly the last thing he had expected to find upon his arrival was his prey so self-possessed. "I merely repeated my earlier question. Why did you not inform me?"

"Because," Lillian replied simply, "I was with the family that night."

He was so astonished he sloshed his tea. "You were *where*?"

"You told me to grow close to them, did you not? That is precisely what I have done. So close, in fact, I possess information that is mine and mine alone. Were you to utilize this in any fashion, it would have revealed your source and destroyed any chance I had to be of further use."

"I will be the judge of that!"

She chose to ignore the outburst. "Now it is my turn to ask a question. What precisely are your intentions?"

The banker carefully set his cup upon the side table. He extracted his handkerchief and wiped his hands. "What an extraordinary thing for you to ask."

"Let us look at this arrangement logically. Surely you do not think you shall be able to maintain your grip upon me indefinitely."

"I do not see why not."

"That is unwise, sir. I shall find some way out of this. You know my history, or so you claim. You know that I am, above all, a survivor. You have me in your grip now. You shall not have this forever."

Bartholomew's gaze grew piercing, and Lillian felt a strong tremor of nerves. She knew he was at his most dangerous now. She gripped her hands together with the effort to maintain her calm. "I repeat my question, sir. What is it you seek? If I am to help you, I must know this."

Finally the banker rose and walked to the front window. He wore his customary black suit, the long tails of his coat sweeping down to the striped black and gray trouser legs. No color at all in the man. No notion of humanity. "There are two families," he said eventually. "The Aldridges are one."

"And the other?"

"You do not know them. The woman is an American. Langston. Of Washington. Merchants. She has married one Gareth Powers."

"The pamphleteer?"

"Just so."

The banker's clipped manner of speech suggested something unspoken to Lillian's attentive ear. "They have wronged you?"

"That is not of your concern. What you must reveal to me is a means by which I can destroy them all."

The studied manner in which Bartholomew spoke those words chilled Lillian to the bone.

"There is more," Bartholomew added.

"Yes?"

"I have heard . . ." Bartholomew hesitated a moment. Finally he continued, "The last time we met, I told you of the ire these Dissenters and anti-slavers have raised within the royal court."

"Indeed."

"This ire is uncommonly strong. Were someone to offer a lever that might genuinely halt their reforming efforts, they would be well rewarded."

The awareness came with shocking clarity. "You seek to be rewarded with a title," Lillian interpreted. "You have come out of the woodwork with your long-standing desire for revenge, over some long-dead matter. They wronged you in the past. You have done nothing to retaliate until now. But the king and his cronies are with you. Finally there is an opportunity to destroy your enemies and gain titles for yourself."

Simon Bartholomew turned from the window. The sunlight cast his features into a series of dismal caverns. "I dislike your belief that you know my motives so clearly."

"How else am I to serve you?" This knowledge gave her a lever. What it signified she had no idea. But she knew the tides had altered somewhat. Her calm restored, it was possible to

release the tight grip her hands had kept in her lap and say, "I
wish to enter into a bargain."

Bartholomew barked a single laugh. "Really, this is too
absurd."

"Bargain," she repeated. "I will seek out the information
you desire. In return, you will agree to dissolve all my debts
and vow never to use your knowledge against me, or my family,
ever again."

The intent examination returned. "And if I refuse?"

"You will not," she said simply. "You know you cannot
hold this blade poised over me forever. This gives you what I
want, and vice versa. Does that not make up an ideal bargain?"

"I will consider . . ." Something outside the window dis-
tracted him.

"What is it?"

"A carriage has pulled up in front of your house." His eyes
widened. "It is the Aldridges!"

"Step away from there!" She leaped to her feet. "Did they
see you?"

He glanced out. "Apparently not. What are they doing
here?"

"Did I not say I was with them in their hour of need?
Where is your own carriage?"

"I came from the bank by transom."

"This way!" She opened the parlor's rear door and said to
the startled maid, "Bring the gentleman's cloak!"

"I had none," Bartholomew told her.

"Follow me." She hastened down the narrow servant's hallway and through the kitchen. Lillian unbolted the rear door
and ushered him out. When Bartholomew stood upon the rear
stoop, she said, "You risk undermining your own cause by
coming here. From now on you will send written word, and I
shall present myself to your premises when I am able."

Before he could reply, she shut the door in his face.

Lillian turned back to face the cook and said, "It appears

we are to have additional guests, these far more welcome than
the last."

The cook understood instantly. "There's some of the lovely
cherry gateau I made up for yesterday's visitors."

"Serve that with tea for three perhaps, or four—I'm not
certain."

"Very good, mum."

She heard the front bellpull jingle and hurried back down
the hall. She arrived in the main foyer just as the maid was
about to answer the door. "Remain as you are for one
moment, please."

"Yes, mum."

Lillian turned to the oval hall mirror. Her appearance was
one of the few givens that remained steadfast in her life. It was
her eyes she wanted to inspect. What precisely had Bartholomew observed? The sky-blue irises stared back at her, as lovely
and placid as ever.

Lillian was struck by a sudden urge to give the banker
nothing. She studied her reflection and wondered how such a
perilous concept could grip her with such wrenching force.
No matter how appealing the prospect, to refuse to do Bartholomew's bidding meant to risk everything. Were she to fail
him, Lillian had no doubt whatever the banker would destroy
her. Yet her mind returned once more to the utter goodness in
Lavinia Aldridge. And her daughter. No matter what nonsense
the broadsheets might be spouting. She had seen the young
woman in her direst hour declare that she would only accept
freedom if her friends were released as well. What a remarkable
strength of will this young woman held. So very much like a
younger Lillian, she reflected. And so very different.

Yet with the blade hung poised over her head, what could
she possibly do? Lillian found no pleasure in the fact that her
features shone with the lie of surreal calm. A life of lies, she
mused. Why was she growing so distressed over just a few
more?

The bell jangled a second time.

"My lady?"

Lillian touched a perfectly coiffed strand of hair, smoothed the collar to her frock, and turned from the mirror. "You may open the door."

As soon as she heard the front door's jangling bell, Abigail knew it was for her. She had been expecting the call, had known ever since Sunday morning that it had to come. Even before Horace came trumping up the stairs and down the long central hallway, she knew it was a visitor for her. Which was why, when her brother knocked upon her door, Abigail was already at her little dressing table.

"Come in."

"Nora is downstairs."

Abigail buttoned her collar and refitted the little cloth fasteners at the wrists. "Thank you, brother."

"Are you all better now?"

That was all it took, and the tears started pressing against her eyes. As if she had not already cried enough for an entire lifetime.

But Horace did not notice. "I hate it around the house these days."

Abigail could only nod her mournful agreement.

He took her silence as license to continue. "It's no *fun*. It used to be so jolly here. Why can't things go back to the way they were before?"

Abigail's curls defied easy grooming. She had two brushes, one stiff enough to force its way through the tightest knots. She used the other one now, so soft it did little save polish the red surface. She picked up the powder puff and dusted her cheeks. The paleness of her complexion caused every tiny freckle to stand out like a beacon.

Horace was ten years old and tall for his age. He wore stout corded trousers and boots and a starched white shirt. He was attending a local grammar school and was scheduled to enroll at Eton beginning the next term. He was both eager to go and frightened at the prospect of leaving home, which only added to his foul mood. He kicked at the doorframe and muttered, "Nora's man is downstairs with her. I don't like him."

Abigail turned from her dressing table and opened her arms. "Come here."

Horace had long been a great friend, the little man of her life. She found him utterly exasperating at times, of course. He was, after all, a younger brother.

He allowed her to hug him, something he was growing to detest as he grew older. "Are you all better now?" he asked again.

Abigail hugged him harder still and found herself recalling him as a baby. How he wriggled when she held him, and the way he smelled. And how much he cried. Baby Horace had always seemed to be squalling.

Abigail released him and stood. Strange how her younger brother was the only one whose presence seemed to calm her. "Come."

Horace took her hand, the most natural gesture in the world. And why not? He had been doing it all his life. "Why did she have to bring that man with her?"

"His name is Tyler. Tyler Brock."

"He sniffs when he talks to me. Like this." Horace snorted like a mule with the grippe.

"Don't make such sounds."

But he had caught the hint of a smile in her voice. So he made the noise again, even louder this time. "It's ever so annoying."

Abigail heard their voices in the front parlor and tightened her grip upon Horace's hand. She would be strong. "The house is so quiet."

"It's the Talbots' half day off," Horace said, glancing at her in surprise.

"Of course." She had no idea what day it was. Time had mingled together in a colorless muddle, and for the first time she could remember, the days had not seemed an hour or so too short. Now it was the exact opposite. Now the clock seemed to taunt her with the impossibly slow passage of empty minutes. Particularly the nights. She had come to dread hearing the hours chime away.

"And Mother and Father are off on some errand." Horace hesitated, then added, "I heard them talking before they left. It was about you."

But they had arrived at the parlor door. Abigail released her brother's hand, lifted her chin, and took a deep breath.

Horace caught the change. His worried expression returned. "Are you quite all right?"

There was no way she could answer that honestly and not worry him further. "Do you think you could be the proper English gentleman and serve us tea?"

"I've done it for Mother before."

"Of course you have. Don't burn yourself with the kettle."

He gave her a look full of a ten-year-old's disdain and turned away.

Abigail opened the parlor door and entered the front room. "Hello, Nora."

"Well. I'm surprised you even remember my name." Her dearest friend came over and embraced her. "Especially after ignoring me like you did on Sunday."

Abigail could not quite suppress the shudder over hearing the day so casually referred to. The church service had been a scalding affair. People she had counted as friends all her life long had seared her with their looks. She had been shunned.

The same as the previous Sunday. And it was all to happen again next Sunday. And every Sunday after that.

Abigail forced herself to confront the slender young man and his knowing smirk. "Good afternoon, Mr. Brock."

Tyler Brock was a fastidious man who used a pungent oil on his hair. Stray curls popped up here and there, glistening in the afternoon light. He was sharp featured and favored high collars with brightly colored foulards. His lips were a tight red line. "Miss Abigail. I trust you are well?"

That particular question deserved no response. Abigail said to Nora, "I have asked Horace to serve tea. I fear it shall be dreadful."

"Oh, good heavens, Abigail. Who cares about tea?" Nora's hands were busy, fluttering about, as though trying desperately to keep her nerves bundled up. "I came to see *you*."

"Did you?"

"Whatever do you mean?"

"Won't you sit down?" Abigail hesitated, then clasped her friend's arm and pulled her over to the sofa even while directing Tyler to the one opposite.

"How *are* you?" began Nora.

"You know perfectly well how I am."

"My parents were frightfully upset. I'm sure it's been just dreadful."

Abigail found she could not bear it. The tearing sensation in her heart was awful. Here she sat, next to her dearest friend in the entire world, and there were so many things she desperately wanted to share with her. But she couldn't. Particularly while her young man sat opposite them, watching Abigail with such disdain.

"Won't you talk with me, Abigail? Aren't we still friends?"

"Of course we are." But Tyler was such a distraction, she could not put much strength into the words. "I'm so sorry I got you into such trouble, Nora."

"It was rather tense around the house, I don't mind telling you." She lowered her voice conspiratorially. "My mother was so upset when she heard I'd been in Soho, she took to her bed for three days."

Abigail found Tyler's tight little grin was visible no matter how she turned in her seat. So she stopped trying to ignore him and instead confronted him directly. "Did Nora's parents insist upon your coming along, Mr. Brock?"

"They suggested that Nora might care for some company."

"And you always do what your betters say, don't you?"

He was not to be cowed. "I find it keeps me in good stead with those in positions of responsibility. As you no doubt are fully aware now."

"Tyler," Nora protested nervously, "you promised."

Normally such a comment would have been enough to raise Abigail's temper to the boiling point. Today, however, she observed the young man as from a very great distance. "What about adventure, Mr. Brock?"

"What about it?"

"Do you not find yourself yearning to be involved in the new horizons unfolding about us?"

He removed a fleck of lint from his trousers. "Hardly."

Somehow the act of speaking was enough to ease the pressure in her heart. She spoke as much for herself as for Tyler. As though she plumbed her own reasons for acting as she had. "They say we are entering into a new age, Mr. Brock. One of great industrial might. One where inventions will transform the way we live our lives."

Nora seemed pleased that for once they were not quarreling. She offered, "Father is very excited by the prospects of steam."

Tyler Brock had developed his sniff into an exact science. "Mr. Mills, the general director of our firm, feels all this interest in steam is utter stuff and nonsense. A flash in the pan. A momentary sensation, a distraction, nothing more. The horse is as perfect a form of transport as will ever be developed."

Abigail waited a moment, hoping Nora might disagree. But of course her oldest friend merely sat and looked adoringly at her fiancé.

Abigail asked him, "And what of all the great strides made in exploration? New lands being discovered, new peoples identified, the westward expansion in America. Does all this not thrill you?"

"I find nothing quite so thrilling as the careful measure of accounts, the knowledge of a good day's wage for a good day's work, and the probability of a long future lived in this fair land."

"With me," Nora added brightly.

"But so much is happening, so much is changing," Abigail protested. Yet her voice remained mild. She was too busy listening to her own thoughts being expressed to find Tyler irritating. After all, she knew his responses even before she spoke. "The broadsheets are filled with this newest land sale in America. They call it the greatest such expansion in the history of humankind."

Nora asked, "You read the papers?"

Abigail turned to look at her friend. Her oldest, sweetest, and dearest friend. "Every day," she quietly replied.

Tyler Brock inquired, "And does your good father know of this?"

"He observes me from time to time," she responded, not taking her eyes from her friend. "But I doubt he is aware how avidly I study the information."

"I would have thought," he paused for a sniff, "that you would have learned by now the perils of such misbehavior."

Thankfully Horace chose that moment to knock and enter. He balanced the tray with great diligence and had even donned a jacket to give himself a proper appearance. He concentrated so hard his forehead creased in a dozen furrows as he poured the tea and offered each a cup. As Abigail had expected, the tea was so weak as to appear almost clear. "You have done a marvelous job, Horace. I can't thank you enough."

Tyler Brock sniffed his opinion.

Abigail decided she had had enough. She said to Nora, "You might as well go ahead and tell me the bad news."

Her friend's hands could not alight anywhere for long. "What—what do you mean?"

"Here, I shall make it easy for you." She waited until Horace shut the door upon his departure. "Your parents have informed you that I shall not be your bridesmaid."

"How did you know?"

It had been clear as day at the church. How everyone looked at her, or avoided looking. Abigail could not have said which had been worse. But Nora's mother had looked. Oh my, yes. A scathing glance that burned long after the woman had turned away. "It's all right, Nora. I understand perfectly."

"I tried and tried. But they won't budge."

"You can hardly expect otherwise," Tyler Brock offered. "After all—"

But Abigail had no interest in hearing the man's opinion of her actions. Her own condemnation was harsh enough. Abigail rose and drew her friend with her. "I wish you only happiness, Nora."

"Oh, Abigail."

She endured Nora's embrace as long as she was able without breaking down. She then turned to Tyler and found the strength to remain steady, simply by looking at his smirk. "Good-bye, Mr. Brock."

"Miss Abigail." His mocking bow felt like a slap in the face, and Abigail took an involuntary step back.

Nora cried, "Oh, do at least promise you shall be there with me on our wedding day!"

She could not lie, not about this, not to her dear friend. So Abigail embraced her once more and said simply, "Be happy. For us both."

Chapter 10

Once the Aldridges were seated in Lillian's formal parlor, Samuel Aldridge told her, "I knew your late husband, the count."

"Did you, now? I don't recall his ever mentioning this."

"No, he wouldn't have. One of his partners approached me in regard to a venture he was entering." Samuel Aldridge nodded his thanks to the maid as she handed him a cup of tea. "One to be based in Lisbon."

"I see." Thoughtfully she stirred her tea with the little silver spoon. Samuel Aldridge was a powerfully built man. There was no sign of the dissipated living so fashionable in London these days. Stocky and stalwart, his muttonchops were flecked with gray. His chin was as determined as his gaze. This was not a man who did anything lightly. Surely he would know of just how that Portugal venture had ended in disaster.

"They invited me to the Carlton Club and hosted a most pleasant meal. The only thanks I gave was to warn them not to become involved. I fear I upset them considerably."

"If only he and his partner had shown the wisdom to heed your words, Mr. Aldridge."

"I understand it wiped out Lord Houghton's partner entirely."

"Indeed." She nodded her understanding. The message was finally received. Samuel Aldridge intended to address the day's difficult issues with honesty.

At least, they would be honest. And she, how would she respond?

Lillian studied her guests over the rim of her porcelain cup. They both bore the pale shadows of great strain. Neither had slept well for quite some time, of that Lillian was certain. Lavinia might as well have been wearing black, her face was so creased with a mourner's lines. Samuel was scarce in better form, hunched over his cup, his eyes encircled by plum-colored stains.

"It was this very same venture which caused my husband's demise," Lillian said quietly.

Samuel Aldridge looked up. "I did not know, Lady Houghton."

"How could you."

"Forgive me for bringing up the matter."

"I understand why you did so."

"There was no ulterior motive, madam, of that I assure you."

"You wished to begin our first conversation together with my knowledge of the only other contact you have had with my family. You wished to be utterly open with me." Lillian took a sip from her cup. "You have come because you would like to speak of some grave matter. Something so vital there could be no hint of subterfuge between us."

Lavinia and her husband exchanged glances. Samuel replied, "Just so, madam."

"Where, might I ask, is your daughter?"

Irritation flickered across Samuel Aldridge's features. "Who can say where my daughter has elected to while away her hours?"

Lavinia spoke for the first time. A soft whisper, the sigh of a bereaved mother. "Abigail is at home in her room."

Samuel glanced at his wife, but addressed Lillian with, "I cannot begin to thank you for all you have done for my wife, my daughter, and my good name." He dropped his eyes to his cup and added quietly, "What is left of it."

"None of that," Lillian said sharply enough to lift his gaze. "We both know the broadsheets that have slandered you have never cared for any of your ilk. Those who admire you will think no less of you for the lies they have printed."

"They are using this matter to slander the entire Dissenter movement!" he protested.

"Then they are desperate indeed. As you have no doubt been hearing from others who know your true worth, sir. As you would be saying yourself were it someone else's daughter who had become so enmeshed in this."

"But it is not someone else's daughter," he retorted.

"Indeed not."

"For this reason, I find myself in your debt, my lady. If there is anything I might ever do to aid you, please, I beg you—"

"Do not speak thus, sir. It demeans us both."

"Ma'am?"

Lillian set her cup aside, rose, and walked to the window. Outside was a lovely display of summer sunlight, a wondrous clear day, though rather chilly for late July. The utterly blue sky was teased by hundreds of white ribbons rising from the city's chimneys. The townhouses across the street were of the same dressed white stone as her own, stalwart monuments to wealth and power. She studied the empty windows across from her and fleetingly wondered what lies they held, what desperation.

"My husband was no friend of the new royal court," Lillian said to the window. "His allegiances were too closely tied to the old king. When the Portuguese venture failed, these same broadsheets which slander you took vast delight in proclaiming to the world just what a failure my late husband was. What a fool, they jested. The headlines went on day after day, week after week. It was not the financial ruin alone which demolished Grantlyn's health. Added to that was the shame." The sunlight was hot upon her skin, but not nearly as searing as the memories. "I was shunned. For over a year I did not set foot outside my own home. The next time I saw any of my friends was at my husband's funeral."

"Ma'am, I can only say how sorry—"

"*That* is true shame, sir. *This* is nothing. A week, perhaps two, and another scandal will shove this one aside. A month more, and people will again recognize you for the fine man you no doubt are." Lillian turned back to the room and gazed directly at Samuel. "And your daughter as the fine woman she is."

Lavinia met her eyes now, sheer gratitude flush upon her features.

"Is that what you wished to speak with me about?" Lillian asked Samuel.

"No." Samuel Aldridge set his own cup aside. "No ma'am, it is not. My wife urged me to come and seek your advice. She said your wisdom meant more than your aid on that night, and now I see what she meant."

"Lavinia is most kind, sir."

"We are faced with a conundrum, my lady. One which confounds us utterly. I do not see what you can do to help us. But I also have no idea where else . . ."

Lillian walked back over and settled herself into the chair. She composed herself to wait as long as was required.

Samuel Aldridge reached to the side table and retrieved the little silver teaspoon, in order to give his fingers something to do. "Are you familiar with William Wilberforce?"

"The name only. I have never had occasion to meet the gentleman."

"He is a wonderful man," Lavinia said softly.

"He is indeed," agreed her husband. "A good and wise counselor, and a friend. We have been involved with Mr. Wilberforce for years, and I can honestly say, ma'am, it has never been my honor to meet a finer man."

"I should wish to meet him for myself."

"Something we can gladly arrange." Samuel Aldridge twirled the spoon such that it reflected the sunlight in scattered prisms about the room. "William, our dear friend, well, ma'am, that is . . ."

Lavinia finished for her husband, "He has urged us to send Abigail to America."

"I do not understand—"

"America," Samuel intoned.

"Her life here is intolerable," Lavinia said.

"Only because she has made it such herself," Samuel retorted, the annoyance creasing his features once more.

Lavinia winced slightly but continued, "The church is furious with her."

"Again, only because of Abigail's own actions. And rightly so, I might add." When Lavinia did not respond, Samuel asked Lillian, "Forgive me for speaking of such a personal issue, my lady. My wife tells me you are not a believer."

"That is correct."

"Then it is scarcely possible for you to fathom the importance the church plays in our life."

"All of Abigail's friends are of the church community," Lavinia added. "Most have been ordered by their parents to have nothing whatsoever to do with her."

"She is more than alone," Samuel said, pain creasing his voice as it did his wife's face. "She is distraught."

"Abigail will not leave the house," Lavinia said, suddenly close to tears. "She will not speak. She scarcely eats enough to keep body and soul together."

"How can this be?" Lillian's gaze swept from one parent to the other. "All because of one minor misstep?"

"You consider this, this *scandal* to be something *minor*?"

"Forgive me, sir. But yes, I do."

Samuel Aldridge's mouth worked, but no sound came out.

"This, sir, is *nothing*. You daughter struck me as a beautiful, vibrant, intelligent young lady. Of course, she has made a grievous error. But how can she believe she has ruined her life?"

"This, effectively, is what dear William has told us as well,"

Lavinia offered, watching her husband as she spoke. "He feels that everyone has reacted too strongly. He suggests that Abigail be granted a respite, I believe was the word he used. From us, from the church community, and from this city."

"I cannot leave now," Samuel said, speaking directly to his wife. "You have heard something of the problems we face on the Continent," he added, turning to Lillian. "It will take months to resolve these, longer still to arrange my affairs here such that I could return to America."

"William did not suggest," Lavinia replied, "that we accompany her."

"You would do this?" he asked his wife. "You would let your daughter go?"

"She needs this, Samuel. You are the observant one. You are the wise leader. Surely you must see this for yourself."

"What I see is that my daughter has placed her life in peril and damaged our family's good name, not to mention the causes we hold dearest!"

"Yes, all this is true. No one is denying this. Not me, and certainly not your daughter. But did you not hear what William told us? We must look *beyond* this."

"You were not so certain of all this when we met with William."

"The idea came as a great shock. Of course I don't want to let my daughter travel halfway around the world without us." Lavinia wiped her eyes impatiently. "But I also know she cannot stay. You heard her speak. She yearns for adventure. What possibly could we—"

"She is a child! How is she to know what she wants?"

"You are wrong there, husband. I am sorry, but it is true. Abigail is an adult."

"How can you say that? She refuses to even *consider* taking a husband!"

"That is far from the only measure of a woman's maturity," Lavinia reminded him quietly.

Both of them must have become aware of Lillian observing

them. Samuel Aldridge collected himself. "Please forgive us, madam. Here we have come to thank you and seek your wisdom, but all we do is return to the same discussion—"

"I shall accompany her."

Her guests froze with shock.

"I shall go with her to America," Lillian said. "It is the perfect resolution to this matter. Does she have anyone with whom she might live?"

"B-both our families, y-yes. They would be most happy to receive her."

"She adores her grandmother," Lavinia added, new hope in her voice. "My parents live in Georgetown, the port city adjacent to our capital."

Samuel reluctantly allowed, "William Wilberforce has suggested that she go and work with Gareth and Erica Powers. They live just half a mile from my wife's parents and have been longtime friends."

Hearing the name spoken so soon after the banker's departure rocked Lillian hard. "The Powers, did you say?"

"You know them?"

It was Lillian's turn to stumble over her words. "Th-the name only. P-Powers is a famous pamphleteer, is he not?"

"Indeed. And a valued ally in our struggle against the evils of slavery." The words seemed to emerge of their own accord. "My dear Lady Houghton, how could you possibly consider leaving all this and going to America on our behalf?"

How? How indeed was she ever to be anything but completely honest with these fine people? Lillian looked from one to the other, as moved by their evident love for each other and their daughter as she had ever been moved by anything. "I assure you, Mr. Aldridge, I would not be doing this solely for your daughter. I need to make this journey. Desperately."

"Need?"

"The Portugal venture came far closer to wiping us out than anyone knows." There. It was said. The secret she had sought to hold back for so long. The first of many.

"Forgive me, ma'am. I did not know."

"Of course not. How could you possibly? But the fact remains. I am perched upon a knife's edge. At any moment I could be encased in ruin and woe." A thought occurred to her. "There is something you could do for me, as a matter of fact."

"Anything."

The blank offer, so boldly stated, left her desperately tempted to tell him everything. For an instant she was very jealous of Lavinia Aldridge. To be married to a good strong man, a man with a head for business, a man who loved her and their child more than his own life. What would this mean?

"Just say the words, ma'am, and I will be happy to do everything in my power to assist you."

The world returned to proper focus. What possible good could come from telling them of the merchant banker who had acquired all her husband's debts? Simon Bartholomew was a world removed from fine people like these. He was one of the Crown's own bankers and a man who loved vengeance for vengeance's own sake. Samuel Aldridge might well be ruined.

Lillian said, "I seek to sell my jewelry."

Samuel Aldridge was clearly disappointed by the paltry nature of her request. "That is not necessary, my lady. Allow me to forward you whatever sum you might care to name."

"Upon what guarantee, sir? I have nothing. My own house is secured by a note, held by a banker. . . ."

"Yes, you were saying something about a bank?"

She steeled herself. "Never mind that. I already face substantial debts, sir. I must seek to start over. I understand there are lands for sale in America?"

At this, Samuel Aldridge brightened. "Indeed so, my lady. The Great Land Purchase, they are calling it. Why, my own family is in the process of acquiring several thousand acres."

"And this land, it is both fertile and inexpensive, do I understand this correctly?"

"From the reports I am receiving, ma'am, the land is the

finest on earth. And it is selling for three American dollars an acre."

"That is most astonishing. I would scarcely believe it save I have read similar reports myself." This was her answer. This is what she would do. Begin a new estate, far removed from all the turmoil and disgrace. "I wish to ask your assistance in selling my jewelry and my paintings. It is all I have, sir. That and my silver plate."

"But—"

"Everything must go, and in great secrecy. I cannot possibly approach an auctioneer myself. Word would emerge, and I would be ruined as well as dishonored."

"Of course, I am happy to help. But I repeat what I said earlier, my lady, I am quite willing to offer you a personal loan." The man's features shone with a resolute force. "Your good name is all the guarantee I could possibly ask."

To be offered such kindness, and over money, and only moments after the merchant banker had departed, was too much. Lillian could not quite stifle the first sob.

"Here," Lavinia said, bolting to her feet. "Have a sip of tea."

"I'm all right, thank you. Forgive me. I was not expecting such kindness."

"After all you have done for us." Samuel Aldridge appeared genuinely astonished. "What else are we to show you?"

"Even so, I am most grateful."

"As you have yourself said earlier, ma'am, let us speak no more of it."

"Then we are decided?" Lavinia asked her husband.

"On the face of such an offer," Samuel Aldridge replied slowly, "I confess to thinking that perhaps God's hand is at work here."

Lavinia anxiously asked their hostess, "I must request your honest and open opinion. Do you feel that we are doing the right thing in permitting our daughter to travel so far from her home and family?"

"I know your daughter hardly at all," Lillian answered

thoughtfully. "But I do know human nature. And if I am certain of anything, it is this: if you chain a person down to hold them, when they finally break free they will never return. And break free she will, if anything you say of her strong and independent nature is true."

The piercing quality of Lavinia's gaze surfaced for the first time that day. "You seem to speak with some experience."

This time Lillian retreated to her cup. In truth, she spoke from more experience than either of them could imagine. But there was nothing to be gained from speaking of that. Though the strange urge to unburden herself remained strong as it had since their arrival.

"Might I ask when you would be prepared to depart for America?" Samuel asked Lillian.

"As soon as I see to a few personal affairs and make arrangements for my son."

"I believe I recall my wife saying he is at boarding school?"

"Eton."

"Our Horace begins at Eton next term!" Samuel exclaimed.

"Your boy must come spend his holidays in our home," Lavinia said.

"God's hand is most certainly upon this," Samuel declared. "What could possibly come from such a meeting other than His perfect good?"

Chapter 11

Lillian Houghton sat at the confectioner's tiny table and watched her son consume an enormous amount of sweets. The lad's appetite was astonishing. "Do they not feed you at Eton?"

The boy's face was liberally sprinkled with sugar dust and chocolate sauce. He laughed delightedly. "Of course they do, Mama. What nonsense."

"Don't talk like that to your mother, Byron," she admonished dutifully.

"Well, it's true." He took another great bite of a round cake filled with raspberry sauce, then licked his fingers. "I say, this one is especially fine."

"You are making such a mess. You have jam on your collar." She dipped her napkin in her water glass and leaned forward. "Here, let me tidy you up."

"Oh, Mama, please don't go on so. People are looking at us."

She smiled through her hurt. "I should think you would like to have your mother make a fuss over you."

Byron's face reddened. "I'm almost a man now, Mama."

"Yes," she ruefully agreed. "I can see that."

He took the napkin from her and bent at an awkward angle, trying to find the stain himself. "Where is the spot?"

"Never you mind, it's almost vanished now." By leaning over, Byron had decorated his shirt with chocolate. "Are those friends of yours at the window table?"

"Probably." Byron did not turn around. "But I don't want to talk with them now, all right?"

"Whatever you wish, my dear."

"It's just—well, all the boys want to meet you." He fumbled with his words in the manner of one who wished he was more grown than he actually was. "They go on about you in the silliest of manners."

This she could understand. The headmaster was no different, nor was the senior teacher Lillian had just met with. Both gentlemen were apparently dumbstruck in her presence. Normally she took such male adulation as her due. But today it was simply another distraction from the matters at hand. "Byron, I must speak—"

"The senior lad wishes to meet you, Mama. He has made rather a point of it. He can make life ever so difficult for me. Would you mind terribly if we stopped by his room after?"

"No, dear. But you mustn't interrupt me."

"Sorry, Mama."

He really was a darling child. Lillian caught herself. Child no longer. He was sprouting up at an alarming rate. She was fairly certain he had grown another three inches since he had been home at Christmas. Byron was a mirror image of his father, with the same sandy hair falling over his broad forehead, the same rather pronounced chin that would grow strong and manly in time, the same keen gray eyes. His father, the late count, had never been a particularly handsome man. But his rather oversized head had contained a remarkably keen insight and a prodigious appetite for learning. "Your headmaster says you might be head boy material."

Byron also shared his father's habit of flushing far too easily to ever lie well. "He never."

"Have I not just come from speaking with the gentleman? He tells me you are at the top of your class in almost every subject. And you are becoming quite the cricketer."

Lillian found herself blurting out, "Darling, would you care to take a trip with me to America?"

He froze in the process of selecting another cake. "Leave Eton?"

"Just for a year. Perhaps even less than that."

"But Mama . . ." Byron sat back in his chair. "All my friends would move on without me."

"You can catch up with them. Besides, think of the adventure. America, darling. The great frontiers. Does that not excite you?"

He looked stricken. "I would rather stay with my pals, actually."

"But I must go, my darling. Wouldn't you miss me?"

"Yes, of course, Mama. But . . ," He fidgeted in his chair.

Lillian perused the confectionery shop while her son contemplated his answer. It had three bow windows, each forming a discreet alcove. The windows were veiled with translucent white curtains and framed by heavy velvet drapes of emerald green. The tables were round and marble topped. The servers padded softly across deep plush carpeting. It was the sort of place designed to appeal to Eton's wealthiest families. Lillian nodded to a titled gentleman she knew vaguely, who was having tea with his own son. The man twirled his moustache and gave her a sparkling eye. Lillian turned away.

Why not marry? She certainly had enough offers. The answer was obvious. Whoever took her hand in marriage would have to know about her past and accept responsibility for covering her debts. Plus there was the risk that the scandal might erupt, unless of course she married someone powerful enough to threaten the banker with ruin. . . .

Her mind had traveled this same circuitous route so often she stifled the thoughts before they descended again into frustration and woe. The fact was, were she to give herself in marriage under these circumstances, she would face the constant threat of having her secrets used against her. Lillian had been fortunate with her first husband. Grantlyn had been a man of his word, and in his own way had been affectionate enough.

Lillian was a woman of the world and knew just how disastrous such arrangements often were. No. There had to be another means of escape.

She focused upon her son, who had returned to devouring another sweet. "I must travel to America, my darling. Do you understand what I am saying?"

"I suppose so."

"Won't you miss me?"

"Oh yes. Very much." He fumbled and almost dropped the oversized teapot. "I say, the handle has grown rather hot."

"Here, use the tea cloth." She poured for him. One characteristic Byron had inherited from her in abundance was fierce independence. It had been his defining trait even as an infant. Byron had resisted being held. Or stroked, or cuddled. Lillian's late husband had taken humorous pride in this, calling it a sign of good British breeding, but she knew better. Her aunt had described Lillian's infancy in the same way. Lillian had been the only baby girl her aunt had ever known who refused a cuddle. Who liked nothing more than to crawl into an empty corner and play all by herself.

Which was why Lillian had elected to send her son off to school. At nine years of age Byron had already begun to explore beyond the safe boundaries. He would disappear for hours, sneak away from the most careful minder and race into the unknown, as though he heard some secret call, a silent trumpet whose invitation he could not resist.

Just like his mother.

"Mama? Did you not hear a word I said?"

"I'm sorry, my darling. I was drifting."

"The school has planned an outing to Scotland. Two days in Edinburgh and then a week hiking the Highlands. It sounds like ever so much fun. Might I go along?"

In fact, she had already discussed this with the headmaster. Byron had been in trouble several times his first year, usually for slipping out of school bounds. His punishments had been rather severe, and at one point Lillian had feared he might be sent down. But the prospect of leaving his new friends behind had done what Lillian could not, which was to teach her boy an acceptance of regulations, at least so far as the authorities were aware. The Highland trip was restricted to those who looked to become honor students. It was a rare privilege to be included.

"Mama?"

"I will agree, but on one condition."

A genuine fear shone in his eyes, and she knew he was expecting her to say he must go to America. Lillian felt her heart fill with burning sorrow. She loved her boy so. Loved him so much, in fact, that she saw with a mother's wisdom that he had already grown beyond her arms.

"What is it you want, Mama?"

"I wish—" she stopped and cleared her throat—"I wish for you to spend your holidays with a family in London."

"Who?"

"You don't know them. Their name is Aldridge. They are Americans."

"But I'm sure my friends would have me home with them if I asked."

"You may spend half the time with them," she conceded. "But the other half I wish for you to stay with the Aldridges."

"Why, Mama?"

Why indeed? Because there was a goodness to these people that she could not fathom. Because she wished for Byron to have a connection to a way of life that was lost to her, or so it felt. "They have a son who will start at Eton next term."

He made a face. "A new lad?"

"You were a new boy not so long ago yourself."

Byron caught the change in tone and no doubt knew his mother would not bend further. He gave his most charming smile. "Of course I shall do as you say."

She resisted the urge to sweep him up in her arms and sob from a mother's broken heart. It would only embarrass him. She struggled to frame the words around a trembling smile.

"And you shall miss your mother just a little. You must promise me that as well."

Lavinia Aldridge did not intend to pry. Well, perhaps she did. She released a breath that might have been a sigh had it not been necessary for her to remain silent. Because she was eavesdropping, of course. She was desperately concerned and needed to know precisely what was happening.

When Lillian Houghton had requested time to speak with Abigail alone, Lavinia had naturally agreed. After all, the two would need to know and trust one another. They would be living in each other's pockets for a very long time. And yet, now that the decision had been taken and things were moving forward, Lavinia lived with an almost constant fear. Who was this Countess Houghton? Was she truly the sort of person to whom Lavinia could trust her only daughter? The thought of her dear sweet child traveling so far away was a noose that threatened to rob her body of breath.

There were so many unknowns, so many perils. The dowager countess had no daughter. What if her intent was to steal their Abigail away? Clearly she was a lady of experience—after all, she managed her late husband's household and estate now. What if she taught Abigail improper ways? And worst of all was the woman's stated lack of faith. This seized Lavinia's heart like a fist. She knew her husband was fearful of the same thing, though Samuel did not speak of it. He had himself stated in the woman's front parlor that God's hand was upon this journey. Yet how could that be, if Lillian Houghton was not a believer?

Lavinia sat in the dining room, which was separated from the parlor by a set of tall sliding doors. When the Aldridges entertained a large number of people, it was possible to remove the dining table and open up the doors to form one elegant chamber. Now the doors were tightly closed, yet Lavinia had long since learned that every sound carried from the front parlor to where she sat. The polished oval table was strewn with papers, matters related to the upcoming journey and unfinished letters Abigail would carry to her family and friends. Lavinia touched none of them. She stared straight ahead, her entire being focused upon what was happening in the next room.

Lavinia heard Ben Talbot enter the front parlor and say, "Begging your pardon, ladies. Mrs. Aldridge suggested I serve you tea."

"A very good afternoon, I'm sure, Mr. Talbot."

"How are you, my lady?"

"As well as can be expected, given this dreadful weather. I don't believe I have had an occasion to thank you for your services that awful night, sir."

"It is I who am grateful, my lady. I don't know what my mistress would have done without you, or Miss Aldridge here either, and that's the honest truth."

"You care for the young lady very much, I see." Lavinia heard Lillian's tone soften.

"She's like the daughter my wife and I never had, ma'am. Can't tell you how pleased we are to know she's got you as a traveling companion."

"Yes, well, that is what we are here to discuss."

The words caused Lavinia to sit up straighter. This was unexpected. Lillian made it sound as though the decision was not yet final.

"Then I'll just set the tray down here, ma'am," Ben said, "and leave you to it."

"Good day, Mr. Talbot."

Lavinia heard the door close and Lillian ask, "Shall I pour you a cup?"

Abigail spoke for the first time since Lillian had arrived. "Yes, please, and thank you, ma'am."

Lavinia heard the tinkling sound of a spoon being set upon a porcelain saucer. Then nothing. Outside the dining room window was a world awash in thunderous gloom. The glass was streaked by heavy rain. Carriages trundling around Grosvenor Square were mere smudges in a gray, wet landscape. The absence of color reflected how their house had seemed ever since that dreadful night. Abigail's cheery brightness had utterly vanished. Previously she'd had an opinion about everything and no sense of restraint whatsoever. When she was happy, the entire world sang. When sad or tired or angry, the household ached with her. Thankfully, her foul moods had been few and short-lived. Until now.

"May I call you Abigail? And you must call me Lillian. I should not abide traveling halfway around the world with someone whose first name is forbidden to my use."

There was yet another silence. Lavinia stared at the rain-washed window, yet in her mind's eye she saw clearly the two of them seated in the next room. Their front parlor was painted a creamy yellow, with the fireplace and windows dressed in white. The sofas and high-backed chairs were covered in matching silk fabric striped the same bright tones. Flowers rose from a crystal vase upon the sofa table, and more stood upon the mantel. Even the painting over the fireplace was a cheerful rendition of children playing with a little dog. The intention had been to create a room that defied the often gray world beyond the drapes. But nothing could overcome the gloom Abigail transported about with her these days.

Except, perhaps, for Lillian Houghton. "It is rather vexing not to have a response from you. I find myself wanting to address you as 'child.' Which of course cannot be if we are to travel together as friends. Do you wish to travel? Or is this something being pressed upon you?"

"I suppose I want it." Lavinia's daughter's voice sounded distressingly weak.

"You suppose. That is hardly the sort of response I had hoped for, given the ardor of the journey ahead of us. Do you not have a strong opinion one way or the other?"

"Yes, but, well . . ."

Lillian's tone turned testy. "I have asked you a proper

enough question. I wish to receive a proper reply."

Abigail blurted out the words, "I am afraid of making another mistake!"

"Excellent. Progress is being made. Why, pray tell, are you so afflicted with such concerns over your future?"

"You were there! You saw what a blunder I made!"

"Indeed I did."

"Well, then."

"Yes? Go on."

"Do you not see?" Abigail seemed disconcerted by Lillian Houghton's response.

"Clearly not."

"How can I be certain that I shall not make such a terrible mistake again?"

"Are you saying that the only way you can give yourself fully to this voyage is if you can be certain of making no errors?"

"No, of course not. That is—"

"That would be utterly futile, would it not? Because of course none of us is perfect. We all make mistakes."

"I have shamed my family so!"

"Indeed you have. And I see that there has been no need for anyone to punish you, for you have succeeded in doing a far better job of it than they ever could."

Lavinia found herself unable to sit quietly any longer. Silently she rose from her chair and walked over to the window.

"Now I want you to listen to me," she heard Lillian continue. "I am not completely certain of what you feel has happened. I would hazard a guess that you are not certain yourself."

"I have failed those I hold dearest. Is that not enough?"

"Abigail, I want you to listen to me. I will share with you something I have never told another living soul. If my life has taught me anything, it is this: we cannot help but fail those closest to us from time to time."

"I-I don't know what you mean."

"I can scarcely believe I am saying such a thing. But your parents . . ."

"Yes, please go on. My parents . . . ?"

"Your parents have left a most remarkable impression upon me. Particularly your mother. I do not understand it. But I cannot deny the fact that in them I see something I do not possess. It is for this reason as much as anything else that I have agreed to make this journey. And it is why I am speaking to you about matters you cannot possibly understand." Lavinia heard the sound of a cup being set down upon the tray. "Listen to me, Abigail. My husband has left me strapped with debts so burdensome I feel at times as though I am crippled. He *failed* me. Yet I do not condemn him. How could I? He did his best by me. He was an honorable man, quite a good husband in his own way. Yet he failed. I could spend my very existence bemoaning his errors. But I do not. How could I, in all honesty, when my own failures are so much graver than his?"

"I–I don't think I understand."

"No. I can see that. And perhaps I was wrong to speak with you as I did. But hear me out. I am going to America because I must. For the sake of my child and our heritage, I must begin anew. There. You know a secret that I have shared with none other save your parents. Not even my own son is aware of our current financial state. So now we are even."

"Even?"

"Is that not part of why you are so distressed around me? Because I have seen you at your worst moment? So now you know of my own." Lillian paused, then said in a much lower voice, "Or at least one of them."

"I am afraid," Abigail confessed quietly.

"I can see that."

"I want to go. So very much. And yet . . ."

"Yes?"

"I don't trust myself anymore." The confession came with a crack in Abigail's voice. "I am frightened of . . ."

"Of failing." Lillian waited. But Abigail did not reply. Or

could not. "Of course you are. It is not merely the mistake as such. You fear the character trait that caused you to err as you did."

From her position by the dining room window, Lavinia raised one hand to press hard against her mouth. The force of her sudden realization was so strong, she had to fight back the sobs. It was one thing to tell herself that her daughter was growing up. It was another thing entirely to realize her daughter's course was no longer hers to shape. Lillian Houghton was here in this house to do what Lavinia could not. She would not merely travel to America with Abigail. Lillian would introduce new worlds. She would help Abigail fashion her direction and name her dreams. Lavinia's eyes became as cast with tears as the windows.

"I would say you have made a great realization," Lillian observed. "You have begun the process of examining yourself."

"I don't feel as though I have learned anything at all." Abigail's words seemed drenched in sorrow.

"No. I can see that. But you have, of this I am certain. And I am much further down this murky road than you." There was the rustling of skirts, as though Lillian were shifting over closer to the younger woman. "Now I want you to promise me something," she said, her voice lower so Lavinia had to strain to hear the words. "You shall give yourself over fully to this voyage. There will be none of this mourning about as you are doing now. Either that or we shall not go at all."

"But you said—"

"That I *must* go. Indeed so. Were I a believer like you and your parents I would say that this entire idea is a godsend. But there is no set time. We can go whenever the time is right."

"My father is already seeking berths."

"Plans can be changed." Lillian sounded firm now. "I shall travel only when you have become fully ready, my dear. And not until then."

Chapter 12

Abigail did not require much time to make the first move. She acted tentatively and with great trepidation, Lillian was certain of that. But Abigail seemed to have accepted her challenge and sought to prepare herself for the journey ahead. Three days later a letter arrived, a brief note thanking Lillian for her visit and saying that her parents had mentioned Lillian wished to meet Mr. William Wilberforce. The gentleman had invited Abigail to visit Parliament. Might Lillian wish to join her?

Lillian's midnight vigils had altered considerably since beginning to plan this journey to America. She had rarely slept through an entire night since her husband's demise. Her worries were hardly the sort of thing to make for easy slumber, and sleeplessness had become a habit. Yet things had changed. She woke still, but more often than not she reflected upon a future without her current burdens. She almost dared hope for herself. There was no logic to this, nor could she say why she continually found her thoughts returning to the Aldridge family. But they did.

And now this. The letter had arrived precisely ten minutes after a letter of her own had left. One requesting a meeting that same afternoon with Simon Bartholomew.

She knew the word religious folk used for such matters. They called it *providential*. She had heard her aunt and uncle use the word so often it had lost all meaning. Yet here she stood, fastening the cloak about her shoulders while Abigail waited in the coach outside, and finding no other word that fit the moment quite so well.

She had sent word back to the Aldridges that she would be delighted to accompany Abigail to Parliament if they might start off early enough for her to see to a rather tedious and unavoidable chore on the way.

Only now that the hour had arrived and the carriage had pulled up in front of her townhouse, Lillian Houghton was afraid.

She stared out the door being held open by her maid. It was truly high summer, with a splash of light as soft and shimmering as the leaves that shaded her lane. Even so, she had to fight down a burning urge to turn and flee back to her bedroom, lock the door, and hide away from all she was risking. Lillian forced her head up straight and walked into the day.

"Good day, Mr. Talbot." She accepted his hand into the carriage. "I hope I did not inconvenience the family, asking to be fetched so early."

"Not at all, ma'am." The houseman tipped his hat as he helped her into the carriage. "Truth be known, I suspect there's little you could do that would displease the Aldridge family."

Ah, but you're wrong there, Lillian wanted to say. "Have you been told where we are to go?"

"Only that I'm to take you wherever your ladyship wishes."

"Bartholomew's Merchant Bank, if you please. Do you know it?"

"On Threadneedle Street. Aye, my lady. The family once had some dealings there." Lillian halted in the process of greeting Abigail. "Did they?"

"Some time back, that was." Talbot shut the door and said through the open window. "But I know it, sure enough."

Lillian wanted to lean out and ask precisely what the Aldridges had done to raise such ire from Simon Bartholomew. But there was nothing to be gained and much perhaps lost from open curiosity. Instead, she turned and said to Abigail, "What an adorable gown."

"It's my mother's. She insisted I wear the finest day frock she owns." Abigail was cloaked head to toe in pale green silk. The collar was rimmed with a stiff frothy trim of the same color. Abigail patted nervously at the small hat pinned at a jaunty angle. "I do so hope I won't spill anything on it."

Lillian felt the carriage shift as Ben Talbot climbed onto the driver's seat. "It is heartening to find us conversing together this day."

"I-I have thought a great deal about what you have said."

"And?"

"My mother says you are right."

"What your mother says is less important to me than what you yourself think." Lillian caught herself. "Forgive me. I have no reason to speak so crossly with you."

Abigail blinked. Clearly she was unaccustomed to having adults apologize to her for anything.

"It is this meeting, you see, that has gotten me out of sorts. I hope you never know the pain of addressing a banker to whom you owe money you cannot pay."

"It must be dreadful."

Lillian more closely examined the girl seated beside her and decided Abigail was not a girl at all. The clear light to her face was deceptive, as well as her youthful dejection over her first great fall in life. But she looked back with the steady gaze of one open to accept a woman's wisdom. There was considerable strength there, even now when she appeared so weakened by her own self-condemnation.

Lillian said simply, "Yes, more so than I ever imagined possible."

"My father once said a strong man is one who can hold his head up even when the entire world is bearing down on his shoulders." Abigail's hair looked aflame in the afternoon light, as though she had managed to claim autumn's finery as her own. "I wish I had your strength."

"You have your own."

"I haven't been very strong lately."

"No. But everyone is laid flat the first time they realize just how harsh life can be."

"How old were *you* when that happened?"

"Fourteen." How easy it was to talk with this girl-woman. How easy and how dangerous. "I was fourteen, and we shall not sully this day with more burdens than it already has."

"Yes. Of course. I'm so sorry."

"Don't apologize. It was once said a proper lady never apologizes. I disagree with that. It reeks of silliness and false pride. But a woman must be sparse with apologies. She must move through the world as though it is her right and all the doors are meant to be open in advance of her arrival. There are so many obstacles placed in our way, you see. We must take great care to guard those few opportunities which are granted to us."

Abigail's gaze had not wavered one iota. "Mother says I shall learn a great deal from you if I am willing."

The words caused a shiver to course through Lillian's form. "Are you all right?"

"As right as I can be. Look, we have arrived." Lillian was already moving for the door before Ben drew the horses to a halt. "No, you must stay here. Your presence here in the carriage will be my excuse for making this as brief a visit as possible."

Abigail leaned out the open carriage door to say, "Then I shall sit here and pray for you as hard as I know how."

The young woman's words only propelled Lillian more swiftly inside. How could she deceive these good people? And that was precisely what she was doing. Her silence was a constant lie. Lillian spotted Simon Bartholomew walking toward her and willed herself to be strong. To be resolute. To put all distractions aside.

But she could not.

"Lady Houghton." He bowed precisely, a slender aging man in black broadcloth. His one hint of color today was a silver foulard held in place with an emerald stickpin. "You do my establishment great honor."

"Mr. Bartholomew."

"Will you take tea, my lady?" He spoke loudly enough to signal her presence to all who observed the exchange. "Or perhaps a cup of chocolate and fresh cream. My vessel has just returned from a passage around the Horn. It carried beans of a most exquisite aroma. My warehouse is positively awash in the fragrance of cocoa."

"Another time. I am due at Parliament."

The piercing quality returned to his dark gaze. "Indeed?"

"Might I perhaps have a word in private?"

"Of course, my lady. This way, if you please."

He led her down the length of the dark-paneled banking chamber. A uniformed porter held open the door at the back. She followed the banker down a hall lined with the portraits of his forebears, all of whom stared at her with undisguised hostility. They passed through a long chamber filled with clerks at high counting tables. He opened the door to his private office and bowed her inside.

All such civility vanished, however, the instant he shut the door. "Parliament?"

"Aren't you even going to ask me to sit down?"

He abruptly motioned her toward a chair. "You have taken a sudden interest in politics?"

Her reply was halted by the sight of the bound file resting at the center of the polished meeting table. The leather binding was tied shut with a faded purple ribbon. The cover was stamped with her husband's crest.

Simon Bartholomew took great pleasure in whatever he saw there upon her features. "I see that no further threats are required."

She sat out of necessity.

"No further warnings must be issued." He picked up a gold dagger he used as a letter opener and swished the air as he paraded around behind the table. "No further admonishments to do *precisely* as I command."

Lillian knew the folder contained the deeds to all her husband's estates. The country manor, the lands that had been in his family for six generations, the South American holdings, the London townhouse. Everything signed over as collateral for a venture the count had been certain would make them the most powerful family in Europe after the monarchs. The venture whose failure had felled him as absolutely as a bullet to the heart.

Lillian looked from the file to the banker's gleaming gaze. And she knew then that Simon Bartholomew would never let her go.

No matter what bargain she might make. No matter what he might promise. This banker lived for the power that money gave him over others. It was more precious to him than his own life's blood. As far as Simon Bartholomew was concerned, she was his forever.

Though Lillian felt she would most likely choke on anything served in this establishment, still she wished she had agreed to his offer of tea. Her throat was so dry she sounded hoarse as she said, "I am going to meet with William Wilberforce."

"You are what?"

"It has been arranged by the Aldridge family. Their coach has brought me here."

The banker sank into the chair opposite her.

"Abigail Aldridge is waiting for me outside."

"The daughter? Here?"

Suddenly she felt weary. What could she do? What good was any of this maneuvering? She was trapped. And trapped she would remain.

"How dare you bring the daughter to my bank!"

"How *dare* I?" Even her ire seemed false this day. "I am doing precisely what you ordered me to do. I am as involved with the family as . . ."

"Yes? Go on."

She waved it away. They had been through all this before. Why bother with futile arguments? She was trapped. What was more, she could not help but feel that it was all her own fault.

Oh, of course she had nothing to do with the Portugal venture. In fact, she had begged her late husband not to proceed. Why should he seek more wealth when they already had more than they needed? But it was not this last argument that held Lillian prisoner.

Her past, the distant time before her husband had rescued her, the horrid mistakes she had made in her early life—they all loomed up like specters rising from an unearthed grave. She had been so certain they had all been left far behind. Yet now it seemed as though she was forever trapped by the lie of her entire life, the lie that said she was a lady.

"Don't keep me waiting!"

She forced herself to focus once more on the banker. "I am accompanying the young woman to America."

"Miss Aldridge? When?"

"Soon. Mr. Wilberforce has some task he wishes for Abigail to accomplish there."

"So it is Abigail now, is it? You are now on such familiar terms with all the family?"

She ignored both the words and his sneer. "I gather this voyage has something to do with the work of Gareth Powers and his wife."

He sat up straight as the color drained from his face. "Are you certain?"

"No." She was certain of nothing save that she wanted to be away. "I suspect that is what we shall be discussing this afternoon."

He rose to his feet, pretending to a casual air they both knew was false. "You have succeeded beyond my wildest expectations, my lady."

Lillian started to ask for another assurance that the banker would release her from the debts and his dire threats. But the day's clarity was too keen. Why insist upon words she knew were a lie even before they were uttered?

Instead, she found herself caught by how lucid everything seemed. She examined not only this moment, but everything that had come together to place her here. She saw the present and all the past forces of her life, and for once she could fathom how she had set this course herself. It was not random chance that had brought her here. Rather, it was her own wrong choices.

The banker was talking now. Speaking about how she should maintain contact with him via certain vessels. She could not bring herself to pay attention. Lillian stared out the window behind his desk. There was nothing to be seen save the brick wall at the rear of the bank's small courtyard. But she was not interested in the view. She wanted to *understand.*

She found herself recalling what Abigail had said upon their arrival at the bank. Was this clarity due to a young woman's prayers? The concept shook her more than being seated here in the banker's lair. When was the last time anyone had prayed for her? The answer was swift in coming. Not since she was fourteen.

"I believe that is everything for the moment," Simon Bartholomew concluded.

Lillian heard only that she was free to leave. She rose from her chair and permitted the banker to lead her back through the chambers, past all the staring faces, through the tall front foyer with its scents of beeswax and money. She allowed him to bow her through the front doors because it was expected of her. She was, after all, a lady.

When Lillian returned to the carriage, she found Abigail watching her with a fretful look. She had scarcely settled into her seat when the young woman burst out, "I need to ask a favor. It's not my place, I know. After everything you've done. But I must."

"Thank you," Lillian said quietly.

"Whatever for?"

"I'm not sure, actually." The air of the carriage seemed to sparkle. Which of course was silly. "You said you would pray for me."

"Yes. And I did. Or rather, well . . ."

"Go on."

"I started." Her hands fidgeted with the folds of her dress. "I had the strongest impression while you were in there. You see, I have tried so very often to write to Derrick Aimes, the pastor with whom, that is . . ."

"The reverend who was arrested with you and taken to Newgate?"

A visible shudder went through the young woman's form. "Yes. But everything I have said has felt so inadequate. So I asked my mother if I might go to the church in Soho and speak with him."

"I can imagine that did not go over well."

"At first I was certain she would say no. But she asked me why, and I explained that I felt a great need to apologize. Not just for the night. For how I was. For my motives. And how wrong I was to ignore his warning. And how right he was in what he told me."

There was a knock on the carriage door. "Begging your pardon, ladies. But I was wondering where it is we are headed."

"One moment, if you please, Mr. Talbot." Lillian turned back to her companion. "Please continue."

"Mother said I might go, but only if you would accompany me."

Lillian nodded her understanding. Abigail's mother did not feel up to revisiting that night.

"Mother works in the most dreadful of places, helping Mr. Wilberforce in his hospital for the poor and such. But she said she had no interest in taking a closer look at Soho just now." Abigail gave her a plaintive look. "Today is already so full. I was going to wait until another time. But when I was praying, I had the strongest impression that I needed to do this immediately."

"When are we scheduled to meet with Mr. Wilberforce?"

"Not until five o'clock."

She asked the driver, "Can you spy a church tower and read us the time, good sir?"

He craned about and replied, "Just gone three, ma'am."

Impossible. She had only been inside the bank for a quarter of an hour? It had seemed like days. "Would you be so kind as to retrace our way so far as Soho?"

He had clearly expected nothing less. "Very good, ma'am."

"Where is it we need to go, Abigail?"

"The church at Soho Square."

Without further ado, Ben Talbot climbed up top, released the reins and handbrake, and started the horses off with a crack of his whip.

Entering Soho was for Lillian yet another wearisome trek into her own past. Not that she had been here exactly in her youth. But every English town possessed such a quarter. One that lay close to the wealthier districts so that the clientele need not travel too far, but safely removed from the truly vile districts. Soho was dangerous in its own way, but nothing like the area south of the river. Soho's allure was its mixture of vice and mystery. But that was by night. In the daylight the seamy nature was all too vivid. The buildings were as gray as most of the folk. The lanes were crowded with tired-faced people who had greeted too many dawns from the wrong side.

Runners scampered along the road, outpacing the carriage horses. They headed into Soho carrying long paper streamers dotted with inked designs, and returned with partially sewn garments. The clothiers of Saville Row and Bond Street were far too cramped to sew their wares from scratch. So the designs were measured out on full-scale sheets of blank newsprint, then sent down to the Soho sewing shops. There were hundreds of such establishments. Lillian had known several. Some were brilliantly lit and served as parlors where ladies might stop for chocolate and gossip along with their fittings. Others were foul chambers employing the smallest children they could hire.

121

These were poorly lit and so confined the children sang in unison to keep their sewing arms rising and falling in tandem.

Lillian stared out the window and saw other inns and other towns. Manchester, Glasgow, Warwick, Birmingham, York. Strange how her earlier travels had never brought her to London. The count had been relieved to hear this when they had first met.

"I am so very sorry for bringing you down here," Abigail said, obviously misreading her expression.

"Don't be silly. It is no trouble at all."

"You look so sad."

"It is not over this journey, I assure you."

"What is it, then?"

Lillian sighed her way around to look into the face of the young woman. Abigail's features were creased with deep concern. "You are," she quietly decided, "a most remarkable young lady."

"I feel like ten kinds of fool." She tasted a tiny smile. "Father would not like knowing I used one of his sayings."

The carriage approached the front of a squalid plaza. Even the tall elms sheltering the church looked dusty and stooped. Hawkers plied their wares in great numbers. The air was filled with the scents of roasting chestnuts and sausages. Children flocked around, screaming as they ran about playing some game. A ragman croaked his goods, walking alongside a tired nag that pulled an overloaded cart. Behind that was a brewery wagon pulled by six dray horses. Ben Talbot halted the carriage in front of crumbling stone steps, and the children immediately swarmed outside the windows, their dirty faces pleading for alms.

"Here, here, none of that!" they heard a gravelly voice shout. "Off with you lot or you'll feel the back of my hand!" The children laughed and scampered. Jack's seamed face appeared in the window. He grinned widely. "Don't see many such fine vehicles 'round these parts, Miss Abigail."

"How are you, Jack?"

"Free and alive and praising our Lord, ma'am." He tipped his filthy cap in Lillian's direction. "Good day to you, my lady."

"How nice to see a friendly face in these quarters, sir."

Abigail inquired, "Is Reverend Aimes about?"

A booming voice responded, "He is indeed!" Jack stepped aside for a younger and stronger man. "A grand good afternoon to you, Miss Abigail. And to you as well, my lady. It's high time I had the chance to thank you both for what you did."

They all realized at the same moment that Abigail was not going to respond because she couldn't. Tears streamed down her face. Lillian moved to the opposite seat to make room beside Abigail and said, "Do be so kind as to join us."

The carriage creaked as Derrick Aimes climbed inside. The man seemed to compress the carriage's air with his bulk. He seated himself and patted Abigail's hand. "There, there."

"I'm so, so sorry."

"And didn't I already know that, lass? Whoever could have predicted the night would turn out as it did?" He cast a grateful glance across the carriage. "I for one believe the Lord's hand was on our meeting on the street."

"How can you possibly suggest such a thing?" Abigail gasped out.

He reached into his pocket and withdrew a clean handkerchief. "Here, now, wipe your eyes. Were it not for her ladyship, we all would still be in a world of woe. And wasn't it your doing that brought her around?"

"My mother brought her."

"That's the same thing from where I sit." He addressed his words to Lillian. "So it's I who have to apologize for troubling the whole world. Never did I expect to be shipped off to Newgate for preaching the Gospel from a Soho stage."

"It's not just that." Abigail forced a huge breath, in and out, struggling to steady herself. "Everything you said to me that night was the truth."

"Was it, now? I don't recall."

"You said I was being frivolous. You said I didn't belong there." The tears started afresh. "You said I was not acting out of faith. You said my motives were selfish. You said—"

"Enough, lass. Enough."

"It was true. All of it. I lied to you and I lied to my parents and I lied to myself and I lied to God."

"And all of us have forgiven you," he replied quietly. "So perhaps it's time you do the same."

Again she fought for control. "I don't know how."

"Aye, it's a hard lesson, that. Sometimes when heaven's light shines upon our weaknesses, we can scarce lift our gazes up again from the shame of what we find exposed." He smiled at her, but it was not a happy expression. "Do you think you're the first who's stumbled? The first who's tried and failed?"

She sniffed. "No, of course not."

"Well, then. Listen and I'll tell you something. I haven't been a pastor for very long. Won't even be fully ordained until this winter. But I've already discovered something that astonishes me. There's a lot of folks out there who shy away from ever changing. They hide, don't you see. They hide behind whatever's closest at hand. And many's the time they hide behind mistakes they've made."

Abigail was listening too intently now to cry. "Please, what are you saying?"

"Aye, it sounds mad, but it's the truth nonetheless. They spend hours remembering the badness. They look around and all they see is what they did wrong. It's an excuse, don't you see? Secretly they claim to themselves that they don't deserve to grow or improve or find a better lot in life."

Lillian found herself wanting to speak. Which was absurd. Address a stranger as she would a lifelong confidant? Yet the pressure built up in her heart like an overheated kettle, the words scalding her throat as she strained to remain silent.

Then, to her amazement, she heard the young woman across from her ask the question on her behalf.

Abigail asked, "But how can I leave such past errors behind?"

"Through prayer, lass. You know that answer as well as I do. What we cannot do alone, God will do for us."

It was astonishing to hear such a gentle tone coming from such a man. His face was mottled with the wounds of ancient battles, his nose looked pounded and reshaped a multitude of times. Scars crisscrossed beneath his left eye, and his long dark hair could not entirely mask the misshaped ear. His knuckles were huge and raw, his fingers like staves. The rolled-back sleeves revealed arms like cordwood. Yet here he sat, speaking so softly Lillian had to lean forward to catch his words. His tone was as soothing as what he had to say.

Abigail was speaking clearly now. "I've asked Him for forgiveness."

"Aye, and He's pardoned you as well. Sometimes the hardest challenge we poor humans face is accepting the gift. What have we done to deserve it? You know the answer well as I. But it's one thing to hear Christ died on the Cross for our sins, and another to come face to face with just how much we need His grace. Not once. But every single day, every moment we're here upon this earth."

She nodded slowly. "I think I see."

"Of course you do." He patted her hand once more. "There is a consolation I can offer you in the here and now, one coming from my own hard-earned lessons. You can best reach the unwashed when you see yourself as having been brought to the same level, do you see? Drawn down to needing the Cross by our own failings, we are neither better nor cleaner than any of them. That is my only gift, frail and meager as it is. But it is a reward nonetheless for all the mistakes I made before arriving at my knees."

Derrick rose and moved for the carriage door. Every motion caused the carriage to shift and creak. "You'll have to forgive me, but I'm due to be teaching this bunch of young scallywags how to read. If I leave them any longer, next thing you know we'll have the church burned down around our ears."

The soft-voiced former fighter shut the carriage door, then said through the open window, "The questions you should be asking our Maker are these: What comes next? You have forgiven me, Father. What lesson do I take from this? How can I turn my hard-earned wisdom into something that serves thee? And what would thou have me do? That's where your future lies; that's where hope lives." Derrick Aimes nodded to the driver and lifted his hand in farewell. "Come see us any time, lass. You are always welcome at this house."

Chapter 13

On the way from Soho to Parliament, Abigail sensed something she had not felt since all the recent events had started. At first she could not even identify the mood, as though she tasted a flavor so novel her tongue had to search out a totally new description.

She felt excited.

She did not feel as though she sat in a stuffy carriage trundling down the tarmacadam roads linking the West End with the River Thames. She did not notice their passage past St. James Palace. She paid scant notice as they turned onto Horse Guards Road, winding their way along the back of the barracks of the king's regiment and Whitehall. She did not see the crowds or hear the hawkers. Instead, her mind was held by a vision of a wave-capped ocean. And beyond that lay a land of endless adventure.

Not until they left Great George Street and trundled around Parliament Square did Abigail realize she had not spoken a word to her companion since leaving Soho. She said to Lillian, "Forgive me. I have been very rude."

Lillian seemed to start awake. "In what way?"

"Is everything all right?"

"No, no, it is nothing."

"Please tell me."

Lillian hesitated a moment longer. "I have been trying to

127

fathom what seemed so strange about our encounter."

"With Pastor Aimes?"

"Indeed. The gentleman showed no interest whatsoever in my presence. I am unable to recall the last time that has occurred."

As Ben Talbot held the door open for the two ladies to disembark, Abigail said, "Prepare yourself for another surprising encounter."

Parliament was not housed in a particularly impressive building. Abigail had been in several manors which were far larger. Vague talk of expanding the structure and even adding a clock tower had swirled for years. Yet the yellow stone held a gemlike quality in the afternoon light. The gothic peaks and high narrow windows were both austere and elegant. She had come several times with her father and always looked forward to her visits. But never had she anticipated one more than now.

A guard in splendid scarlet uniform directed them to the Black Rod entrance. They passed through high-peaked doors and crossed an interior courtyard illuminated by brilliant sunlight. Another guard asked their business, eyed the countess, then pointed them down a long high-ceilinged hallway. They passed a number of formal chambers where crowds of robed officials talked in low yet passionate tones.

Abigail noticed that whenever men spotted the countess, all conversation halted. She had never considered Countess Houghton's beauty as anything but an attribute until now. Abigail corrected herself and mentally spoke the lady's first name. *Lillian.* She had never addressed a titled older woman by her first name before. It would require some practice. They passed another open doorway, this one crammed with gentlemen holding leather portfolios and official-looking documents dressed with ribbons and seals. Once more Abigail noticed how the men stopped their discussions to observe their passage, particularly Lillian's. One of the men stared in slack-jawed wonder. Abigail had not realized what a burden such beauty might actually be.

128

"There you are!" William Wilberforce extricated himself from a mass of berobed gentlemen, most of whom wore powdered wigs and the ermine collars of royal appointments. "I was just going to see if perhaps the guards had refused my two lovely guests entry for fear of disrupting the affairs of state."

Abigail felt herself almost overwhelmed by the excitement and force of this small gentleman. "How are you today, sir?"

"Eh? Oh, you mean my recent bout of ill health." He waved it aside. "Thankfully, when those episodes end I can scarcely recall having felt unwell at all."

Abigail said, "Might I have the pleasure of introducing the Countess Houghton?"

His elegant manners made Wilberforce's small stature unimportant. He bowed over the lady's hand. "You do me great honor with your presence, my lady."

"I hope I am not untoward in joining Miss Aldridge on her visit, sir."

"Quite the contrary, my lady. I shall be the envy of all Parliament for many months to come." Indeed, the hall was frozen solid, all eyes trained in their direction. "Might I suggest we retire to chambers where I have ordered tea be served?"

He led them into a smaller side room adorned with stained glass windows, fine Gothic paneling, and a high domed ceiling. A sterling tea service was laid out on the ancient table. "My dear, perhaps you will do the honors?"

"Of course." For once, Abigail was enormously grateful for her mother's insistence upon teaching her the polite art of serving tea. She waited for Wilberforce to hold Lillian's chair, then served them both a cup before pouring one for herself. She seated herself opposite Lillian, so that they sat to either side of Wilberforce.

The gentleman tasted his tea and nodded approval. "I of course knew your late husband, my lady," he addressed the countess.

"Indeed. He never mentioned the fact."

Abigail noticed how Lillian's voice had become muted

since their arrival, such that it sounded almost faint. She could well understand. William Wilberforce was an astounding individual. So much power was encased within this diminutive figure. Even when seated and still, he seemed nearly bursting with sheer unbridled force.

"I am hardly surprised." Wilberforce took no notice of the lady's subdued nature. "Since we normally occupied opposite sides of the hall."

Abigail understood his expression because of her father's work in politics. When votes were called in Parliament, many times its members were required to move to opposite sides of the chamber, such that all could see how each stood upon issues. This also lessened the risk of any miscount.

Wilberforce went on, "Might I ask, my lady, if you share your late husband's views?"

When Lillian hesitated in responding, William Wilberforce leaned forward to say, "I implore you, my lady, to take no offense. I ask only because I understand that you might be traveling with my dear young friend."

"It is not that, sir." Lillian patted her lips with the starched napkin. "To be perfectly frank, at present I am uncertain precisely how I feel on any number of issues."

"Is that a fact." Wilberforce leaned back in his seat. For reasons Abigail could not fathom, he seemed rather pleased by the lady's response. "You don't say."

Wilberforce waited, but Lillian said nothing further. Instead the lady lowered her gaze and traced one finger along the royal crest adorning the cup she held.

Again Wilberforce seemed to take delight in Lillian's response. He turned to Abigail and examined her closely. "You appear much recovered, my dear."

"I scarcely know what to say," she replied, mirroring Lillian's reaction. "In truth, it seems I should ever remain overwhelmed with remorse."

The gentleman's entire frame rocked in accord. "If only we could go back and change the past," he gravely agreed. "You know the story of Lazarus, of course."

"Yes, sir."

"Why should I mention this now, you may well ask. After all, what does the old story of a dead man locked in a tomb have to do with a young woman positively filled with life and hope? Perhaps nothing. Who am I to seek and impart wisdom to such a lovely and intelligent young woman?"

"You are a dear, dear friend," Abigail softly replied.

"Thank you. But you see, I was reading about Lazarus this very morning, and I find myself captured anew by the man's story. It seems that death is not a future problem. Death is *now*. Death is the state where all dwell until—what? Until the hour comes where we choose life, choose Jesus, choose to rise again."

Lillian's gaze rose to fasten upon the gentleman. Wilberforce's eyes remained intent upon Abigail. Yet he seemed to be aware even of this silent act. For he pushed his chair back a trifle, opening the space to include Lillian.

"If only we could change our past," Wilberforce repeated. "If only we could have more control over our present, cleanse away all the tainted memories we carry with us. If only we could rise from this burden that feels almost as heavy as death. If only we could *improve* ourselves and our future lot in life."

Abigail was held from speaking, but not by the gentleman's words. Rather she was restrained by her companion's expression. Lillian's lovely gaze looked mortally stricken. Her lips parted, her eyes stared unblinkingly at the gentleman. She did not even appear to breathe.

"When the sisters of Lazarus turn to Jesus in their grief, our Lord tells them, Be not concerned with the past. Your brother will rise again. Even the impossible is given to you. Your future has burst into the present. Redemption lives in the here and now. If only you are able to face your fears and your pains and your errors. If only you can seek the *eternal* truth. If only you can *believe*."

Wilberforce then did an astonishing thing. He turned and

peered directly into Lillian's solemn gaze. And he smiled. It was a gentle smile, one filled with the silent speech that Abigail could not understand. Yet it did not matter, she realized, for this communication was not intended for her at all.

The countess did not respond. She did not move, save to blink once. This was enough to dislodge a single tear. It ran down her otherwise perfect cheek. She did not lift a hand to wipe it away. She did nothing save continue to meet Wilberforce's gaze, as though she had neither will nor strength for anything else.

Wilberforce's delight over this silent exchange was so great the chair could no longer contain him. He bounded up and exclaimed, "My dear Abigail, I wish to settle a commission upon you."

The sudden change of direction was most shocking. "Upon—upon . . . ?"

"None other. First I must explain the situation. You shall forgive me, Countess, if I burden you with facts you might prefer not to hear."

His address to her released Lillian so that she could swiftly wipe the tear from her cheek. Her voice cracked slightly as she replied, "Pray continue, sir."

"Miss Abigail, no doubt your father speaks of the dire situation faced by so many of our more impoverished brethren in the countryside. The past two planting seasons have been murderously bad. Last summer's wheat, barley, and corn crops were destroyed by constant rain. The village workhouses of York are so full that people are being left to starve in the gateways. There is famine in Wales and Ireland both. And what does our ruling government in London do? I will tell you. They do nothing! They sit in their well-lit rooms and dine at their gleaming tables, while outside their very windows a nation starves!"

Wilberforce began pacing the front of the chamber. "Some of our church leaders have begun speaking of following our Pilgrim ancestors and leaving these shores. They hear rumors of a bright new future opening in America's western reaches."

To Abigail's surprise, it was Lillian who quietly responded, "Land."

"Just so. Land and more land. I have been handed yet another missive this very morning. The price of land in Missouri has dropped to a dollar and a quarter an acre."

Lillian exclaimed, "That can't be!"

"Perhaps not. I find it astounding myself. But that is what the pamphlet says. Here, I have brought it with me." Wilberforce withdrew the leaflet from his inner pocket and handed it to the countess. Then he moved over behind her so he could read over her shoulder.

"A dollar and a quarter per acre," Wilberforce read again. "And only twenty percent as deposit. One is obliged to purchase lots no smaller than half a square mile. Why, that is larger than the former commons land of most English villages."

He resumed his pacing. "I have received one distressing letter after another from Erica Powers. Their battle against slavery in the Americas does not go at all well. They beg to return to England, where they feel their efforts might bear more fruit. They are disheartened. They feel they have wasted their years in Washington. I want you to go straight to them and tell them that nothing could be further from the truth."

"Of course I will do—"

"Wait, my dear Abigail. Wait. There is more. I want you to tell Gareth and Erica that before they return to England, they must help me with this matter. I wish for them to proceed forthwith westward. They must evaluate this land issue personally. They have never written on this. Their pamphlets are trusted all over England. All over the Continent for that matter. Their word is known to be steadfast and true. People *rely* upon them. Tell them of the dire straits faced by so many here in Britain. Better still, I shall write them. But I wish for you to reinforce my words. This is not an entreaty. If ever they have sought to do my bidding, it is now. We must know for certain the truth behind these rumors. Is the land fertile? Can it be farmed? Is there indeed hope to be found in these claims?"

"I will do as you say, sir."

"Excellent. I wish for the Powerses to write with first-hand authority. We must know for certain if these rumors are to be trusted." He pointed at the pamphlet in Lillian's hands. "Do we see here a great opportunity, or a terrible risk?"

Wilberforce held Abigail with a gaze that wrenched her with its urgency. "Not a moment is to be wasted. You must proceed with all haste and tell Gareth and Erica to do the same. We must know, and know quickly."

Packing for America proved a much more difficult affair than Abigail had imagined. It was not simply the matter of putting things in order. A trunk and matching case were purchased, offering far more space than Abigail supposed she would need. The folding of her gowns and other garments was done in less than an hour and took up only half of the trunk. That proved the easy part.

Her mother arrived then, with half a dozen of her own finest frocks bundled in her arms. "What are these, Mother?"

"Items you will need far more than I."

Abigail spied a hint of palest lavender at the bottom of the pile. "Mama, I can't take that one."

"Why not, may I ask?"

"It is your favorite day dress!"

"And one which looks far better on you than it does on me." Briskly Lavinia began folding the items and stowing them away. "The day you wore it to the tea dance, I thought my heart would seize up, you were that lovely."

Abigail was wrenched by a pair of sudden realizations. The barrier that had separated her from her mother was gone.

And she was going away.

"Oh, Mama."

"Don't—don't, my daughter." Lavinia's actions grew swifter

still. "We have wept all we need to."

"I'm so—"

"You needn't say it again. Not ever. Not to me, the one who loves you more than life itself."

They hugged then, a clumsy affair with dresses spilling at their feet and the remaining pile cascading off the bed. Abigail felt pierced anew, this time with relief. "It's over."

"Over and gone," her mother agreed, stroking her hair. "My dearest darling child."

"Perhaps I shouldn't go."

"Shah, now, none of that. My heart isn't strong enough to keep from agreeing if you were to start with any such suggestion. And we both know it's a good decision." Lavinia released her and stooped to retrieve the dresses. She repeated in a determined fashion, "A good decision."

Abigail felt sick with conflicting desires. She was thrilled to be going, yet she longed to stay. "But why?"

Lavinia's response was interrupted by a knock upon the open doorway. "Perhaps I should be the one to answer that," Samuel Aldridge said. "May I come in?"

Abigail could not halt the sudden flood of tension. "Of course, Father."

"You're home early," Lavinia said. Her own voice had heightened in tone, as though sharing her daughter's strain.

"Ah, well." Samuel Aldridge held to such a preoccupied air he no doubt did not notice the change in the room's atmosphere. "Further work proved impossible. I found myself missing my little girl so fiercely."

The admission from her stalwart father was utterly unexpected. Abigail's response rose from the core of her being of its own accord. "Oh, Father," she said as she pressed into his outstretched arms.

"The office seemed so bare, don't you know. And the day so empty of the joy you have always brought me."

Abigail nestled into her father's strong embrace. She felt her mother's hands upon her shoulders. Finally she managed to whisper, "Then I shouldn't go."

"I've been busy trying to convince myself of that very same thing," her father intoned. "And I have come to see it not only as selfish but wrong."

"And I the same," Lavinia agreed. "Though it breaks my poor heart to say so."

"Our dear friend William Wilberforce has been the mirror to my own soul," Samuel said. "He has illuminated a truth I have tried very hard not to see."

Gently he pushed his daughter back to where he could peer into her eyes. "You have grown up on me."

Abigail tried hard to seize the moment and hold it fast, as a proper lady should. But the image of her father's face swam in and out of focus, and her words emerged broken and ill formed. "I'm not—not sure I want to."

"You have become a fine young lady with a will and a strength all her own. Who has only done what she has because I refused to accept her as she is."

"I'm so sorry, Father."

"And don't I just know that."

Lavinia whispered, "Could we not perhaps wait a while longer?"

"Whenever would we find a better moment? The church is still reeling from the so-called scandal. This will take time to die down. They are currently making too much fuss over a young woman's innocent mistake, as did I. They need time to see the error of their accusations."

"Father, I—"

"Shah, my beloved child. We have spoken of this enough. It is no longer your actions which concern us. The king's court and their broadsheets have turned this into a scandal based upon lies. Soon enough the church will see what William has already recognized, and now I have as well."

Lavinia sniffed loudly. "And that is?"

"Were it not this, it would be something else. They attack

us not because of our dear daughter. They attack us because they oppose everything we stand for." His own voice trembled at that point, and drawing a new breath seemed to take great effort. "So you will go to America, and you will go now. You are my lovely young daughter who will go off on her adventure of serving God. And you will make us all very proud."

PART

TWO

Chapter 14

Lillian was enjoying the most splendid dream.

She was lying not upon a bed at all, but rather she was inside her carriage. Not the one she had used in London. The one her late husband had acquired just before his financial disaster. Lillian had ridden in the new coach only three times. It was gilded in real gold leaf and had seats of leather with headrests of softest suede. It was gone, of course. She knew this even in her dream. Yet for this blissful moment her world was undisturbed by debts or foreclosures or bankers or the constant fear of loss. Here she lay, surrounded by quilting soft as the clouds she admired outside her carriage window.

The vehicle sparkled with new varnish. Lillian snuggled into her coverlets and gazed through the small window. She would never have lain so in a coach. It was hardly a proper position for a lady, particularly a countess in such a lovely carriage as this. But just then it did not matter. Dawn touched the sky overhead with a wan gleam. Then she saw her coachmen lead six high-stepping horses past her window. She wanted to cry out with delight, for she had bought and named every one. They had been lost to her and yet here they were again. Their hooves clipped sharply against the stones as they stepped friskily toward their stations, their breath misting in the early chill. She listened to the belts and buckles being fitted into place and the soft chatter of men whose only role was to do her bidding.

They set off. The carriage gave a glorious ride. Back and forth it swayed, gentle as a cradle. She knew this road so very well. It was a journey she had feared she would never make again.

Another milestone swept by. This one marked their final turning. How she could see this while lying down mattered not a whit. A trio of horse patrol, known as Redbreasts for their bright hunting jackets, fell in to either side of her carriage. They served as the only protection against highwaymen in the outlying districts and were drawn from retired cavalry regiments. They tipped their hard felt-covered hats to her as she lay there in the gently swaying carriage, then sped on to take their proper stations just ahead.

She had the most remarkable ability to lie down and yet see all she wished. They swept past fields heavily laden with crops of wheat and rye and barley. None of the recent unpleasant summers of rain and cold and want pervaded this perfect scene. Hedgerows grew to either side, dusted white by the passage of her fine carriage. The coachman blew his curved horn, signaling a village up ahead, warning all who occupied the lane to give way. The carriage swept grandly through a hamlet of stone houses and laughing children.

Soon after the hamlet, the wall began. Lillian cried with joy at the sight. The wall was shoulder high and ran for just under two miles, marking the front of her estate. The one now occupied by that vile banker. The one she had promised herself she would never return to unless it was hers free and clear. Yet here she came, which could mean only one thing. Lillian snuggled deeper into her coverlets and reveled in the sight of that lovely stone wall.

The carriage slowed and the horn blew again, this time warning the occupants of the house that the mistress was returning.

They turned through tall stone gates, carved as a miniature triumphal arch. The gates were open, of course. The horn blew again, and Lillian wanted to rise. She should be properly seated for her return. But she could not. And somehow it was all right. Sunlight flickered in and out of the tall poplars bordering the entranceway. The light played with her eyes. If she could but lift her hand and shield her gaze from the flickering light, then she might catch a glimpse of the manor. The horn blew once more, and the light grew stronger still.

Then she sneezed.

Lillian opened her eyes and stared in dismay about the cramped cabin. "Oh no, tell me it is not so."

"Good morning. How do you feel?"

"Oh, let me sleep. Please let me sleep."

Instantly Abigail was by her side. "Here, won't you take a bit of cold tea? You know it settles your stomach."

"No thank you." It had been a dream. Lillian felt like weeping. Just a dream.

"Are you ill? What a pity. You're usually at your best in the morning."

"No, it's not that." Lillian knew it was not a horn at all she had heard in her dream, but rather the boatswain calling to the watch high in the riggings.

She recognized the swaying now as well. How could she not, after two weeks and two days at sea. The boat pitched and yawed in steady yet jerking motions. She had come to consider the movement as among her worst enemies.

"Here, let me help you up."

Lillian raised her arm to the customary position for Abigail to take hold. She had been continually ill, almost from the moment the ship had left the Thames estuary. She had never thought an illness could be this severe and not mortally fell its victim.

"The captain says we continue to make astonishing time." Abigail had been her constant nurse, day and night trying to ease her distress. Always cheerful, always patient, she had been a true angel. "He assures us we will be close to breaking the record for a late summer crossing."

The days had been endless hours of nausea and agony.

Although her anguish was less severe in the morning, these early hours remained distressing because ahead of her stretched another dismal day. Abigail would force her to eat a morsel of something before the nausea grew worse. Then she would do her utmost to ease Lillian's descent with cheerful talk and reading from Byron's last letter.

Two days prior to their departure, Lillian had traveled up to Eton to visit with her son one final time. Byron had surprised her with a gift. One of his schoolteachers had explained to the boy the journey his mother was taking and how it might be several months before letters could be exchanged. Only then had Byron truly understood the distance and the time that would soon separate them. He remained fiercely adamant that he wished to stay at school. But he had conjured up a parting gift that continued to touch Lillian deeply.

At that final meeting, Byron had presented Lillian with a vellum packet containing the longest letter her son had ever written. It was a journal, really, a glimpse into the life of a boy at the cusp of manhood. He had walked her through several of his days, describing his mates and his teachers and his sports and his life. But it had been more than mere descriptions. Byron had sought to examine his own changing heart. He had stumbled often and slipped into formality and even chastised himself for writing as he did. But that he had tried at all had reduced Lillian to tears. And his boyish open-hearted charm had proved a wonderful balm to her body and spirit on the long sea journey.

But today was to prove quite different. For Lillian abruptly realized that something had changed, and at a fundamental level. The sensation was so alien, Lillian was halfway across the cabin before she realized she felt no nausea. "Let me go, would you?"

"I'm not certain that's a good idea. The ship is pitching something dreadful this morning."

"Please. I'd like to stand unaided."

"But you were so ill when you first awoke. I'd hate to see you fall again."

"It was a dream."

"Truly?"

"I cried out over a dream I was having. I thought it was real, but it was only a dream."

Abigail released her arm but remained hovering nearby.

Lillian was almost flung flat by the ship striking a great wave. She caught herself on the bunk's railing.

"Shouldn't you sit down?"

Lillian said in disbelief, "I'm all right."

Abigail could not believe it either. "Are you certain?"

Lillian looked at the younger woman and said in wonder, "I'm hungry."

Abigail gasped, "Really?"

"I can scarce believe it, but I feel absolutely famished."

Abigail cried, "You wait right there!"

Abigail hurried from the room. Lillian remained as she was, protecting herself against the ship's violent rocking motion with one hand on the bunk. Yet the motion was no longer an enemy. She was so weak her head spun. But there was none of the horrid nausea and cramps that had devastated her every waking moment and turned the past sixteen days into endless torment.

The cabin had a small window in the wall opposite the narrow door. Gingerly she made her way across the cabin, wrenched the lever, and opened the window wide. She took draughts of the air and stared out at the heaving blue waves. The ocean was no longer her foe. She laughed out loud at the morning's liberty.

Steps hastened down the hall and the door was flung back. "Are you ill yet?" Abigail asked anxiously. "Do you still feel—"

"I have never been better."

Abigail's eyes sparkled with a joy so great the ailment might have been her own. "All I could find was this morning's gruel. But I persuaded the cook to part with a bit of honey."

Her stomach seemed to reach across the cabin with her hands. "Please give it to me. I feel the hunger in my bones."

This statement caused both women to laugh out loud, for the few scraps Lillian had eaten during the journey had been forced upon her, and most came back soon after.

She sat on her bed and devoured every bite.

Lillian set the bowl aside and declared, "That was the most splendid meal I have ever enjoyed. A six-course meal at the Berkeley Hotel could not be any finer."

The two ladies shared yet another laugh. Lillian gathered enough breath to say, "I have been such a dreadful burden."

"You have been no such thing."

"I most certainly—" Her words were halted by a knock upon the door.

Abigail stepped to the door and cracked it slightly open. "Lieutenant, I had not expected you to deliver the water yourself."

"Captain's compliments, Miss Abigail. He is heartily glad to hear the countess is better." The young officer's voice sounded both formal and mildly flirtatious to Lillian's ear. "I am to say this is the officers' entire Sunday allotment of shaving water."

"Lady Houghton will no doubt be most grateful. Thank you for your kindness, sir."

"It is nothing, Miss Abigail. Will we be seeing you on deck?"

"Anon, sir."

Lillian waited for the door to shut and the footsteps to retreat to comment, "Miss Abigail, is it?"

Abigail set the steaming wooden pail down by her bunk. "He is quite handsome. And he has gone to great pains to explain his prospects."

Suddenly the two were giggling like schoolchildren.

Lillian gathered herself and reached for Abigail's hand. "Thank you, dear sweet girl. Thank you. You have saved my life. I must apologize for all the trouble I have caused you."

Abigail's gaze was as direct as the light coming in through the open portal. "Do you recall how you refused to accept my own apologies and gratitude?"

"Vividly. And with great shame."

"But you were right. It is as my mother predicted. Already I have gained such wisdom from our time together."

A swift pain came and went, one that scraped across her heart and vanished.

"It's not the nausea, is it?"

"No, no, I'm fine." Lillian forced herself to smile. "Really."

"Do you feel up to joining us on the deck for the Sabbath service?"

Lillian could see the younger woman expected her refusal. And in truth she had no desire whatsoever to endure the ceremony. The memories would no doubt resurface. But Abigail had done so much for her over the past two weeks, it was hardly possible to refuse her anything.

"Let me put this water to good use," Lillian replied brightly, "and see if I can repair some of the damage these weeks have inflicted on me."

"You'll join us?"

The delight was so evident on Abigail's features Lillian knew she had made the right choice. "I should be honored."

The church Lillian's uncle had overseen had been a dismal and cold affair, dating back to the eleventh century with a thirteenth-century tower. He and her aunt had been so proud of the fact they made a point of mentioning it to everyone they met. Lillian had thoroughly disliked the building. It had seemed much smaller inside than out, and no wonder, for the walls were four-and-a-half-feet thick at the base, built at a time before pillars and supporting columns and the like. The windows, narrow slits set far back, meant that the church's interior always resided in shadows, even on the sunniest day. The exterior was a mottled yellowish brown, the color of dried mud. The slate roof was ancient and buried beneath a growth of lichen and moss. The edifice sat in a medieval graveyard, with the tombstones so lashed by wind and rain and time that the names were unreadable.

The congregation had all seemed as gray and stone-faced as her aunt and uncle. No one ever smiled at her. They knew her dark little secret even before she had heard it herself. As a child, all she knew was they had looked at her askance, and whispered behind her back, and refused to let her play with the other children. Lillian's early years had become peopled by the ghosts she had made up, her invisible friends with whom she played hide-and-seek among the weather-beaten tombstones.

As Lillian dressed for the service topside, she found herself recalling that first glimpse of her own hidden secret. One chilly evening when she was nine, while her uncle was busy with his church duties, her aunt had spirited the young Lillian across town to a prison. That distant night, the prison's keeper led Lillian and her aunt down a dank stone hall mired with fetid odors and the misery of centuries. They entered a stone chamber with low beams darkened by eons of woe. There sat a woman who looked somehow familiar to the child.

Lillian now stared out the porthole as she brushed her hair, but in truth she saw nothing save that dread night. She recalled how everyone had cried then. Lillian's aunt had sobbed as she hugged the woman. The woman was dressed in rags, and she cried as she reached out for Lillian, who screamed in horror and drew away, or tried to. Her aunt and the woman only cried the harder. Her aunt forced Lillian to step forward. But the woman did not attempt to hold the child again. Instead, the woman caressed Lillian's hair and face, over and over, as though seeking to draw in the child's beauty through her grimy fingers.

Now, as Lillian stared out the window at the dancing sunlit sea, she could feel the woman's touch sliding down her cheek in time to her strokes of the brush. How strange life was, she reflected, that the further she moved from that time, the more vivid the memories became. As though some unseen force was determined that she would never leave that early pain behind.

In truth, today's ceremony was vastly different from anything Lillian had known as a child. Today's church was an open space upon the ship's heaving deck. Their ceiling was a new sail, lashed to the masts and the side railings. The canopy billowed and boiled with the wind. The crew and passengers were joyous. They welcomed her with smiles, and the pastor even made mention of their guest, one newly risen from what must have come to feel like the grave. Lillian marveled at how all the people responded with chuckles and smiles her way. She had never heard humor from the pulpit before.

The pulpit really was nothing more than stairs leading to the quarterdeck. The pastor wore a suit of rough-woven black cloth and a matching round hat. He smiled at all and sundry. He spoke about the great adventure they had set themselves upon, and he compared it with the Israelites' trek through the wilderness, following the path their God set out for them. Lillian tried to listen to what the man said. But her mind was too caught up in how astonishingly different the service was from anything she had ever known before. When they rose to sing again, she looked about her. The people responded to her gaze with nods and smiles.

Their ship was one of a new class called clippers, meant to be far swifter than anything ever before built. The shape of the vessel, narrower than the older ships known as square-riggers, required even the nicest of passenger cabins to be very restricted in size. The ship now cleaved the waves ahead, sending froth over the windward bow. This bucking and heaving was far more severe than with the older ships, or so Abigail had reported from talks with more experienced passengers. At the time, Lillian had bemoaned the fate that had granted them passage. But now, as she sat upon the hard bench and breathed the sea-spiced air, she was exhilarated by the sense of speed. The boat moved with such determined force it might as well have been powered by great canvas wings.

Lillian spied the ship's lieutenant leaning against the quarterdeck railing. He really was rather handsome, in a rakish way. His eyes were as dark as his hair and his sun-drenched skin. He kept his gaze fastened upon Abigail with singular intensity. Such open attention would not be accepted in polite society. But here the customs were not so well defined. Lillian would need to offer Abigail a warning.

The thought caused a return of the guilt that had stabbed her in the cabin. Lillian cast a swift glance at the young woman seated beside her. Abigail's attention was as tightly focused upon the pastor as the lieutenant's was upon her. She had such a pure spirit; she was such a *good* person.

Strangely enough, Lillian found the moment acted as a clarifying potion on her mind. She was able to sit beneath the sun-dappled canopy and feel a powerful lucidity to her thoughts. What was the truth behind her own motives? The fact was, her motives had *never* been clear. She had always carried her secrets, and in a way it was because they remained hidden that they had held such power over her.

She caught her breath as the truth of it filled her being. The sound was enough to turn Abigail's face toward her. Lillian dredged up a smile to show she was not becoming ill again. But the thought remained shockingly vivid. She had been chained to secrets she thought were not only hidden, but gone. And that had been a terrible lie. The banker had revealed this. The past had merely waited in the shadows until it was time to strike.

So how was she to escape?

The pastor called to his little flock, raising them to their feet for a final song of praise and thanksgiving. Lillian glanced about her at the shining faces, and for the first time in her life she envied them. The religion she had scorned her entire life gave these people a simple joy, a *freedom*, that was not hers. She sighed deeply. A freedom she would never know. How could she?

Chapter 15

Abigail was once again worried about the countess. That morning they passed the Chesapeake Bay headlands and entered calmer waters. If anything, Lillian should have been delighted. Yet since the previous Sunday when her nausea disappeared, Lillian had become increasingly withdrawn. A subtle change at first, now she hardly spoke at all. Lillian still took pains over her hair and face and dress, yet even this seemed to be mere habit. She dined at the captain's table, as did all the upper-decks passengers. She could go the entire meal, with every man at the table agape at her loveliness, and notice nothing at all. Her eyes, normally so open and aware, remained blank. The candlelight might as well have been reflected from two blue-tinted mirrors. If someone spoke directly to her, she started as though coming awake and responded with such brevity they eventually turned away. Abigail was very worried Lillian had overcome her illness only to succumb to something far worse. But she would not speak of it.

Lillian now sat upon an empty water cask lashed to the lee railing. She stared out to sea, yet Abigail knew she saw nothing. Not the low marshlands that turned the western horizon into an emerald ribbon. Nor the clouds of water birds that swarmed so thick they created shadows beneath the sun. That morning Abigail had spoken as clearly as she had dared, insisting that Lillian tell her what was the matter. She had refused to respond.

Abigail had then asked if she had done something to offend the older woman. Lillian had finally looked at her, but all she would say was, "You dear, sweet young lady. How could you possibly have been anything other than angelic?"

But Abigail did not feel angelic just then. She was mightily concerned.

A male voice at her side said, "My dear Miss Abigail, I fear you have not heard a single word I have spoken."

She wrenched her gaze away from Lillian. "Forgive me, Lieutenant. It is just that I am worried about my friend."

"The countess? She looks splendid as always."

He really was a dashing fellow. He stood upon the quarterdeck with feet set well apart, a man accustomed to remaining steady in the foulest of conditions. The inland sea was calm here, however. Yet the low marsh headlands made no dint upon the wind. Their vessel sped along, the waters murmuring in a sibilant rush.

The captain had retired to his day cabin, leaving his young officer in command. The lieutenant had taken this opportunity to invite Abigail to join him on the quarterdeck. Much of the deck was open to the upper deck passengers, but one corner was reserved for the senior officer on duty. Not even another ship's officer could cross the invisible line without permission. They were chaperoned by the entire watch and all the passengers on deck. Yet the wind caught up their words as soon as they were spoken and flung them over the railing. It was as private an area as the ship offered.

"I was saying," the young lieutenant continued, "that so long as the wind remains off our stern, the captain feels we might head straight for the Georgetown docks. It would be quite a feat, making the entire journey in just four weeks' time. Or less, perhaps, by a day."

Abigail could see that a polite comment was expected, maybe even a regret over how their time together was about to end. Something he might use as an opening for speaking of the future. But out of the corner of her eye she spotted Lillian heave a great sigh and slump slightly. Abigail had to resist the urge to rush over and hold her. Lillian was not the sort of person to accept such aid, particularly in public.

Abigail knew the lieutenant was awaiting her response. "But that's not what we're speaking about, is it."

"Pardon me?"

"The wind. The tides. The headwaters. Our journey. That's not what is on your mind."

The lieutenant's mouth worked a moment. He was tall, with a strong cleft jaw and features carved from wind and fierce determination. "Miss Abigail . . ."

"Oh, I know I am impetuous and I speak far too often without thinking. But I dislike all this talking around and about, like we were waltzing upon the quarterdeck." She turned slightly, so that she could no longer see Lillian. It was the only way to direct her attention fully upon the lieutenant. "Listen to me, sir. There is many a young lady who would be most thrilled by your attentions."

"But I do not want just any young woman's favors." He responded to the directness of her gaze and words. "I want yours, Miss Abigail."

"That is a pity, sir. A very great pity."

"Why, pray tell?"

"Does it matter?"

"Of course it does. It matters a great deal. Why else would I ask?"

"Because you are looking for some way to change my mind. Which, I assure you, will not happen."

He parried her thrust with a smile. "How can you be so certain unless you try?"

"Very well." Abigail crossed her arms. "Who am I?"

"Miss Abigail, forgive me, but that is the first comment you have ever uttered which has not made sense."

"It makes perfect sense to me, sir. I ask you who I am because it is a question I myself cannot answer. I have often wondered why it is I have never felt inclined toward—toward a gentleman."

"I can perhaps answer that one." Dark eyes flashed. "You have never given yourself the chance."

"No. I am sorry, sir, but you are wrong. I cannot give myself to a man until I know who I am. And that is a quest I must accomplish myself, with God's help."

"Your God can join you upon this quest but I cannot. Is that your response?"

"In its entirety, sir," she replied firmly.

His smile turned bitter. "How convenient."

It was done then. The connection was severed. Abigail felt a lancing regret as she observed the cold hardness enter the lieutenant's gaze. She nodded her head. "Good day, sir."

"Miss Aldridge."

Abigail let the lieutenant be the one to turn away. It was his due, this gesture of pride and dismissal. She jumped slightly at the angry bellow which he then used to order the watch aloft. She walked over to where Lillian sat staring out at the sea.

Abigail leaned against the railing. The water glinted slate gray and cold beneath the scuttling clouds. They were surrounded by the raucous call of countless birds, and the wind was a constant chilling force against her back. Abigail pressed the hair from her face and asked, "Why could I have not handled that better?"

"You did remarkably well."

The response was so unexpected Abigail wondered if perhaps someone other than the countess had responded. "You heard?"

Lillian raised an eyebrow toward the sea and the marshlands. "The wind carried your words."

"He is angry with me now."

"The lieutenant lives by pride." Lillian continued to aim her words out to sea. "He cannot accept that any woman would refuse his advances. Particularly one surrounded by the world where he is master."

"I should have—"

"You could have done no better."

"I am so impetuous."

Lillian turned to her. "Why do you consider this a fault?"

"Because it is."

Lillian started to respond, then turned her gaze back to the sea.

Abigail settled herself upon the neighboring cask. "Would you tell me what you were going to say?"

"I was thinking," Lillian slowly replied, "I have no platform from which to advise you at all."

"Why ever not? Other than my mother, you are the finest woman I have ever met."

"Stop. Please. Do not—"

"Do not what? Say that I admire you almost more than I can say? Tell you how worried I have been about you these past days? Wish that you would confide in me—"

"No." Lillian bolted upright. She pushed herself off the railing and rushed for the stairs.

Abigail started to call after her, then sighed herself to lonely silence. Once more she had said the wrong thing. Once more she had accomplished nothing save offend someone close to her.

If only she could do better.

The wind did not hold in their favor. They awoke the next morning to a storm determined to press them away from land. All day the ship tacked back and forth across the Chesapeake Bay and the mouth of the Potomac. Finally they managed to berth at Owen, the port of Fredericksburg, just as the last glimmer of daylight faded to rainy dark. In fourteen hours of tacking they had advanced only thirty-nine miles. The storm passed, but the wind remained steadfast against them. The decision was taken to off-load. That night Abigail was awakened several times as the deckhands emptied the holds of cargo. When she rose at daybreak, three long river barges were lashed alongside their vessel.

The captain made a brief speech of farewell, mostly congratulating himself and his crew for their rapid and safe passage. Abigail stood on the foredeck and observed a strange occurrence. The lower-decks passengers were both eager to leave and slow in their farewells. They had been together for four weeks on this cramped wooden island. One adventure was over, another was about to begin. Friendships had been made, secrets shared. Now they were going off in a multitude of directions, perhaps never to see one another again. Abigail watched as two women clung together and shed many tears. Their husbands looked on with the embarrassed expressions of men who had no idea what to say to one another. Abigail felt a trace of jealousy—not over the sorrow, but rather what the journey had held for them. For herself, she had spent the first two weeks nursing a prostrate Lillian, and the final two weeks worrying over her. Here she came now, stepping from the cabin hold. Apparently Lillian did not even see the captain as he bowed his formal farewell.

"We have spaces held for us in the first barge," Abigail told her companion. She spoke with the gentle cadence of one addressing a child. "We should arrive in Georgetown by early evening."

Lillian glanced over the side of the ship and inspected the barge far below. "Our luggage?"

"I've already seen everything but your small hand case on board."

This time the captain inserted himself so closely Lillian had no choice but to accept his presence. "It has been an honor to have you on board, Countess."

"I cannot thank you enough, sir," she replied. Her words were perfect, her manners impeccable. But Abigail knew her companion well enough to realize that Lillian was not really

157

there at all. "Both for seeing us along this journey and for your hospitality."

He bent over the offered hand. "It would be an honor to welcome you on board again soon, my lady."

Abigail assumed the conversation was over and began leading Lillian toward the temporary stairs leading down to the barge. But again the captain stepped forward. "A word of advice, my lady."

"Yes?"

"The Yanks, well, ma'am, that is . . ." He fumbled with his thoughts for a moment. "Might I ask where you are headed?"

"That depends upon a number of things out of our control, sir. But I would imagine a journey into the interior is required. We are thinking of acquiring land, you see."

The captain nodded, as though his suspicions had been confirmed. "In that case, my lady, you'd best be aware that there are those among the frontiersmen who don't take kindly to titled folk."

"Why is that, do you think?"

"They're seen as land-grabbers, ma'am. Speculators, they're called. Folks who are not interested in farming, or even clearing the land. Just paying top dollar for the best and the biggest, then holding it for gain or even just for prestige."

"That is not my intent at all, sir."

"They won't be knowing that, my lady."

"Indeed not." For the first time that day, Lillian seemed to draw the world into focus. "You are saying it would be best to refrain from mentioning who I am. I am indeed most grateful, sir. Come, Abigail. I see the others are on board and await us."

But as soon as they were settled into the bow station and the barge was cast free, Lillian seemed to return to her internal world. For once, however, Abigail refused to be affected by her companion's secret ailment. The surroundings were simply too captivating.

Thankfully, the sun lanced through the sky's coverlet. But the wind held its aim straight for their faces. The swift-flowing current and the wind proved too strong an adversary for the barge's six oars. They halted a brief distance upstream as two strong horses were attached to a yoke and long lead rope. One of the oarsmen led the horses on a path alongside the river, while another rode backward and kept an eye on both the line and the barge. All traffic moving downstream kept to the opposite bank. Their progress remained slow but constant.

The landscape was varied and beautiful. Gentle hills seemed carved by the farms that blanketed their sides. There was a prosperous and contented air. The hamlets were far more open and expansive than the villages Abigail knew in England. There were neither ancient fortress walls nor tightly restricted lanes curving through densely clustered houses. And the air was rich with scents—autumn foliage and late fruit and woodsmoke and the river's sweet smell.

Her first sighting of Georgetown was a shock. Even Lillian roused from her reverie enough to ask what the matter was. Abigail replied, "I-I don't recall it being so—so large, important looking."

"When were you last here?"

"Four years ago. But most of my time was spent with my father's family in New York." Abigail stared at the sight drawing steadily into view. "I do not recognize anything."

The port of Georgetown was nowhere near as expansive as London's eastern docklands. Yet the noise and bustle resounded across the waters and punched at her chest. Even as dusk fell upon the river and the surrounding hills, the activity continued. A constant stream of heavily laden wagons plied back and forth at quayside. Men shouted and horses neighed and an endless line of stevedores shifted cargo. Scores of blacksmiths pounded steel in a neighboring open-sided building. Farther upstream a dozen mills spouted great plumes from brick smokestacks.

As the barge pulled alongside one of the long piers, men swiftly appeared and began off-loading cargo, shouting so harshly Abigail could not make out the words. She could not even tell if they were speaking English. Their hands and arms and faces were black with dirt and sweat, and they were never still. Everything about the place seemed frenetic and jarring.

The passengers were shepherded up the landing and off to one side. Abigail identified all their baggage, counted the pieces a second time, then allowed one of the jostling carriage drivers to load their goods. Everything seemed to be taking place at an impossibly swift pace, as though the entire scene were driven by some unseen hand.

Once away from the river port, however, Abigail was reassured by familiar sights. She had found herself wondering if everything would be alien. Yet here she was, traveling down a long cobblestone street that she was almost positive she had been on before.

They turned one corner, another, and a third. And she cried out loud.

"What is it?"

"There's the house." The familiar redbrick Colonial house with its emerald green shutters welcomed her with its memories. "That is where . . ."

"Yes?"

Abigail alighted before the carriage had fully halted. "Hurry!"

"Abigail, wait a moment, please."

She forced herself to turn back. "Yes, what is it?"

Lillian said, "Perhaps I should have the driver take me on to a hotel. Your grandparents do not expect us, you see. As I have noted before, most certainly they are not prepared for a stranger arriving from halfway around the globe at dusk—"

Abigail could listen no longer. The house was there and beckoning, with candles in the windows just like she remembered from childhood. She wheeled about and tossed back over her shoulder, "Oh, Lillian, I *know* they won't hear of you staying any place but here."

A narrow brick walkway led from the street to the three-story manor. Abigail lifted her skirts and raced beneath the magnolia tree and the dogwood, the cherry tree and the dark-leafed maple she had climbed as a child. She flew up the six steps where she had danced and spun her childhood fantasies.

She paused there a moment, resisting the urge to turn the polished brass handle and call to the house. Abigail smoothed her dress, patted her hair, and pushed her hat into place. She wished suddenly for a hand mirror to check her appearance. But there was nothing to be done about that now, nor any way to correct the ravages of wind and sea. She raised the knocker and hammered once, twice, three times. *What if they are not at home?*

The wait seemed as long as their sea voyage. Finally the door was opened by a housemaid in starched apron. "Yes?"

"Is Mrs. Cutter at home?"

"Who should I say is calling?"

"I . . . Please excuse me, but I'd rather it be a surprise."

"Who is it, Matilda?" came from behind the maid.

"She won't say, ma'am."

"Won't say?" A slender woman with her hair pulled back in a steel-gray bun entered the front hall. "Why on earth not?"

Then the older woman faltered. She gripped her throat with one hand.

"Mrs. Cutter? Ma'am? Are you all right?"

Abigail stepped into the light. But she could not say precisely what was happening, because the room now was swimming. She bit her lip and wiped at her eyes.

A voice called, "Mother? What is the matter?"

A man appeared in the side entryway. Abigail recognized him instantly as her uncle Horace, after whom her brother was named. "Who is this, Mother?" Horace questioned once more.

But her grandmother did not speak.

Abigail took a very shaky breath and said, "Good evening, Grandmother."

"Oh, my dear, sweet child." The older woman came rushing forward now, her arms outstretched. She embraced Abigail with the force of one who had yearned for years. "My dear darling Abbie, you've grown up on me."

After awkward hugs with Horace, she was brought into the front parlor where her grandfather struggled to rise from his chair. Abigail recalled a burly man with a great booming voice and pockets full of sweets for his granddaughter, not this ailing man with snow-white hair and limbs that could not stop their shaking. She wept then, both for joy and for all the years that were lost to her.

When she regained a semblance of control, Abigail was introduced to a man she did not recognize but instantly knew his name. Reginald Langston was Erica's brother. He was a tall, strong-looking man with a handsome face. And Abigail felt her heart pierced anew by that strange mixture of sorrow and joy, for she could see in his features a mirror image of her childhood friend. Erica Langston, now married to Gareth Powers, had been the most wonderful person in Abigail's young world. And now she stood before Erica's brother and again felt a rushing back through the years, echoes of long discussions with Erica about her family and friends.

But the man did not completely reflect the descriptions Erica had drawn of her brother. Both in their time together in England and in the letters that had followed her return to America, Erica had described her brother as full of joy and energy and great good humor. Yet this handsome man now stood motionless by the fireplace with a slightly haunted look upon his well-carved features. Then Abigail remembered a letter, some two years back, relating how Reginald Langston's beloved wife had died in childbirth. The baby had died just hours after the mother. A son, if she recalled correctly. Erica had noted that her brother had taken this very hard. Even now, two years later, the stain of sorrow remained in his gaze.

Abigail abruptly remembered Lillian. "Forgive me, Grandmother, but my companion awaits outside in the carriage."

"My goodness, child, why on earth did you not invite her in?"

Abigail decided any longer explanation could wait. "She

has not been particularly well. The journey was very hard on her."

"Even more the reason to bring her in out of the night."

"She was thinking that perhaps she should find lodging in a hotel. I assured her that you—"

"After escorting my granddaughter all the way from England? And with six upstairs rooms sitting empty? I won't hear of such a thing." Mrs. Cutter hurried to the front door.

Soon enough there came the sounds of protest outside the entrance. "Surely you must understand, madam. I have no wish to intrude upon your reunion—"

"I understand nothing of the kind" was the firm response. "You are a friend of my family, and I will not hear any further discussion of your staying anywhere but with us. Now up the stairs with you, if you please."

Abigail's grandmother propelled Lillian forward with a firm grip upon her arm. The woman looked to protest further, but Mrs. Cutter was busy with her own arrangements. "Horace, be so good as to see to the carriage and their luggage. Granddaughter, perhaps you might formally introduce your companion."

"Yes, please, I would be most happy to do so. This is the Countess of Wantage, Lady Lillian Houghton."

"Eh? What's that you say?" A trace of her grandfather's stout manner returned. "We're entertaining a countess this night?"

Abigail nodded and looked at Lillian, who stood frozen in the doorway, her hand to her throat. Abigail followed Lillian's gaze across to where Reginald Langston stood by the mantel. If anything, he was even more still than Lillian.

Chapter 16

Abigail moaned in terror. She was back in Newgate Prison, crouched in the narrow recess between the empty fireplace and the side wall. The association room, the jailer called it, leering at her as he rattled his keys.

Everything she thought had come since then had been only a dream. The surprise arrival of Lady Houghton, the anguish she caused her family, the meetings with Wilberforce, the travel to America. All a myth, a fabrication created by her fevered mind.

She had only imagined that a countess would appear like a delivering angel to sweep her away. Abigail struggled to see the fetid room with its flickering shadows and gloomy tallow candles, and knew she would never escape. Never.

The far door opened. The creaking hinges sounded like the wails of prisoners trapped inside forever. The stone walls glistened with centuries of tears.

The jailer entered, his stained leather apron stretched taut over his enormous belly. He started walking toward her, jangling his keys like a snake rattling its tail. She saw in his hard flashing gaze all the unthinkable dreads that made up his daily life. And now were hers as well.

She awoke calling out in panic.

"Child, child, I heard your whimpers in my dressing room." Her grandmother's voice and hand soothed her. "I thought at first it was a kitten." Mrs. Cutter set the hairbrush she had carried with her down on the bedside table. "There, shah now, you're safe and sound. Open your eyes, my darling little girl."

"I had the most awful nightmare!"

"Look at you, trembling like a leaf. Your nightclothes are drenched. Do you have a fever?" Her grandmother pressed the back of her hand to Abigail's forehead. "No, you feel all right. Come, let's get you into some dry clothes."

Abigail allowed herself to be treated like a young child. The nightdress was pulled over her head, and a fresh one was slipped on and buttoned up the front. She was settled back into bed and the covers were nestled under her chin. Her grandmother stroked her forehead. "There. Do you feel better now?"

"It was the most awful of dreams, Grandmother."

"Do you want to tell me about it?"

The fact was, she did. She lay there snuggled deep in the bed where she had slept as a little child. The room had been reserved for her whenever she had visited her mother's family in Georgetown. The morning light was strong and clear and golden. It poured through the window across from her bed and vividly illuminated each detail in contrast to all the appalling memories. But it was not of the nightmare that Abigail spoke. Instead, she told of the reality that had brought her to America.

Midway through the telling, Abigail found she could remain prone no longer and rose to a sitting position. Even that was not enough. She swung her feet around to the floor. Her grandmother seemed to understand, for she took Abigail's hand and led her to the straight-backed parson's bench beneath the window. The light was even stronger here and lay across her shoulders like a warming hand. Which was very good indeed, for the telling had chilled Abigail to her bones.

When she was finished, her grandmother remained silent for a very long time. Abigail felt no urgent need for her response. Instead, Abigail inspected this woman who was both an intimate part of her life and a new person entirely. Her grandmother had aged into a slender and stately woman. Her hair was pulled back into the same bun as the previous night. A silver and black lacquered hairpin rose like a miniature Spanish fan at the back of her head. A matching brooch was pinned at the collar of her high-waisted dress made from rose-colored linen. The frock shone in the morning light like a late summer flower.

"What are you thinking, Grandmother?"

"That I should not call you Abbie any longer."

"Have I done something so awful you wish—"

"Oh, my darling child. You have grown up. That is what I mean." She took hold of her granddaughter's hand and said solemnly, "I want you to know I am honored you would entrust me with such a secret."

"I want to ask you something. Will you please be truthful with me?"

"I hope I have always been such, and always will be."

"I wish the barest of truth, Grandmother. Now that you have heard what I have done, what do you think of me? What do you see when you look at me?"

Her grandmother had her mother's eyes, now framed by lines and skin turned fragile as porcelain in the light. "An intelligent and adventurous spirit, who until recently was trapped inside a place she yearns to outgrow."

"You are just saying what you think I want to hear." When her grandmother did not respond, Abigail pressed, "How can you say such a thing?"

"Because I know your mother," she replied simply. "Now I want to tell you a secret of my own. When you were very young, the British invaded Washington and burned a great deal of the city to the ground. Your dear childhood friend, Erica Langston Powers, lost her father that day. The family's business caught on fire. Her father died when a soldier struck him on the head with a musket as he tried to get through the line of soldiers to the water trough. Erica later discovered that the fire was not caused by the British soldiers who invaded Washington. Instead, an unscrupulous London merchant banker used foreknowledge of the British invasion to fire the Langston business. He was holding a great deal of the family's gold, you see, and he wanted to keep it for himself. But Erica went to England and stayed with your family and successfully forced the banker to return her family's gold."

"And while she was there she met Gareth Powers," Abigail said as she filled in the rest. "They fell in love and then returned to Washington together because William Wilberforce asked them to become involved in America's battle against the slave trade," she finished. "I know this, Grandmother."

"Indeed you do. But what you don't know is that during the very hard years between the loss of her father and her departure for England, Erica came to me for help. And being the busybody that I am, I gave her advice as well."

"You're not a busybody, Grandmother."

"Oh, that I most certainly am. Just as certainly as your mother, God bless her, would like to go through her entire life without making a single wrong step."

"Why should she need to?" Abigail felt a great lump of sadness building within. "After all, she has this impetuous daughter who will make more than enough mistakes for the whole family."

"That I very much doubt."

Her grandmother's calm tone defeated her. How could she possibly remain upset with herself when her grandmother did not seem the least bit fazed? "I have a letter for you from Mother."

"In which I am sure she has been very diplomatic in explaining why you are here. Again, child, I am grateful that you would share your confidences with me as you did."

"I-I was dreaming that I was back in Newgate Prison, locked up forever."

"Well, you're not. You are here in your family's Georgetown home, safe and sound." Her grandmother reached around Abigail's shoulders and hugged her close. "You came to me for help, just as Erica did all those years ago. Shall I give you advice as I did her?"

"Of course, Grandmother."

"Very well. Here is what I think. Don't let the world ever take away what makes you unique. And of even more importance, don't ever count your gift as a burden."

Abigail sat straight, breaking free of the embrace. "How can you say that? It is this very impetuousness of mine that has caused everyone so much trouble!"

"Gift I said, and gift I mean," her grandmother said firmly. "The deed may be wrong, but God has given you this characteristic for a reason. There is nothing wrong with impetuousness, if tamed and correctly employed."

"But . . ." The concept was so novel she had to work her mind around words that could frame her confusion. "How can I use something that causes me to act before I think?"

"I have no idea." Her grandmother was smiling now, and she gave Abigail another hug. The sunlight seemed to be captured by her grandmother's features and reflected back in a glow that warmed Abigail's heart. "Why don't you take that question to God? After all, it is He who gave you the gift in the first place. Why not see what He has in mind?"

Abigail dressed and went down for breakfast, fearful that the entire household had heard her cries on awakening from her nightmare. She entered the kitchen hesitantly. Gazes all turned her way, inquiring, inspecting. She lowered her head and took aim at the chair her grandmother pulled out for her. A bowl of porridge was settled in front of her, then a steaming cup of tea followed by a little pitcher of fresh cream. Her grandmother began introductions. The cook stood by the stove, preparing her grandfather's breakfast. A younger woman, the maid, stood polishing silverware by the big rear window.

Abigail did not catch their names. She focused upon her bowl of porridge and remained silent after her acknowledging nods.

The door behind her opened and another woman came in, this one introduced as a nurse employed to help with Abigail's grandfather. He had, according to her grandmother, become increasingly doddery this past year. A man stumped into the kitchen from the rear door, wishing Mrs. Cutter a grand good morning and calling for his tea. He was introduced as the gardener. The kitchen now held six people and felt very cramped. Abigail did not need to lift her head to feel the eyes watching her.

Abigail finished and placed her spoon in the bowl.

"Would you care for more porridge?" her grandmother asked.

"No, thank you, ma'am."

"Susie, pour the young lady another cup of tea."

"I'm fine, really, thank you."

Her grandmother seemed to take that as the signal she had been waiting for. She pulled her chair up close.

"My dear, I want you to tell me about your companion."

The question was not expected, and Abigail required a moment to understand properly.

"The countess. She really is a titled lady?"

"Y-yes. Her husband was the count of Wantage."

"Was?"

"He has died."

"Do you know when?"

Abigail lifted her gaze. "Over a year ago."

"Land sakes," the cook said at the stove.

"It's Providence," the maid declared as she refilled Mrs. Cutter's cup. "Mark my words. Providence is here among us this very morn."

At the end of the table, the gardener asked, "Where is she now?"

"Pacing the front parlor," the maid reported. "I asked did she want tea, but the lady didn't hear me at all."

"Is she as lovely as they are telling me?" the gardener asked.

"You wait till you see her," the cook answered stoutly. "Take the breath right out of your body, that woman will."

Her grandmother ignored them all and focused her gaze on Abigail. "How old is she? Do you know?"

"Not for certain," Abigail replied slowly. "But she has a son."

"Providence," the maid said with a firm nod of her head. "Mark my words."

"How old is the boy?" the cook asked her.

"I'm not . . . Yes, I remember now. Byron is fifteen."

"That's not possible," the cook said, banging her spoon against the pot. "That lady isn't old enough to have a child nearing man size."

"But she does. I recall distinctly my parents talking about this."

Abigail's grandmother asked, "What can you tell me about her?"

Abigail looked around the room, puzzled by their curiosity. All of them—even the gardener—seemed filled with the most remarkable sense of anticipation. As though they could scarcely wait for something to happen.

"Don't mind them," her grandmother said to Abigail's hesitation. "If you and I were to have this conversation at the bottom of a deep dark well, they'd learn of every word the instant it was spoken."

"It's Master Reginald, you see, miss," the cook explained. "We think ever so much of the gentleman."

"He's mourned long enough." The gardener nodded his agreement. "If I've said it once, I've said it a thousand times."

"If anyone deserves a bit of joy in his life, it's that gentleman," the cook said.

"The finest man to ever walk this earth, Master Reginald is," the nurse agreed.

"Our Horace is starting a business with him," Mrs. Cutter

explained. "Only it's not really with Reginald, but with his sister, Mrs. Erica Powers."

The maid put in, "She's the brains in that family."

"Master Reginald is no sluggard," the cook commented slowly.

"No, but it's Mrs. Powers what's driving them forward. Her with the child and the writing and the troubles."

"Troubles?" Abigail wondered. "What troubles are these?"

"Mrs. Powers, she's been ever so busy with this anti-slave business," the maid answered.

"A right tragedy, that is as well," the gardener agreed. "Worn her down to a nub."

Her grandmother tapped the table with a the sugar spoon. Just one quick rap. But it was enough to silence the room. She turned to her granddaughter and said, "Erica's situation can wait. It most certainly isn't going anywhere, what with this pending presidential election. As for Reginald, my dear, you know of course about his losing his wife in childbirth."

"Only what Erica wrote in a letter."

"It was a tragedy such as you can't imagine," her grandmother said. "He adored that little lady."

"Ripped the heart right out of his chest, it did," the cook said, wiping her eye with the corner of her apron. "Spent these two years mourning. Losing himself in work and pining for his lost lady and their little son."

The gardener used his cup to point out the front window. "Here comes the gentleman now."

Abigail's grandmother bolted to her feet. "All of you, stay right here. I'll see to the door. Cook, prepare tea. Use the silver teapot and the Meissen porcelain. I'll serve them myself."

"Providence," the maid said as the cook pointed her toward the dining room and the silver service. "You mark my words."

Chapter 17

Lillian hardly saw the parlor where she had stayed since arising that morning. One set of reasons for distress had been exchanged, not for others, but rather for the same plus even more. Though an ocean apart, she was still caught in the banker's snare. Piled upon this were pressures that rose from a past she had thought was faded and forgotten. Yet now here it was, coming at her from all sides. These new forces were far more confining than the room's walls. They went with her everywhere, even into her dreams.

Pages from her son's letter, written more than a month ago as his gift to her before their separation, dangled from her hand. She had hoped to find a sense of peace in his caring words. Today, however, Byron's letter only magnified her inner tumult.

She had tossed and turned all night. Her thoughts were like wolves, baying at her heels, tracking her every move. They surrounded her now, their howls so confusing she could not distinguish one from the other.

If only I had not attended that Sabbath service on the boat, she remonstrated with herself. She would prefer to have remained ill, yes, even that! It had all started then. The feeling remained with her still. That day, for the first time in years, she had felt a spark of hope. She wanted to tell herself it was just a lie. Yet she could not. She yearned for this. She *hungered* to believe it was real. But how could she? For every time her mind touched upon this yearning, she was attacked. She was back in her uncle's cold house, trapped inside restrictions and rules and silent condemnation. How could a religion that had so confined her soul now give her such a sense of beckoning new life? It was impossible. Oh, if only she could still believe it was impossible! She thought she had reconciled herself to a life of hidden secrets, fear of their disclosure, and now a banker's blackmail.

But she could not ignore the flame that had been ignited within her. She had sat alongside young Abigail and peered into her very soul. She had seen the truth. Yes. Even now, trapped and hounded as she was, she could not refuse the fact that she had seen there what she did not have, what she had *never* had. And what she so desperately wanted.

Peace.

A chance to set down her burdens and dwell in the strength of One who was able to carry them all for her. Yet how could she? Of all people, she was the most outcast! This banker demanded that she damage these very same people who had revealed to her a living mystery. A chance at hope eternal. And to compound her guilt, she was using their very goodness and kindness to carry out her evil assignment.

Oh, if only she could dismiss their faith as myth and turn away!

The knock on the outer door froze her mental wandering. Lillian folded her son's letter and slipped it into the pocket of her day dress. She heard the sound of a man's voice at the front door. A murmur of voices in the hall was followed by a softer knock, then the parlor door opened. Mrs. Cutter smiled. "Good morning, Countess. I hope you slept well."

"Y-yes, thank you," she stammered out.

Abigail Cutter said, "You met Reginald Langston last evening. May he join you here? I have called for some tea." She motioned them both to chairs near the fireplace. "I won't be but a moment."

The man who entered the parlor seemed equally speechless. When they had finally made their way to the offered seating, Mrs. Cutter said, "Tea it is, then," as she backed from the room and shut the door.

Lillian had no idea how long they sat across the fireplace from each other. The mantel clock droned steadily.

Finally Reginald Langston said softly, "I do not know how to address you. Should I call you 'my lady'? Or is 'Countess' the correct term?"

"Whichever you wish," Lillian answered, her voice low.

The two quietly watched the fire until the maid entered and placed a silver tray on the low table between the sofa and the fireplace. She quietly departed.

Lillian said, "I shall pour us tea. Will you please tell me about yourself?"

"I think I would prefer that we begin with your story. I'm afraid mine is rather ordinary."

"How do you take your tea?" Lillian asked, feeling her cheeks grow warm. He told her a bit of cream and sugar would do. Her hands trembled as she passed him his cup and picked up her own.

"Now then," she said demurely, "I asked first. Please tell me."

"Well," he said simply, "you have perhaps heard from Abigail about my sister, Erica. After she returned from England, I helped her rebuild our family business. For years the work consumed me. Four years back, I met and married Agatha. She was lovely, and we were very happy. She died giving birth to our first child. A little boy. He died later that very same wretched day. My life since then has been no life at all."

Lillian could barely hear his last sentences. She saw the way each word was pushed out against a great wall of grief.

"I am so terribly sorry," she whispered, reaching a hand toward him, then slowly returning it to her lap.

He spent a long moment looking down at the floor. When he spoke it was to her hand. "I have spent the last two years thinking that the sun should never rise again. Not for me. That joy is something reserved for others. That I could never . . ."

Lillian wanted to hear him finish that sentence. But she could not ask it of him. How could she, and then hold back her own secrets?

Reginald raised his gaze to hers, eyes the color of smoke laid upon the glow of a winter's dawn. They were set in a strong and handsome face, with high cheekbones and a cleft chin. A strand of dark hair fell over his forehead, like a little boy's.

He said, "Today is the anniversary of my wife's passage."

"Oh," she breathed out like a sigh.

"I am planning on driving out to visit her grave this afternoon—hers and that of our little son."

He paused a long moment. "Would it be—I mean, is it too forward of me to invite you along for the drive?"

Lillian's breath caught in her throat. She began her answer with a nod, then said, "It would be a privilege to pay my respects."

"And it will be your turn to tell your story," he said with a smile. But Lillian felt her heart squeeze with foreboding. How could she tell him of her past?

Only Mrs. Cutter was at the front door when the carriage with the driver up front departed. But the staff were at the windows. Lillian studied their expressions through the open carriage window. They obviously cared deeply about this man who sat beside her.

"I say, you have only arrived in America last night," Reginald noted. "Are you certain this is how you would care to spend this afternoon?"

"Yes, as a matter of fact. I am quite sure." When they turned onto the main avenue, she spied a shop up ahead. "Would you have your driver halt for a moment?" she asked.

But when the carriage pulled up in front, she realized she had not brought along her purse. "I am terribly sorry, but I left the house without a farthing to my name."

Reginald was already climbing down and held out his hand to her. Together they entered the flower stall. She selected a bouquet of late-summer blossoms—dahlias and delicate pink roses. He paid for them and walked her back to the carriage.

They rode in silence to the Oak Hill Cemetery. Lillian felt relieved he was not asking questions. The cemetery gates were framed by maples so large their boughs formed a canopy over them. The grounds were quiet and almost empty. The white-washed church shone in the afternoon sunshine.

The carriage halted before a broad tombstone. Reginald helped Lillian down and they walked across the grass.

"This is where my boy lies," Reginald said softly.

Lillian gently read the name, "Charles Harrow Langston." The infant's mother's name was engraved above his.

"He was named after a distant relative. It was done to honor my mother, who passed away . . ." But Reginald did not finish the sentence.

"And where does she lie?"

Silently he crossed the well-trimmed grass to a neighboring stone, one that bore two names, Forrest and Mildred Langston. Beneath the woman's name was the same year of departure as Reginald's wife and son. "You poor man," Lillian murmured. "All at the same time."

Together they returned to the first grave. Lillian knelt and placed the flowers in the stone urn. She remained where she was for a long time, then slowly rose to her feet.

Behind her, Reginald asked, "Do you think it might be possible for someone to truly set the past aside and start anew?"

Lillian brushed the grass from her dress with slow, deliberate motions. "I was about to ask you the very same thing."

Abigail chatted with her grandmother about several differences she noticed in Georgetown as their carriage took them into town. There was a definite change in the atmosphere since their bedside conversation. Abigail knew her grandmother loved her. She always had and always would. But now, things were different. A threshold had been passed. Confidences had been shared. They rode companionably together now as adults. And as friends.

Langston's was no longer merely a trading center and coffeehouse. Where the original warehouse had once stood now rose a grand structure of cream-colored wood and yellow brick. A large sign above the second-story windows proclaimed this to be Langston's Emporium.

Abigail alighted from the carriage and took in the uniformed doorman tipping his hat as he opened the portals. "Why, this is as nice as anything I have seen in London!"

"Be sure to tell Erica," her grandmother said, nodding to an elegant lady departing from the store. "She will be so pleased."

They left the bustling public areas behind and moved upstairs to the central offices. An attendant left them in an antechamber lanced by afternoon sunlight. There was a fine old carpet on the plank flooring and horsehair chairs from another age. The mantel brimmed with drawings and small oils of faces Abigail faintly recognized.

She was both excited and nervous over the coming meeting. Her grandmother noticed the tension. "What is troubling you?"

"I was just wondering," Abigail slowly replied, "whether I should tell her."

Her grandmother did not need to ask of what she spoke. "You will tell her what you wish, and only when it seems suitable."

"But the scandal was in all the broadsheets. Possibly she would have read about it . . ." A thought occurred to Abigail. "Had you heard about all this before I told you?"

"I do not bother with nonsense from the British royal court," her grandmother replied crisply.

"So you *had* heard."

"Only enough to be certain it was all a pack of lies."

"But Erica—"

"Was a dear friend," her grandmother finished for her, "who trusts you as I do and who knows the British court to be full of ruffians and scoundrels."

"Just so." The side door creaked open. A lovely woman entered, dressed in gray muslin with white collar and cuffs that would have been severe were it not for the warm glow on her features. "I could not have said it any better myself."

For a moment Abigail was uncertain whom she faced. Though she recognized Erica instantly, still she knew this was a very different woman from her childhood friend. Here was a woman of calm authority and very deep resolve. Intelligence shone from her eyes. Then she smiled, and the young Erica came into view. "My dear, sweet Abigail! What a lovely young woman you have become."

In that first embrace, Abigail felt the bundle of nerves recede to mere excitement at the reunion. They held hands as Erica led them into the next room and announced, "This was the chief clerk's office when I was a child. Then the British troops invaded and the warehouse was burned and Father killed. You know that story, of course. Afterwards it became my mother's bedroom. The chamber has returned to its original purpose, I'm happy to say. Reginald's protégé occupies it now."

"I have so wanted to meet this young man," Abigail's grandmother said. "Reginald speaks very highly of him."

"As well he should." Erica turned at the sound of footsteps. "And here he comes now."

Abigail found herself singularly unimpressed with the man who came through the door. He might have been handsome were he to pay the slightest attention to his appearance. Which he most certainly did not. Nor did he seem the least bit concerned with greeting unexpected guests. His attention was completely focused upon their hostess. "Mrs. Powers, the shipment from France has arrived!"

"What, already?"

"Three weeks early!" He bore a double armful of documents. The way he clenched the papers to his chest revealed two poorly patched elbows on a dark coat shiny with age. Rings of ink adorned both shirt cuffs. His pants were intended for a much larger man and were held up by threadbare suspenders. "The company has employed a new clipper ship, and it has made the crossing in record time!"

"Might I introduce two dear friends, Mrs. Abigail Cutter and Miss Abigail Aldridge. This is Abraham Childes."

"Ladies." It was unlikely the young man saw them at all. "The customs officer is downstairs, Mrs. Powers. He has the bill of lading and wishes for payment in full." He spoke in excited bursts, as if he had run the entire length of the emporium. Which perhaps he had. Ink was streaked across his forehead, where he had no doubt sought to clear his unruly dark hair from his eyes. "I have served him coffee and told him I would seek you out."

"Can you see to this matter yourself?"

The young man was brought up sharp. "Well, I suppose, that is, if you're sure—"

"Excellent. Tell the good gentleman I am otherwise engaged. You will find the banker's drafts in Reginald's top drawer."

"V-very well, Mrs. Powers. That is, if you're sure."

"I most certainly am." Erica waited until he had bowed to the visitors and turned away before quietly saying, "I apologize for Abe's—well, his appearance and his brusqueness."

"There is no need," Mrs. Cutter replied. "It is nice to see such young and vibrant energy about the place. And Reginald claims the young man is most remarkable. Why not invite him to lunch with us on Sunday?" Mrs. Cutter asked Erica.

"Oh, Reginald would be delighted. He has been urging

Abe to visit our church. It will prove the perfect opportunity." She led them across the chamber and through the next doorway. "I am very sorry Gareth is not here to greet you as well, Abigail. He is midway through a tour of the southern states. There is a national election, you see. It is staggered in time, stretching from August right on through until November. Gareth wanted to observe some of the results firsthand."

"I am sorry to have missed him." Abigail followed Erica into a long room with oiled paneling and a row of tall sash windows overlooking the street. "This is just as I imagined! You described it well, Erica."

Erica gave another of her warm smiles. The sunlight was brilliant enough to reveal a shadow of weariness upon her strong features. "My father's desk belongs to Reginald now." She pointed to a long table set by the first window, with a smaller desk forming an L to the right. "That desk was a special birthday gift from my father. I use it now for my pamphlet writing. Though I have less time for this now than I would like, what with the care of our darling little girl and the requirements of this business." She lowered her voice. "And the harsh times we face with our work on the cause."

"Your work is valiant and vital and will bear great fruit," Abigail's grandmother stoutly declared.

Erica started to say something, then seemed to change her mind and gave another smile, this one slightly forced. "Let me serve you coffee."

When they were seated at an oval table set by the unlit fireplace and coffee had been poured, Abigail ventured, "I met several times with Mr. Wilberforce before we departed."

Erica brightened. "And how is the dear man?"

"He has bad days and good, with his ailment and all," Abigail said.

"So I have heard." Erica set her cup down untasted. "And what news do you carry of our struggles in England?"

"Work goes well on some fronts and less well on others," Abigail said, feeling rather ashamed. For in truth the words were simply a repetition of what she had often heard her father say, not derived from any knowledge of her own.

"And of slavery? Have there been many victories to count?"

She lowered her gaze. "I fear my parents have felt I was too young to become involved in that particular battle."

Erica recovered the moment swiftly. "And they were well advised to take this course. Were you my own daughter I would have insisted upon the same."

Abigail took enough heart from those kind words to offer, "I understand things are not all that we would hope. I have heard my father speak of many defeats and few victories."

"So we are being vanquished there as well," Erica said disconsolately.

Abigail Cutter interjected, "Only on the surface, my dear. Only on the surface. You are too involved to realize just how great is the opposition's foment and fear. The anti-slavers are growing in force. Pamphleteers such as you and your husband are generating great support for the cause. This you would recognize yourself were you only to take a step back and view your efforts from a distance."

Abigail decided no better cue could be offered. "Mr. Wilberforce has sent you a letter."

"For me?"

"It is addressed to you and Gareth. He asked me to convey personally that it is more than a request. He says that if ever you have treated anything he has said as a directive, do so with this."

"May I see it?"

"Of course." Abigail withdrew the letter from her handbag. She observed the intensity with which Erica fed upon the pages. She found herself yearning for something that would give such purpose to her days and her life.

Erica refolded the letter and stowed it away. Her cheeks were flushed and her eyes sparkled. "As soon as Gareth returns, we shall begin," Erica declared, excitement coloring her voice.

Abigail tried to maintain an interest in the conversation. Yet her mind continually returned to the new fervor that gripped her friend. How would it feel, she wondered, to have something that *ignited* her in such a way as this?

Chapter 18

When Lillian awoke the next morning, she tried to tell herself it was just an ordinary day. She rose in the four-poster bed and went through her morning preparations with a deliberate air. She chose a gown she thought seemed suitable. She decided not to wear any jewelry except a small silver brooch. She brushed her hair, pinned it up, and carefully inspected her reflection. She heard sounds from the kitchen directly below her room. The family was gathering for breakfast. Lillian rose from the dressing table and walked to the window. There was no rain, but there was also no sunshine. Nor was there wind. The day seemed trapped inside a stillness. Lillian turned from the window. The day's tranquility moved with her. She looked around the room, the walls cast in shadows by the dim light. It really was a lovely room. The furniture was all maple and elm. The hardwood floor was as polished as the furniture and graced with a hooked rug in autumn colors. The curtains framing the tall sash window matched the rug and the bedspread. Lillian moved about the room, tidying up her things and making the bed. She had not truly noticed the room before now. In fact, it seemed as though she had moved through the past weeks since the shipboard service noticing little save the internal turmoil that held her captive. If she opened her heart to forgiveness and hope, how was she to protect her secrets? How could she keep her blackmailer at bay?

The previous night had begun like all the others since her seasickness had passed. She had gone to bed exhausted and slept poorly. Sometime in the night she had awakened. This was when her worst struggles commenced. All the raging voices were loudest then, all the memories clearest. Only this past night had been different. She had lain there waiting for the battle to begin. Instead, there had been an eerie calm. Lillian had been filled with the knowledge that the conflict was over. Her indecision was gone. She had not realized a decision had been reached until that moment. Then she had turned over and slept without dreaming.

Even now, as she started down the front stairs, she was tempted to pretend to herself that no choice had been made.

"Good morning, Countess." Mrs. Cutter rose from her place at the kitchen table as Lillian came through the door. To one side sat Abigail. On her other side sat a woman Lillian did not know. "I hope you slept well," her hostess continued.

"Very well, thank you. Must we rest upon formalities here among us?"

"Not necessarily," Mrs. Cutter replied. She spoke slowly, as though testing the words. "No doubt you would prefer to take your breakfast in the dining room?"

"A place here at the kitchen table would be fine."

"I'm not sure . . ." But Mrs. Cutter stopped midsentence because Lillian had already seated herself. "May I introduce a very dear friend, Mrs. Erica Powers."

"A pleasure, Mrs. Powers. I have heard a very great deal about you. Abigail admires you to the highest degree."

"Likewise, my lady."

"Please, I would be most grateful if we might use a less formal address. I am Lillian—or if you prefer, Mrs. Houghton."

Erica smiled. "A truly American sentiment."

"So I am told. Everyone in London speaks so highly of you and your husband—except of course those who profit from slavery. But no doubt Abigail has already told you of this."

"London," Erica repeated. "I would very much like to

return there. It has been far too long."

Mrs. Cutter chided gently, "Your work here is not done."

"And I am telling you that all efforts at this point are futile." Erica wearily rubbed the side of her face. "Forgive me. I was up half the night with our daughter. She has a fever that will not ease. Fortunately, she is better this morning and her nanny urged me to get out for a bit." She stopped and sighed. "Also I received a letter from Gareth saying he will be away longer than expected. I do miss him so."

The cook asked Lillian, "Will you be having tea this morning, my lady?"

"Yes, thank you."

"And a bit of porridge, perhaps? I just made some up fresh for Mr. Cutter."

"That would be lovely." She asked Mrs. Cutter, "How is your husband this morning?"

"The same. Always the same." Clearly this was not a preferred topic. "Mrs. Houghton, Erica was just telling Abigail about the coming election. Do you mind if we continue with our discussion?"

"Not at all. And please, I would be most grateful if you would call me Lillian."

"Yes, I understand and I will abide by your wishes."

"I am told that titles hold little value in this country."

"That is both true and not true. Within some circles, titles are all the rage. Were I to let it be known I harbored a countess in my back bedroom, I would be flooded with invitations."

"Then please do not tell a soul," Lillian replied with a small smile.

Erica said to Lillian, "I hope you will excuse me for saying this. But thank you for accompanying my brother to the cemetery yesterday."

"I was unsure whether to mention it myself," Mrs. Cutter said. "But now that it is out, I must agree. All of us who care for him are most grateful."

"Reginald has mourned long enough," Erica added. "Even

he says this. But it is one thing to speak the words and another thing entirely to live the act. Yesterday when he told me of your outing, I dared hope for the first time in a very long while."

"Please," Lillian said after a pause, "you were going to speak about an election?"

She was glad to see the gathered ladies took this as a signal to change the subject. Erica now turned to Abigail and resumed her conversation. "Originally there were five candidates running for the presidency—Crawford, Calhoun, Clay, Adams, and Jackson. All but one own slaves. All of them give lip service to abolishing the practice, but only while they visit the Northern states. When they travel south they sing an entirely different tune. The political race has come down to just two men now, Jackson and Adams. What is perhaps more telling of the nation's mood is the fact that one man, John C. Calhoun, will run as the vice-presidential candidate on *both* tickets."

"You do not support this man," Abigail observed.

"John Calhoun has spent his entire political career defending slavery. He is an eloquent master of the half-truth." Erica Powers's voice had hardened. "But he merely represents the views of many Americans. These days, all talk is of expansion. Of opportunity. Of new wealth and growth. The fact is that our fair land is besieged with suffering and wickedness."

Erica paused, then added more quietly, "Gareth has written of rumors that the election may be stolen."

Mrs. Cutter protested, "Surely that is an exaggeration."

"Perhaps." Erica did not sound convinced. "As you know, the more distant states began their elections last month. The final votes from these eastern states are due in November. Jackson is sure to win substantial majorities in almost all of these outlying states. Adams has formed an alliance with Clay, a most unscrupulous politician. Clay masterminded the admittance of Missouri as a slave state and Maine as a free state, thus maintaining the balance in Congress. Clay has won a tremendous amount of power with the Southern states as a result. It appears that Jackson will win the popular vote. But the choice of president lies with members of the electoral college. They can be swayed. Or so Gareth reports. This is why he has delayed his return. To determine the truth to these rumors."

"All this is beyond me," Mrs. Cutter said, waving her handkerchief. "But to think of the president being chosen by wrongful means, well, it's a bit too much to fathom."

"You know as well as I that corruption in Washington is rampant," Erica replied. "There is bribing and thievery from the public purse. Our constitutional integrity is undermined by secret deals. Politicians are using public office for private gain. Private interests are being granted priority over public welfare."

"Yes, of course you are right; we all know of this and condemn the practices. But the office of the president? Surely not."

"Gareth is working with his contacts throughout the states in question," Erica said, clearly not able to hope she was wrong. "He is trying to establish what is really happening."

Lillian spooned her oatmeal and sipped at her tea, and all the while she observed the women gathered in this cozy kitchen. Even amidst these harsh tidings, there could be no denying their closeness, their strength, their sheer goodness. They were unlike any Lillian had come upon before. They sat and spoke together as concerned friends, filled with compassion for those they did not know. The safe confines of wealth and power could easily have shielded them from needing to think of such matters. Instead they sought to use their affluence to help those less fortunate. They were passionate in their causes.

"Begging your pardon," the cook said over the voices at the table. "Mr. Reginald's coach has just arrived."

Lillian was immediately on her feet. "You must excuse me."

"My dear, you haven't finished your breakfast."

"I'm not . . . That is, I must hurry. Thank you." There was little reason for such haste, but her heart was tripping so fast that were she to tarry, it might give her away.

There may have been a cough in the kitchen as she shut the door, or even a soft chuckle, but she did not care. She hurried to the stairway to flee to her room just as Reginald sounded the front door knocker. Heart fluttering, she turned and opened the door.

"Madam." He tipped his hat, his smile warming her through and through. "I hope this morning finds you well."

"Thank you, yes, and do please call me Lillian."

"I should be delighted, but only if you will leave behind the 'sirs' yourself and use my name as well."

"Reginald," she said. It was silly, this fluttering of her nerves that caused her voice to catch.

"Would you join me on a drive this morning?" he asked.

"Yes, yes, please, I have something to . . . Well, yes, that would be lovely. I'll get my wrap."

Reginald drove the light open rig himself, and Lillian sat beside him. The wheels were very high, rising up almost to her shoulder as she sat upon the jouncing seat. Reginald explained it was designed for rough tracks or bad weather, both of which this part of the country experienced in abundance. Lillian listened, yet she could not say whether she heard him or not.

They passed the Oak Hill Cemetery they had visited the previous day and continued along a winding river Reginald identified as Rock Creek. They left Georgetown behind, or so it seemed, for the pastures stretched out broad and green. Trees rose here and there, beacons to summer's close.

Reginald pulled up by an overhang that gave them a view of the fields and the creek and the city of Washington beyond. "I often ride out here of late," he confessed. "It has become a place where I try to make sense of the jumble in my head."

"It is very nice," she observed. Then she slid as far from him as the bench would permit and turned to face him. "I must speak with you of something, Reginald. And I fear I shall be rather long in the telling."

"Wait a moment, then." He slipped from the seat and eased the tension on the two horses' traces. The conveyance rocked gently as he climbed back on board. He wrapped the reins around the hand-brake handle. "All right, Lillian. Speak away."

"I fear you may not—not think very well of me when I finish."

Reginald, dressed in an overcoat of forest green with a matching cravat and a high-collared white shirt, nodded as he crossed his arms and leaned back to wait.

She liked this about him, Lillian decided. He was a man of means, yet he held no sense of impatience. At least he did not demonstrate this with her. For some reason finding yet another quality to admire in Reginald acted like a key. She felt the door to her heart creak open. A door she had not even realized existed.

"I am not going to bandy words, Reginald. I scarcely know you at all. Please forgive me if I sound too forward. But I find myself caring for you—caring what you think of me."

"Lillian—"

"No. Please." She stopped his movement toward her with an upraised hand. "Wait, I beg you. I am not who I appear, you see. Far from it. I have never spoken of these matters to a soul. My late husband knew some of this. In fact, he put together the charade of my present life. I was very fond of him, I suppose. No, I do know that as a certainty. We appreciated and cared for one another well enough. All my life until now I assumed that was as much affection as I was capable of, except for my son, whom I adore. Now . . ."

"Now things are very different indeed," Reginald softly offered.

"Do not look at me so, I beg you."

"And how, please, am I looking at you?"

"As though you are about to hear something good. As though I am pleasing you with my words."

She thought he might respond with some offer of affection, of gratitude over her honesty. Instead, Reginald merely nodded. Up and down, very slowly. Then he looked away. Out over the fields and the river and the still day.

Lillian was again struck by how astonishing this man truly was. All her life she had dismissed the concept of love at first sight as sheerest folly. Yet here she sat with a man she hardly knew at all. And she was thinking of opening her heart and soul to him, to tell him everything. Her darkest and her wildest.

In profile he displayed an even stronger visage than straight on. Lillian found herself asking, "How can you wait so patiently, not even looking my way?"

It seemed that Reginald had been expecting such a query. "Some things must come at their own time. And I find such matters are easier to address when not gazing directly into another's soul."

How could he affect her so with the simplest of words? "I am very afraid you will not care for me at all once you hear my confession."

"You must put that fear aside right now."

"How can you be so certain?"

"I cannot answer you that. I am a simple man, Lillian. My sister will attest to that fact. But I know what I know. And sure as God reigns on high, my love for you will not be shaken by what you say."

His words echoed in her mind. She gathered her trembling hands into her lap and addressed her words to the river, to the fields, to the featureless sky overhead. "All the world thinks I am the daughter of a vicar. That is a lie. I was in fact raised in a vicarage. But I was born to a woman whose name I was never told. I met her once. At least I think I did. I believe she was sister to the woman who raised me. The vicar and his wife told me to call them aunt and uncle. Perhaps I was merely a waif left upon their doorstep—I know nothing with any certainty. But once I was taken by my aunt into a prison. There I met a woman who looked very much like my aunt. This strange woman wept over me. That is as close to my true heritage as I have ever come. My aunt refused to ever speak of that prison visit or that woman again."

A mockingbird took up residence in the neighboring maple. The song was piercing in its clarity. Lillian felt as though her body was turned to crystal by her recounting of these secrets, open even to the force of birdsong.

"It was a joyless home, as dismal a place as ever I hope to see," she continued, now aware of Reginald's head turning and his eyes on her. "My uncle was a cheerless man. He was severe in manner and dry in tone. I cannot ever recall seeing him smile. I do not think he cared for me at all. When I was ten I ran away from home. He brought me back and thrashed me. I was locked in my room for three weeks. When he released me, he said if ever I ran away again, he would not come after me. He would disown me. He would claim to all the world I had died. Which, in his eyes, I would have done. As he spoke the words, I was filled with an absolute certainty that this was in fact what he hoped would happen."

Had she ever imagined such a moment, when the truth she had spent a lifetime hiding was revealed, Lillian would have supposed she would be weeping so hard she should fight for breath. Instead, she felt nothing save a most remarkable calm.

"At fourteen I ran away again. I began singing with a wandering troupe. I had a good enough voice. My youth was enough of an attraction for them to see profit in my company. That and my features, of course. I had to be very careful about that. But the leader was a kindly old soul who treated me as a favorite relation. I stayed with them for almost two years. Then the old man grew ill and he knew his time was near. He knew also what would happen to a lass like me out on the road, with no one to protect her."

The surrounding countryside became painted with visions of times long gone. Lillian knew full well Reginald would soon be seeking a way to set her down and ride away, never again to appear. Still, she knew this was the right action. The *only* action. She had never expected to feel this way about anyone. She had lived a life of one lie piled upon the other. This one day, this one moment, she would honor her feelings with the truth.

"At sixteen I was given work singing in a tavern in the city of Manchester," she said, her tone somber in her ears. "One night the man who ran the city's largest theatre came to hear me. He wanted to make me a star of the stage, he said. I accepted his offer and before I knew it I was singing in his theatre. My third night there, I met my husband. He was visiting a friend and they had come in to hear me, or so he always said. He claimed word of me had spread far and wide. What he wanted was me."

So much effort had gone into hiding the truth. So much energy, and for so very long. She could hear the toneless quality to her voice now, as though it had come to match the overcast day.

"He was a most eccentric sort of British gentleman, the fifth in his line. He had held power and wealth since the moment of his birth. He was accustomed to having the entire world do his bidding. I was no different. He wanted me as his wife. That, as far as he was concerned, was all that mattered.

"He obtained the services of a local solicitor and went to work. The man approached my uncle and offered what to him must have seemed an astonishing sum. He was asked to sign documents making me his rightful daughter. In return for his silence over my true heritage, he would receive an annual stipend for the rest of his life.

"A series of tutors taught me proper etiquette. I went to Paris and met with more tutors who taught me what a proper lady would know about history and style. I was attended by the finest dressmakers in the world. In time, when the myth was complete, we were wed in St. Paul's Cathedral. My new husband found this deception delightfully humorous. He was so accustomed to wealth and power, you see, pulling the wool over the eyes of the entire British society was just the sort of joke he would relish all his life. He never spoke of my past. He did not need to. But I could see it in his eyes, particularly when we were surrounded by the pompous and the vain. How these courtiers fawned over a woman who was in truth nothing but a tavern singer in silk and diamonds. I never went north again, of course. I never sang again. There was too much chance someone might recognize me. It seemed a small enough price to pay. I was now, after all, a lady of the realm."

The sun lanced through the clouds. She squinted against the unaccustomed brilliance and forged on. "We had a son, Byron. He is a wonderful and independent lad. Byron is now at Eton."

Reginald spoke for the first time. He quietly murmured, "A son."

Lillian waited for Reginald to say more. But when he returned his gaze to the horizon, she continued, "My husband died over a year ago. I discovered soon after that he had lost everything in a most preposterous venture in Portugal. I am here because of that. My poverty has driven me here. I am in possession of a banker's draft from Abigail's father. A loan, I wish to call it, though I have nothing to offer as collateral. But a loan nonetheless."

She could go no further. Though there was not a sense of hiding anymore, the truth of Simon Bartholomew would be revealed soon enough. But not now. "I have more I wish to say. But it is a different story entirely, and I suppose . . . Well, forgive me, but I wish to speak with someone else about this first, as it pertains specifically to her."

Reginald responded with a single nod. But his attention had returned to the river, whose waters now sparkled green and blue in the gathering light.

Lillian sat beside him and waited. She felt both drained from the telling and tense over the coming response. She could examine him minutely now. Reginald sat with his arms crossed across his chest. His legs were extended out as far as the vehicle's confines permitted. His chin had lowered to where it almost rested upon his foulard. His eyes stared unblinking at the water.

Finally she could wait no longer. "Oh, please, do tell me what you are thinking."

"Very well." He lifted his face to the sun. "I was wondering who owned this knoll and the surrounding pastures, and how much I must pay to buy these from him."

Her surprise was so great she could say nothing in response.

"It would make a wonderful place for a house, don't you think?"

"A house? I have told you the worst of tales and you are thinking of a house?"

"Indeed so." He turned to her, and the golden flecks in his eyes reflected the light. "For it is at this place I have come to know of love once more."

She had to struggle to shape just the one word. "Love?"

"Yes, indeed. I have no such experience with the world as you do, but I know what I know. And in love, there is only now."

"Then . . . you do care for me?" And she was weeping.

"Here, here, my darling Lillian." Reginald gathered her up in arms as strong as she knew they would be. "Don't cry so, else my own heart will soon be breaking as well."

She tried to stop, and gradually the sobs faded away. But she did not break from his embrace, and he did not release her. Lillian turned her face to the sky. She mouthed the word, tasting it anew, hearing it in her heart for the very first time.

Love.

Chapter 19

The next morning, Lillian awoke determined to make this the day she unfolded her remaining secret.

Of course the old arguments were allied against her. She sat at the dressing table and argued with her reflection. She brushed her hair with such firm strokes the tresses billowed around her head. There was no going back. She said this over and over. Yes, she was greatly afraid that Simon Bartholomew would do as he threatened. For him to reveal her secrets would mean as great a disgrace as calling in her debts. She would be ruined. Her titles would be stripped away. He would foreclose on all her properties. Her son would be left with nothing. Yes, all true. The silent menace was so great she fought down tears.

She would not weep over this. She would not change her course. There was indeed no going back.

She was pushed from her reverie by a knock on her door. "Yes?"

"I hope I'm not disturbing. I thought I heard you moving about."

"Not at all. Please come in."

Abigail wore a dress of sky blue with matching cloth buttons. Her hair was pulled back in a silk ribbon of the same shade. She wore no jewelry. "I have been sent to ask if you were aware that today is Sunday."

"Do you know, I had forgotten it entirely."

"As had I." Abigail waited.

"The family is going to church?"

"We leave in less than an hour."

"Do they wish for me to join them?"

Abigail replied carefully, "You are an honored guest in this house. You are under no constraints."

"You are quoting someone, are you not?"

Abigail gave an impish smile. "My grandmother made me repeat it twice before sending me upstairs."

"Very well. You have fulfilled your mission with great dispatch." Lillian returned her smile. "Now tell me, would they like for me to come?"

"Nothing would give them greater happiness."

At Lillian's nod, Abigail added, "They attend the same church as Erica's family. Reginald, no doubt, will be there."

The two women looked for a long moment into the other's eyes, and they both knew the question and its answer. Lillian replied, "I should be honored to join you."

The moment passed, and Abigail studied Lillian's form. "Do you intend—is that what you will wear to church?"

Lillian glanced down at her dress, a striped affair of palest yellow and blue silk, the latest fashion from Paris. "Is this not appropriate?"

"Ladies tend to dress rather modestly for church," Abigail said, then hastened to add, "but I'm sure you will be fine."

"You must tell me the truth."

"If you wear that to church, those who think black is the only color for Sabbath dress will have something to discuss besides the sermon after the service." Abigail's hand flew to her mouth. "I can't believe I said that."

"Nor I. And shame on you."

The two ladies shared a look, then began to chuckle. Lillian said, "Now you must help me select something appropriate."

"First let me bring you tea and toast. Otherwise you will be famished long before dinner."

Abigail was soon back bearing a tray. "Grandmother is thrilled that you are going."

"I do hope she won't introduce me by my title."

"She won't need to. Everyone knows."

Lillian drew in a sharp breath. "They what?"

"Don't ask me how. But they do." Her hands were busy with the tea as she talked, with milk and one sugar as Lillian preferred. "Grandmother has been stopped on the street. She has received a pile of notes and invitations. This lady wishes to call. That one wants to invite Mrs. Cutter to an afternoon tea dance. And of course her houseguests must come along."

"Is this the normal way things happen here in America?"

"Grandmother says she has received more invitations in the past three days than she has in the past two dozen years." Abigail spread butter liberally over a piece of toast. "Will you take marmalade? Cook cooks it up fresh with figs from our own garden."

"To tell the truth, I am rather hungry."

Abigail settled herself in a straight-back chair. "Do you think I should ever fall in love?"

"A lovely young maiden like yourself, I'm astonished it hasn't already happened."

"Mother has long since despaired of me. She says I can turn away suitors faster than anyone she has ever met. One young man actually told her he would rather face a brace of pistols on a dueling ground at dawn than spend another hour in my company."

Lillian lifted a second piece of toast from the plate. "Umm, this marmalade is delicious. I'm sure the young man did not mean that."

"He did, I fear."

"But whatever for?"

"I informed him that I failed to see how his money permitted him to harbor such a vast collection of miserable failings."

"Oh Abigail, I wish I could have heard it!" They both laughed.

"My mother says I am both impetuous and incorrigible," Abigail said. "Do you suppose she is right?"

"Impetuous, certainly. And I find it one of your most endearing traits."

"Then you will forgive me for asking you again why you were so morose for the second half of our journey. I thought you were deathly ill."

"Ill, yes. But in spirit only." Lillian was tempted to tell her the whole story then and there. But she quailed at the prospect.

"I'm sorry . . . Are you all right?"

"Yes. Yes. Please do not be concerned." Lillian tried hard to reassure the anxious young woman. "It has to do with something I wish to speak with you about this afternoon, you see."

"I suppose if we start now we should be late for church," remarked Abigail slowly.

"Precisely."

"You may find this difficult to believe, but I positively detest having to wait for anything." Again their laughter mingled in the morning sunlight.

Lillian said briskly, "Now you really must show me what might be a proper gown for church."

The day was sunny but blustery, with a slight hint of bite to the wind. Lillian wore a spare cloak from Mrs. Cutter. Abigail had pulled a similar one from the recesses of her trunk. The charcoal gray cloaks made a suitably somber impression. For the journey to church Lillian sat alone on the carriage seat, facing a frail Mr. Cutter with his wife holding his arm on one side and Abigail on his other. With every jostle or turn, Mr. Cutter threatened to slip from his seat. But Abigail and her grandmother's steadying hands kept him upright. He examined the world outside with alert eyes, and twice when their gazes met he gave Lillian an observant smile.

When they arrived at church, Lillian remained in the coach with him while the other two saw to his chair. The old man said to his houseguest, "I fear I have made rough going of my duties as host, my lady."

"Nonsense, sir. I could not have been made more welcome to your wonderful home and family."

He attempted to dab a wet spot at the corner of his mouth, but his shaking hand could not seem to make proper contact. Lillian moved to the seat beside him. "Here, sir. Allow me."

He permitted her to take the handkerchief from his grasp and apply it to his mouth. "It is a sad day when I must rely on a grand lady such as yourself to dry my chin."

"Sir, I must tell you . . ." She had to stop there. For reasons she could not explain, the small gesture of assistance had left her throat closed with emotion. She swallowed. "I have never known a finer family, nor felt more indebted to new friends, than with your household. They do you great credit, sir. They are . . ."

Mr. Cutter studied her anew. "Yes?"

She forced herself to continue. "They somehow humble me at the same time they are showing such great care."

He sighed, a contented sound. "I do so appreciate my Sabbath meetings. So long as I can make the journey to church each week, my life is not in vain."

"No matter what happens to you, sir, no matter how cruel life's hand may turn, I assure you with all my heart your days are far from futile."

"I see my wife was correct in her thinking." Outside the open carriage door, the coach driver had unlashed the wicker chair with its wooden wheels. As the driver lowered it, Mr. Cutter went on, "You will take an old man's advice?"

"With deepest gratitude."

"My wife tells me you do not share our faith."

"I-I regret to say I do not." She wanted to add *yet* but held back for reasons she could not have explained.

"Might I ask why?"

"I . . ." Lillian stopped when Mrs. Cutter reappeared in the carriage doorway.

Her husband said, "May I have a moment longer with the countess?"

"I can hear them beginning with the music," Mrs. Cutter began, but stopped as she looked at her husband.

"We won't be long." He turned back to Lillian. "You were saying?"

"I would be so grateful if you would not let titles stand between us, sir."

A trembling hand waved the air between them. "We were addressing the issue of faith, madam."

"I was raised by a vicar and his wife. It was not a pleasant experience."

"Ah. A forlorn and loveless home, I take it."

"Such that I can scarce call it a home at all, sir."

He studied one of several stains on his greatcoat. "Such experiences are near impossible to overcome."

The absence of platitudes struck her hard. "Yes?"

He lifted his gaze to hers, revealing a trace of the power that had certainly once filled his now frail frame. "Without God, madam. Without God we are but bruised reeds, ever threatened by the prospect of being crushed by life's uncaring millstone. Without God we are nothing, our lives worthless, our days an endless circular tread. Without God we stand condemned, doomed to a life without the precious gift of hope."

There were many people awaiting them by the church doorway. Reginald stood among them, and it seemed to Lillian that all the others faded slightly. Reginald did not speak, but she could feel his gaze on her face. Lillian endured an endless stream of introductions, wishing she were back on that wind-swept hill with him again.

Horace pushed the wheelchair holding his father up the brick path. Alongside Horace now stood his wife, Beatrice, and four strapping young lads, all in dark suits and hand-tied bows. Reginald was joined by his sister Erica and her young daughter, Hannah. Abigail was on her knees, adjusting the child's petticoats and chattering in a soft manner. The child smiled shyly in reply. Lillian knew she should be paying attention, yet her mind seemed capable of just two thoughts: Reginald's presence and the old man's words.

The Bridge Street Church's cornerstone announced that it had been erected in 1782. The edifice was stone and wood, the interior gloriously unadorned. They hung their wraps on wooden pegs in the vestibule. Lillian was wearing the most sedate dress she had brought, a blue velvet with pale chalky stripes running from hem to neckline. They walked up the central aisle as the congregation rose to sing a hymn. Lillian could feel eyes watching the progress of the group to the Cutter family pew, and she heard someone whisper *countess* as she passed. But it could not distract her from the feeling that she was in a hallowed place.

And hallowed it was. Of that she had no doubt. A line of whitewashed iron pillars marched down either side of the church, supporting a broad balcony encircling the rear. The same intensity of spirit she had felt beneath the ship's billowing white canopy was here as well. Perhaps it was even stronger, she reflected as she slipped into the pew. The group accompanying Lillian filled two entire rows. The pews were entered through little waist-high doors, upon which were named the families who occupied them.

The song ended, the pastor spoke words of welcome, and a second hymn began. A well-worn book was slipped into Lillian's hands. She did not need it. She knew the words. Oh yes. She knew them intimately.

She had first known of her musical gift when she was seven

years old. Long before then, she had loved singing. In fact, it was one of her greatest joys in an otherwise colorless childhood. Lillian had sung with all her heart. Perhaps she had done it for as long as she had known the hymns. But when she was seven, she began to experiment with sounds. At the time Lillian had not known such words as chord structure and tonal elements. Nor could she read music. She had merely wondered one Sunday what would happen if she sang a different note below or above the melody. Would this not add something to the music? She had done so very softly at first. Even then, several of the people around them had stopped singing and listened to the child. The young Lillian found great pleasure in this. She had never had anyone look at her in such a way before. The weeks passed, and she became increasingly comfortable with this exploration. She began to move further and further from the hymn's standard course. And those clear, confident tones were noticed by her uncle from the pulpit.

Lillian stood in the pew and recalled that horrid night. How her uncle had thrashed her after church! He had called her a bad seed. She remembered it vividly. He had said there was no hope for her. Her uncle had declared that Lillian carried all the elements of doom, just like the one who was lost to them now, another singer who had let her voice take her off into the dark. Lillian had not understood her uncle at the time. But she had seen the rage in his eyes and his voice and his hand as he commanded her to never sing like that again. And she had obeyed him. Until she ran away.

Lillian realized her eyes had clouded over. And at the worst possible moment. The pastor had done something quite remarkable. He had invited the congregation to offer the sign of peace to one another. And then he himself came down from the pulpit and was now walking toward her!

Lillian wiped the tears that marred the carefully applied powder upon her cheeks. The pastor did not seem to notice. He took her hand in both of his and welcomed her. Welcomed her so warmly, in fact, that the tears fell even harder.

Then she was being turned and other hands were taking her own. So many people wished to greet her. And she could see none of them clearly.

Abigail leaned across the people between them to take both Lillian's hands and say, "Sabbath blessings to you."

Lillian could not reply, so she merely squeezed Abigail's hands.

"Grandfather asks if you might wish to come sit beside him."

She did not know why this offered the solace it did. But Lillian slipped past the people and waited while a place was made for her at the end of the pew. Mr. Cutter remained in his wheelchair, positioned alongside in the aisle. She seated herself, reached over the little swinging door, and allowed the old man's quivering hand to take her own. For some reason that simple gesture permitted her to regain control of her emotions.

The congregation now began another hymn. Holding Mr. Cutter's hand gave her the excuse to remain seated and silent. She opened the hymnal and set it in the old man's lap. She read the words along with him as the congregation sang.

> Christ, Whose glory fills the skies,
> Christ, the true, the only Light.

The words echoed through the vast emptiness within her. Lillian had not recognized it until that very moment. But confessing to Reginald the day before had left her hollow inside. Now the words were filling that inner void.

> Sun of Righteousness, arise,
> Triumph o'er the shades of night;
> Dayspring from on high be near;
> Day-star, in my heart appear.

Only it was no longer just a hymn, nor words merely sung by those standing around her. Lillian remained seated by Mr. Cutter, who hummed a tuneless cadence. Now they were words she spoke inside herself. Words spoken to a God she had never truly known until now.

> Dark and cheerless is the morn
> Unaccompanied by Thee;
> Joyless is the day's return
> Till Thy mercy's beams I see;
> Till they inward light impart,
> Glad my eyes, and warm my heart.

No doubt it was not a proper prayer. But it was all she could think to do. Her own words seemed so feeble, so marred by all the failings of a squandered life. Yes, even after she had been rescued and refined for polite society, her inner being remained damaged and unclean with selfishness and sin. Why not find comfort and assistance in words she had never truly heard until now?

> Visit then this soul of mine,
> Pierce the gloom of sin and grief.

It seemed to her that she was both returning home and entering a realm she had never before experienced. And in the spreading sense of comfort that came with her silent voicing of these words, Lillian heard something truly remarkable. A little girl's voice echoed faintly within her.

> Fill me, Radiancy divine,
> Scatter all my unbelief;
> More and more Thyself display,
> Shining to the perfect day.

Chapter 20

After the service, Abigail remained in the pew. Her mind held to a sort of Sabbath clarity. She was able to examine herself and the past, even the most painful bits, with ease. People were crowding in about her, but she made no motion to rise. They soon left her alone, assuming that she was still praying. And perhaps in a strange way she was.

The night in Soho had marked a turning point in many ways, she reflected. Some of the changes she was only now beginning to glimpse. Before that night, she had viewed the world . . . how should she put it? Abigail tried to shut out the voices around her by tensing her closed eyes. Yes. She understood now. She had looked at everything as though she were the center of the universe. She had justified her actions simply because they were what *she* wanted. As though that were always enough. As though that made things right.

It would be painful to acknowledge that God's hand may have been directing Lillian's illness during the voyage. But from where Abigail sat, that was how it seemed. Looking back, it appeared to Abigail as though she had spent those long days and nights learning to put herself aside.

Her mind drifted back to the recent afternoon in Erica's office. Abigail had sat and listened to her exclaim over the letter from William Wilberforce. Erica had explained how they had been planning just such a journey west. Not only that, but her brother Reginald wanted to establish a Langston's Emporium in Wheeling. This city was the end of the newly opened National Road and the jumping-off point for pioneers headed to the Indiana and Missouri provinces. Abigail had sat and watched as Erica's previous weariness had dropped away, and she had come alive before her very eyes.

Erica's brother was not known for original ideas. Erica related how there were myriads of reasons why Erica might have dismissed his notion. They were doing exceedingly well with the Georgetown emporium and their trading business. They had entered into a partnership with Horace Cutter, now director of the trading company established by Abigail's grandfather. What need was there, Erica had wondered, for them to take on more? And yet, because it was Reginald's idea, the man who previously had been content to follow someone else's vision and direction for the firm, Erica had been reluctant to object. It had felt, Erica said several times as she related the situation to Abigail and Mrs. Cutter, as though God had been urging her to remain silent. And now, finally, she understood.

Abigail had sat there between Erica and her grandmother and felt thrilled over being the herald of such glad tidings from their friend Wilberforce. Abigail had spent an afternoon talking and making plans. And her thoughts had been directed toward the needs and wishes of *others*.

Abigail now noticed that the commotion around her was beginning to dim. She knew it was time to depart. Her grandfather needed to be getting home. But she was reluctant to let go of the moment. God felt so close just then. Abigail clasped her hands in her lap and prayed, *Help me, oh my God, to make this a real change. Take these little seeds and help them grow. Make me into someone thou might truly use. Make me into someone thou can indeed call a good and faithful servant. Amen.*

She rose and walked down the central aisle. As she stood in the vestibule and fastened her mantle about her neck, a single ray of sunshine managed to pierce the day's gray cloak. Motes sparkled and danced in the air about her, and the church's peaked doors appeared framed in heaven's holy light. Abigail took a deep breath and stepped outside.

Momentarily blinded, she realized she was staring at the young man from Erica's office. Tall and straight, he stood rail thin in his poorly fitting clothes, and with an almost bashful air he spoke with Reginald Langston. Yet the two men seemed to fit together somehow. Reginald said something and the young man laughed out loud, for a moment seeming to drop his hesitant air.

A group of young ladies stood to one side, waiting for his conversation with Reginald to end. Abigail noted their flushed excitement and the way they whispered among themselves, their eyes never leaving the young man. She found that very odd. She looked at him again and decided he could be handsome, with his dark wavy hair, if someone could take him in hand and attire him properly.

"Ah, there you are." Horace approached the bottom of the church stairs. "Are you ready to depart?"

Her uncle led her to where Lillian and her grandmother stood by the wheelchair. "There have been so many people wishing to speak with you I have forgotten all their names."

Her grandmother asked, "Did you enjoy returning to our old church, my dear?"

"Yes, thank you. So very much." Abigail fell into step with her family. Behind her came a peal of girlish laughter. For reasons she could not explain, Abigail found the noise grating. Which was silly, of course. She had never paid attention to girlish flirtations before.

She matched her pace to that of Horace as he pushed her grandfather's chair. Lillian remained both silent and withdrawn, walking alongside the wheelchair. Further feminine laughter behind them drew her grandmother around. "The young gentleman from Erica's office seems to have a way with the young ladies. What was the young man's name, Horace?"

"Abraham Childes. But we call him Abe. It was so kind of you to invite him to lunch today, Mother." Horace eased the chair over a rough spot in the walk. "A finer young man it has never been my privilege to meet."

"And so very handsome," her grandmother said. "Don't you agree, my dear?" she added, turning to Abigail.

"I really wouldn't know." Abigail could not keep herself from glancing back. Abe, surrounded by the young ladies, smiled at something one of the girls said. Abigail shrugged and turned around, wondering why she had never found any man so interesting as to hang upon his every word.

She asked her grandmother, "Do you think God has a sense of humor?"

"What a remarkable question, granddaughter. I should certainly hope so. Sometimes I find myself in situations where I am forced to choose between laughing and raging at the heavens above. It is only because I hope God is laughing with me that I am able to bear it at all."

Abigail slipped her hand around her grandmother's elbow. "You are such a wise lady."

"Thank you for thinking so. I should hope I would have learned something after all these years!" Her warm laugh drew a similar chuckle from Abigail.

The table was crowded with Horace and his wife along with Erica Powers, Lillian, Reginald, her grandmother, and across from Abigail sat Abraham Childes. Mr. Cutter had retired to his chambers, fatigued from the morning outing. Horace's four boys and Erica's daughter took places at the kitchen table, where Cook could keep an eye on them while they enjoyed a meal liberated from adult formality. Every time the kitchen door swung open, their soft chatter and laughter emanated with the fragrance of each dish.

Now that she was seated across from the young man, Abigail could not say precisely why she had been rather dismissive of him. He was remarkably self-contained and seemed most comfortable watching others and having no attention paid to him at all. He said nothing unless he was directly addressed. Then he replied in a soft, agreeable voice, using the sparsest words possible.

As Reginald sliced the glistening brown turkey, he said, "I was hoping to hear you sing today."

For an instant Abigail thought Reginald might have been speaking to her. Then she realized it was Lillian, and she turned to look at her companion. Lillian's face was flushed, and she spoke softly to the plate in front of her, "Oh, no. Certainly not."

"Do you sing, my dear?" Mrs. Cutter asked.

"Not for years. Not since . . . not since before my son was born."

"But why not, may I ask?"

Lillian still had not lifted her gaze. "I couldn't possibly."

Reginald sounded contrite. "I am so sorry. I shouldn't have spoken."

Mrs. Cutter looked from one to the other in bewilderment. "What is secret about being able to sing?"

Abigail realized the attentive silence was painful to Lillian. She turned to the young man opposite her and spoke the first words that came to mind. "Where do you hail from, Mr. Childes?"

He looked at her for a moment with eyes of palest blue-gray. He replied in his soft voice, "That is a difficult question to answer, Miss Aldridge."

"Why is that?"

"I was orphaned when I was five. My family were farmers along the Shenandoah. My parents and my two sisters all fell ill with scarlet fever. None survived."

"Oh, I cannot tell you how sorry I am. It must have been so very painful."

"I fear I do not remember them very well. It frightens me

at times, forgetting my mother's face. But I know of nothing I can do about it."

"I do." Abigail knew she was speaking without proper thought. But only two things mattered just then. First, the table was now observing their exchange and not Lillian. And second, she thought she had an idea to address the pain in those eyes. "Every time you feel the connection to your parents fading, you must inspect your own face very closely in a mirror. When you do, realize that your mother and your father must be so very proud of you."

Abraham's jaw clenched hard for a moment, but his gaze did not waver. "How—how can you say that, ma'am?"

"The fact that you are seated with us here today, sir, bears witness to how you are a credit to your beginnings. I know my family well enough to know that is why they invited you."

"Hear, hear," Horace agreed.

Lillian lifted her gaze and gave Abigail a look of purest gratitude. Abigail heard Reginald's sigh of relief from his place beside her. Which gave her the courage to continue, "Where did you live after that?"

"I lodged with an uncle who had three boys and farmed a piece not far from Georgetown. He had lost his wife to the same fever. When I was twelve he married a woman who had two children of her own. She felt I was old enough to fend for myself."

A plate piled high with sliced turkey was placed in front of Abigail. Someone spooned vegetables onto her plate, but she paid them no attention. "Where did you go?"

"I lodged for a time in a shed behind the church. The pastor's wife saw to it I had enough to eat. I did odd jobs around the place."

"What a sorrowful beginning," Abigail said softly.

He gave a shrug. "Lonely, perhaps. But I had ample time to read."

"You enjoy books, do you?"

"For the longest time, ma'am, they were my only friends."

"He's never to be found without a book on him," Reginald added. "Devours them, Abe does."

"Are you reading something now, may I ask?"

"In my coat pocket in the hall, ma'am, I have two books."

"And they are . . . ?"

"Homer's *Odyssey*. And a Greek grammar."

"Do you mean—well, are you teaching yourself Greek?"

"I have so loved the hero's tale, ma'am. I would like to read it in the writer's own words."

"Four years back, this young lad appeared at the warehouse door asking for any work I might have," Reginald told the table at large.

"The pastor and his wife had moved on," Abe explained as the looks turned his way again. "The new pastor didn't think it was fitting for me to stay in their woodshed."

"Not fitting?" Abigail asked, appalled.

Reginald continued, "This lad did whatever task I set to him. Nothing was beyond his ability. If he did not understand something, he asked for an explanation."

"I did a bit of asking, didn't I?" Abraham Childes commented, then joined in the chuckles around the table.

"He works at twice the pace of anyone I have ever met, including myself," Reginald continued. "And every spare moment, he reads. Whenever we receive a barrel of books, he dives inside. He borrows them one by one—usually overnight is enough. His knowledge and understanding surpass many I've known with university diplomas."

Abigail's grandmother rapped the tablecloth with her spoon. "This is all well and good. But the meal Cook has prepared for us is growing cold. Horace, will you please be so kind as to bless this food?"

They gave their full attention to the meal. When the forks were put down for the final time, Reginald picked up the conversation where they had left off. "I have asked Abe to become the manager of our new Wheeling emporium. We need a man we can trust, someone we are confident will have the good sense to adapt to all the things we cannot anticipate in advance. We are offering to take him on as partner in this new venture."

All eyes turned to where Abraham fiddled with his fork, but the young man did not speak.

"Do you want this to happen?" her grandmother asked.

Abraham addressed his response to the tablecloth. "More than I can say, ma'am."

"Then why," Reginald asked, "have I been waiting all these months for your answer?"

"I don't see how I can accept, sir."

When no one else spoke up, Abigail asked, "Why not, please tell us."

Abraham raised his eyes to hers. "Life's not been so good to me, Miss Aldridge. I've never known a family like this one nor hours like the ones I've spent in their company, the work I've been entrusted with."

"Yes?"

He seemed to struggle to form the words. "I couldn't bear it if I let them down."

Abigail could barely hear his statement. She wanted to assure him, but the conversation had taken another turn, and she held her thoughts inside during the dessert and coffee. She would watch for an opportunity to discuss the offer being made to him.

Mrs. Cutter pushed back from the table. "I fear I have eaten more than is healthy and really must have a breath of air. Horace, do you think I might have the strength of your arm for a turn about the neighborhood?"

"Of course, Mother."

"If anyone else wishes to join us, you are most welcome," she said as the two moved toward the door.

Abigail rose along with several others, and she found herself beside Abe as they stepped out onto the front porch.

"I shan't be a moment, Abigail," her grandmother said. "You young people wait for us in the front garden while I get my cloak. You had better wear one yourself, young lady."

Abigail went back inside for her own cloak, and as she fastened it at her neck, the sound of voices drew her back a few paces. She tiptoed over to the narrow hall table and pretended to inspect the clasp in the oval mirror above.

"I have known the lad for just over four years now," Reginald was saying, "and I have never heard him speak of his past before."

"You knew something of his beginnings, surely."

"Aye, a few sparse words, granted only after I wrestled them out of him. But to lay it out calm as you please like that? Never."

There was a moment's silence, then Horace asked, "Is it true what he says? He's teaching himself Greek so he can read Homer in the original?"

"I've never known the lad to lie. About anything."

"You've got yourself a prize there, Reggie. He thinks the world of you, sure enough."

"If only I could manage to build a little gumption in the lad. He fears his own shadow at times."

"No wonder, given his difficult start in life."

"I tell you the truth, if the lad had a bit more spark, he could become anything he wanted. Why, I wouldn't be surprised to find him governor or senator or even president of these United States one day. If only he—"

Abigail hurried for the door as the voices grew louder. Abe stood on the top step waiting. He smiled as he turned toward her, causing a little catch inside. His story had profoundly moved her.

Chapter 21

At Mrs. Cutter's suggestion, the little group turned away from the river. The waterfront taverns, according to Abigail's grandmother, did a booming business on the Sabbath. Instead, the four headed inland and wandered through streets Abigail did not recognize. The day remained overcast, with a rising wind that tasted of coming rain.

Her grandmother and uncle set the pace, with Abigail and Abe gradually falling behind. Even when the lane in front of them provided enough privacy, Abigail was uncertain how to begin the conversation.

Abe finally ventured, "May I ask, Miss Abigail, what you are thinking?"

"I was wondering whether you would continue talking with me as you did inside."

He appeared pleased by her comment. "Do you know, I was thinking the same thing. I never have been one for sharing confidences, you see."

"I'm not the least surprised, given your upbringing. Only books for friends, never a family to shelter you through the hard times. I should think you'd scarcely have learned to communicate at all," she finished in a rush, then quickly covered her mouth. "Oh, I am sorry—"

"Not at all," he assured her.

"But it was a truly dreadful thing to say," she argued, cheeks hot with embarrassment. Exasperation with herself rose like a wave. "Oh, why must I always speak before thinking? If I could find out precisely where my impetuous nature resides, I would physically cut it out!"

"Oh, no," Abe said, shaking his head.

"But it's always getting me into the most terrible messes."

"I never can seem to do anything without fear and trembling." He tried to smile at his own little joke, but the uncertainty in his eyes came through clearly. "I am awfully fearful, you see."

"But look at everything you have overcome to arrive at where you are now," she protested.

"Ah, but you don't know all the mistakes I've made along the way."

"Mistakes? You think *you* have made mistakes? I don't think you want to hear about all the mistakes my impetuousness has dragged me into."

"Oh, but I do," he said, then they both laughed at the irony.

But Abe turned serious again, and his interest was so genuine, his face so open, Abigail told him everything. How she had lied to them all, most especially to herself. Over and over and over. Then of the night in Soho. And the arrest. And the prison.

She was so busy with the telling, gesturing with her hands and her voice rising and falling with the emotions of the moment, that she did not immediately recognize the wetness on her face as rain. But when she realized his face was wet as well, and his hair, and his coat, she exclaimed, "Look at me! Here I am babbling away while we become drenched."

Abe shrugged. "Rain never hurt me before."

Abigail spotted her grandmother and uncle sheltering beneath a shop's awning. They were observing the two young people with affectionate smiles and waved but said nothing. "It was so very impulsive of me to tell you all that." She shook her head, creating a shower of raindrops from her hair. Abigail had no interest just then in joining her relatives. Instead, she waved back and started toward a nearby elm whose branches were so thick the lane underneath remained dry. "Oh, this reckless nature will be the death of me!"

"Please don't say such a thing!"

She stopped at the entreaty in his voice. "But—"

"You probably have no idea of the gift you have. Can you imagine never taking a single step without fearing it is the wrong one? Can you conceive of people only wanting the best for you, fully knowing this, and still seeing only the prospects of failure?"

Her heart constricted at the strain in his voice and on his face. She reached for his arm and began pulling him toward the sheltering elm. "Come, Abe. Let's at least have the sense to take cover from the rain."

Once they had wiped the moisture from their faces, she looked up at him. She could see raindrops caught by his dark lashes and the ache in his gaze—all the lonely hours, all the emptiness he had struggled against for so long. "Abe, I promise you, to fail is not your lot in life."

"How can you be sure of that, Miss Abigail?"

"Because," she declared with soft and utter certainty, "you will not let it happen." *And neither will I,* she promised herself silently.

The rain halted as suddenly as it had begun, and a soft call was heard from their chaperones. "Let us return home before the deluge truly arrives."

The horses clip-clopped down the length of Pennsylvania Avenue. Their hooves striking the brick pavement made a contented Sunday afternoon sound. Lillian sat upon the landau's high fore seat next to Reginald. She had seldom had the opportunity to view the world from this perspective. But

Americans did not seem to go in for drivers, particularly for the smaller open carriages such as Reginald's landau. He clearly enjoyed handling the matched bays himself, and he was quite skilled with the reins. Although the day remained gray and the wind brisk, Lillian was comfortable in her cloak with the travel rug over her lap. Tall oaks and hickory and birch lined the road. It was a fine day for a ride, especially with Reginald at her side.

If only she could truly enjoy herself.

Reginald was making the ride an introduction to the nation's capital. He drove by the president's residence, which had been painted white when rebuilt after the British invasion of 1814, and ever since had been known as the White House. He explained how the city had been designed by Pierre L'Enfant and laid out by the surveyor Andrew Ellicott, and how it was constantly growing. He took obvious satisfaction in the city's six miles of brick paving. Past the expanded building known as Congress House, they drove up to where Pennsylvania Avenue joined Thirteenth Street at the Rotunda. There he halted to enjoy the panoramic view of the surrounding forests.

Lillian scarcely saw any of it at all.

"I fear I am boring you with my enthusiasm for my nation's capital. Britishers have every right to consider us infants —"

"It's not that at all."

"I believe I just saw you shiver." He took a firmer grip of the reins. "We'll have you back to the warmth of the house and fireplace in no time."

"Please, no—"

"But I saw—"

"It is not the weather. Or your fine city. It is my own . . ." But she could not complete the thought.

"You are ill?"

"In spirit only." Her hands were clenched so tightly she scarcely could feel them. "Will I never know a moment's peace?"

"Please, Lillian," he said, his voice catching on her name, "I do wish you would tell me what is the matter."

"And I would so . . ." She bit her lip. "I owe Abigail and her family a great debt. I feel it is only right to speak with her first."

"Are you sure it matters all that much, the order of the conversation?" He bent to look at her.

"I am certain of nothing these days." She gazed into the eyes of this kind, strong man. "I prayed today."

The delight shone in his face. "In church?"

"It was not much, as prayers go. But I tried."

"Lillian, my dear, you don't know how much joy this brings me."

She shook her head in wonder. "I am astonished at how I feel I can speak with you about the most intimate of matters, and do so with such ease. I have spent my entire life harboring secrets as though they were my only companions."

"But a lady of your wealth and standing must have had any number of friends."

"It is remarkable how lonely one can be in the company of others," she replied softly.

"I do wish you would tell me what makes you so downcast."

"Perhaps I should. Perhaps . . ."

The first drops of rain began, carried by the wind. It did not rain heavily nor for very long. It seemed as though Reginald had just raised the landau's top before the rain halted. When he returned to his seat and Lillian remained silent, he picked up the reins and clicked the horses back into a trot.

Lillian sat upon the high seat, trying to take an interest in Reginald's world. She knew he was attempting, hoping, to captivate her with this burgeoning city, to make her feel as happy here as he clearly was. In truth, it was an extraordinary place, with an energy that even a quiet Sunday afternoon could not disguise.

But she could not reside here. Lillian knew that all too well. Her only hope was to lose herself in this new country's vast hinterlands. Find some distant town or outpost where British scandals—or bankers—could not reach. Or if they ever did, it would not matter. For Lillian was under no illusions. Once Simon Bartholomew realized she was no longer of use to him, he would do his utmost to destroy her. No, she could not stay here in this new nation's capital, much as her heart yearned to call this wonderful family's peace and strength her own.

Revelers chose that moment to burst out of a boarding-house set back from the road. Reginald flicked the reins and urged the horses to greater speed. "Pay them no mind."

"Who are they, may I ask?"

"Freelanders would be my guess. Some months back, rumors started that if General Jackson wins the election he will give land away."

"Why, that seems absurd."

"You'd think so, wouldn't you? But rabble-rousers from all about the union have been gathering here, intent on pressing Congress to make good on the claim." Once safely past the noisy throng, he slowed the horses back to a canter. "The Land Office is our nation's greatest source of income. It pays for the military, the government, even the National Road."

She started to ask what that was, then decided that in truth she really was not very interested. Reginald obviously caught her introspective mood, for he said nothing else until they arrived in front of the Cutter home. He fastened the reins to the brake lever, leaped down, and helped Lillian alight. "Perhaps you would prefer to go in and rest?"

"I have explained to you, Reginald, that I am not the least bit weary."

"But—"

Lillian motioned to where Mrs. Cutter had already opened the front door and stood waiting for them to enter. "Do please come with me. Otherwise the lady of the house will think we have quarreled."

Midway up the walk, however, Lillian knew something was wrong. The solemn cast to Mrs. Cutter's features caused her insides to clench with foreboding. "What—what is the matter?"

Mrs. Cutter waited until they had climbed the front steps to reply, "You have a visitor."

No walk seemed longer than the one Lillian took from the front stairs of Mrs. Cutter's house across the foyer and down the hall. She was halted by the sight of several people seated in the parlor, silent and staring forward. She could not see who was the focus of their attention.

She looked at Reginald, feeling helpless to enter the room. But he was wise enough to understand and offered, "Shall I go in for you and see what it's about?"

The words granted her the clarity she needed. She whispered, "Would you please stay nearby?"

"Of course," he replied, offering his arm.

She could feel his strength through her fingertips. They stepped into the parlor.

The tableau would remain etched upon her mind. Erica Powers sat closest to the visitor, occupying a straight-backed chair by the window table. Abigail, looking a bit rain-spattered, sat on the parson's bench closest to the fire, alongside an equally damp Abraham Childes. Old Mr. Cutter sat opposite them, the parlor's most comfortable chair turned so he could be near the fire and still observe the room. Horace Cutter and his wife, Beatrice, occupied the sofa next to the spot Mrs. Cutter must have vacated to watch out the front door.

A solitary chair, isolated on the window-table's other side, was occupied by a stranger. One glance was enough for Lillian to be certain they had never met before. Even so, she knew him and why he had come. Oh yes, she knew.

This gentleman was stouter and far taller than Simon Bartholomew. He cut a commanding figure from the gray light pouring through the window behind him. No color to his dress, no break from the stern black save the starched collar rising to envelop his substantial jowls. But there was no doubt in her mind who Lillian faced.

Reginald must have sensed her tension and her fear. He demanded, his tone civil but direct, "Perhaps you would care to state your name and the purpose of your visit, sir?"

"I believe Lady Houghton is well aware of this matter," the man replied, "and understands why it should remain confidential." He had a deeper voice than Bartholomew but the same pompous overbearing tone.

"Your name, please," Reginald pressed.

Erica Powers was the one who answered. "His name is Andrew Smathers."

Reginald tensed. "The banker?"

"The very same." Erica's cold voice continued. "Financier to the nation's slavers. Backer of the most despicable trade—"

"My business is with the countess!"

"—the world has ever known," Erica said, not to be deterred. "Trader in misery and death. Profiteer of chains and anguish."

Lillian quickly realized the man was nervous. And why not? He was in the presence of the very opponents he and Bartholomew were hoping to crush. The people they had intended to use her to destroy.

The indecision she had been carrying slipped away. *No.* She would not be used by them anymore. It was time. They were gathered, and they would hear.

Even so, she trembled with fear, no longer only from concern over her son's fate. She was desperately afraid of what these new friends would think of her.

Lillian sighed deeply. What would be, would be. This day, this hour, she would do the right thing.

For once.

Her hand trembled on Reginald's arm. "Do you need to seat yourself?" he whispered.

"No, well, that is, perhaps . . ."

Reginald guided her to the place alongside Horace. Mrs. Cutter had remained standing by the parlor entrance. Reginald took his station beside her.

"I have stated as clearly as I know how," the banker intoned. "My business with the countess is strictly a private matter."

"No, it is not," Lillian asserted. "There will be no secrets in this house. No longer."

"Lady Houghton, I assure you I come well armed."

"And precisely what do you mean by those words?" Reginald asked, moving forward a step.

The banker sought to mask his rising nervousness with bluster. "It would most certainly be in Lady Houghton's best interests, sir, if you were to refrain from involving yourself in matters that are none of your concern!"

"But they are his concern," Lillian said. "They are most certainly his concern."

Reginald's hand came to rest upon her shoulder. Once more his touch gave her the strength to go on. "Allow me to hazard a guess, Mr. Smathers. The same vessel which carried us to America also contained a mail packet. From a certain banker in London."

"My lady, I must warn you—"

"A banker," Lillian cut in, "by the name of Simon Bartholomew."

To her astonishment, Erica Powers cried aloud. "It can't be!"

"Bartholomew," Lillian continued, "is your ally in the financing of the slave trade, I would imagine."

Smathers glowered at them all, but his words remained directed with swordlike precision at Lillian. "You trifle with danger, my lady."

Well she knew it. But neither her fear nor her tremors would halt her words. She declared to all the family, "I have come here on false pretenses. The whole wretched story will come out. I intend to hold nothing back from any of you ever again. But I do not care to reveal all my distasteful secrets in this man's presence. My guess is, Simon Bartholomew has only told him the barest of details, keeping the greatest ammunition safely under his sole control."

Erica had risen to her feet. "How do you know Simon Bartholomew?"

"His bank holds all the papers to my late husband's estate. The count was ruined by a failed venture. We lost everything."

"This is a misguided confession." The banker leaped to his feet. "As you well know."

"I know only that these secrets are over. The subterfuge is ended. Your bank's hold over me is finished. Did you hear me? *Finished!*"

She found she was breathless. Reginald squeezed her shoulder. She reached up and took a grip of his hand with her own. It might be the last time she held it, this good, strong hand.

She took a long breath. "Simon Bartholomew approached me last summer. He had come into possession of all my late husband's outstanding debts, his land, his manor, the London house, everything. But more than that, he had uncovered a dread secret. One Reginald is aware of, and one I shall share with you when this man has—has taken his leave."

"Which will happen immediately," Reginald said, his meaning clear.

"No, let him stay a moment longer. He needs to hear enough to know his power over me is ended." Her voice was wracked now by the same tremors that coursed through her frame. "My entire life is a lie. My titles, my son's good name, his right to hold his head up in British society—all will come crashing down if Simon Bartholomew reveals what he knows about my past. And this he has sworn to do."

Erica took a step toward the banker. "Will his evil maneuverings never end?"

Something in her features caused the man to back up a step, knocking against the chair.

Lillian continued because she had to. Though *why* was now lost to her, and the words burned her throat like acid. But speak she must. "Bartholomew threatened to ruin me entirely.

He would cast me out into the street. He would reveal my dark secrets. I would be penniless and without friends or allies, and my son would be scorned and destitute." She took the hardest breath of her entire life. "Unless I agreed to spy upon the family of Samuel and Lavinia Aldridge."

Now Abigail was on her feet, her hand to her lips.

"Added to this were the names of two strangers, at least strangers then. Erica and Gareth Powers. Bartholomew wanted information that would subvert their antislavery campaign or do them personal harm."

"It can't be!" Reginald's voice was like a knife through the tension in the room.

"The threat was delivered the very same night Abigail's mother and I met at a dinner given by the earl of Lansdowne."

"No!" Abigail gave a stricken cry.

"The same night you were arrested in Soho." Lillian could not seem to bring the young woman into focus. "I am so very, very sorry. I did not know what to do or how to avoid his cruel task. But that same night, when your mother sat in the coach outside the gates of Newgate Prison . . ."

She stopped and found a handkerchief had been slipped into her free hand. She wiped her face as best she could and drew as much breath as her aching chest would allow.

"Lavinia Aldridge is the finest woman it has ever been my honor to meet. And you stand close behind her, Abigail. But what was I to do? How was I to free myself from this foul task? How was I to protect myself and my son?"

Again she halted. The room was utterly still. Even the banker did not move.

Finally she managed to continue, but only by keeping her gaze downcast. "And so I traveled to America under false pretenses. I accepted a banker's draft from your father, a man I had agreed to help destroy. A man as stalwart and fair as any who has ever walked this earth."

The pain in her chest was now so great she could no longer hold herself erect. Lillian clenched her arms across her stomach and bowed herself over her knees. "I am so utterly, wretchedly sorry," she gasped, tears dripping down her face.

Other arms were there now, wrapping about her back, touching her face and her hair. Lillian heard a voice she recognized as Abigail's. And another. Could it be Erica Powers? But had she not just confessed to seeking their downfall? Oh, nothing in this world made sense. Not even her confession.

Reginald's voice came from somewhere above her. "You will remove yourself from this room and this family. And do so this very instant!"

"Yes," Lillian whispered. Of course. What else was there for her to do but flee? "I will go and gather my things."

"Shah, my sister, you will do no such thing." This from Erica Powers.

"But . . ." Lillian raised her face. Could those be tears she saw upon the woman's face?

"He was not speaking to you," Abigail said quickly.

Lillian lifted herself further, supported now by a woman on either side. She wiped her eyes in time to see a furious Reginald escorting the banker from the room. And to hear him declare, "If ever I learn that you have had a hand in damaging this lady in any way, Mr. Smathers, you will rue the day you ever heard of her, do you hear me, sir? You will rue the day!"

Chapter 22

Lillian woke and felt the house stirring about her. She had no idea what time it was, but most certainly she had slept later than usual. Her limbs felt languid. Though she had slept deeply, still she felt weary. The strain of a lifetime would not be healed by one good night.

She had taken a cold supper with the others, remnants of the Sunday dinner. They had gathered comfortably together in the kitchen, so many of them the men had stood by the counter. Horace's youngsters had noticed nothing untoward. Indeed, the atmosphere had been that of just a normal extended family at the end of a long day. A slap-up meal, Horace had called it, and meant it as a compliment. Other than the children, none of them had been particularly hungry. No further mention had been made of Lillian's confession, but the adults all bore a thoughtful air as they concluded their meal and said their farewells. Lillian had excused herself as early as was polite and retreated to her bedroom.

In the distance Lillian heard a church bell begin to chime. She counted, and with alarm, Lillian realized it was ringing eleven o'clock. She leaped from bed and hastily began to dress. She had not slept this late in years.

She was taken aback to find almost the same gathering awaiting her downstairs. Horace was there, this time without Beatrice and their children. Erica Powers was deep in conversation with Mrs. Cutter and Abraham Childes, Abigail hovering nearby. Even old Mr. Cutter was in his high-backed padded chair, pulled up close to the range fire. Everyone wore a somewhat preoccupied air. Lillian cast quick glances at Erica and Abigail as she sat down at the kitchen table, but she was not able to catch the eye of either. Abigail murmured something about getting her some tea and moved to the stove. Mrs. Cutter offered toast, but Lillian declined.

"Are you sure I can't offer you anything? Maybe a bowl of porridge? That's not difficult at all—"

"You are very kind, Mrs. Cutter. But I really can't disturb your routine any more than I already have." She found herself addressing the entire room, as all had turned her way. She felt she had to make some explanation for her lateness. "I can't remember the last time I have slept so long into the day."

"You have been under a great strain," Mrs. Cutter soothed.

She nodded and sipped her tea. Reginald cleared his throat. "Lillian, might I have a word?"

"Yes, of course." She sighed. Perhaps it was best coming from Reginald.

"Would you care to take a turn with me? The day is brisk for September, but not unkind."

"Yes, thank you. I will get my wrap."

As she rose from her place, old Mr. Cutter said in his trembling voice, "My dear."

"Sir?"

"My wife speaks for the both of us." He was not in particularly good form this day, for shaping the words seemed almost too much for him. "It is important that you understand this."

"I do indeed, sir." With all the grace she could muster, Lillian offered the old gentleman a full curtsy, the same she had learned before her first presentation at Buckingham Palace. The gentleman deserved nothing less. "And I in turn can offer you only my sincerest gratitude. And my heartfelt apologies as well."

"There is nothing for which you need apologize." His

voice quivered, but his gaze was direct and clear.

Lillian decided not to respond. She would depart from this place as much of a lady as she could muster. "Good day, sir."

Mrs. Cutter followed them into the front hall. The older woman seemed unable to decide what to do with her hands. They flitted about, touching everything, remaining nowhere for very long. The normally unflappable woman seemed distraught, agitated.

As Reginald settled the cloak about her shoulders, Lillian said to her hostess, "Please don't concern yourself further, ma'am."

"Nothing about this entire affair is all right."

"No," Lillian conceded. "I quite agree."

But Mrs. Cutter did not seem to hear her. "I want you to know one thing. You are not being pressured into making any decision."

Reginald protested, "Mrs. Cutter—"

"You will permit me to say what my husband and I have decided," she insisted. Mrs. Cutter continued to Lillian, "They say there is suddenly a great need for haste. That is all well and good in the world of business. But you are my guest and I shall not have you feeling pressured to do anything except what you feel is correct."

Lillian felt as though she had missed an important part of the conversation. "Ma'am?"

"It is vital that you understand this one thing." Mrs. Cutter shot Reginald a rather stern glance. "You are welcome to remain here for as long as you like."

"No one is intent upon pressuring Lillian," Reginald quietly insisted.

Mrs. Cutter paid him no mind. "As far as I am concerned, you are welcome to consider that upstairs room your new home." Finally her hands managed to fasten themselves together before her waist. "There. I've had my say. Now you two may go about your business."

Reginald sighed as he opened the front door. Lillian forced

her legs to carry her outside and down the front steps. Once upon the brick pathway, however, she found she could go no further.

Reginald showed no interest in walking on either. He led her over to a garden bench. When they were seated, he turned to her. "I fear what I must address cannot wait."

"Please speak, then." Lillian dropped her head to stare at her folded hands.

"There are two principal roads heading west from this central portion of our nation," he began. "One was fashioned by Daniel Boone himself and is known as the Wilderness Trail," he continued. "Though the region it traverses is no longer wilderness, it remains little more than a trail. In many places it is a marshy, narrow, convoluted track that is good only for men on foot and pack animals. But it has remained the principal route for settlers headed through the Cumberland Gap to the bottomlands of Kentucky. Only these lands are now almost all taken, at least those worth farming. And still the immigrants keep arriving on our shores. Now, as you may have heard, other lands are opening. Missouri might be a state, but only half of the land within its borders has been claimed, much less farmed."

Lillian knew he was talking of something vital. But precisely what he was addressing, she could not be sure. Over and over her mind returned to the same astonishing fact. These people did not seek to discard her. She was not to be punished for her ways. They *accepted* her. Lillian raised her face to Reginald's. His hair was tossed by the rising wind, and she now realized he must have spent considerable time preparing what he wanted to say to her. How was this possible? Was it not just the previous day that she had confessed her terrible truths? And of course poor Lavinia and Samuel did not know her evil deception yet.

"The name on everyone's lips these days is the state of Indiana," Reginald continued. "It has recently been opened to cultivation, and the stories that come back from new settlers are of a land that is bursting with promise. Dreadful winters, by all account, but the hardy Scots and Swedes and Germans who are settling there have no doubt survived worse. What is remarkable is that these lands, Missouri and Indiana and Illinois between them, are being made accessible through something called the National Road. Even now they are surveying as far west as St. Louis, and already they are laying the rock well beyond Wheeling. Broad as the largest Conestoga wagon and well structured for easy travel, it is financed by these very same land purchases. What's more, there's never a grade more than five percent. I don't suppose that means anything to you. But for a drover carting a full load of produce, a level road means the world, I assure you. It means the very world itself."

She nodded, but mostly to keep him talking. She turned slightly so as to be able to see the house. It was a fine place of dressed brick with tall white windows framed with green shutters. A chimney rose at each end of the slate roof, standing with the grace of Corinthian columns, or so it seemed to her. The six trees in the front lawn stood like sentinels against the world's troubles. She glanced at the front door, now shut. Mrs. Cutter's words still rang clear and strong, causing her heart to shimmer with surprised delight. She was invited to call this place *home*.

"This National Road is now open all the way from here to Wheeling," she heard Reginald say. "This town on the Virginia-Ohio border has become a jumping-off place for settlers headed west and north. It is a remarkable place, by all accounts, with many an opportunity to be had. But this you already know."

Do I? she wanted to say. But Reginald was talking so spiritedly he did not seem to need further encouragement. So she did her best to listen, while still examining the lovely day about her. Had she even really noticed this place before? Had she seen this village? She could not for the life of her recall.

"What has us all in such a dither is the timing, don't you see. Here we've spent the entire summer talking about sending Abraham out to establish an emporium. We've dawdled for almost four months now. Horace and I needed to frame the new partnership. Then we've had the hardest time convincing Abe he could manage well enough. To tell the truth, we had almost given up hope of having the man agree to take it on. Then you arrived on our doorstep."

Lillian returned her full attention to Reginald.

At her unspoken question, he said, "Well, you and Abigail. And you brought word from that Wilberforce fellow, asking Gareth and Erica to determine the truth to the land tales. Then there is your desire to seek out land for a new estate for yourself. And now Abigail turns Abe's head straight around. Why, it's divine Providence is what it is. A whole string of events directed by the Almighty, I'm convinced. Never have I seen such a change in a young person."

Reginald stood up and started pacing in front of her. "It's the snows, you see. That's the hurry."

"Snows?"

"Not here. On the road. There's perilous risk of being stranded. We'd need to remain out there for a time, of course, to make sure things are settled right in the beginning. But I can't remain for the entire winter. Not with the business to run here. And William Wilberforce has placed such urgency to his request that Erica has written her husband and asked if perhaps she should go in his stead. Not only that, but Abigail says she's ready to go immediately, if you are."

"Abigail?"

"No, you didn't hear of that, I expect. The young ones, they sat in the front parlor and talked well into the night, by Mrs. Cutter's account. Abigail won't say where it's headed beyond tomorrow. Abe, well, the young man's so overwhelmed it's all he can do to focus on his next step."

She felt she could do no more than repeat the last person's name she had heard. "Abe?"

"Him and the rest of us, if truth be known. We have to hurry now, don't you see." He stopped and fastened an inscrutable gaze upon her. "That is, if you'll be agreeing to accompany us."

"Accompany?"

"Well, that is . . ." He leaned toward Lillian and asked, "Why are you crying?"

"Am I?" She touched her face and was astonished to find her hand was wet.

"Did I say something wrong?"

"Wrong?" She looked at him and found his head seemed to be rimmed with rainbow light. "Since last evening I've been waiting to find myself turned out."

It was his turn to repeat. "Turned out? Of here?"

"How can you look so surprised? Did no one hear what I had to say yesterday?"

"Of course we understood."

"Well, then."

"Well, what?"

"Reginald, I confessed to treachery and deceit."

"You also spoke of how you have done your best to resist their manipulations and blackmail, even when it put everything you have at risk."

"I have nothing."

"Which makes your bravery even more astonishing."

"You speak of bravery?" Her laughter held a sharp edge. "I have been nothing but a coward and a liar."

"No, my dear, you are neither."

She started to argue, but something in his expression stopped the words before she could form them.

"Say you'll come," he said, a smile curving his lips.

"Where?"

"Now it's you who haven't been listening. To Wheeling."

"You wish for me to accompany you? After everything—"

"My dear Lillian, I will only go at all if you will come with me."

"But why? Why is it you want me to accompany you?"

He struggled to frame a response. "Because I love you, Lillian."

"But that was . . . before."

"And you think my love would be such a frivolous matter that it could be swayed by your confession?"

"Well . . . yes."

"Then I fear you do not know me very well at all."

She worked hard to form the words. "Reginald, never in my wildest dreams did I ever think I would hear words of love from a man such as you. I can scarcely believe . . ."

"Yes?" he encouraged.

"I do not deserve your love, Reginald."

He reached over and took her hand. "Lillian, outside of my own blood-kin, I have loved three people in my entire life. A wife snatched from me by death, a child I knew but for a few heartbeats of time, and now you. Yes, I will admit my tolerance for your past errors is no doubt strengthened by this love. But the truth is, you are a remarkable woman who has survived what would have crushed a weaker spirit. I know what I know. You are here with me now. And nothing, not even the fiercest whirlwind of time and fate, will keep us apart. Come westward with me, and you will learn this is true."

Chapter 23

Dearest Mama, dearest Father,

Hello and greetings from Washington. It is fast approaching midnight. Never did I think I would arrive at a point where my only chance to sit and write you would be when the rest of the family is abed, but the days have become immensely full. Not in a displeasing way, mind. In fact, I have never been happier. I hope you will not think ill of me, being able to say such a thing when you, my beloved family, are so far away. I miss you all terribly, especially now as I set pen to paper.

Abigail used a taper from the fire to light another candle. The brass holders glowed with a ruddy cheer, as though glad to be used for such a purpose. Abigail sat at the writing table stationed in the home's second parlor, the one where family gathered when not entertaining guests. The room faced onto the back garden and was filled with furniture that was no longer considered suitable for the more formal front room. In the far corner was an old pianoforte, one that did not appear to have been used in years. The room smelled rather musty, overlaid with the scent of her grandfather's liniments.

Grandmother Abigail could not be kinder. She does her best each day to fill the void caused by my being separated from you. She is kind and loving and so very wise. Also, I see a great deal of Erica Powers. Gareth is away writing pamphlets on the upcoming national elections, and Erica is working hard in his absence and delighting in little Hannah, as am I. And I have had several lovely visits with Erica's brother, Reginald Langston. Grandmother remains a great pillar of the church community here and asks that I send you her deepest affection. Which of course is accompanied by my own as well.

She rose and went to the back window. Moonlight illuminated the row of staves in the kitchen garden, there to support the squash plants and runner beans and blackberries. She found a sense of calm staring out at the orderly rows of plants. She sighed heavily enough to cloud the glass by her face. She turned and looked back at the writing desk with its trio of flickering candles. There was no putting it off. She must tell them. She crossed the room, seated herself, dipped the quill into the inkstand, and wrote.

I am in love.

When her husband had started growing ill, Abigail Cutter had debated selling the large old home and moving into something more manageable. But, thankfully, her husband's mind was not deteriorating along with his body, and he informed her in no uncertain terms that he wished to die where he had lived. When she had protested about the upkeep and responsibility, he had assured her that she would never need to stand alone. And so it had proven. The more frail her husband became, the closer her friends had drawn. They had so many friends. Even the staff had become very close, with their daily lives now so inextricably bound to her own that she fretted over their children and relatives as she would her own kin. Which, in many respects, they now were.

When it became clear that her husband would no longer

manage the stairs by himself again, she had wanted to turn the downstairs back parlor into a bedroom. Again she had been overruled. Her husband was a private man and had no interest in bringing his ailments into what he considered to be the public area of their home.

So they had arranged for a high-backed chair to be built of ash, the lightest of hardwoods. She had sewn cushions that could be threaded into the back and seat and tied in place, with yet more ties to hold her husband fast. The gardener and her son, Horace, had become adept at tilting the chair back and carrying her husband up and down the stairs as they would a stretcher. The sight of that first transport had left her so bereft she had sobbed her eyes dry. But her husband had professed himself satisfied and thanked them all profusely.

Her husband's sensible attitude had aided her mightily in adjusting to this new era. She did not like the casual brutality of time's passage, but there was nothing she could do. And Abigail Cutter had always been a practical woman. If the dear, sweet, ailing man was able to make peace with his state, then how could she do otherwise?

This practical determination aided her as she now set the candlestick down on her upstairs desk. She had brought in workmen and refashioned two of the upstairs rooms into an elongated station without doors. She called one her dayroom and the other her dressing alcove. In truth, it was merely space in which she could get on with the affairs of life while remaining as close as possible to her husband.

She trimmed a new quill with steady, deliberate motions. She knew what needed to be said. And say it she would.

My Dearest Samuel and Lavinia,

How very good of you to send me your angel of a daughter. In this difficult time, with my beloved husband growing increasingly frail, Abigail has brought into this home a new light. It is as though one of God's own has come to remind me of life's constant cycle. Of birth, and growth, and partings, and coming home. I realize the situation that brought Abigail to us was not an easy one for you. But her coming has, from my own perspective, been as great a gift as any I have ever received.

A noise in the next room raised her from the chair. Candle in hand, she padded across the carpeted floor and peeked into the bedroom. Her husband seemed to be resting well. He slept so much these days. She remained standing over him, for the candle bathed him in a glow so soft it eased back time's cover and revealed a younger form. She sighed softly. They had known so many good years together. Finally she withdrew from the room and returned to the task at hand.

You know me as a direct woman, and that is precisely how I shall speak with you now. Your daughter has fallen in love with a gentleman by the name of Abraham Childes. I suppose you shall hear of all his merits soon enough, for Abigail informed me that she would also be writing to you this evening. It should be my own duty to offer a more balanced perspective, by granting you insight into his faults. But I find this a strange task. Because what might be faults in another man are in this instance not faults at all. Rather, Abe has done his utmost to compensate for his weaknesses.

Abe has no family. He was orphaned young and raised in circumstances that might have crippled another, yet in Abe they have only left him both stronger and wiser. He is parsimonious, perhaps too much so, for I would dearly love to see him spend a bit on better clothes and someplace worth calling home. He is shy, and by that I mean not awkward about people but rather hesitant in accepting responsibilities at which he might fail. A highly unlikely possibility, in my opinion, based on his strength and stature and immense intelligence. Oh, I know I should do a better job of telling you why this romance should not progress, but I cannot. With God as my guide and witness, I feel His hand is upon these two young people coming together.

Abe's tentative nature seems to form a perfect foil for

your daughter's lively energy. She inspires him in a manner that is deeply touching to see. All who care for Abe, and that includes every member of our family here in Washington, as well as all the Langstons, feel that Abigail is coming to be a remarkable tonic for our young Mr. Childes.

Since dear Reginald lost his wife and baby, this orphaned young man has done more than anyone to keep Reginald from pining away. And now, of course, there is the burgeoning romance between Reginald and Lillian. I suppose it must seem forward of me to use her first name. But she has remained a guest in our home since her arrival and has done us all a world of good, most especially my dear husband. Who, I must add, grows more affectionate with her each day, and she with him. There are revelations here regarding Lillian as well, and soon enough I must pen a second letter and disclose these. But this particular letter is not about Lillian. It is about your precious daughter, whom I hold so very dearly.

I have been forced to act as her guardian on this matter, but only after spending numerous hours in discussion with my husband, with Erica, and with our dear Lord. You may dislike what I have to say. But I feel that I can now stand before you and before our Maker and state that I have discharged my duties to Abigail to the very best of my abilities.

I shall put it bluntly. My son and Reginald are expanding their partnership. They have written to you in order to inform you of everything related to the business, Samuel, so I shall not go into that here. They are granting Abraham Childes a minority share in this new venture. Abe will travel to Wheeling on the National Road and reside there for two years. At the end of this time he shall be free to return to Georgetown if he so wishes. But for two years he will manage the new Langston-Cutter Emporium.

Abigail and Abe are in love. But there has not been time for them to see whether this is a temporary infatuation or the genuine article, as they say. So Abigail has asked for my blessing to travel with the young man and the others, Reginald and Lillian. If Gareth can be reached and grants his permission, Erica and her daughter, Hannah, intend to journey with them. They travel to fulfill the mission requested by William Wilberforce. Lillian Houghton is going to seek a tract of land. Reginald is traveling as well and will remain out there for one month. The plan is to leave in one to two weeks' time, as soon as they can gather all their supplies. Together they will find a suitable property and begin work on the buildings. At the end of that time, Abigail will either return home to us here in Georgetown or she will not. If she remains, it will be as Mrs. Childes.

My dear daughter, I know how those words send an arrow through your heart. But even if you are unable to come for the wedding, I am most confident that pain would soon turn to joy if you could witness their love as I have.

Now let me try and describe for you what this means to me, your old mother. There have been nights, many of them and not so long ago, when I have sat at this very desk. I have stared at the candle and felt a darkness so great that neither the tallow's flame nor my most fervent prayers could keep it at bay. Fear of what the future holds has become an affliction so profound I might as well be laid up alongside my dear husband, who I fear is not long for this earth. It is the first time I have uttered these words. There you are. They are laid out as real as the pain they cause to my heart. Oh, I love him so.

And then your daughter arrived. Your wonderful daughter, with her internal flame as brilliant as her beautiful hair and a love of life so great it has banished these shadows from my heart and mind. She has become my dearest companion. It would be so easy to refuse Abigail's request. The temptation to be selfish this one time, and insist that she remain here with me, is as great as any I have ever known.

But I cannot.

Your daughter has found her lifelong match. It is love.

She is happy. They are intended for one another. And I, for one, must offer them what I hope you would were you here in my stead.

They go. Together. With my blessing. And my prayers.

PART
THREE

Chapter 24

Abigail moved about the house in a cloud of tension. Which was hardly surprising, Lillian reflected. In perhaps a week they were all departing. This journey could well change Abigail's life forever.

But Abigail was not alone in facing such difficult issues. Erica's frantic attempts to reach her husband by post had been futile. Gareth was moving from one state capital to another, following the elections and meeting with people involved in their cause. Erica had spent several sleepless nights in prayer and conversation with her family. Finally, only two days earlier, a letter by postrider had arrived. Gareth could not return. Matters were coming to a critical juncture. But he understood the urgency both to Wilberforce's request and the timing of this journey west. He urged Erica to take their daughter and go with the others. If he could, he would follow their path and join them. If not, they would meet upon their return to Washington. But by all means, he trusted her to aid Wilberforce and their allies in England with this vital task. Erica now sat at the dining room table along with Lillian and Mrs. Cutter, her face etched with sleepless strain.

For herself, Lillian served where she was needed. Half fearfully, half in calm expectation, she waited for someone to speak to her about the confession. But no one did. Not even Reginald. She intended to bring it up with him, but the man had the look of one who scarcely stopped to eat, much less sleep. Time and again they had refashioned their departure dates. Or rather the others made such plans while Lillian sat and listened. She could not bring herself to take part. Instead, she made herself busy around the households and the emporium. Langston's was a sizeable establishment, drawing customers from as far afield as Baltimore and even Philadelphia. Along the upstairs hall where the family had their offices, hung paintings of the clippers in which the company owned part interests.

Erica Langston wrote to her mother's relatives, the Harrows, who owned a vast estate in western Pennsylvania. She asked if they might reside with them and rest for a day or so toward the end of their journey. The hope was that they might perhaps make friends with folks who lived close to their final destination.

Several days back, Reginald had asked the women to take no finery on this journey. He had heard enough about Wheeling to know it was a borderland town run by frontiersmen. Silks and the like would only stand out. He apologized profusely for such a suggestion, but Lillian assured him she would rather hear it now than discover it herself in the town. She and Abigail and Erica acquired bolts of cotton prints from Langston's Emporium and had Mrs. Cutter's favorite seamstress fashion clothes of simple cut.

The banker had not shown his face again. Lillian worried, but not overmuch. The die was now cast. She must establish a new estate for her son and be done with the old life.

This morning the men had deposited yet another task into their laps. Reginald had rushed in and told them to go through the inventory list line by line. What were they neglecting to bring for the new emporium? What further supplies might a woman client wish to find? They must remember these customers would be setting out upon the journey of a lifetime, and Wheeling might be the last provisioning stage for a year and more.

They had entered into the duty reluctantly. But now they

were deep into the work, filling pages with more items the men had overlooked. But several times Abigail had leaped up to look through the front windows.

"What in the world could be keeping them so long?" she demanded as she checked outside once more.

The women exchanged glances across the paper-strewn table. Mrs. Cutter asked, "Who, dear?"

"The men!"

"Why, they are not due back for another hour," Beatrice Cutter explained.

Abigail crossed the parlor to glare at the mantel clock. "I'm sure this wretched timepiece has stopped!"

"It has done no such thing," Mrs. Cutter clucked. "I wound it myself this very morning, and I can hear it ticking cheerfully from where I sit."

"But . . ." Abigail spun about and returned to her place at the table, although her attention obviously was elsewhere.

The women resumed their work. Mrs. Cutter finally declared, "I do believe we have made as complete a list as is possible for the time allotted."

"How they could have included thread and scissors and then forgotten sewing needles is utterly beyond me," Erica noted with a chuckle.

"They are three men and a great swath of male clerks, all of whom assume they know everything there is worth knowing," Mrs. Cutter replied crisply.

Abigail sighed and looked once more at the clock. "Oh, why does time choose this day of all days to slow to a crawl?"

Beatrice rose from her seat and crossed to the front window to peer out herself. "Won't you tell me what is troubling you?"

"I can't!"

Mrs. Cutter approached as well. "Well, why not, my dear?"

"Because . . ." The young woman's expression held frustration. "It is not my place," she finished lamely.

The women exchanged astonished glances. These were not words they expected from Abigail.

When Abigail spoke once more, it was to her own reflection in the windowpanes. "He has to do this himself."

"Whom are you speaking of, my dear? Young Abe?"

Abigail might have nodded, or it could have been a shiver. "We talked and talked. If I am going to always say what he is too shy to tell, how ever can he learn confidence in his own abilities?"

Lillian reached for Abigail's arm. "Come sit with me by the fire."

Abigail permitted herself to be led over to the settee. "It's his plan. Not mine. All I did was, well . . ."

"You have urged Abe to speak with the others about some idea of his?"

"He didn't want to at first. But I insisted. Abe has agreed to talk this through, but only if I am present." She looked back at the clock. "The hands have not moved at all!"

"They will be here soon enough," Lillian assured her. "You have done all you can. Now the task is to put your mind upon something else."

Abigail stared at her. Finally she asked, "Is it true what I heard at dinner after church on Sunday, that you sing?"

Now it was Lillian who felt time freeze to a halt. "I used to," she finally said cautiously.

"But why do you not sing anymore?"

"Abigail," her grandmother quietly admonished.

"No, it's all right." Lillian copied Abigail's position, with her hands clenched tightly in her lap. "I promised myself I would harbor no more secrets in this house."

"I'm sorry," Abigail said, contrite. "You really needn't—"

"I sang in taverns for my keep. After I ran away."

For the first time that morning, Abigail's attention was drawn from whatever lay beyond the sun-drenched curtains. "You ran away?"

"Twice. The second time I did not return to the loveless home where I was raised by people who might have been relatives; I'm not really certain. My late husband, the count, found me singing in a theatre. He fashioned a new past for me out of myths. That is the short version of a long and tawdry tale."

"But . . ." Abigail had difficulty deciding which question to ask first.

Mrs. Cutter used the moment to interject, "My dear, perhaps it is not right for us to pry."

"But I want to know . . ."

Before the older woman could object again, Lillian said to Abigail, "Ask what you will."

"Why did you stop singing?"

"Because my late husband so wished. He claimed it was for fear someone would hear my voice and recognize me for who I really was. But I often wondered if perhaps there was some other reason. He was a very furtive man, you see. He loved owning possessions in secret. He kept paintings in a vault, portraits I never even knew we owned, which now hang in the offices of Simon Bartholomew."

"That wicked man," Erica Powers murmured.

"Perhaps my late husband merely wished to count my singing as yet another possession that was his and his alone. In truth, I had little desire to sing. It was part of a cheap and dismal past, one I was happy to leave well behind."

"But if you sang in a theatre, you must have a nice voice."

Lillian smiled through the sorrow and the memories. "They once called me the Siren of Manchester."

Abigail clapped her hands. "Oh, sing for us now!"

"Not if she does not wish," Mrs. Cutter hurried to say, but her eyes shone with excitement.

"None of the songs I knew then would be fitting for this home," Lillian replied.

"But what about a hymn? You know some of them, don't you?"

"Some, yes. From my early childhood."

"So they must bring back many memories. Is it too awful for you?"

"No, actually, my fondest memories of the early years are of my singing. But I don't recall many hymns well after all this time. Certainly not well enough to sing without accompaniment."

Mrs. Cutter offered, "There's the pianoforte in the back room. But it hasn't been played, oh, since before my husband became ill. He did so love his music."

Abigail offered, "Abe plays."

Mrs. Cutter exclaimed, "I don't recall ever hearing of this."

"It's like everything else. He loves to play but he won't when others might hear him. His mother was a musician. The old pastor where he lived used to give him lessons. He plays sometimes in the church, but only when it's empty. He says it draws him close to the family he once had."

Mrs. Cutter glanced out the front window. "Here they are now."

"Finally!" Abigail sprang from her seat and hurried to the front door.

"Steady, my dear," Lillian said quietly. "Steady."

"Yes, of course. You are right." She forced herself to take a step back into the front parlor.

Lillian walked over to join her. As the front door opened and the men entered, she said, "You are showing restraint."

"Oh, Lillian, I wish that were so!" Abigail's face was pale.

"Much as you would like to 'help,' you are leaving Abe to chart his own course." Lillian patted her arm. "I am proud of you."

Before Abigail could respond, Abe entered the room, looking rather terrified. His dark gaze fastened upon Abigail with desperate appeal.

Lillian walked over and placed herself directly between him and Abigail. "Good morning, sir. I was wondering if I might ask your assistance."

Abe forced his attention to her. "Of course, Mrs. Houghton."

"I am nearly petrified with fear, you see."

His gaze focused more intently upon her. "Ma'am?"

"They have asked me to do something which frightens me utterly."

"Really, my dear," Mrs. Cutter protested. "You mustn't feel pressured."

Lillian held Abe fast with her gaze. "You see, Abe, I have not sung in more than fifteen very long years. Now it is time. And I am very nervous about this. I was wondering, well, might I please lean upon your strength and skill at the pianoforte?"

"Y-you wish me to accompany you?"

"I could not do this alone," she replied simply. "It would be beyond me. As it is, the thought of singing in front of anyone, even more before these new, dear friends, leaves me scarce able to stand."

She held out her hand. "What I am asking, Abe, is if you would please be strong for me."

Now that the moment was actually here, she was in fact as weak with fear as she had professed. The pianoforte was contained in its own little alcove off the rear parlor. To protect the surface, a tapestry had been used as a dust cover. The silver candlesticks were removed and the tapestry folded and set aside. A chair was brought from the dining room. Abe seated himself and ran his fingers down the keyboard. Lillian noticed two notes that were flat, but the instrument's sound was not displeasing. Abe signaled a similar conclusion by nodding at her, but seemed to be ignoring the rest of the room entirely, as she was doing. Perhaps Abe felt the same way as she, that by intently holding each other's gaze they were able to keep out the almost overpowering sense of anxiety.

"What song have you selected, ma'am?"

"I'm not sure—I suppose one of the hymns I sang as a little

girl, though I can scarce recall the titles, much less the melodies. Perhaps you might suggest a tune you know?"

Abe thought a moment as his fingers continued to test the keys. His touch was sure, his hands very strong. There was a rustling sound as the others found chairs and settled down. But neither of the performers looked over at the group.

Mrs. Cutter slipped in and set a hymnal upon the stand above the keys. The woman's appearance within Abe's range of vision caused him to falter, and he hit his first wrong notes.

Lillian turned her back entirely to the room and set her hand upon his shoulder. Their gazes remained locked. *This is just you and me,* she said with her eyes. It was the only way she could continue. For a moment, she wished with all her heart that she had never started upon this foolhardy course. But she was not doing this for herself. She must seek to show her gratitude to these good people with the little she had at her disposal. And help Abe's confidence through it also. Lillian took a very deep breath. No more lies. No more secrets.

Abe seemed to draw strength from her silent determination, or perhaps it was the genuine fear he saw in her face. For he straightened in his chair and said, "How about this, ma'am?"

His fingers began playing a melody that she recognized in an instant. "Of course! I used to be very fond of that one!"

"Let me find the words for you." He reached for the hymnal and turned swiftly to the page. He then returned to the keys.

Lillian began humming softly to test her voice. The hymnal granted her an excuse to keep her back turned to the room. Abe played well enough to avoid hitting the off-tune keys any more than absolutely necessary. He moved the bass down one octave and fashioned his chords minus the worst key. He played the melody through twice. Gradually Lillian allowed her voice to gain in strength. By the third round she was humming almost at a strength to match his playing. She looked up from the notes and nodded.

Abe paused for two beats, long enough for her to draw a full breath, then began.

She sang,

> "Crown Him with many crowns, the Lamb upon His
>   throne;
> Hark! How the heavenly anthem drowns all music but its
>   own."

The memories were a force as strong as the music itself. She sang and seemed to become two people. One stood with her back to the room and studied every word, every note, every breath. It might be more than fifteen years, but the lessons she had learned were with her still. She heard the accuracy in her voice—and the weakness. Her throat was constricted somewhat, and her notes were too reedy. But the clarity was there, and the slight hint of bell-like power.

But there was another person there inside her, a little child of seven, who could scarcely contain herself with the joy of singing again.

> "Crown Him the Lord of peace, Whose power a scepter
>   sways
> From pole to pole, that wars may cease, and all be prayer
>   and praise."

Lillian closed her eyes. Only for an instant. She no longer recalled the words from memory, so she could not look away from the music for longer than it took her to sing the line.

She remembered how the old church smelled. She recalled the scent of dust and incense and age. She remembered how she could make her voice resound off the high rafters, so clearly she could identify her voice among all the others in the church.

> "Crown Him the Lord of love, behold His hands and side,
> Those wounds, yet visible above, in beauty glorified."

The meaning of the words had mostly escaped her conscious understanding as a child, but each stanza caught her heart now with its truth and power.

They finished the stanza, and Abe looked a question at her. She understood and nodded assent. Briefly he permitted himself to escape the bounds of the hymn's written notes. Lillian felt a thrill run through her being. She knew the man was allowing himself this only because he was caught up in the moment. Here and now, it was only them. Here and now, it was safe to fly.

Lillian turned partway around to face both Abe and the room. She kept her gaze upon the young man and heard as he moved further afield, experimenting with tone and tempo. She nodded in time to his playing and smiled. It was, in all truth under heaven, a moment of pure beauty. Further than that she need not dwell, not for the moment.

Abe returned to the hymn's precise notes and played his way through the last bars of the verse, finishing with a half-step key change. Lillian hummed a pair of notes, preparing herself.

Abe lifted himself up, the musician's signal to the singer. Then came the downbeat.

Lillian opened her mouth and soared away.

She did not test her outermost limits. The years had brought her a different voice than the one she had known as a young woman. It was vital that she take time to try out its new borders. Even so, the hymn became a platform from which she might take flight. She moved off into the distance, returning only to remind herself and the listeners where she began and what remained her base. Lifting herself away from the years that had kept her silent. She joined once more with the spirit of the bright-eyed little girl and sang to hear her voice echo off distant rafters.

"Awake, my soul, and sing of Him who died for thee,
And hail Him as thy matchless King through all eternity."

A long silence ensued, filled with the emotions of each listener. Abe and Lillian exchanged glances. They both had won something here. Very different for each of them, yet the same. At least that was how it felt to Lillian.

Mrs. Cutter was the first to recover. "What an utter astonishment."

"An angel," Erica murmured. "I feel as though I have just heard the voice of heaven."

Then all of them were talking at once. The voices were the best sort of applause, the response of an audience that just had to make some noise of their own. Lillian reached over and let Abe take her hand. Together they stood and let the tumult wash over them.

Reginald rose from his chair and came to embrace her with a spontaneous joy. "My dear, my very dearest Lillian."

"I'm so glad you liked it," she murmured against his shoulder, not in the least awkward about this private moment in a public setting.

"My dear, I am transported beyond words." He turned and offered Abe his free hand. "My congratulations, young man."

"Thank you," he said. "It was her singing—"

"You caused this wooden beast to sing with a voice almost as fine as the lady's here." He refused to release either of them.

Abe flushed with pleasure as Abigail rushed forward to embrace him. "Oh, Abe, that was wonderful."

He smiled his appreciation.

"I have loved that hymn since I was a child," Abigail hurried on. "Never have I heard it played as well." Her eyes were filled with unshed tears as she looked at Lillian and added, "Or sung."

Abe straightened further, standing as tall as ever Lillian had seen. He said to Reginald, "Sir, I have something I wish to talk to you about."

"Speak your mind, lad. There is hardly a thing I could refuse you this day."

"It has to do with business, Mr. Langston. Perhaps we should seek a more private corner?"

"Nonsense. We are a family. I may not know much, lad. But I am assured our success stands or falls upon the strength of this family and these friends."

The others stepped away until Abe stood alone in the little alcove.

A pair of glances, first at Abigail and then at Lillian, gave him the strength he needed. "I have an idea for a new business," he began. "One tied to our plans for Wheeling and the West."

"Please proceed."

"As you know, sir, there are but two stagecoach companies operating along the new turnpike to Wheeling. Both of these use a coach of old-fashioned design. One that is reported to be extremely uncomfortable for the passengers."

"How is it you know this?"

"I lived next door to the stables for a time, sir. Many a time I heard complaints from passengers. They wouldn't ride the coach into Washington, much less all the way to Wheeling."

Horace Cutter spoke up. "I've heard it called 'cruel and unusual punishment.'"

"There is a new system just developed," Abe went on. "The coach's base is strengthened by iron bands, and these bands rest on something called through-braces. These thick pads are made of oxen leather. The system does much to steady the ride."

"You've ridden in one?"

"Several times, sir. I've also had one of the manufacturers explain the idea. The braces act as a sort of hammock system. The coach swings over bumps like a cradle."

"Is the coach as large as the standard build?"

"The interior is the same—three passengers to a side. But the coach can carry a greater total weight. So the boot, the step at the back, has been extended to carry cases strapped into place with leather bands. And up top the coach is ringed by a low brass railing to hold more luggage."

Reginald and Horace exchanged glances. "I gather you've discussed the purchase of these coaches?"

Abe flushed. "I didn't mean to overstep my bounds, sir."

"You've done nothing of the sort. Tell us the rest."

"The authorities are now planning to extend the National Road all the way to St. Louis," Abe continued in a rush. "Nobody has yet to make a bid for carrying the post beyond Wheeling. If we were to make them an offer, agreeing to carry the post as far as the road is open, they would also grant us rights to carry a third of the post destined for Wheeling."

"Would they indeed. You've been busy, young man."

"Miss Abigail helped me, sir."

"Of that I have no doubt whatsoever. Our womenfolk have an indisputable amount of strength and wisdom." His gaze came to rest on Lillian, and then he turned back to the young man. "I suppose there is a bit of bad news."

"How—how did you know that, sir?"

"When you've been in business as long as I have, you'll learn to expect the hidden cost, the unknown roadblocks to success. Go on, out with it."

"Well, sir, there are two coaches to be had. And the price is not unreasonable. But there are no horses."

"Horses trained to a coach's tethers we can most certainly obtain," Horace responded with a firm nod. "Long as our competitors don't know what we're about."

Abe added, "Nor have I been able to find drivers."

Even Lillian understood the significance of this. Coach drivers were a rare breed. With four or sometimes six horses held to a long series of traces, the risks were vastly multiplied. A good driver needed to be able to sense each horse's mood through the reins and keep them pulling equally. He needed the strength to quiet a restless horse long before panic could cause a tragedy. The worse the condition of the road, the more skills the driver required. A thrown wheel in Indian country could mean the death of everyone on board. Where cities remained few and far between, a driver must also be a skilled carpenter, blacksmith, leather worker, and horse doctor.

Reginald said, "I assume you have an idea here as well."

"Well, sir, that is . . ."

"Go on, speak up, lad. We're all on your side here."

Lillian shivered and scanned the room. *All on your side here.* It was true. Despite the worst she had to reveal, despite all the trickery and the falsehoods, still they accepted her. They drew her in as *family.*

Abe continued in a rush, "I've been taking lessons from the stable where I used to berth. And you and Mr. Cutter both can handle a trace. I've seen it. So I was thinking, rather than riding on someone else's coaches . . ."

"We take our own and look for drivers out Wheeling way," Reginald finished. He turned to his partner and asked, "How would you feel about making the journey with us?"

"Been wondering about that very same thing. If I'm going to invest out that way, I should see the lay of the land for myself." Horace glanced at Beatrice. "As long as you and the children can do without me for a time."

"We shall miss you terribly," she replied after a moment. "But if you feel it is important, then you shall journey with my blessing."

"Then it's settled," Horace concluded.

"We're bound to find settlers in Wheeling who can handle a full trace," Reginald continued. "Men willing to be away from home part of each month in return for good hard cash."

"We could carry a good deal of the first wares ourselves this way, and have the rest transported by oxen train."

"Slower and far cheaper," Horace agreed. "But if we're carrying enough to make a start, what difference does it make?"

Reginald turned to Abe once more. "Does this mean you'd commit to running this as well as our Wheeling company?"

Abe took time for one hard breath and one long look at Abigail. Lillian followed his eyes. The younger woman's face shone with such pride and love Lillian wanted to weep with shared joy.

Abe straightened his shoulders and replied, "Yes, Mr. Langston, sir. I am."

"Partners ought to address one another by their given names, Abe."

Abe flushed more deeply. He gripped Reginald's hand, but kept his gaze upon Abigail as he replied, "Partners, yes, Reginald." He walked across the room. "Horace," he said and shook the man's hand.

Chapter 25

The adventurers departed at dawn on the following Monday. Their hopes were to arrive at the Harrow home in southwestern Pennsylvania before the next Sabbath. Lillian took great joy in one final church service with old Mr. Cutter. She sang along with the church hymns, but only loud enough for him to hear her voice. It was more than enough.

The closer they all had come to departure, the faster the world had spun. Such was the pressure to keep to the imposed schedule that none of them slept more than a few hours the last two nights. The group had been working together, both those going and those remaining, and all of them shared tasks and called upon one another without hesitation. Lillian had forged ahead with whatever was set in front of her, including packing bolts of cloth, counting blocks of soap, and checking wares off a long list as Abigail and Erica sorted through piles destined for the later oxcarts. By the time they had left, the travelers were all beyond the point of exhaustion.

They had elected not to seek additional passengers for the journey, but rather use the extra carriage space for further supplies. Reginald and Abe traveled in one coach with Lillian and Abigail. The one professional driver they had managed to hire was a taciturn older gentleman married to the nanny Erica Powers employed for her daughter. Erica would be accompanied in this second coach by her daughter, Hannah, the nanny, and Horace Cutter. The nanny was a rather colorless lady who spoke scarcely a word to anyone, just like her husband, the driver. When not tending the child, the nanny kept her nose buried in a threadbare copy of *Pilgrim's Progress*.

That first afternoon the two men sat above with the driver while the two women napped inside. They berthed at a roadside inn long after dark and started again soon after dawn. That second morning they fashioned a bed up top so the man not driving could rest within the fencing. The road was very crowded this close to the nation's capital, but there were laybys every quarter mile, where the slower carts would pull in and allow the faster coaches to speed ahead. That second afternoon it rained so hard they were forced to shut all the windows, and Reginald accepted Abe's encouragement to retreat inside with the ladies. That night as Abe sat by the tavern's roaring fire, drying his boots and his oilskin on the back of his chair, he took paper and quill to a list of figures. They had averaged a full eleven miles an hour for the first two days of their journey, he declared. A most remarkable pace, they all agreed.

For Lillian, banked-up fatigue was joined now with the tiring journey. She rested when she wished. She chatted with Abigail, mostly about lighthearted matters, for Lillian did not wish to speak of the dark cloud she felt still looming over her personal horizon. Abigail also was very weary and clearly in no frame of mind to discuss anything weighty.

Lillian was seeing the land firsthand out the carriage window as the miles slowly ticked by. The country appeared endless. It was not a matter of traveling out a distance and buying land. The arable lands neighboring Washington were either going at very high prices or already taken. No, the land sale was out West. Lillian had heard people say this any number of times. But only now did she understand what it truly meant.

On the third morning they crested a rise, and up ahead of them they spotted the first ridgeline of the Appalachians. Reginald explained how they would take the National Road north of the highest peaks, heading through the Pennsylvania farmlands for several more days before entering the steep hills. Lillian saw how the others received the news with equal mixture of excitement and acceptance. She, however, was utterly alarmed and discouraged. The hills rose like blue-tinted walls, barriers she would cross because she had to. Yet on the other side, what then? She listened with a heavy heart as Reginald described more of the landscape and Abe calculated time and distance.

Lillian turned her face to the window. The forested hillside sloped down to yet another valley, endless land in vast array, stretching out for days and weeks and months. How had she permitted herself to fall in love with a man who would return to his Georgetown life and be lost to her forever? How could she have ever dreamed they might find a way to maintain their romance?

She was traveling to some western land because she had no choice. And once there, she would say her farewells to this fine man beside her. And he would return to his city, where already her scandals were beginning to be hinted at. Her confessions were not enough to diffuse the tirade of half-truths and bitter denunciations the bankers would send forth. She would make a new life in the distant West beyond these faceless hills. She had no choice in the matter.

And she would have to do so alone.

On the fourth morning they shifted positions so that Horace, Reginald, and Abe might travel together and discuss business. Abe took the reins of one coach, sharing the bench with his partners, while the taciturn driver handled the other team. Lillian offered to sit with the nanny and Erica's slumbering child, insisting that a time alone with her thoughts would do her a world of good.

For her part, Erica spent the first hour completing work on a journal article. She carried a small wooden case that opened into a lady's traveling secretary, with a scrolled leather top and compartments for quills and paper and ink. Abigail observed Erica with a strange pleasure. She had known this woman since childhood, most of that time only through letters, yet she felt in some ways she knew Erica not at all. Letters were fine, of course, for Erica was an excellent writer and diligent in maintaining the friendship. Abigail now felt a great sense of ease. She knew Erica cared for her very deeply. She also knew their time together would soon be ended, as they went their separate ways. So what should they talk of? For a moment Abigail was tempted to bring up the incident in London. Yet something held her back. It took only a moment for her to realize that was the past. What Abigail wanted to address with her oldest friend was who they were *now*.

Erica cleared the quill tip and laid it in the recessed cavity. She dusted the ink, set the page onto the pile of completed work, and closed the box. "There has scarce been time to gather my thoughts and keep up with the journaling Gareth asked me to do," Erica said. "Even with the nanny traveling with us, Hannah demands a great deal of attention."

"You two look so lovely and happy together."

"She is such a blessing to us both," Erica said. Merely speaking about her daughter brought a new shine to her eyes. "Gareth and I had to wait so long, we feared we would never have children. We had almost decided God wished for our work and our cause to be the sole bonds between us and Him."

"That possibility must have made you awfully sad at times."

"Yes, but it also drew me closer not only to Gareth, but also to God and more devoted to our shared work."

"The pamphlets and the antislavery movement."

"Just so."

"What is it like to have such a cause, I wonder?"

Erica spent several thoughtful minutes finishing latching up her little box and stowing it away. "I would say that it draws me out of my own comfortable and somewhat selfish world more than I should ever have thought possible."

Abigail felt the faintest tremor run through her form.

"It teaches me to care for others, people beyond the reach of my family and comfortable church community. And through this, I have come to care more deeply for our Savior."

"How is that, please?"

"Because I am drawn to care deeply for those that are dear to Him. The voiceless, the infirm, the innocents in chains. I learn through my actions what Jesus meant in His lesson about loving my neighbor, whoever and wherever he might be."

Another tremor touched the core of her being, stronger even than the first. "I would so very much like to have such a cause," Abigail whispered.

"Then you shall be granted one."

"How can you be so certain?"

" 'The harvest truly is plenteous, but the labourers are few,' " Erica quoted. "Our Lord will use all who seek to do service, according to His calling."

Abigail could hardly contain her enthusiasm and impatience to discover what her calling might be. Erica told her to wait, watch, and pray—it would come.

Almost a week had passed when they began climbing the hills of southwestern Pennsylvania beneath a clear sky with the air fragrant with autumn's spices. The coach rocked a good deal more than Lillian's English carriage and had none of the gloss and ornate grillwork. But it was an extremely sturdy conveyance and remained well balanced even with the mountain of supplies stored up top and strapped to the rear boot. The road had good enough drainage that the previous night's torrential rain did not slow them down overmuch.

The villages along the National Road were becoming

home to an increasing number of inns. Many of these towns had been founded by religious groups, and many still banned the sale of spirits. It was in such places they intended to over-night, for these were also the safest villages. But their midday halts could not be so well planned. That day, the village where they had hoped to stop contained more than three dozen un-licensed roadside taverns. They were known as tippling inns and already had a notorious reputation. So they halted only long enough to buy fresh bread and continued on to the next lay-by. They picnicked beside one of the whitewashed mile-stones, a triangular marker noting the distance from Washing-ton on one side and Wheeling on the other.

As he ate, Abe made hasty calculations and declared, "We're now making better than twelve miles per hour, despite the train of Conestoga wagons that slowed us just after dawn."

"I do wish you would set your work aside for a time," Abi-gail complained, only half jokingly. "Your brain needs a rest."

"I have never discovered a means by which to turn off my thoughts." He stopped then, but gave the impression of having more to say.

"You may finish your thought, Abe," Abigail invited with a wry look.

Abe turned red and lowered his voice. "I was going to add, except when I look at you. Then my thinking scatters to the winds!"

Abigail turned a brighter shade of red than Abe. "Well, thank you, Mr. Childes."

Reginald returned from inspecting the horses. One of the men repeated this task every midday and evening, loosening buckles and fitting nosebags. While the speediest coach com-panies arranged to trade teams at various stages along their journeys, private travelers continued with the same horses for the entire journey.

"The day looks to be fine," Reginald said to Lillian. "Would you care to join me up top for the next leg of our journey?"

Lillian could tell there was something on his mind, but she kept her tone light in the others' presence. "I should be most pleased," she responded with a smile.

"I gather Abe and Miss Abigail shall have no difficulty finding some topic to occupy them in the coach," Erica noted to kind laughter.

Reginald scarcely waited until he had tightened the braces and helped Lillian climb on board before saying, "There was something I wanted to speak with you about before we left. But things became awfully busy there toward the end, don't you know."

"I do indeed." Lillian was feeling very comfortable with this man and no longer felt a need to prepare herself for the worst. Whatever it was, she knew he would only speak with her best interests at heart. "We have scarcely had a single moment these last few days."

"Now that I have no reason to hold back, still I find it difficult to speak. But Erica insists I should put this off no longer."

Even with such an introduction, Lillian felt no threat. "You trust your sister so. It is a lovely thing to see."

"She is as much the leader of our little company as I— perhaps more. Oh, I manage the day-to-day affairs and take care of all the strenuous work. I always have preferred working with my muscles, over my head."

"You will miss her terribly when she goes back to England," Lillian softly observed.

"It is something I can scarce think of without very real sorrow," he said, his voice low.

"I am certain you will do fine, Reginald. You are a man with far more talent and abilities than you give yourself credit for."

"I wish . . ."

When he did not continue, she urged, "Pray finish that thought, Reginald."

Reginald cleared his throat and said, "On the Friday before

our departure, I visited with several allies within the Washington community. I explained to them that I was concerned about a possible threat posed by one certain local banker. You know of whom I speak?"

She sat up straighter. "Of course."

"I was joined by Horace, who has once again proven himself to be a staunch friend and ally. We did not explain things fully to the others, of course. Merely that there were matters which we feared might be used in an insulting and untrue fashion." He kept his eyes upon the road ahead. "Our concerns were apparently well founded."

Lillian's hand rose to her throat. "What did they tell you?"

"Only that the banker had indeed been making scurrilous references to certain company we kept." Reginald's features had taken on an iron cast. "I fear this is not the last we have heard from this scoundrel."

"Reginald—"

"Oh, I know I should have discussed it with you. But I feared you would beg me not to proceed as I have. I could not bear the thought of departing Washington with you so vulnerable. It was a minor matter, but it had to be done. I discussed it with Erica, and she agreed."

"It was not minor at all," Lillian protested.

"What I meant to say was that I wish I could do more. With the departure looming all I could do was alert our trusted allies to this matter and ask that they speak on our behalf until my return." He glanced anxiously at her. "Have I made an error?"

"You have sought to be my protector and friend. For that I am most grateful." But even more than this was the gnawing certainty that she would be a constant burden to these people so long as she was to remain with them. She had no choice but to flee far and deep into this country's seemingly endless depths. Perhaps even take a new name. Find someplace safe for her and her son to start afresh.

Reginald interrupted her bleak thoughts. "Then you are not angry with me?"

"Dear, dear Reginald. Of course not. I only wish . . ." It was now her turn to leave the thought unfinished.

But he understood and spoke for them both. "That none of this had happened, or was hanging over you still. As do I. So very much."

Lillian shook her head. This man continued to astonish her so. "Does it not trouble you in the slightest that I am—I am a fallen woman?"

"You are nothing of the sort," he admonished hotly.

"But I was, Reginald. I was. Though it pierces my very soul to speak of it, I shall have no illusions between us. I have done many wrong things and spent years hiding behind a title and station that were not mine to claim."

He paused so long she feared he might actually agree with her, which caused such pain she could scarcely breathe. Or, worse still, suggest that soon they would part and the problem would no longer be a concern to either of them. Her heart wrenched with the terrible certainty of coming loss. Of all the worries besetting her—the thought of withdrawing her son from his beloved Eton, the two of them leaving England forever, scandal chasing them across the Atlantic, forging a new life in an utterly alien world—this one, losing a man she knew but for a short time, caused her by far the greatest agony.

Yet when Reginald responded, it was with a thoughtful air. "I have seen you bow your head and pray."

"Yes."

"You have done this quietly. No fanfare, no thought of being observed. But you have done something that you have denied all your life long."

"It is true." She found herself missing the hours with Mr. Cutter. If only she could sit with him now, and feel his calm certainty, and pray with the strength and the clarity she had known in his presence. "And I am the better for it."

"There is a passage in the Bible that reads, 'As far as the

east is from the west . . .' speaking of how God separates us from the mistakes we have made in the past. *All* of us have made such errors. I don't know much—"

"I do wish you would stop saying that, Reginald. You are a man of great strength and wisdom."

"You mistake my sister's intelligence for my own."

"Stop, please, I beseech you. How could anyone possibly consider you anything but brilliant?"

He looked at her in astonishment.

"Brilliant," she repeated, more softly this time. "You might not have all the book learning in the world, but you have built for yourself a position of success. This was not accomplished because of your sister. You are the man who leads this company. You are the man Abe looks up to. And from what I have seen, this is a sentiment shared by almost all of your other employees. You are a truly great man, Reginald Langston, and it is high time you recognized this."

He seemed to mull that over for a time. "Forgive me, I have completely lost track of the conversation."

"Mistakes," she replied glumly. "My own."

"All of us have made errors, Lillian. All of us require God's saving grace."

"But these mistakes could well mean the loss of everything I have. Title, position, and damage to the reputation of those I care about."

"Who in all these reaches will be concerned with such matters?" Reginald swept his hand in a broad arc. "Look around you. This is a new land. We have founded this nation upon the principle that a man is what he is. We are not bound by titles or inherited position. We are who we make ourselves to be."

Yes, and it was this same land that soon would tear them apart. Lillian stiffened her resolve, determined not to give in to her yearnings. "How can I simply pretend that my previous life never existed?"

"How can we deny what has brought us to this point? All

these years later, I still wake up in the middle of the night from dreaded dreams of the fire that left me fatherless."

"But of course that was not your fault."

"No, but it *happened*. It *shaped* me. And with God's help, I have found lessons and wisdom even in this most bitter of experiences." He gave her a piercing look. "This is America, Lillian. A man's worth is measured by the man himself. His own words and his own deeds. That's what I love about this land. God has helped me grow into a man of worth and taught me to accept the good and the bad, both in my own past and in those around me."

Lillian nodded slowly. She realized that here in these words lay the deeper significance to the acceptance she had received from these fine people. Here was why they had been so open to her, even after her confession. They were not friends of hers because of the title she had so valued, or the riches she no longer possessed, or her false friends in the royal court. It was astonishing that she could find such clarity in such a heartrending moment. And such love. "You are such a wise man," she murmured.

"I know what I know, Lillian. You have a fine heart, a great spirit. You sing like an angel. You are the most beautiful woman I have ever met." Reginald's voice cracked at that point and he tried to cover it with a cough. But he could not quite keep his voice steady as he continued, "And as I sat in church and saw you take the old man's hand in yours and bow your head . . ."

At that point his voice failed him entirely.

Lillian saw no need for further conversation. Instead, she reached over and settled her hand upon his arm. The effort of controlling the reins bunched and knotted his muscles beneath her touch. The knowledge that Reginald would soon be lost to her left her so undone the road ahead shimmered and swam in a pool of unshed tears.

Abigail mostly delighted in the hours of travel. Much of the time Abe was utterly involved with his work, and she did not mind this at all. With each day, she was discovering new things about herself. She had always known she was independent and willful. Because she had never spent time in the company of a man she loved, she had not realized before that she did not need to be the center of attention, nor did she require to be entertained. She was indeed content with time for herself and her own thoughts and plans.

Except for the occasional sound of voices drifting back into the coach from the driver's bench, this day might have been theirs and theirs alone. Abe had his maps spread out upon the opposite seat. One was a copy of the surveyor's map used to construct this very road. Abe found this fascinating. There were numerous circles with tiny numbers written in here and there. Away from the road upon which they traveled, the world became shaded and ill-defined. Beside the maps were two geography texts of the region, along with reams of paper. Abe hummed as he perused the maps and the books and his notes from the previous evening.

Abruptly he looked up and caught her watching him. "Forgive me. I have been ignoring you."

"Is that so? I'm sure I hadn't noticed."

"You are making sport of me now."

"Only a little."

"I am sorry, Abigail. There is so much for me to study."

"This is important for you, isn't it?"

"The study? Why, it is vital. I feed upon it as I do upon nourishment for my body. Sometimes I hunger for this more than I do normal food."

"Not to mention how the journey itself fascinates you."

"I have never been anywhere. Of course, I journeyed from my family's home and eventually arrived in Washington. But I was so, well . . ."

"Afraid," she offered.

"Terrified," he solemnly agreed. "Suffering and alone. I did not understand how God could allow such things to happen to me. I still do not fathom this entirely. I have learned to accept it, though."

Abigail marveled at his simple yet profound view of life.

Abe asked, "Why are you looking at me like that?"

She gave him as simple an answer as she had received. "Because I am learning to love you."

He blinked slowly. "I do not deserve this."

She reached out her hand.

"I have nothing to offer you," he said, enclosing her hand in both of his.

"Except yourself. Which is as great a gift as anyone has ever received."

"Last night I lay awake and tried to describe for myself what it is you brought into my life."

"Tell me."

"You have brought me *vision*."

"My dearest Abe, you see more clearly than any person I have ever met."

"That is not what I meant. Let us take this coach in which we are traveling. I saw it as a splendid contraption, one that could serve a company well. What did you do, but urge me to see this as *my* company. You found the people I needed to speak with—"

"No, Abe." She shook her head.

"You pointed out where I should look, then. You urged me to research the concept and work the figures and talk with the coach people. . . ." His gaze was a reward all unto itself. "I would never have done this without you."

"I don't know that for a certainty, but it's nice of you to say so."

"How could you see such things as possible?"

"I didn't. I simply saw the potential in you."

"I don't understand."

"You can do whatever it is you put your mind to."

"No—"

"Listen to me, Abe. I have heard the others speak of you in this manner, and I know it to be the truth. You have astonishing potential."

"And you," Abe replied, "could have anyone you wish."

"But I don't want just anyone. I want you."

"This is the marvel that escapes my understanding." Just then one of the carriage wheels hit a pothole and jostled them apart. Abigail nearly lost her place on the seat. When Abe determined she was all right, he began to laugh, and she soon joined him.

When they had regained their composure, Abigail examined the frank openness in his features, a face more honest and intelligent than any she had seen before. "I had come to consider my impetuous nature a curse. Until I met you. And now I see myself in an entirely different light. I can see how God was shaping me. He even used that disastrous night in Soho to open my eyes to the truth so that I might begin to learn and change. I was broken so that I might come to recognize just how much I needed God—and you."

He looked stunned.

"You," she repeated, reaching again for his hand. "You are the man who possesses none of what I have in far too great abundance."

"Beauty? Grace?" He hesitated, then added, "Family?"

"Impetuosity," she replied. "The fire to move forward. The urge to take what is known and *apply* it. You speak of hunger. I suppose that describes what I have as well as anything. I absolutely hunger to act. But until the moment when God brought us together, I had no true *purpose*."

"Purpose," Abe finally repeated after a moment. "For some reason, the way you speak of that leaves me enthralled."

"Then let me share with you one other word," Abigail replied. "Cause. I have watched the way Erica speaks of her work against slavery, and have yearned so for something which stirs in me such passion and fervor. She and I spoke of this, and I have come to see that it is not something I can decide upon. I must seek this from God. It is His gift to bestow. I wish it, and I am afraid of it."

"You, afraid? Why?"

"Because I fear I will be found wanting. I fear I will not be strong enough or good enough."

Abe looked down at her hand in his and said softly, "I would like nothing more than to add my strength to yours."

"And I," Abigail said, striving to keep her voice steady, "would like nothing more than to share a cause with you, my beloved."

"Do you think we might pray for guidance on this?"

They did just that, holding hands in the rocking coach, speaking both with each other and with God, using the same conversational tone with their Lord as they did with each other, as though He were sharing the day and the ride with them. This lasted until the tilled fields and softly undulating hills suddenly gave way to the bustling cacophony of a market town. Abruptly Abe broke free to peer out the coach window. "Why, this must be Farmington!"

Amen, Abigail silently amended. *Amen and thank you for this day and this wonderful man.* She said, "Is it?"

He began rooting through his maps and notations. "I am certain of it! We have arrived in Farmington, and we are . . . Yes! A full two hours ahead of schedule."

"Are we indeed. How utterly remarkable."

Finally her tone must have gotten his attention. "You are making fun of me again."

"Perhaps just a touch."

"But this is extraordinary."

"Tell me why."

"We have traversed the better part of a state and arrived at the point where we depart from the National Road, and we have done so on schedule! Do you have any idea what this means?"

"No, but I want to learn," she replied, seeking to match his enthusiasm. "Please do explain."

"We are negotiating unknown territory, with untrained drivers, in unfamiliar coaches. We have not been able to take on fresh horses, which has slowed us immensely. And yet we have managed to hold to a proper schedule! This means we can make precise timetables for our coach service. Which means we can calculate reliable costs for the journey!"

She shook her head, not over the news, but rather over the man's unbounded energy. "Tell me what you are seeing."

"The National Road," he said, his face back now at the side window. "It is an utter marvel of modern engineering. And you shall see just what I mean when we turn here and begin traveling north on a more primitive road to your relatives' estate."

"Not my relatives. Reginald and Erica's."

"Of course. Forgive me. It is just that your families are so intertwined I often think of them as one." This was spoken as he looked out on the noisy market square. "Before the turnpike was completed, Farmington was just one more village in the Pennsylvania foothills. Now just look at it! A picture of the prosperity that such roads promise." He pointed ahead. "I do believe we are approaching the turning now."

And indeed Abe was right, both about the juncture and the sudden change in the road's condition. The carriage bucked hard as it maneuvered over rain-washed gullies and ruts.

"My goodness," Abigail exclaimed as she was thrown against the side.

"There, do you see? The National Road measures thirty-two feet in width, of which the center twenty feet is made of broken stones placed to a depth of eighteen inches."

None of this was new information for Abigail, of course, as he had been extolling the virtues of the road for days now. Nevertheless, she listened patiently.

"The bottom twelve inches are of stones smaller than seven inches in diameter," he continued, "and the top six inches are of gravel and sand pressed into a solid surface using a specially designed three-ton roller." Abe addressed this thrilling news to both windows as he bounded from one side of the rocking carriage to the other. "It is a road to be proud of. It is a road that carries the future of our great nation!"

Abigail watched this astonishing man with a love so great she felt her whole being was smiling.

Just beyond the town's market square, a broad circle had been formed around a pair of long watering troughs. The turning was large enough to permit several coaches to halt, water their steeds, or return in the direction from which they had come. Without such turning circles, a driver was required to unhitch their horses, lead them around, manhandle the coach about, then reattach the horses. When their coach slowed to a halt, Abigail poked her head out the door in time to see Reginald leap easily down. "Is everything all right?"

"I just want to check on something." Reginald walked around to examine the traces of the right front horse. "Stay as you are. We won't be stopping for long."

Abigail started to retreat into the coach when she saw Reginald looking back to where the second coach was pulling up behind them. She watched him walk back and begin a conversation with Horace. "Please would you go and see what they're talking about?"

Abe caught her tone. "Is something wrong?"

"I couldn't say. But they look rather serious."

Without further comment, Abe slipped past her, opened the coach door, and stepped down.

He was not gone long. When he returned, he wore an expression as grim as Reginald's. Abigail demanded, "Is something wrong? Maybe a horse—"

"The horses are fine," Abe said quietly, shutting the door.

The coach rocked as Reginald climbed back on board. "They think we're being followed."

"Whatever do you mean?"

"Come over here." Abe pushed aside some bundles and made room for her on the seat facing backward. "Don't let him see you. The man rides a roan with a white patch on its forehead."

"I see it. There by the hitching post."

"Reginald says he's noticed that same horse for the past two days. Never coming close enough for inspection. But dogging our path."

"Strange for a horseman to match the pace of a pair of heavily laden wagons," Abigail said softly, suddenly feeling breathless and a tightness in her chest.

"Those were Reginald's thoughts exactly."

"But who . . ." Abigail answered her unformed question. "Lillian."

"That is what Reginald fears."

"It must be someone sent by that banker."

"It could be. It could also be that they are after Erica. Or perhaps even us."

"But why?"

"We are no doubt seen as a threat. We may take away part of the very prosperous business of carrying passengers and mail west." Abe was as somber as Abigail had ever seen.

"What do we do?"

"Up to now the road has had so much traffic we have remained safe from anyone intending mischief." Abe glanced over at his unfurled maps. "But between here and Wheeling we enter the forested highlands. The road is much tighter, the way ahead harder to see."

"A minute ago you said *they*. Do you think there are others who might attack?" Her heart thudded in her chest.

"That is precisely what we must determine," Abe replied as

Reginald assisted Lillian back into the coach.

"I think it will be better for the women to travel inside the rest of the day," he said with a meaningful glance at Abe. "Keep an eye on things."

Chapter 26

As it turned out, the elusive scout on their tail did not approach the entourage. That evening the travelers approached the Harrow estate. The house itself commanded the crest of a flat-topped hill. The views as the carriages wound along the tree-lined lane were spectacular. A broad river flowed through a distant valley, and the surrounding vista revealed tilled fields and hardwood forests dressed in autumn glory. A cluster of stables and several dozen workers' cottages formed a tiny hamlet in the distance. Smoke rose from the cottages' chimneys and drifted lazily across the sinking sun.

The redbrick manor with white-trimmed sash windows was most impressive, though not as grand as some of the country estates Lillian had known in England. But it most certainly held a certain sprawling majesty. A broad front portico was bordered by six Corinthian columns supporting a high sloping roof. To either side extended sheltered walks. Here the columns were both shorter and thinner, giving the impression of two classical arms outstretched to greet any new arrival. At the end of these walkways rose miniature versions of the central house. One looked like it contained the cookhouse; the other seemed to be apartments for the house servants.

As they all stepped down from the coaches, Lillian turned in a slow sweep of the surrounding vista. There was no other house to be seen, save the cottages in the valley below. In fact, she could find no other estate at all. Nor was there any road visible save the lane leading up to the house. The overall feeling was one of rustic elegance carved from an almost endless land. And isolation.

There before her stretched a future that was hers by force and by fate, but not by choice. Oh, she had elected to come. But not because it was where she wished to live. She came because all other paths were barred. She came to leave a lifetime of half-truths and outright lies and scandal behind. She came to find a secure place for herself and her son.

Yet as she stood on the manor's broad front lawn and surveyed the farmlands and valley and forested hills beyond, she did not feel at all safe. Instead, she felt like an outsider, trapped in a role for which she was not made.

Their hosts, distant relatives of Erica, proved as welcoming and hospitable as their home was lovely. Erica's letter of introduction had arrived only two days earlier, but this hardly mattered. Had they not received word at all, Lillian had the impression these kind people would have greeted them with open arms. She swiftly gathered that such chance meetings made up much of the social life of these far-flung American landholders.

They were all shown to inviting guest rooms and encouraged to rest and freshen up before supper.

Lillian was to share a room with Abigail, one that looked out over the front of the house. Dressing for dinner took little time, for like the others she had brought no finery on this journey. Once she had washed and changed into a fresh gown, Lillian pulled a book from her carrying case and sat by the front window. But her attention remained held by the view. The lands looked both rich in promise and beautiful in the softening light. Yet she was filled with the same sense of foreboding she had known when pulling up the drive.

"Lillian, did you hear what I just said?"

Lillian turned from the sunset and the pastures. "Forgive me, I was miles away."

"Shall I leave you be?"

"No, please don't." Lillian turned from the window. "Tell me again what you said."

"It's nothing, really. Only that I shall miss dressing up."

"So you think you shall remain in Wheeling?"

The younger woman replied simply, "I could not bear being separated from Abe. To even consider such a thing threatens to pluck my heart from my body."

"I understand." And she did. Yet agreeing with Abigail left her wanting to weep.

"It's silly, I know," Abigail said. "To be sorry over a trifling like nice dresses. I never did much care for the socials and ladies' gatherings Or opera."

"I for one should miss the fine meals," Lillian confessed, then silently added, *and so much else from my former life.* Such thoughts again drew her toward the parting from Reginald. She could no longer lie to herself and hope their Wheeling business might hold him there or even bring him back. The prospect of a new life in this alien world, heartbroken and alone, pierced her anew.

Abigail inspected her companion. "Are you feeling all right?"

"I was just reflecting upon all that will soon change." Lillian forced herself to sound cheerful. There was nothing to be gained from keening over circumstances she could not change. She touched the letter she always carried in her pocket and reminded herself that another life was at stake here. "I must confess that I do miss my son very much."

"I have never before thought of starting a family," Abigail confessed, and blushed deeply. "Until now."

Lillian found comfort in this young woman's burgeoning love and the joy it brought. For Lillian, the future was bleak. But she could still find strength in the hopes of these others, and for her son. Lillian forced herself to smile through her pain. She would not destroy this woman's fragile joy with her own sorrow. Not now, not ever. "Abe is truly a fine young man."

"Yes," Abigail softly agreed. "He is."

A bell sounded from somewhere down below. "I suppose that is our call to table."

Abe joined them on the upstairs landing. "Miss Lillian, did you spy the pianoforte in the second parlor?"

"I did not, Abe." Once again, Lillian found solace in the young man's affectionate eagerness. "Would you care to play again?"

"Only if it would not inconvenience you to sing."

Perhaps her voice might indeed prove a comfort in this new land, Lillian reflected. Perhaps this tainted talent might be turned into an instrument of truth and light in her new life. "I have no objections."

Reginald appeared as Abe and Abigail started down the stairs. "Might I have the pleasure of leading you into dinner?" he asked formally.

"It would be my distinct honor." The effort of speaking evenly was a great challenge.

"You look troubled." When she did not respond, he added, "May I be of help?"

If only, she replied, but silently. Even so, the yearning and distress must have been there in her gaze. Reginald touched her arm, a simple gesture but one which left her fighting the urge to fling herself into his embrace. *My son,* she repeated over and over. *I must be strong for the future of my son.*

"I can do nothing unless you tell me," Reginald said, his voice low.

"I am beset by problems for which there are no earthly answers," she whispered.

"Are you certain?"

"Yes."

"What one finds impossible, two can often overcome."

"You are most kind, sir." She spoke through lips stiff with the effort of control. "But in this case I know I face the prospect alone."

Reginald's own voice sounded strained. "Perhaps you should pray on it."

She started to dismiss the words, yet in the same instant she felt a strong sense of harmony, of righteousness. "I-I really don't know how."

"God is not concerned that you say the proper words," Reginald said, starting down the stairs with her hand on his elbow. "He merely wishes to have you ask with a contrite and open heart."

Before the meal, Franklin Harrow led them through the main rooms. They were invited to inspect a framed document hanging above the great room's fireplace. Lillian read how a grateful Continental Congress had affirmed an earlier Harrow's ownership of this estate. She was surprised over the particular wording used and asked, "Do I understand correctly that your forebear was an earl?"

"He lost his titles," Franklin said, "and all his British holdings for backing the Americans in the War of Independence."

Sylvia Harrow held herself upright, seeming stiff and a bit distant. "My husband has made numerous appeals to the Crown, requesting that the earldom be restored. All to no avail."

"Aye, well, it would be a falsehood to say I don't wish for the titles. Especially now," Franklin conceded.

"Why is that, sir?"

"Coal!" Franklin Harrow was a big-boned man, not as tall as Reginald but considerably heavier. He wore his hair long and was dressed in a crimson housecoat over a starched white shirt. But his hands bore the scars and callouses of a lifetime of hard work. He was an incongruous figure, part frontiersman and part Eastern socialite. "The hills about these parts are full of the finest grade coal you could ever hope to see. I've acquired land to the south of here, just over the Virginia border. There are veins so rich you can pull the stuff from the earth with your bare hands."

"Franklin has tripled the size of the holdings he inherited from his father," Sylvia Harrow interjected proudly.

"The new mills around Boston are paying top dollar for good coal. Top dollar! Now that the National Road is open, I'm filling two wagon trains a week. There's a new turnpike abuilding that will take me as far as Philadelphia. From there the roads are straight and open all the way to Boston. The mills want ten times what I'm supplying now, and I intend to deliver."

"Franklin has acquired a house on the same square as Paul Revere's silversmith shop," Sylvia put in.

"The Boston merchants were making more money off my coal than I was. Gouging me, they were. So I'm going to sell directly to the mills. Which means Sylvia and I are up and moving to the big city."

"I was raised in Philadelphia," Sylvia said. "I have always missed the life in town."

"And now she will have it again."

"But the folks in Boston won't afford Franklin the respect he deserves," Sylvia commented.

Franklin Harrow blew out his cheeks. "They're some of the oldest families in America."

"They treat us like paupers and miscreants," Sylvia said, sounding incensed by the notion.

"It's not so bad," Franklin said, putting on a jovial tone.

"It is and you know it. They put on the most dreadful airs and turn their nose up at us, like, like . . ."

"Like we didn't belong," Franklin finished, shrugging his big shoulders.

"Never did I think I'd be hearing that Americans would not measure a man by his own accomplishments," Reginald offered.

"They say Boston is a world unto itself," Franklin replied.

"And they're right." He rubbed his hands together. "Well, enough of that. Let's go to the dining room."

They were joined at dinner by the local vicar. John Stout certainly lived up to his name, for his girth was almost as great as his height. But genuine intelligence and warmth gleamed from his brown eyes. And his clean-shaven face held an interest in everything about him. Most particularly the unexpected guests. "Mrs. Erica Powers at the same table as myself. What a delight. What an unexpected delight. My wife will be doubly sad to learn what this bout of croup has kept her from enjoying. I can't tell you what your and your husband's writings have meant."

"You do us great honor, sir."

"Stuff and nonsense. I am but a minor servant fighting this dire plague called slavery. But you two, why, here before me stands a portion of the struggle's very heart."

"We are able to do very little," Erica replied. "And so far none of it to great success."

"Why, you know that is not true," he protested. "We out here in the hinterland hear how much ire you are raising with your writings, both in the nation's capital and farther south."

"Yet still the slave trade flourishes."

"For the moment. For the moment. But the day shall come when we will look back upon our struggles in triumph. And triumph we most certainly shall, you mark my words. We shall then see that your honest reporting has sparked the flames that grew to sweep across our nation."

"My husband and I are soon departing for England," Erica confessed, "and we feel as though we leave nothing save defeat in our wake."

"Not defeat. Not at all. Merely a temporary setback. But we shall win, of that you can be sure. With God's help, the seeds you have planted shall erase this scourge from our great nation once and for all."

The dining table was large enough to comfortably seat them all. The three Harrow children, aged between seven and twelve, sat at the table's far end. Their mother's stern gaze was sufficient to keep their antics to a quiet minimum. The driver and his wife and little Hannah sat with them as well. Three servants helped Sylvia Harrow bring out the feast. And feast it was. There was roast goose and smoked pork and wild turkey served with cranberry sauce. There was a stew of beef and another of venison along with fresh okra, potatoes, white corn, and beets with onions. A sweet potato casserole and green beans joined the freshly baked bread to be topped with churned butter and cheese still sweating from the cool house. The food just came and came. After the sparse fare of roadside inns, the travelers gaped in wonder.

As the vicar blessed the food and the gathering, Lillian found herself reflecting on Reginald's advice. Did she truly know God so well as to be able to pray for guidance? She had only recently begun to bow her head at mealtimes and in church. Also at bedtimes she had occasionally offered up a few words. But to pray and ask for help, this suggested a new element to her relationship with the divine. Was God truly close enough that she might seek His specific direction?

The vicar's words intoned directly across the table from where she sat. Lillian heard them with one part of her mind, but with the other she saw with utter clarity that if there was a barrier to her drawing near to God, it lay wholly on her side. God was the constant. She was the one who had held to a distance from Him.

She found herself praying an apology. *For all the days and weeks and years I have spent too far from Thee, God, I am most humbly sorry.*

She knew the vicar had finished with his prayers and the rest had echoed his amen. But she had no inclination to raise her head. Let them wonder, if they would. She felt a welling up inside her, a force so strong she could not be drawn away from this encounter with the Almighty.

I have not been the person I should. I have remained determined to live life utterly on my own. Perhaps love has been offered me in the past. But I was too proud and too defensive to see it. Perhaps thou hast sought me out. Perhaps thou mightest even have protected me when I was a hurt and frightened child. But I would neither heed nor accept thy presence. Yet I do so now. I ask, please guide me and share with me the wisdom and the comfort that is thine alone to offer. If I am to be on my own for the rest of my days, lost from the world I know and the man I have come to love, let me draw ever nearer to thee. Let me learn to call thee friend.

It was not seemly to cry at the dinner table, but the burning sensation behind her eyes was such that she was forced to raise one hand and press hard against them. Yet it was not from sorrow. Instead, her heart seemed afire. There was such great strength to the moment now. Such a sense of love, yes, and *welcome.*

Lillian knew the moment was ended then. She could open her eyes and raise her head because she felt an absolute certainty that there would be many more such moments to come.

The vicar responded to her upraised head with an almost imperceptible smile, then turned his attention to where Franklin Harrow was standing to carve the turkey at the end of the table. "Are you still intent upon making the move to Boston next spring?"

"The new house should be ready by the time the thaws arrive that far north," Franklin confirmed.

"What about next year's planting and harvest?"

"We have two excellent overseers, men I would trust with my life."

"You will be sorely missed here," the vicar said.

"We shall be back from time to time, of that you can rest assured."

"It shall not be the same, as you well know."

From his place alongside the vicar, Reginald held Lillian with his gaze. She knew he was wondering about her, and she gave a hint of a nod.

Sylvia Harrow interjected, "Unless we can find a means of entering Boston's social world, I fear my dear husband might insist upon a more permanent return."

"That would put an end to our commercial quest," Franklin responded. "My goal has been to move onward from Boston to Europe, becoming a supplier of hardwoods from our forests and coal from our hills."

"But Franklin is a man who loves good company and warm welcomes," his wife amplified, as seemed to be her pattern. "Which we have yet to find in Boston."

Lillian was struck with an idea. Before she had time to consider it, she said, "Sir, what you said earlier about a title perhaps helping your entry into society. Is that true?"

"There is no 'perhaps' about it," he replied instantly. "They might be firmly bound to the rest of America, but they also lay claim to British aristocracy. And take great pride in the fact."

She hesitated only a moment further. It was a logical move. Everyone from the ship's captain to these newfound friends gathered about this table had warned her that titles held no value in the interior of the country. And other than her title, what else did she hold of value?

Lillian sensed she had an opportunity here to set aside both the source of scandals and many of her past falsehoods. This act seemed a natural response to her prayer.

She drew the table back into focus. "Sir, I have a title you might secure. That is, if you truly think it might be of some use to you and your family."

The table fell to utter silence. Franklin Harrow's mouth worked a moment to form the words. "Please, I don't understand—"

"I am the Dowager Countess Lillian Houghton, widow of Grantlyn Houghton, fifth lord of Wantage and one-time equerry to His Royal Highness, the former Prince Regent and now King George the Fourth."

Franklin had gone absolutely still, his fork frozen in place.

"At the end of his life, my late husband made a series of disastrous business decisions which left me with ruinous debts. I am here to attempt to begin anew and carve out a place for my son and myself." She opened her hands. "The titles reside with me. I must warn you, sir, that a scandal now envelopes my reputation. But this does not affect my titles, unless the king himself withdraws them. Until that time, I have every right to do with them as I please. Were I to sell them, the scandal would not pass to you. It is a personal matter and would not affect your own station."

"Y-you would do this?" He stared down the long table to where his wife sat, equally stunned. "You would sell us your titles?"

"They shall do me little good, particularly with the risk of scandal, as I said."

"Wh-what do you wish in return?"

No one touched their food while she mulled this over. Lillian decided, "I should ask that you pay off the portion of my late husband's debts so that I might retain ownership of my London townhouse. It would not be for me. I have no interest in ever living in England again. But I would like my son to have this possibility, if he so wished. Until then we could rent it out and apply the income to his future. I would also ask for a sum of money sufficient to buy land here in America."

It was Sylvia Harrow who asked, "What are the legal requirements?"

"Any transfer of titles must be approved by the royal equerry. With England's current king, this can be assured with a proper gift."

"You mean I am to bribe the king?" Franklin had regained his equanimity, and there were some smiles around the table at his small jest.

"You are to offer the gift to his aide," Lillian corrected carefully. "This regime is constantly in debt. The king gambles, you see. The Parliament has refused to meet his personal expenses. The royal household is strapped for cash. All this works in your favor."

"This practice, it's been done before?"

"Rest assured, sir, in recent years any number of highborn

families have been brought to penury. The disastrous harvests have beggared many. They have sold their titles in an attempt to keep their land. In my case, this is not possible. But if I can at least offer my son a London residence and grant myself new land free of debt, then it is a worthy exchange. That is, if you are interested."

"Am I interested?" Franklin clapped his hands to his lap. "Am I interested? Why, I would call your arrival in this house a godsend, my lady."

Lillian risked a glance across the table. Reginald observed her with equal measures of joy and pain. She forced herself to turn away and rose from her chair to meet Franklin Harrow's approach. Even in the midst of such commotion, Reginald managed to share her innermost feelings. Even now, as the hour of their final separation approached.

"It is my habit to seal such agreements with the shaking of hands," their host said. "I hope you will not think me forward if I ask this of you, my lady."

Despite the moment's deep distress, she felt as right about this as anything she had ever done. She offered Franklin Harrow her hand and said, "Perhaps you should address me simply as Mrs. Houghton."

Chapter 27

Lillian's offer dismissed any prospect of her singing that evening. She thought Abe might be somewhat disappointed, but she was grateful for the reprieve. The longer the evening wore on, the more despondent she became. Sylvia and Franklin Harrow continued to query her about the title, its heritage, and the royal court. She did not object. At least she was saved from mulling over worries for which she had no answers.

The next morning, though it was the Sabbath, was hardly different. Abigail had sought out the vicar before he had departed the previous evening and spoken to him about Lillian's singing ability. As soon as Lillian was awake and had taken her morning tea, she found herself in the back room practicing a new hymn with Abe. Once again, remaining active held her only sense of solace. As Abe began the song's introduction, Sylvia appeared in the doorway. A few minutes later, Sylvia was joined by her husband, as well as Erica and Abigail. Reginald was nowhere to be seen.

Sylvia's stiff manner evaporated as the music filled the room. "That is most beautiful," she commented when the practice was over. "Mr. Langston should have been here to hear it."

"The gentleman decided to take one of my horses for an early morning run," Franklin explained.

Lillian lowered her gaze so that none could see her sorrow.

Reginald was no doubt aware of the permanence of their coming farewell. He was easing his way into it. As should she.

Midway on the long ride to the town and church, a horse and rider cantered up alongside their carriage. Reginald tipped his hat to one and all, then fell in behind without once meeting Lillian's eye. As they disembarked in the church forecourt and started up the walk, Reginald was intently conversing with an iron-jawed gentleman burned dark by the sun and a second burly man in a wide-brimmed leather hat. Lillian could not help but inquire, "Who, may I ask, is Reginald speaking with there?"

"The slender fellow is one of my overseers. A most capable gentleman."

She felt her host's hand grip her elbow and guide her forward. "And the other man?"

"Ah, that would be the sheriff of Farmington. A friend of my overseer, by all accounts." He led her up the church's front stairs. "Of course you remember the good reverend."

The vicar greeted everyone, then said to Lillian, "Thank you for your willingness to participate in our service this morning. You are ready?"

"I know the song," she confirmed. "But I fear . . ." She could not finish.

In his Sunday robes, the man looked even larger than in his suit the previous evening. Yet his jollity was now replaced with a dignified aura. "Then we shall join together in asking the Lord to aid you in accomplishing what none of us can do alone."

"Please, Reverend Stout, I'm not sure what you mean."

The vicar replied simply, "What all of us should be at the altar. An example, a beacon, a worthy servant." He turned to the next arrivals.

As Lillian entered the pew, Reginald hastened up the aisle and seated himself on Franklin's other side. She quailed at the thought of rising and stepping forward and facing this packed chamber. And Reginald. She glanced over at him. He still did not meet her eye.

The vicar pronounced the opening benediction, led the congregation through a first hymn, and then said, "We have with us this day travelers from afar, guests in the home of our friends and church elder, Franklin and Sylvia Harrow. Two of their guests have kindly agreed to grace us with song. I could not think of a more appropriate message for us to hear than the words of this next hymn. For we are, all of us, travelers upon this weary road of life."

The vicar motioned the two forward.

Lillian followed Abe around the altar. He seated himself at the organ, and she took up a station where she could both see the music on the stand and watch his lead. Thankfully, now that she was standing and facing the church, there was a sense of peace and focus on the task at hand. The nervousness she felt was merely a part of the moment's intensity.

Reginald continued to examine the hands in his lap and not look up at her, yet even so she felt a small thrill. Her talents and experience were finally being put to a worthy use. Not even her worries over Reginald and the lonely days ahead could erase this sense of finding purpose for her gift.

Abe watched for her signal. When she nodded, he played the introduction he had rehearsed. She sang,

> "Our God, our help in ages past,
> Our hope for years to come,
> Our shelter from the stormy blast,
> And our eternal home."

Reginald had lifted his gaze. They locked eyes, and it was hard for Lillian to tear herself away long enough to find her place in the song. There was such tenderness in his gaze, such yearning. And such grief. She scarcely heard herself sing.

> "Before the hills in order stood,
> Or earth received her frame,
> From everlasting Thou art God,
> To endless years the same."

She lifted her voice to soar, singing now not to the rafters nor to the congregation, but to her Lord. Life may dictate that she and Reginald would remain apart. God in His infinite wisdom knew what was best for both of them. Yet she would love this man with her dying breath.

> "Our God, our help in ages past,
> Our hope for years to come,
> Be Thou our guard while troubles last,
> And our eternal home."

Their departure from the Harrow manor was put off a day. Early Monday, Franklin Harrow brought his solicitor up from Farmington. Together they drew up the appropriate papers. Any remaining hesitations the Harrows might have felt about Lillian's offer were dissolved by her insistence that no payment be made until the titles were officially transferred. Letters of introduction to Lavinia and Samuel Aldridge were prepared with requests for their help. The solicitor's eager aide was thrilled beyond words to find himself appointed emissary. The young man was sent off that very day upon Franklin's fastest steed, aimed for the New York ports and the first clipper leaving for England.

Lillian saw nothing of Reginald throughout much of the day. He had departed with the dawn, taken on a tour of the estate by one of the Harrow overseers, and did not return until they were seeing off the solicitor late in the afternoon. Reginald greeted the man and news of the day's events with an air of grim fatigue. Lillian tried to speak with him and tell him she understood, but her throat closed up tight and she could not utter the first word. Reginald excused himself and went off to bathe before dinner.

When they all sat down for an early meal, there was a sense

that distant relatives and new acquaintances had been transformed into friends and allies. The mood was now one of eagerness to help one another however possible. The talk soon turned to Wheeling and what they would find up ahead. Franklin Harrow proved an excellent source of useful information.

"The distance you've yet to cover is not that great. From Farmington to Wheeling is only forty or so miles as the crow flies. But between here and there lies the last of the Appalachians. One final spine of mountains is just beyond the western horizon. The National Road maintains its maximum five percent grade through long sweeping turns. The distance is increased by half again. Even so, the road is a marvel of modern engineering."

Sylvia Harrow noted somewhat disdainfully, "If it was such a marvel, I don't see why they couldn't have erected a few decent inns along the way."

"No one in their right mind would remain in the last hills before the plains," her husband explained. "Especially at this time of year. What we experience here as cold autumn rain could well be snow in the higher reaches."

Sylvia was not satisfied. "If you find yourself behind one of my husband's coal trains or any other line of oxen carts, this last leg of your journey can well take another three days. Which means either camping in forests or sleeping in a miserable tippling inn. Both ways, you run the risk of meeting up with the dread highwaymen."

"Now, now, there's no need worrying our guests. The weather is their real concern," her husband responded. "It always seems to be raining in these hills to the west of us. Either that or they're blanketed by a fog so thick you can't see the hand in front of your face. Many a time I've been unable to observe my own lead animals."

Lillian listened to the exchange with only half an ear. Once again she was seated across from Reginald. Her position at the table afforded her a perfect station to observe Reginald's inner turmoil.

It pained her to even glance his way. Taking another forkful of the excellent fare became a chore. Silently Lillian implored him to lift his gaze, to just look in her direction.

But he remained withdrawn, tense, and downcast.

Once again she found herself drawn by her own helplessness to prayer. She could not wait for a private moment.

Her eyes open and steadfast in their gaze across the table, she offered a new sort of prayer. It seemed to her that the communication was being shaped even before she thought through the words. The prayer changed from one where she intended to plea for herself into one directed outward. *Father, I pray for this good man. Whatever I might do to ease his burden, help me to see this clearly. Grant me the strength and the wisdom to do whatever I might to heal his woes and calm his heart. Use me however Thou wilt, Lord, to return the light to his gaze and the happiness to his features.*

"Mr. Langston, I hope you enjoyed your tour of my lands," Franklin was saying.

Reluctantly Reginald raised his head. "It was most informative."

"My overseer was able to answer your questions?"

"I could not have asked for a better guide. He thinks the world of you, sir."

"And I of him, I assure you. I suppose he told you that I am granting him and his partner a third of everything they gain from their work."

"He did, and he marvels at your generosity."

"I have always found that long-standing relationships are best built upon fairness."

"I agree."

"And honesty," Sylvia added. "And a chance for all to advance together."

Abigail spoke up, "Mr. Langston and Mr. Cutter are taking Abraham in as a partner in their Wheeling venture."

"There, did I not say it? It is a wise course, and one that will bear great fruit for everyone involved." Franklin Harrow smiled down the length of the table. "Will there be other reasons for celebrating in the near future?"

As Abigail blushed, Sylvia chided her husband, "I cannot imagine anything that might be more inappropriate for you to ask the young lady."

"I mean no offense," he said, still smiling.

"None taken, sir," Abigail replied, gazing now at Abe, who was equally embarrassed.

Franklin Harrow turned his attention to Reginald. "Would you call your quest successful, sir?"

Reginald sat in silence for a moment, then responded quietly to the plate set before him, "I must see this through to completion."

Franklin nodded. "Please let me know if there is anything I can do, sir."

Lillian understood Reginald's message. The ending was upon them. She might wish for another day, another week, or month, but to what purpose? To love him even more deeply? To face a parting that would wrench them both even worse?

Yes, her heart mourned. *Yes, even a single heartbeat more!*

But as she studied the downcast gentleman seated across from her, she knew their parting should come as soon as possible.

Lillian took a deep breath and tried to control the trembling of her hands. She would not remain in Wheeling as she had intended, drawing out their time together to the last dying gasp. As soon as they arrived, she would make plans to depart for the West.

Lillian realized the conversation had moved on without her. Franklin was addressing Abe, "I gather you see Wheeling as your very own land of opportunity."

"I can but hope at this stage, sir," Abe replied. "Having never been there before."

Abigail asked, "What can you tell us of the place, sir?"

"The city lives up to its name," he replied. "A more free-wheeling town you will never hope to find. But if I were you, I would not see myself putting down permanent roots in that place."

"Why is that, sir?"

"Because before long the world of opportunity will be moving further west. Soon as the National Road opens to St. Louis, Wheeling will become just another way station and river port."

Horace Cutter pointed out, "There will still be the settlers bound for Indiana. From Wheeling they will keep heading west."

"Not if trekking to St. Louis means bridges across the great rivers and a closer point from which to begin the overland adventure," Franklin replied. "You have not seen what it is like west of here, sir. Other than the National Road, there is nothing in the way of decent transportation. Nothing! Crossing a flood-swollen river can mean losing half your herd—either that or paying a ferryman whatever he chooses to charge. There is pestilence and bad water and Indians to tend with. No, you mark my words. The immigrants will take whatever course is safest, and take it as far as they can."

"St. Louis," Abe said thoughtfully.

"Aye, that's your world of opportunity. Why, if I was your age, I'd be making for there this very instant! You mark my words. There are lands out beyond our reach that will soon be opening up. Lands the likes of which you've never dreamed of."

"I've read accounts," Abe said.

"As have I," Horace agreed. "And always dismissed them as fables drawn from the blandishments of frontiersmen and fur traders." This was greeted with chuckles.

"Fables they might be, but there's truth enough as well." Their host thumped the table for emphasis. "Mark my words. St. Louis is the gateway to new worlds. That's where the future lies!"

The entire table became caught up in excited discussion. All, that is, save Lillian and Reginald. The two of them remained locked in silence. Lillian continued to study his face, reading there the truth hidden from her before.

As they rose from the table, she gave Reginald's downcast features one more moment of scrutiny, seeking to brand his face upon her memory. Three days. She would give herself just three days more, then move on to the void of a future without him.

Chapter 28

Lillian was emotionally and physically exhausted. Yet a shared excitement seemed to run like a current through the dark house. Beside her in the large four-poster bed, Abigail had tried to be silent, but the young woman had been restless and stirring constantly through the long hours. Lillian could well understand her anticipation. A day's journey, two or three at most, and her future would stand there before her. Who would not be both thrilled and terrified at such a prospect. From somewhere down below their bedroom came the quiet rumble of male voices.

Finally Abigail whispered, "Are you awake?"

"I am."

"I have disturbed your sleep. I am so sorry."

"It is not you."

"You are excited about tomorrow's journey?"

The determination neither to lie to her dear young friend nor dampen her enthusiasm left Lillian in a quandary. Finally she replied, "Everything is mingled together into a great knot that extends from my mind to my stomach."

"I know precisely what you mean."

No, Lillian silently replied. *No, you do not. And may you never be faced with such a dilemma, or such a night.* "Whatever do you suppose the men are still talking over downstairs?"

Abigail said, "No doubt they are planning the route ahead."

"No doubt."

Abigail rolled over on her back. "Might I ask what you are thinking about?"

What to tell her? "I wish God were closer just now. Such a desire would never have occurred to me before. But now I yearn for it desperately."

"Closer than any brother, that is what the Scriptures promise."

"Never did I imagine that such a desire could be possible. Especially for me." Her throat constricted. Or that she should ever need a friend so desperately.

"Sometimes the only way I can fathom the Savior's grace," Abigail said, "is by light of who I am without Him."

Lillian mulled that over for a time, then turned to Abigail's profile in the moonlight. "Now it is my turn. What are you thinking?"

"Two things," she replied slowly. "What my calling might be, beyond that of being Abe's helpmate and support. And I was also thinking about St. Louis."

"You think Abe will want to go there?"

"I know it. Did you not see his face when Mr. Harrow was speaking?"

"I am unable to read him as well as you."

"I will go where he wishes to lead," Abigail said, speaking as much to herself as to Lillian. "I will not hold him back."

"You will make him a good wife."

"Oh, I do hope so."

"I am certain of it."

Abigail scrunched the covers up close to her chin. Lillian dreaded that she might inquire about her relationship with Reginald. But the young woman merely said, "Might we pray together about tomorrow?"

"For our futures," Lillian whispered.

"Yes," Abigail agreed. "For God's help with all that lies ahead."

They arose long before dawn. Breakfast was as vast a meal as dinner, and eating enough to satisfy Sylvia Harrow was a terrible chore for Lillian. Reginald's place at the table was empty. When he finally arrived, he displayed dark circles beneath his eyes and carried the same tensely preoccupied air as the previous night. Lillian could scarcely look his way.

As they climbed into the carriages, the early-morning sky was star-studded and brilliantly clear, with a moon just three days from full. The lane stretched away from the manor like a silver river, waiting to ferry them into a future Lillian dreaded with all her might.

Abe and Reginald shared the coach's top seat. The air held an uncommon chill for September, a bite just a fraction off a hard freeze. Abigail and Lillian bundled into blankets tucked up around their knees. Remnants of both breakfast and the previous dinner were wrapped and stowed in the coach with them. Farewells were said, and said again. With the aid of the moon and lanterns hung from the top posts of each coach, they were away.

Abigail bobbed from window to window as they passed through Farmington, but the village was dark and silent. They knew when they rejoined the National Road because the coaches' heavy jolting softened to a constant rocking, and the horses' cadence picked up to a swift-moving canter. Abigail and Lillian were both exhausted. Soon enough the coach's steady sway granted them what the four-poster with its down mattress could not, and they fell fast asleep.

Lillian woke to the brilliant sunshine of a full-fledged day. Abigail slumbered on, her head in Lillian's lap. They were rising through a heavily forested stretch, with nothing to be seen through either window save rocky promontories and ancient woodlands.

The road traversed a steep hillside in a series of cutbacks.

She could see the roof of the second coach as it negotiated the passage directly below them. Horace was handling the reins, and as he passed below them he whistled and called to the lead horses. But that was not what captured Lillian's attention. To her astonishment, she realized that the nanny's husband, seated beside Horace, held a rifle to his chest. She had not even been aware that they carried weapons on the coaches at all. Both men wore taut expressions as they scanned the forests to either side. Lillian glanced back and forth, but as far as she could see the road was empty.

Lillian craned forward to follow the other coach's progress. Her motions woke Abigail. "What is it?"

"I'm not quite—"

Her words were cut off as the forest about them erupted.

Shots rang out from the forests to either side. Abigail shrieked and tumbled off the seat and onto the coach's floor. When she made to rise, Lillian slipped down alongside her. "Stay as you are!"

"Are they highwaymen?" Abigail's face still bore the creases of slumber. Yet her features stretched tight in fear. "Abe!"

More shots were fired. The horses cried in shrill terror. Lillian gripped Abigail harder. "You must stay down!"

"But he's exposed up top!"

"There's nothing you can do for him except stay safe!" Gunfire seemed to explode from all sides. And shouting, yet she could not make out a single word.

Then she was terrified further by the sound of Reginald calling for the horses to halt. This could only mean one thing. They were encircled by too large a gang.

A voice yelled out of the general fray, "We've got you surrounded! Throw down your arms!"

Beside her, Abigail whimpered.

Lillian felt a deep dread rise to her throat as the coach creaked and the two men jumped down. When the door opened, she could not bring herself to raise her head.

Then she heard Reginald say, "It's all right. You're safe now. You can both come out."

Lillian descended from the coach on shaking legs to find herself among grim-faced armed men. Abigail clung to Abe and would not release him. Erica clutched her whimpering child to her chest. Then Lillian spotted Franklin Harrow among the armed horsemen. Beside him was the overseer she had spied outside church. Franklin tipped his hat to her and said, "All right, Mrs. Houghton?"

"Thanks to you. Thanks to all of you." She turned to Reginald and asked, "Is anyone hurt?"

"One of the attackers was winged; he's laid out back there around the far bend," Franklin informed her. "But we're all safe. Thanks to your man here, we got the jump on them. Been tracking them along hunting trails only the locals know about."

My man. The words created a false echo of relief and regret. *My man.* She asked Reginald, "You knew of this in advance?"

"We suspected."

"Reginald spied a horseman following us outside Farmington," Horace explained.

"The plan was all his," Franklin said. "Brilliant, it was."

"We're not done yet," Reginald replied grimly.

"Right you are," Franklin agreed, and called over his shoulder, "Bring them forward!"

Three men shambled up, their wrists bound and ropes tied to the horns of three saddles. Reginald asked Lillian, "Do you recognize any of them?"

"How could I possibly?" She tried to hold back the tremors racking her frame. "Were they after me?"

A burly man she recognized as the sheriff who had spoken to Reginald outside church barked, "Who's the leader of this band?"

None of the trio spoke. But two cast furtive glances at the third, a leathery skinned man with a scar that creased his left cheek and eyebrow.

"You there! I'm the sheriff of Farmington and these are my

deputies. I'm telling you this so you understand what's about here. You attacked folks on the National Road. That's a hanging offense."

The leader spat into the dust at his feet. But the younger of his men cried out, "We was just doing what we was told."

"Shut your gob," the leader snarled.

"That's right," the sheriff agreed. "Do as he says and swing there beside him."

"I ain't hanging for nobody." The young man was sweating mightily, the whites forming a clear rim around his bulging eyes.

The sheriff was a bull of a man with a waxed moustache and a rough-edged voice. "Who hired you?"

The young attacker pointed with his bound hands at the leader. "Was him what met the man paying. Him alone."

"Where was this?"

"Washington. Leastwise, that's what he told us."

The entire group breathed a tight sigh. The leader snarled once more. At a motion from the sheriff, the deputy turned his horse and dragged the leader away.

When they were out of sight, the sheriff demanded, "Was it just the lady here you were after?"

The young man trembled, his eyes glazed with feverish terror.

"Speak up, man. Your words are all that separate you from the noose."

"We was told to finish 'em all."

The sheriff asked Reginald, "That what you needed to hear, sir?"

Reginald gave a short nod. "We would be indebted to you if you could deliver us the name of the man back in Washington."

"That may be coming soon enough." The sheriff removed his hat and wiped sweat from a brow that was pale compared to his lower features. "They watch the gallows being built, it's remarkable how loose their tongues get."

The young man cried, "I told you what I know!"

"And I'll be telling the judge just how helpful you've been." The sheriff tugged on his reins. "We best be getting this lot back. Don't want to be caught on the road after sundown. That applies to you folks as well. These ain't the only scallywags haunting these hills."

Chapter 29

Later that afternoon, they crested a rise to find themselves atop a hill. The forest disappeared, and the vista opened up before them. As though the wide-open spaces were a signal, the coach pulled into a lay-by and the drivers called for the horses to halt.

Abigail opened the door and called, "Where are we?"

"The end of the hills." Abe leaped down. "Come see your new world," he said, holding out his hand.

And new it was, or so it appeared. Beyond the plateau where the two coaches stood, the world dropped away. Below and to the west stretched a vast golden plain. Forests were adorned with all the season's finery, and the sky was china blue.

Abigail stepped forward to clutch Abe's hand. "Is this heaven?" she asked in wonder.

Lillian moved away from the others. In the far distance, sheathed in a cloud, flowed a broad, still river. The plains below them were a patchwork of brown fields and verdant forests.

Abe asked Abigail, "Do you see Wheeling?"

"Where?"

"Just there, beside the Ohio."

"The Ohio what?"

"Did you not hear anything I said along the journey? The Ohio River, of course."

Abigail searched in all directions. "Can it truly be this lovely?"

Abe looked at her with an expression of deepest adoration. "You do like it, then."

"Like? Like?" She looked ready to weep. "Never in all my life did I imagine it would be this glorious."

"It is just a rough and tumble frontier town, by all accounts."

"But the setting of the town is beautiful beyond description."

Lillian heard footsteps approach. She knew from the tread it was Reginald. Without glancing his way she turned and stepped further from the others. "Why did you not tell me?" she asked.

"Until they struck, all we had were raised suspicions. I saw how distressed you were. We all did. I had no interest in adding to your woes."

"I thought you were drawing away from me. In preparation . . ."

Reginald stared at her in astonishment. "Why would you think that?"

"What else was I to think? You remained so grim and withdrawn." She wrung her hands. "Oh, why must we even discuss this? We both know what lies ahead."

"Do we?"

"Reginald, Wheeling is a week or more from Washington! When you leave me here . . ." She could not continue.

"But I cannot."

"You can't what?"

"You have seen the dangers. Do you really think this will be the last of their attempts? I love you, Lillian. How could I live with myself if I were to leave you alone in such peril?"

"So you'll stay here?"

"I can't. You know I can't. Erica is returning to England. Abe and Abigail will remain here. Someone must watch over our emporium and warehouses in Georgetown." He gripped her hands. "Say you'll come back with me."

She pulled her hands away. "How can you ask such a thing? Haven't I already brought enough havoc and danger upon your family?"

"You did not bring this on anyone."

"Reginald, they attacked you because of *me*. They intended to kill us all."

"No, they attacked us because of the Langston name. Lillian, listen to me. I beg you. You told me of this banker back in London . . ."

"Bartholomew."

"Yes. He approached you because of *us*."

"Reginald is right, you know," Erica said as she approached. "Forgive me for intruding, but I could not remain silent. You know the facts for what they are, Lillian. I first confronted Bartholomew years ago in England to make the bank return the Langston gold it held. Ever since, Gareth and I have battled the slavers as best we can. He and the slavers have remained our enemies. They see those of us who work alongside Wilberforce as a threat to their trade, which we most certainly are."

Lillian found herself trembling without being able to say why. All of their little band were observing them now and listening intently. "I don't . . . I can't . . ."

Erica touched her arm. "Give yourself time. You have suffered a great distress. I pray that you would only think this through. Because what my brother says is indeed right. I feel this at the very core of my being. And he speaks for all of us when he wishes for you to become an even closer part of our family."

Erica turned to her brother. "Reginald, perhaps you should join her in the carriage and have Abe and Abigail occupy the upper seat. Is it safe enough now?"

Reginald assured her that it was.

Erica took a firmer grip upon Lillian's arm and guided her back. As she helped Lillian into the carriage, she said, "The only advice I can give you is to pray. That, and I will repeat what my brother has said. You have brought nothing upon our house save the joy of finding a new friend."

Once the road flattened and straightened, traffic slowed to a crawl. Abigail found herself both impatient and glad for the gentler pace. The attack had shaken her to her core. She felt she had witnessed firsthand the battle being waged against the antislavery movement. Abigail had always deplored slavery, but up to this point she had simply accepted this position because her parents and church opposed it. But only now did she have a faint inkling of what it meant to combat evil.

As they arrived at the town's outskirts, Abigail did her best to put these thoughts away. There was so much to see, so much to take in. Everywhere she looked, she saw things utterly foreign to her previous life. They had passed the outlying farms, then entered a noisome region of corrals and stables and smithies. One enclosure was given over to a livestock auction. The area was full of dust and bleating animals and the cries of farmers shouting their bids.

They then passed a second auction arena. Although it was empty, and though Abigail had never seen one before, she knew instantly what it was. The air seemed tainted here, the sunlight quartered by invisible shades. The auction block was a raised wooden platform, almost like a gallows, for at the rear stood four stout posts. Instead of nooses, however, the posts held chains. Abigail felt gripped with a tension so fierce she could not call it fear, nor rage, nor anything she had ever felt before.

"Turn away," Abe quietly suggested. "Don't look at it."

"No, I must see it. Understand it. We must fight this."

"I agree."

She looked at Abe and was heartened by his firm demeanor. She had not seen this side of him before, the fiercely stern resolve. "Do you recall our discussion of taking on a cause?"

"I do."

"Do you wish to share in this fight with Gareth and Erica?"

His gaze pierced to her depths. "With all my heart."

"Oh, I am glad, Abe. This is right. This is our calling."

The city itself was split into three distinct portions. The area closest to the river was laid out in clearly defined streets, forming square blocks of wooden and yellow-brick structures, framed by roads of packed golden clay. In the distance, the river was broad and smooth flowing.

Surrounding this neat section of town, however, were two less orderly boroughs. North and east of the city, the fields were sectioned into temporary camps. Conestoga wagons with their broad canvas backs were ringed by temporary corrals and yet more animals. Children scampered everywhere. Women tended cooking fires while men worked at their wagons and their horses. A long stream of wagons moved slowly toward the flat-bottomed ferries plying the Ohio River.

South of the central part of town was a ramshackle metropolis of tents. Some were large affairs that seemed to sprout from half-finished structures. This region of tents dwarfed the more permanent structures. Pushing right up to the road's southern border were tents selling everything from healing remedies to pots and pans and wagons and plows. There were even tents holding churches.

"Sorry, I need my other hand."

Abigail looked down. Without knowing, she had taken hold of Abe's hand. "Oh, forgive me."

"Thank you." He hauled on the reins, taking the horses through a gradual turning, and then he checked behind them to make sure the other carriage was still following. "May I ask your impression?"

She heard the intensity in his voice.

"It's all so utterly and completely new to me."

"Are you displeased?"

She took a very long breath. There was so much she wanted to say, but the words just did not seem to fit together in the proper form. "Could we please continue down to the riverfront?"

He glanced at her. "But of course."

The road broadened and became the city of Wheeling's main thoroughfare. A line of cypress and ash trees formed a separation along the center. Traffic for the pair of ferries across the Ohio River waited in a long and almost stationary line. Abe joined the steadily moving stream that made its way past the hotels and the restaurants and the land offices and the haberdasheries and the saloons and the dry goods stores and the courthouse and the jail.

"Can you feel it?" she asked.

"What?"

Again she was unable to find the proper words. The sensations were as strong as the sunlight overhead. People thronged the raised plank walkways fronting the stores. Men tipped their hats and stood aside for ladies walking beneath parasols. Families in the odd dress of immigrants gawked and moved slowly along the street. The town seemed impossibly full, of people and sights and sounds.

Abigail motioned up ahead. "Would you stop here for a moment?"

"I can try." A line of shade trees rimmed the riverbank. Abe found a spot that was not occupied by other wagons. He pulled the horses to a halt and applied the hand brake. "Can I get you anything? A drink of water, perhaps?"

"Just sit here with me for a moment, please."

"Abigail, I don't think I can stand this much longer. What is it?"

She turned in her seat so she could stare back up the crowded central street of Wheeling. Dust hung heavy in the windless afternoon, like a golden veil dropped over the city and the people and the wagons and the river. She asked again, "Can you feel it?"

"Feel what?" he exclaimed in frustration.

"The excitement. The energy. The life!"

He stared at her. "You're pleased?"

"Pleased? Oh, Abe, I have never been so thrilled in all my life."

"But . . ." Now it was he who struggled for words. "But this is just an overcrowded border town."

"No, no, Abe. It is a city of new beginnings. It is a city of the future. It is a new world filled with *adventure*. We are surrounded by people who are staking all they have, including their lives and the lives of their children, on carving a place for themselves in this new world."

"So you like it? You—"

"I have never in all my life dreamed that I should find a place so exciting." She took a breath and felt the energy surge through her. "It is a world of impatience and impetuousness. It is a world of opportunity. It is our world."

"Ours," he repeated.

"Ours. Together." She pointed out over the river. "And look there."

Just upriver from the main ferries, a team of drovers was pulling tar-blackened tree trunks toward the river. Off the opposite bank, a smaller ferry was moored. From it a crew of workers was busy hammering in crossbeams to stanchions rising from the river bottom. "They are building a bridge across the Ohio," Abe observed.

"Just so." She raised her finger a trifle. "And look out on the other side."

A long line of wagons were carting in rocks, and a team of workers were spreading them to form the base for the extended road. Abe stared at it a long moment, then said, "Tell me what you see."

She looked into the eyes of this man she loved and replied, "Our future."

"Would you help me down, please?" Lillian asked.

"Of course." Reginald extended his hand.

"Come along, Hannah," Erica said. "Let's go look at the river." The two of them skipped off hand in hand, while the nanny and her husband followed at a distance.

Lillian and Reginald had spoken scarcely a word since leaving the hilltop. Lillian had regretted the tension and the distance between them. But Erica had been right. The need for a time of prayerful reflection had been so great she accepted Reginald's anxiety as a necessary cost.

"Thank you." She stepped lightly down and kept hold of his hand. She drew him into the trees lining the river until they could stand and look across the gray-green waters at the opposite bank.

They stood there for quite some time. The town's clamor rose behind them with the dust. Up ahead was scarcely less tumult. Where workers were building the road, carters shouted at their beasts and cracked whips twenty feet long. Oxen strained to haul the loads of rock and gravel. The ferry operators handled the long guide ropes while their teams pulled the flat-bottomed vessels against the river's constant flow. As soon as the ferries docked on the other side, the ferry master shouted for the men to swiftly off-load. There was nothing tranquil about the scene. It was dusty, chaotic, tumultuous.

Lillian shivered, but it was neither from fear nor dismay. "I have seen enough."

"Very well." Reginald turned from the water. "I suppose we should see to rooms for the night."

"Yes."

Something in her tone turned him back. "You are already wanting to speak with a land office?"

"No, Reginald."

"I would urge you not to act in haste. There are many scoundrels at work here. Everyone warns—"

"Reginald, you misunderstand. It is not that at all."

"Well, what then?"

She stepped forward until she stood so close she could smell the dust on his clothes and see how it clung to his lashes, as though already the city were working to set its imprint upon his features. "I had to be absolutely certain before I spoke with you. I hope you can see that."

"All I see is that our journey is at an end. Our journey and our time together."

"That is not true."

He encompassed the entire sunlit vista with a wide sweep of his arm. "This is not my world, Lillian."

"I know that."

"You have traveled half the world around to come to this place."

"Yes. What you say is true."

"You must establish a new future for yourself and your son. I understand that. Just as I understand your future holds no place—"

"Nothing could be further from the truth, dear Reginald."

"But . . ."

"Reginald, listen to me. I love you. But I had to be certain that what I had come to find was not here. Do you understand? No, I see that you do not."

"Lillian, hopefully somewhere farther to the west is the place of safety you desire, your destiny."

"So I thought. But I was wrong. I have come to realize through this journey that everything holds risks. Staying can be dangerous, moving the same. Genuine security must be found in love, both human and divine."

Reginald needed a moment to gather himself. "Then you will come back to Washington?"

"Before I answer that, I must know one thing. Here and now, I beg you to speak plainly and in utter honesty. What you said back on the hillside about my not being the cause of this ambush, this was the truth?"

"Never have I spoken with greater truthfulness."

"You understand that my returning with you could well open you and the family to further attacks."

"All of which would be only slander and lies."

"Nonetheless, they will accuse you of harboring a fallen woman." Despite her sternest resolve, her voice broke.

"No, my dearest, a thousand times no. Slander and lies will be met with truth."

"You would do that? Shield me at such a dire cost?"

"How could I do anything less for the woman I hold dearest?"

"Reginald—"

"I know what I know, Lillian. You are a good woman. You are becoming a *godly* woman. You are the woman I would give the world to call my own."

She sighed. "How can I argue against such love?"

"You can't."

"Then whenever it is time for you to depart, I am ready."

"You will do that? Come with me?"

"If there is room for me in your life," she repeated, "I am ready."

He reached for her hand, his strong frame now trembling. "Lillian, my dearest, would you marry me?"

It took her a long moment to whisper, "Yes, I will."

"God has brought to me a gift beyond measure." Reginald looked into her face. "Please, you mustn't cry, my dearest."

"I'm not, am I? Well, perhaps a little. It doesn't matter." She wiped at her face, using just the one hand, for the other was unable to release hold of his fingers. "It is you who have taught me the lesson of love, of finding a place where I belong and a role worth the joy of giving all my days to. All my life."

He smiled as he said, "Do you recall the carriage ride we took on the day you told me of your past?"

"I shall never forget it, nor the goodness of your reply."

"And the knoll and pastures? The riverbank?"

"And what you said there in the carriage, yes, I remember. You spoke of love."

"I spoke also of purchasing that piece of property."

"You didn't!" His grin was all the answer she required. "Oh, Reginald!"

"We will build a house for ourselves there," he declared. "A place of refuge and shelter, of love and friends willing to accept us exactly as we are. And perhaps Byron could join us, at least for a time, and allow me to come to know and care for him."

"A home," Lillian whispered and held him so tight she felt his heart beat against her own. "I have found my safe place."

It seemed to Abigail that all the world was singing. The birds in the boughs overhead added a high tremolo to the workers and the horses and the children. All this river town had to offer was wrapped in a single glorious song. She also knew that when she thought back to this day, she would remember it as a hymn. As though even the sun were humming a bright golden note. As though the angels were choosing to add their own secret tone to this most special of afternoons.

"My darling Abigail," Abe said, turning to her as they stood at the edge of the river, "would you marry me?"

Her own answer came out as a trembling melody. "Yes. Oh yes. It is all I could ever ask for, to marry you, my dearest Abe."

He embraced her and drew her close enough to say into her ear, "You make me the happiest and most fortunate man, dearest Abigail."

Abigail stepped over to the other coach as Erica and Hannah returned from the riverside. Something in Abigail's gaze caused Erica to leave the child with Horace as he tended the horses. "Yes? What is it?"

"Abe has asked me to marry him."

"And you are pleased?"

"I am thrilled beyond words." But then her expression changed. "Erica, I saw the slave auction block."

"Ah." Erica nodded slowly. "I understand."

"There is a terrible risk of this evil spreading west with this expansion, isn't there?"

"You have just described our worst nightmare," Erica replied.

"We must stop this before it has a chance to begin."

"Do you understand what you are saying?"

"No, perhaps not." Abigail took a deep breath. "But I will learn. With God's help."

"Does Abe feel the same?"

"He does."

A look of grave joy took hold of Erica's features. "I have no doubt that you shall both prove a vital part of the cause."

The whole group eventually reconvened near one of the carriages and Abigail pulled Lillian a step away. In the cautious manner of one uncertain about what she would hear, she asked, "Is there news?"

Lillian nodded.

"Indeed so," Reginald confirmed.

Horace Cutter looked from Lillian and Reginald to his young partner. "All I can say, Abe, is you seem like a man in love." The group laughed at Abe's red face as Abigail slipped her arm through his.

"Abe has asked me to marry him," she announced.

Lillian likewise took Reginald's arm and said, "We too are to be wed."

The two women hugged each other, then Erica, and were soon surrounded by a flurry of best wishes.

Abigail finally managed, "There is more." She turned to Abe and urged, "Go ahead, my dear."

"Perhaps it should wait."

"Too late for that," Reginald said. "We are all highly curious about what else we should know."

Abe flushed beneath the attention. "Abigail and I . . . that is . . ." He started again. "We feel, sirs, unless you disagree, of course, in which case we could, well . . ."

"Out with it, man!" Horace cried.

"We think we should establish a small base here in Wheeling, one that can remain as a way station for the stagecoach line. As for everything else, first we must see whether Mr. Harrow is correct in his prediction that things are soon to be moving farther westward."

He looked around at the faces in the circle. "In which case, we believe a better permanent setting for the Langston-Cutter Emporium would be St. Louis."

"But we will stay here until you both agree it is time to relocate," Abigail hurried to add. She glanced at Erica and went on, "There is much to do for the cause before we move on."

"And much to learn," Abe added.

Horace turned to Reginald. "What say you, partner?"

"I say," he declared, "that the new emporium is misnamed."

"So say I as well."

"I say," Reginald continued, "that as half owner of the new business, it should be named after the true master."

Abe asked weakly, "Half?"

Abigail clapped her hands. "Half!"

"Half," Horace repeated, nodding slowly. "All in favor of the new Childes Emporium and Stagecoach Line being moved to St. Louis, say aye!"

The sun was westering before talk moved on from these momentous decisions. The river was a flowing golden current and the day veiled in softest hues when Abigail asked Lillian, "I am wondering what of your dream to establish a new estate here in the west?"

"I have found new dreams," Lillian replied simply. "New and better dreams."

"How long can you remain here?"

"That is for my fiancé to decide."

"Long enough to see you both well settled," Reginald said, joining the conversation. "The road to St. Louis will not be completed for another few years by all accounts. You must view this as your home for the duration."

"I have so much to write my dear parents about," Abigail said distractedly. "But with winter coming and the road soon to be made perilous, it is doubtful that they would be able to come before next summer." She looked from one face to the next. "You are all the friends and family I have here in this new world. Please, please will you stay until we are wed?"

After a pause, Lillian replied, "I think I speak for all of us when I say that nothing could possibly give us greater joy."

"Except one thing," Reginald corrected.

Lillian caught his gaze and saw clearly what he meant. "Yes," she said. "Oh, yes."

"What?" Abigail cried. "That you will sing at my wedding?"

"No," Lillian replied. "That I shall sing at *ours*."

Book Three/HEIRS OF ACADIA
The Noble Fugitive

Serafina, the daughter of a powerful Venetian counselor, has become infatuated with Luca, her dashing art tutor. As the family sets sail for America, she discovers her father has banished Luca forever. Distraught, Serafina secretly abandons ship on the coast of England. Confronting a series of misadventures, she reluctantly takes a job as a chambermaid in an English manor. Her burning desire is to find her way back to her beloved, but a heartrending betrayal may force her into remaining indefinitely at Harrow Hall as a lowly servant.

John Falconer, a world-weary ship captain, unexpectedly seeks refuge at Harrow Hall. Escaping from his past in the slave trade, he is chased by henchmen determined to silence his dark confessions. He works as a stable hand while awaiting the opportunity to steal away to London, where he might tell his tale and revolutionize the antislavery movement.

Gareth and Erica Powers travel across the Atlantic from Washington to rejoin William Wilberforce in his campaign for social reform, and they also find themselves at the Harrow mansion. Gareth has taken ill, and although his life hangs in the balance, he yearns to return to London and his writings against the slave trade.

Deep in the English countryside, the lives of these characters become intertwined in startling ways. The mysteries of Harrow Hall heighten the intrigue as Erica investigates her Harrow family ancestry. A place that once loomed as a dreaded detour becomes a sacred venue for the unveiling of God's Providence.

Watch for this new addition to
the Heirs of Acadia series
in the summer of 2005!

Discover the Beginning of the Saga With

Janette Oke & T. Davis Bunn's

SONG OF ACADIA

A Chance Encounter Will Forever Change Their Lives

The year was 1753, and the lines of separation were firmly drawn. The French had named the region Acadia, their "beloved home." When the British came soon after, they battled with the French on the new continent as they had in Europe for centuries.

The settlers of Acadia were either French or English, and though their villages might be but a stone's throw apart, most could go an entire lifetime without speaking to someone from the other side.

And then the chance encounter of Catherine Price and Louise Belleveau in a meadow of wild flowers.... From this unexpected friendship, Oke and Bunn spin a tale of devotion, loss, renewal, and bonds stronger than blood and faith stronger than tragedy.

◆ BETHANYHOUSE